MW00720550

Deadly

Lessons

by David Russell

Thanks so much for coming to the launch!

David Russell

RendezVous
Crime

Cover art and design Jennifer Harrington

Le Conseil des Arts | The Canada Council
du Canada | for the arts
depuis 1957 | since 1957

We acknowledge the support of the Canada Council for the Arts for our publishing program.

RENDEZVOUS PRESS
an imprint of Napoleon Publishing
Toronto, Ontario, Canada

Printed in Canada

10 09 08 07 06   5 4 3 2 1

Library and Archives Canada Cataloguing in Publication

Russell, David, date-
        Deadly lessons / David Russell.

(RendezVous crime)
ISBN 1-894917-35-9 (pbk.)

        I. Title. II. Series.
PS8635.U877D43 2006   C813'.6   C2006-903889-9

To Barbara, who encourages and inspires me
And Ainsley—who inspires us both

While most of the locations in this novel are real, Sir John A. Macdonald Secondary is a fictional Vancouver high school. All of the characters are, of course, likewise creations of the author. Any perceived similarity to actual people is purely coincidental. Numerous individuals helped me by reading the manuscript and making suggestions—thanks to you all. Thanks also to Sean Vanderfluit, who answered occasional what surely seemed ignorant legal questions: any errors in legal understanding contained herein are certainly mine and not his.

Prologue

Dobrila peered at the clouds swirling just outside the kitchen window. A storm was brewing. Since she was a small child, Dobrila had both feared and delighted at the booming summer thunderstorms that would roll quickly through the countryside when she stayed at her grandparents' farm. She remembered standing in the doorway of the big barn—green as opposed to red like they were supposed to be—laughing and pointing at each flash of lightning, her grandfather counting aloud the seconds between the lightning and the thunder claps. When the storm moved towards them, he would grab her shoulders with each clap of thunder, sending her running with shrieks of delighted terror behind the old rain barrel next to the door. When the storm receded, he would stand in the doorway, hoist Dobrila onto his shoulders and declare their bravery had scared away the storm. When the storm was over, Dobrila's little brother could always be found stepping gingerly out of the empty horse stall at the end of the barn, never admitting his fear. To protect him, neither Dobrila nor her grandfather ever let on they knew how scared he was, and they did not tease him for his obvious lack of courage in the face of atmospheric disturbance.

Turning from the sink, Dobrila smiled at the memory. She smiled too, though quizzically, at the thought of her own daughter, nearly six years old, asleep in the other room, unaware of the thunderous turmoil rolling their way. Her daughter never bothered with conflicts around her. Instead, she was the dreamer, like her father. Her father. Dobrila sighed.

For over two months, she had heard nothing from her husband.

1

Since the beginning of the end of their country, her husband had been home only sporadically. He was an officer, he told her. The Croats could not be allowed to break apart their nation, he had told her. Croatians. Hungarians. Serbians. All her life, Dobrila had known them all, growing up as she had in this very city on the Danube, Novi Sad, so close to the area now reclaiming independence as Croatia. Her friends were Croatian. Her friends were Serbian. She shook her head. As a child, none of that had mattered. How was it that these same people with whom she had run through the woods behind the school, the handsome young Croatian neighbour on the school's soccer team from whom she had stolen her first kiss, the old couple who ran the small store just three doors from her own home, were now her enemy?

That was the danger, her husband was convinced. It was no longer safe to trust anyone. No one's loyalties could be trusted any more. Dobrila wanted to hear none of it. All that mattered to her was that this independence—or failure to achieve it—would conclude before her daughter began school in the fall. She could not bear the thought of her little girl facing danger by simply walking down the street with her classmates, whoever they might be. If it came to it, she would take the family away from Novi Sad, to the south where they would be safe from the country's squabbles. Maybe she'd go to London. She had always wanted to go there. Or even to America. Her brother, long since grown and working with the government, could surely find her passage away from the city of their childhood before it robbed her daughter of her own childhood. Her husband only got angry when she talked of uprooting the family. It was a topic she didn't bother to discuss with him. Though for two months now, there was no topic she had been able to address with her husband.

Dobrila turned back to the window just in time to see the sky awaken as a flash of lightning brought the city aglow in yellows and blues. The lightning was bright, intense, though without forks, for which she was grateful. To this day, some of the fear of the forked tongue from the heavens remained with her, the byproduct of her grandfather's active imagination. In the split second during which

2

the city was illuminated, Dobrila could see as far down the hill as the city centre and the spire of the church, hundreds of years old, that stood steadfastly against the modern downtown developing around it. From the corner of her eye, Dobrila saw movement in the instant of brilliant daylight in her backyard. Her head turned quickly as the shadow of a man passed on the path from the gate. As the lightning disappeared from the sky, so too did the lights from her kitchen, as Novi Sad experienced another of its many power outages.

She wondered if she had only imagined the man on her garden walkway. Fighting had recently broken out within the city limits, but it had been limited largely to small pockets of Croatians on their way to what they saw as their new homeland. But the resistance to the Croatian independence movement had grown in recent months and with it, growing numbers of Croatian militants had infiltrated communities and towns where Serbian officials lived. It was foolish to be worried, she tried to tell herself. She was allowing the passions of the moment to invade her reasonable mind, the power of the storm sparking new fears in her now that she was alone.

Dobrila turned away from the window. It was too dark to see anything outside anyway. The power outages usually lasted only a few minutes, but just the same, Dobrila thought she should find some candles. Feeling her way along the counter's edge, she made her way to the curio cabinet—another remnant of memories from her grandparents' farm. The top drawer stuck, as it had for as long as Dobrila could remember. With effort, she pulled the drawer away from its rails, spilling the contents onto the floor. Dobrila crouched down to gather them, and as she did, she shot her head back up towards the back door. There. She had heard it again. It was more than the contents of the overturned drawer that had made such a racket. The noise she heard was from outside by the garden path.

Dobrila slowly raised herself, pressing her back against the archway that separated the kitchen from the dining room in her small, proud home. Watching the doorway, she found herself momentarily stunned into paralysis. She looked towards the hallway leading down to her daughter's bedroom, thinking for sure that she must by now have woken up. Yet no sound came from that direction. Again Dobrila heard a slight scraping outside, closer now to the back door. She wanted to tell herself that her husband had finally returned. But why would he take so long to open the door? Was he injured? Did he need her help?

Quickly deciding she needed to get to her daughter, if only to hold her and be sure she was safe, Dobrila eased her way towards the sleeping girl's room. She had nearly reached the hallway when she stopped. Had she locked the door? The distance between her and the door seemed so far, but it seemed equally foolish to run to her daughter—who had not yet even woken—if the door was not even locked. Dobrila stepped away from the wall, feeling suddenly exposed as she walked in the dark, arm outstretched, to reach the deadbolt on the door. Reaching the door, she breathed a sigh of relief when she noted it was already locked. After catching her breath, she half-smiled at her own foolish fears.

"Now who is afraid of storms?" she said aloud, and the sound of her own voice brought her even more comfort. A flash of lightning briefly lit the room, confirming for Dobrila that she was alone. So alone, she only then noticed the family dog was not at his usual spot lying near the radiator in the hallway. "Idiot," she told herself, again aloud, realizing it was the dog making the noise in the yard. He was probably terrified by the storm, as she had allowed herself to become. Dobrila unlocked the deadbolt and pulled open the door, whistling quietly so as not to wake her daughter—as if anything could, she smiled again to herself. A flash of lightning illuminated the sky, and in that instant she saw him.

She gasped, unable even to scream as the man leaped forward, covering her mouth with his hand, pushing her back into the kitchen hallway. She struggled to break free, gasping for air. She could taste the salt of his hands, the oil of his skin as his fingers gripped her face. Using his foot, he slammed the door behind him and pushed his way into the kitchen, still holding Dobrila with both arms like an enormous child's toy. He was strong, stronger than Dobrila could even fathom, dragging her along with what seemed little effort on his part. As he pulled her to the floor, his hand across her mouth slipped, momentarily giving Dobrila the freedom to yell.

It was short-lived, for no sooner had she managed to get out the very beginnings of a shriek than the man's hand found its way to her face, his enormous palm covering her mouth and nose until she was certain she would pass out from lack of air. This time, she tasted something different on his hands. It was blood, and she instinctively knew that it was not her own. This man was injured. Slowly, he eased the pressure on her face, lowering his mouth near her ear and whispering. "Will you scream?" he asked. "You cannot scream."

Dobrila shook her head, as much as his grip would allow her. Slowly her attacker raised his hand from her mouth. "Please. Do not hurt me," she said. The man seemed to laugh.

"You are not who I thought you would be," he told her, slightly bemused. Dobrila's head raced as she sought for meaning in the man's strange words. Then she knew. Soldiers, especially officers, were frequent targets of kidnapping and torture.

"My husband is not home," she told him quietly. "He has gone to fight in the wars. Please. Leave me be." Dobrila, thinking quickly, was careful not to mention her daughter in the house and prayed this new noise too would not awaken her. The man was so close to her now, she could smell the tobacco he breathed, sensed the racing of his breath.

"Your husband?" he hissed. "Your husband is with the army? I thought I could find shelter here. I did not think I would find Serbian killers here."

"You haven't," Dobrila whimpered. "I am alone. There is no one but me. My husband, he only goes because it is his job. Please. I beg you. If you need help, I can give it to you." He smiled at her fear, rising up and sitting on his heels to look at the woman he had come across. Dobrila looked at him too, could see that he was wounded but did not go to help him. From down the hallway, Dobrila and the man both heard a sound at the same time. He turned towards the doorway. "No!" she screamed and hurled herself in the direction of her daughter's bedroom.

Before she could reach the hallway, she felt his full weight upon her, pulling her to the floor. Dobrila could keep quiet no longer, screaming, kicking and struggling to free herself. "Stop it!" he ordered, hitting her hard on the back of the head as he brought her to the floor. Dobrila rolled over onto her back and kicked with all her might, connecting with her attacker's abdomen. Even through her stocking she could feel that her foot was wet, warm and sticky with his blood. He screamed, then hit Dobrila again, this time hard in the face with such ferocity that Dobrila thought for certain she would die at his hand.

He fell on top of her, pinning her arms to the floor and covering her mouth. He raised his head and listened for more sound from the hallway. Dobrila screamed but could do nothing to free herself from the bleeding man. He put his face next to hers again, his breathing sounding ever more laboured. "Do you know pain?" he asked. Dobrila's eyes went wide with horror, and she screamed again, but could do nothing. He pinned her arms with one hand while reaching down with his other.

Dobrila's eyes filled with tears as she felt him attack her. His arm smothered her cries, and through her struggles she cried out to God to help her. But no help came, and Dobrila could only pray for her life to end quickly and that the animal on top of her would not find her daughter. The lightning flashed after an eternity, and the man sat up, letting go of her arms and looking down at her with disgust in his eyes. Dobrila could not move, only lie on the floor in their mingled blood and count the seconds until she heard the thunder of the storm moving away. The man got up, leaned against the wall and tried to catch his breath. Finally, he stood up straight, a massive man, well over six feet, Dobrila found herself noticing, and took one final look at her. He spat in her direction, then turned and walked out the door.

As the door to her little house slammed, the insufferably unreliable power of Novi Sad returned, springing the house into light so quickly Dobrila, staring up from the floor, had to squint her eyes in pain. She knew then she would live.

"Momma?" she heard a small voice from beside her ask. Slowly, she turned her head and saw her daughter standing at the edge of the hallway that led to the bedrooms. "Why did he hurt you?" she asked.

Dobrila lay on the floor and wept.

One

He was snoring. If he had just been asleep, I might have been inclined to leave him where he was, but make no mistake about it: the kid was snoring. And everyone had taken notice. At least he hadn't passed out. The forms required to deal with that were endless.

This was not the life I had been anticipating. This was Communications class at Sir John A. Macdonald Secondary School. For the lingo-impaired, "Communications" is a euphemism the education system uses to identify an English class where we often put those students who are, shall we say, challenged when it comes to an understanding of literature and language. They're also often stoned.

At the moment, I was attempting to teach a lesson on how best to prepare a resumé for the work force. Now, I'd be the first to admit my lessons aren't always stimulating, cutting-edge brilliant, but when a student falls into a deep enough sleep that he's actually snoring—and waking other students who are sleeping quietly— one has to take action. My action? Chalk. It always works.

This particular piece of chalk bounced off Justin's head and had no immediate impact. The upside was that the class laughed loudly enough that Justin was, in fact, awakened from his midday slumber.

"What the fuck...?" were the first words his limited vocabulary could muster.

"You were snoring," I informed him.

"Maybe that's because your class is boring." What Justin lacked in written ability, he more than amply made up for with his spunk. The fact I was his teacher in no way limited his willingness to hurl insults at me. It was part of the reason I liked him.

"I see you're practicing your sleeping skills. That should come in handy when you're living under the Granville Street bridge because you can't get a job." Justin, I had learned, also appreciated a well-timed insult tossed in his direction.

"Yeah, well, at least society will know which teacher to blame."

That's really why I got into the teaching business: the respect I get from students.

Justin duly wakened, I returned to the task at hand, attempting to convince my students that while they may never come to appreciate great literature, the least they could do was exit my class with the ability to fill out a job application, write simple business letters and not get screwed over by "record of the month club" agreements. They weren't really all that interested, but fear of chalk missiles kept the rest of the students from dozing off for the remainder of the period. I was beginning to understand how Gabe Kotter must have felt.

Anyone who doesn't think teachers earn their money on a daily basis should stand in front of twenty-four seventeen year olds—with fifty per cent of them high at any given moment—and try to instill some kind of appreciation for language. In November. In Vancouver. In the rain. Better people than I have been driven to the brink of insanity in more favourable circumstances.

Like an audible gift from God, the bell finally rang, dismissing my class from their stupor and me from the interminable dog and pony show I used to keep them in some kind of holding pattern until the end of the period. I liked them, but they tired the hell out of me. Students might think it's weird, but I looked forward to lunch time probably more than they did. I'd been teaching for two months.

I had just finished sliding some papers into my bag—yes, there's an evening work component to this job—when Carl Turbot stepped into my room. "Hey, Winston," he said.

"Hey, how's it going?" I replied.

"Got a minute?" he asked, his tone more serious than I was accustomed to hearing. Carl Turbot was a biology teacher who was the same age as me, which was thirty-five. He was popular: rumour had it that female students in particular were drawn to biology in this school in greater numbers than any other high school in Vancouver. Carl was largely considered the primary reason, for his fine teaching as well as the numerous other characteristics students find appealing.

Despite my pressing need for lunch and a trip to the staff washroom, I stayed because Carl had been a mentor of sorts since my arrival at John A. Macdonald. Many of my private sector friends had tried to convince me of the relative ease of the profession I had newly entered. When we compared the perils of our jobs, it always came to one comparison. I would ask my friends: for example, as a financial advisor, are you able to go to the bathroom whenever you want? The answer being "yes," I was always able to claim undue hardship in the teaching profession. When you have a room full of teenagers, especially some of the winners I worked with, you just couldn't leave them unattended long enough to go to the staff washroom two floors down and half a block away. Nonetheless, I figured I could hold my coffee byproduct for a couple of minutes more to talk to Carl.

"Sure," I told him. "What's up?" Carl stood in the doorway of my classroom. He looked the least sure of himself I'd seen him. "Carl. You can come in."

"Yeah. Okay." The student desks in my classroom were organized in a loose horseshoe shape. It wasn't always the most productive for students, but it was easier to catch the sleepers like Justin. Carl slid his six-foot-frame into the end of the horseshoe and looked away from me like a student caught cheating. "These desks really aren't very comfortable, are they?"

"Nope." A long, palpable silence filled the dusty classroom. I could feel my bladder expanding while I waited for Carl to speak.

"Listen, can I talk to you off the record?" he finally asked.

"I wasn't aware we were supposed to keep notes of conversations between colleagues."

"I just mean...I just need this conversation to be confidential. Okay?"

"Sure." Another pause followed.

"I've got a problem, and I'd like your advice."

"I'll do what I can. Is this a teaching problem?"

"Well, yes and no."

"If it is, you know how new I am to this business. You might be better off talking to another teacher, or maybe the principal if you're..."

"No!" he suddenly blurted. "We can't talk to the principal or anyone else. Please. You're the only one I can trust with this right now."

"Okay, it's all right," I tried to reassure him. "I'm here. You can talk to me." There was another, agonizing wait while he gathered the nerve to continue the conversation.

"I need to speak to you not as a teacher, but...I need your advice in your...your other capacity."

"Oh." It was the worst guarded secret at Sir John A. Macdonald Secondary that the reason I had come to teaching at the relatively late age of thirty-five was that I had given up the practice of law to pursue what I had always assumed would be a less demanding, much less conflict-oriented profession. Of course, the first class I was assigned to was "Law 12", a Social Studies elective course for budding teenage lawyers. Fortunately, there weren't enough of them to make up my entire teaching load; unfortunately, what was left over for me to teach included my Communications class. "Carl, are you in some kind of trouble?"

"I think so."

"Okay. Look. Before we go any further, you should know that while I'm still a member of the bar, I really don't practice law any more. And 'educational law,' if there even is such a thing, is certainly not my area of expertise. I was defence counsel for legal aid."

"Criminal law might be what I'm looking for advice about."

"I see." I didn't, of course. Two months into my new career, I didn't want to get involved in a teacher's legal problems. But Carl had become a friend.

"There's a student in my biology class. Her name is..."

"Better that you don't tell me her name right now," I interrupted.

"Okay. This girl. She threatened me this morning."

"She threatened you how? Like she was going to hurt you?"

"Not physically. I don't think she's gonna pull a Columbine on us or anything. It's me she's after. She threatened to...she threatened to go to the principal, to Dan, to tell him that..."

"Hold it, Carl. Stop." Under British Columbia law, as a teacher, I was obligated to report any sexual misconduct between a student and a teacher. As a lawyer, anything he told me was confidential, but that wasn't the way I was paying my rent any more. "You know I can't really hear this without putting you in jeopardy."

"Shit, Winston, hear me out. I don't know what else to do."

He truly looked pathetic. I had only known Carl for two months, but I had a hard time believing he could actually be guilty of anything that would harm his students. He was the consummate professional. If anything, students would have held him up as someone unapproachable because of his high standards.

"Carl. Give me a dollar."

"What?"

"A dollar. A loonie. Have you got one?"

He reached into his pocket and pulled out a handful of coins. Reaching out, he placed one in my outstretched hand.

"Okay. You've just retained me. What is this student going to tell the principal about you?"

Carl took a deep breath. "She threatened to tell the principal we've been sleeping together."

Two

I'd had cases not unlike this before. When I first took the L-SATs and entered law school—as an honour student, I might add—I really hadn't envisioned myself defending criminals—err, pardon me—"alleged" criminals. Still, by the time I had graduated, corporate, tax and real estate law gave me hives, divorce law (or "family law" as our legal system euphemistically calls it) reminded me too much of my own childhood, there didn't seem to be enough work in intellectual property law, and I refused to wear sandals, which ruled out environmental litigation.

That pretty much left me with criminal law. On the face of it, criminal law seems to be the most exciting: murder, mayhem, chaos, shady characters cutting deals in underlit offices, all of which is how this particular legal genre is played out on television and film. I chuckled watching Sam Waterston give a ninety-second closing to a murder case on *Law and Order*. The truth is criminal law can be more tedious, with a mind-numbingly precise attention to detail, than any other profession. But at least I knew there would always be work to do: despite politicians' promises to the contrary, there is no real hope that the criminal element will straighten itself up and turn to the good life.

There was no way I was going to be Crown Counsel. Two of the friends I had graduated with had chosen that noble calling. "You'll be serving society, Win," they tried to tell me when it came time to seek work. "Ridding the streets of unwanted low-lifes, protecting the innocent from the ravages of criminal activity." Both of them still toil away proudly in the courtrooms on behalf of Her Majesty, working seventy-hour weeks on a civil servant's salary. I chose the other side.

The real money for a lawyer is in criminal defence. It does take a considerable amount of time to build a reputation and really learn the ins and outs of the Criminal Code. But once a good defence counsel's name is known, he or she can almost print their own money. When you travel down to the yacht club and see all those two thousand dollar suits getting out of their Jaguars, they're not the prosecutors.

It isn't all about the money, however. I like to think I was motivated by a real desire to see justice done. I never really wanted to help criminals get away with their crimes, but I never wanted to see an innocent person go to jail either. There's an old saying that it's better to set ten guilty people free than to put one innocent person in jail. I believed that. And while Vancouver isn't exactly a mecca for police brutality and wrongful convictions, the court system, criminal or civil, is intimidating, and no one should have to go through it without someone helping them along the way. Plus, I've always really liked Jaguars.

Since the high-powered firms didn't want me right out of school, I began my career as defence counsel with Legal Aid: the dreaded Public Defender's office. This is the place where those with no real means of buying the high-priced Jaguared lawyers come. It is also the place where some of the most difficult, if unsophisticated, legal grunt work gets done. As a newcomer, I was assigned most of the petty cases: theft, break and enter, minor assaults, even vagrancy. Almost all of my cases were related to drugs.

It seemed like a good place to learn the trade, and it was. I learned it so well that within a few years I was managing a team of lawyers in a small firm doing mostly Legal Aid work. And that Jaguar was nowhere in sight. Within four years of beginning my law career, I realized I was working as many hours as my co-graduates in the major Howe Street law firms, for about a tenth of the income.

Worse, no matter how hard I slaved, how many cases I could plead down to misdemeanours, how many injustices I felt I had undone, the workload never ceased or even slowed down. And despite a fairly steady increase in pay that came with a concurrent increase in working hours, as I hit my seven year itch during a mad bout of work-induced stress and depression, I decided that "lawyering" might not be for me. Thus, after a short, illustrious career defending the downtrodden, the petty thieves, the junky prostitutes and runaways, I fled the world of legal defence to work with kids before they hit the court system.

At least that was my stated, altruistic reason. Secretly, I mostly longed to have summers off to sit outside a lakeside cabin and read Oprah's book club novels. No one can accuse me of insensitivity.

Thus, at the ripe old age of thirty-five, I had begun my second professional career as a high school Social Studies, Law and Communications teacher. Sitting with Carl Turbot now, my former career had just thrust itself brutally into my current one.

Recognizing this conversation with Carl was going to take up a significant portion of our lunch period, I left him stewing in my room while I made the long, arduous trek to the staff washroom, deking out students along the way. I couldn't help but look in the faces of the students I passed along the way, wondering what kind of pain a student experienced when a teacher crossed "that line" between teacher-student relationship and romantic or sexual relationship.

When I returned to my classroom, lunch in hand, Carl hadn't moved from the student desk he had flopped into. He looked defeated and—despite all my legal training, which told me I ought to believe in my client's innocence—I couldn't resist thinking he should look defeated. If the university's teacher training program taught us one thing—and believe me, it didn't teach us all that much—it was that a physical, romantic or sexual relationship between teacher and student is absolutely forbidden. No questions. No exceptions. There was no situation Carl could provide for me that would exonerate him. But since I had rushed into a solicitor-client relationship with him, I was obligated to hear his side of the story. I could only hope he would plead guilty, and I could simply help him get the lightest possible punishment and best rehab.

"Sorry to use up your lunch period."

"That's all right. You sound like you need an ear, but I'm gonna eat while you talk if that's all right."

"Sure," he replied, "go ahead."

I reached down into my lunch bag and pulled out my pathetic meal. Quite recently having returned to bachelorhood, making a decent packed lunch was not a skill I had acquired, and unlike in lawyering, even legal aid lawyering, there are rarely opportunities for going out for a decent lunch when one works as a teacher. Cheez Whiz sandwiches were a staple of my diet. When I was feeling healthy, I also brought carrots, but only if I remembered to buy them pre-cut, pre-peeled and pre-packaged in lunch bag size pouches. I was a busy man, after all.

I waited for Carl to break the awkward silence. After a long pause, he looked at me with doleful eyes and said, "Win, what do I do?"

I sighed, took a bite of a carrot and paused before responding. I have found pregnant pauses often make it look like I'm seriously pondering, when in fact I don't really have a clue what to do next. For the moment, he seemed to be buying it.

"Carl," I began, "this is extremely difficult. I have to admit I don't have much experience in this area of law, but I'm pretty well-versed with the statutes. The bottom line is that this is one area of law that is pretty clear. There's really no grey area at all. I don't know what kind of wiggle room we'd have in a trial."

"Christ, this is unbelievable."

"Why did she come forward now?"

"I don't know."

"Did you have a disagreement? A fight?"

"This is totally out of the blue. I just don't understand it. I always got along really well with her, and suddenly she hits me with this. It's incredible." He got up and began to pace around the room. "It's like some kind of vendetta. The thing is, I don't know what I did to get her so mad at me."

"Well, Carl, in situations like this, it's not uncommon for a student to suddenly turn against a teacher. Something suddenly makes them feel like they've got to take action."

"But why? She'd never given any indication anything was wrong."

"She's young. She's taken in by a good-looking teacher. She feels strong, important. Who knows what other things are going on in her life? This could just have been the final straw, and she feels like she wants to get back at someone."

"Biology is the final straw in a kid's life? My class isn't that bad."

I sighed. This wasn't going to be easy, but I had to know. "Carl," I asked, "how long have you been, umm...with the student?"

"Forever. She's in my Biology Twelve class, but I've had her since she was in my Grade Nine science class."

"And you've been, umm, 'together' all that time?"

"What do you mean?"

He wasn't going to make this easy. "You've been sleeping with her since she was in the ninth grade?"

"Jesus, Win!" he exploded, leaping to his feet and turning to face me head on for the first time. "What kind of an animal do you think I am?"

I was shocked. "Calm down, Carl. I'm just trying to figure out..."

"Shit! I know we haven't known each other for long, but I came to you because I thought you were my friend!"

"I am your friend. I'm trying to help you."

"You think I'd sleep with a kid—fourteen-year-old kid in Grade Nine! I can't believe this!"

"Carl, for God's sake, would you lower your voice! Just sit down and listen for a minute!" For a brief moment we stared each other down. "Sit down. Now."

He dropped back into the chair, his hostility still bubbling at the surface. "I'm sorry, Win. Maybe I shouldn't have come to you with this. I didn't know where else to go. But if you think I would do that..."

"Would you just listen to me?" I told him. "I'm just trying to get the facts. Stop getting all indignant. Whether the kid's in Grade Nine or Twelve it doesn't really matter. Sleeping with a student is the problem. Not her age."

"What? What the hell are you talking about?" He looked genuinely confused.

"I'm saying that whether or not this relationship has been going on for three years or it just started, the charge is equally serious."

"Jesus, Win, you don't get it. I haven't been sleeping with her since Grade Nine or since yesterday, for that matter."

"What?" It was my turn to be confused by his story.

He just shook his head. "Don't you see? That's why I'm so angry and confused. It's not true. She's making it up. That's why I came to see you. She's making the whole thing up."

"Oh," I replied somewhat sheepishly. "That sort of changes things."

Three

Suddenly it felt very hot in the classroom. It was November and it was sunny, which in Vancouver is a rarity. Some people—and by people I mean kids—had actually complained during the morning's classes that it was too bright in the room.

"What are you, vampires or something?" I had asked. In my Communications class, there were a couple of students who looked like they just might be. "I'll consider closing the blinds in June, if and only if there has been more than five consecutive days of sunshine." Did I mention how sensitive I can be?

Generally, when it's sunny in November in Vancouver, it's also cold; that sharp, crisp cold that tingles the senses on your face and makes you want to go skiing. Indoors, however, with the sun shining through a classroom wall full of windows, insulated by heavy layers of dust and dirt on the insides and outsides of the panes, November sun has a way of turning aging classrooms into saunas.

Carl was eyeing me with a look that wavered between incredulity and genuine hurt. I felt like a shite, a term my dad frequently used when he caught me doing something worthy of punishment, which was often. "I thought you knew me better than that," he said quietly, finally calming down enough for polite conversational tones.

"I'm sorry," I told him. "When you said the student was going to report a sexual relationship, I guess I just assumed the problem was the reporting of the relationship, not that there had ever been one."

"Well, you thought wrong."

"I know. I'm sorry. Why don't we start over, and you tell me everything. Right from the beginning." There was the fourth awkward silence of this lunch period, and I could practically hear Carl trying to decide whether to continue. "I may be all you've got," I told him.

"Okay," he finally said. "You're right. I don't know what to do." With a sigh, he stood up and slowly paced the front of the classroom, settling eventually on a spot in the centre of the room with his backside up against the chalkboard ledge to address his class of one. It was a position I had yet to master without covering my pants and the back of my shirt with chalk dust; limited janitorial budgets apparently meant chalk board ledges were never cleaned without enlisting the labour of a student on a detention.

"Can I tell you the student's name now?"

"Yes."

"Her name is Tricia Bellamy. Trish, she likes to be called. Like I said, this is the fourth year I've had in her my science classes. Sometimes it can be a bad thing having the same teacher throughout a kid's high school career. I've had kids transferred to other classes just because they've had me too many times. But I always got along really well with Trish. She's been a good student, good sense of humour. I've never had any problems with her, so I thought it would be fine for her to take Biology with me. Do you know her?"

"No. She's not in either of my law classes."

"No, I guess she wouldn't be. I don't think the humanities are her thing. As long as I've known her, she's been really into sciences. I'm sure she's told me she wants to go straight into sciences next year at university. Pre-med, I think. And I know she could do it. She's very, very bright."

"Has she gone through anything lately? Did her marks drop or anything?"

Carl paused to think for a moment. "No. In fact, I'm sure she's got an 'A' average right now. I can't see what could have happened in class that would send her over the edge."

"What about in her personal life? Has she broken up with her boyfriend? Her parents split up or anything?"

"You know, that's just it. As much as I've taught Trish for over three years now it's just...I mean...You know how with some kids you just have a closer relationship than with others, kids that you're almost friends with?"

"Are you kidding me? Have you seen the group of kids that just left here?"

"But you know what I mean?"

"I think so, yes."

"I like Trish. She's a great kid. But we just don't have that kind of relationship. I haven't seen any information from her counsellor to indicate anything is going wrong. She hasn't seemed any different. I just don't know."

I let this sink in for a moment to allow Carl a moment to collect his thoughts. When a suitable amount of time had passed—the lunch period wasn't terribly long—I reluctantly stepped into the next, most difficult part of the conversation. "I hate to have to even ask this, but since you've taken me on as your legal counsel, we need to be frank with each other. Completely frank, okay?"

He looked back at me with apprehension. "Okay," he replied.

"Carl, is there any truth to Trish's allegations whatsoever?"

"Win, I told you..."

"Hold on," I interrupted. "Hear me out, here." I paused again. It's hard to ask your friends if they're sleeping with teenagers. "Is it possible you've done or said something Tricia could have misconstrued as some sort of sexual or romantic advance?"

I have to admit that watching the expression on Carl's face spoke volumes to me. I'd found in my vast legal career that people's faces very often answer a question much better than their words do. Face reading was a handy skill as well as disadvantageous. Sometimes, as legal counsel, especially as defence counsel, knowing the truth about your client isn't necessarily a good thing.

Everyone deserves to have his legal interests fairly represented by counsel. And as a Legal Aid defence lawyer, I had to know I would be called upon to defend those who not only were guilty, but those who would not, under any circumstances, admit to their own guilt: not to their lawyer, likely not even to themselves.

Of course, at least part of the reason I had become disillusioned with the legal profession was the fact that I had to defend guilty people—defend them vigorously, and attempt to obtain their freedom. Somewhere along the way, a really good legal principle had been perverted: even a guilty person should not use the legal system to avoid justice; only to ensure proper legal procedures are followed in apportioning justice to the accused. In eight years, I'd had to subconsciously look the other way many times when forced to defend a client I knew was guilty. It's a generally accepted defence practice not to ask a client outright about his or her innocence.

In Carl's face, all I could see was confusion and genuine hurt. He not only couldn't understand why Trish was making spurious allegations, it was causing him no small amount of anguish. He didn't really even have to answer my question; he chose to anyway.

"I just don't see how. I honestly don't think we've ever even made physical contact. Ever. Let alone anything sexual. We've never kissed, we've never held hands, brushed shoulders, or bumped into each other in the hallway. Where the hell can she possibly be getting this from?"

"I don't know, Carl. There could be a thousand reasons why she's targeting you as the object of attention. It's unlikely the reasons have anything to do with something you've done or haven't done."

He turned and faced me again. "So you believe me then? You believe I didn't do anything wrong? I would never do anything to hurt a student, Win. I wouldn't."

"I know. I believe you. You're right. I haven't known you for long, but I think I'm a pretty good judge of character. I'm sorry I doubted you."

He smiled slightly for the first time since he'd come into the room. "Thank you. That means a lot to me to have someone on my side." He stood up and walked towards me. "Where do we go from here?"

"For starters," I told him, "I'm going to have to talk to Tricia."

Four

Let's start with the confession right now that from a very early age I have had little success talking with members of the opposite sex. That I managed to talk to a woman long enough to actually get married was an amazing feat. Dissolving the marriage with a bitter, acrimonious divorce was a much easier task to accomplish. For a man who has made two careers essentially out of talking to people, my lack of communication skills was well documented by anyone who'd ever made the "mistake" (generally *their* term) of dating me. I have this uncanny ability not to talk about emotions, desires or anything that has to do with relationships.

Often my lack of skill runs so deep, I found myself destroying relationships I didn't even know I was in. One evening in Grade Ten, a girl I went to school with challenged me to a game of tennis. It took me a long time to agree to play—nearly a minute—because I wasn't much of a tennis player, and I really liked this girl. I mean, I really *liked* her (that's Grade Ten-speak). What chance would I have if I showed her how much I sucked at the game? And why was she asking me anyway?

It was an unusually warm spring evening as we walked up to the tennis courts nearly two miles away. Sweat had formed on my brow, partially from the heat and partially due to my nervousness at spending an evening with this goddess from French class. We were walking past the well manicured lawn of a quaint little two-storey house about a block from home, when suddenly Melissa (a name I'm making up because even I can't remember her actual name) grabbed my hand and pulled me through the oscillating lawn sprinkler, soaking us both in refreshing cold water. As we reached the edge of the lawn, I laughed, let go of Melissa's hand and continued on to the tennis courts. Melissa later told friends she didn't want to see me any more, since I obviously had no interest in pursuing a romance. Who knew that grabbing my hand was an expression of her romantic desires?

With a foundation based upon that type of historical success, I can't say I was looking forward to sitting down to have a heart to heart chat with a female student about her "alleged" relationship with her teacher, my colleague, my friend. Sometimes, so I've been told, a teacher is one of the only people to whom a student is able to open up. A good teacher is often a good counsellor, even more so than the professional counsellors.

There are definitely protocols to follow in the kind of situation Carl had brought to me. Relationships between teachers and students were common enough that formal procedures had been established about how these situations should be handled. I hadn't really gotten around to reading those formal procedures, hoping I would never find myself in a position to have to know them.

I knew at least what the union's position was: no teacher should report on the professional conduct of another without first reporting their concern to the colleague in question. Even after that concern is raised with another teacher, he or she must be informed—in writing—of the intention to raise the issue with school management. The exception to this rule came when any sexual abuse, exploitation or inappropriate relationship between teacher and student was occurring. Then—and only then—was there no obligation to inform the suspect teacher of any intent to report his or her conduct to the principal.

The catch, of course, was the fact that while I didn't practice law any more, I had just been retained for the paltry sum of a dollar by Carl Turbot. Therefore, everything he had told me was protected under the principle of solicitor-client privilege. My options were thus: I could follow the duties of my teaching profession and report Carl's problem to superiors for fear that Trish's story was true, or I could try to defend Carl and defuse the situation before it got any worse. The problem with option "A" was that I risked getting disbarred for violating my client's confidence. I might have given up law for the time being, but it was way too early in my teaching career to determine whether or not I was willing to completely abandon my legal credentials. I was inclined to believe Carl. Call me gullible, but I had to give him the benefit of the doubt at least long enough to investigate his story.

So, at the tail end of lunch hour, I headed down to the main office to seek out the timetable of Trish Bellamy. Fortunately, last period that day I had my preparation period, time allotted to prepare lessons, photocopy, contact parents, mark papers and the myriad other tasks that fill the day of a high school teacher. In my case, add "interviewing potential hostile witness" to the list.

For some reason only a provincial bureaucrat can fathom, Physical Education is not required in high school past the tenth grade. The Ministry of Education feels that by the ripe old age of sixteen, students are ready to begin their adult couch potato years. Still, some senior students take the class out of interest or desire to maintain some degree of physical fitness beyond using the fingers on their right hands to operate their computer mouse to navigate internet chat rooms with their friends. Tricia was one of those.

By the time I wound my way down to the gym, class was already underway, and the students were taking advantage of the rare, late fall sunshine to run outside in the crisp November air. I found the P.E. teacher, Ralph Bremner, standing in the exit doorway of the gym, waiting for the students to return from their fitness sortie. Another educational mystery I had wondered about since my own high school days was why so few P.E. teachers actually ran with their students. Bremner cupped a cigarette in his left hand. Role modelling.

"Oh, hey there, ahhh, umm," Bremner began, surreptitiously tossing his cigarette onto the ground.

"Winston," I reminded him, "Winston Patrick."

"Right, Winston. Sorry about that. You're the lawyer, right?"

"I was. I'm a full-time educator now."

"Right. I was just...."

"Relax, Mr. Bremner."

"Ralph. It's Ralph."

"Okay, relax Ralph. We all have our vices. I'm not here to bust you for smoking."

"Right. I'm sure you've figured out how it is. So few hours in the day. So much to do. Sometimes you need to sneak in your breaks whenever you can get them."

"I understand," I told him, putting on my neutral lawyer face to hide my quasi-disgust at this physical education teacher sucking back a Players Light.

"Wow. So you gave up the courtroom for the classroom. Doesn't that seem like kind of a step backward? No offence."

"None taken. If you met some of the people I got to work with as defence counsel, you might think differently."

Bremner sort of chortled. "You may not have worked here long enough to meet all of our people. Hell, here you're probably just meeting them before they get to the court room." He started to laugh, then graduated into a hacking wheeze. As he choked, his large paunch tottered up and down above the waistband of red and white Adidas pants that looked like they dated at least as far back as my high school days.

"You all right?" I asked.

"I'm fine," Bremner replied, recovering sufficiently to participate in dialogue. "It's this cold weather."

"Yeah, it's a bitch."

"So, what can I do for you, Winston?" Bremner asked, recognizing slowly but surely that I probably had some purpose for standing out in the cold with him.

"I was thinking of going for a run with your class," I replied casually.

"Really?"

"No."

"Ah, shit, you had me going there for a second."

"I'm looking for one of your students. I was hoping I could steal her for a moment."

"You just want one?" he smiled. For a moment I worried he might start laughing again. I don't know CPR.

"One will do for now. Tricia Bellamy."

"Uh-oh. What's she done now?"

"Done? Trish a problem student in your class?"

"Nah, not really a problem. She's just got some attitude at times. Truthfully, she's not really the kind of girl we usually get in elective phys-ed."

"What kind of girl is that?"

"You know. Nothing wrong with her really. She's usually pleasant enough. But when she's in a pisser of a mood, there's almost no working with her. You know how melodramatic teenaged girls can get 'at that time of the month.'" Bremner made those obnoxious quotation marks with his hands.

"Not really, but I guess I'll learn."

"Yes you will, my friend. Luckily for me, when they get bitchy, I can just make them go run outside. Keeps me sane, if you know what I mean."

"Sure. So you don't mind if I take her away for a few minutes?"

He looked across the field as the first of the runners began to appear. "Nah, help yourself." The first four or five runners approached the entrance to the gym. "Here she comes now," he continued.

"Which one?" I asked him.

"You don't know her? She's not one of yours?"

"No. I just need to ask her something to do with one of her classes."

"Oh. Well, that's her. First girl in the group. She's pretty fast, I'll give her that."

I nodded. I had no idea what constitutes fast for a teenager. I wondered if fast to Ralph meant anyone who could complete a run without stopping for a smoke break.

"Trish!" Bremner suddenly bellowed, nearly jolting me into the wall behind us. Smoking hack or no, this man could project his voice. I thought he might double as a drama teacher. A student, still breathing heavily from her run, turned and trotted lightly towards us.

Tricia Bellamy was the kind of girl that sent eighteen-year-old boys for a cold shower. High cheekbones, deep green eyes and an engaging smile peered out from under beautiful, thick brown hair tied back in a tight knot on the back of her head for her P.E. class. For a student who thus far I had come to think of as a bookworm, Trish had the body of an athlete. Muscular arms, rock-firm legs and shoulders that looked like she could probably press her own weight, held together by a torso that seemed never to have heard of the term "body fat." I suddenly thought: if Carl had fallen for a student, at least on appearances, I could see why Tricia Bellamy might be the one.

"Trish," Bremner said, "Mr. Patrick wants to see you for a few minutes."

Trish looked up at me and smiled. "Hi, Mr. Patrick?" If the thought of some strange teacher coming to see her gave her any reason to be worried, Trish didn't show it.

"Hi. Yes. I'm Mr. Patrick. I teach in the Social Studies department."

"Oh, yeah," she replied. "My best friend Jessica McWilliams is in your Law class."

"Sure, yeah, I know Jessica. Do you mind if we talk for a couple of minutes?"

A brief flash of genuine concern passed across her face. "Is everything okay? Is something wrong with Jessica?"

"No, no. She's fine," I told her. "I just need to ask you about something school-related. Why don't we go inside? I may be dressed warmer than you are, but you've had the benefit of cardio exercise."

She relaxed again and smiled. "Sure," she said, following me into the gym. We walked across the gym to the door exiting into the hallway on the far side, small talking about the run the class had just endured. Trish seemed to think it wasn't so bad and had actually enjoyed blowing off steam after her French class the period before.

"You don't have sore *pieds?*" I asked.

"*Non, monsieur,*" she responded with what was becoming a regular smile. I was not looking forward to this conversation. In the just over two months of my teaching career—longer if you count my student teaching practicum the year before—I had by no means become an expert on adolescent behaviour. It was nearly impossible for me to conceptualize this sweet-looking, pleasant student concocting a story of sexual misconduct against a well respected teacher. Still, I've been duped before, and I didn't think it was a good idea for Carl's legal counsel to find himself in a precarious situation with a student. I made sure we stayed out of earshot of the rest of the returning gym class, but within clear view of Ralph Bremner and the rest of Tricia's classmates.

"So," I began badly, "how're you doing?" Did I mention I was never good at talking to the opposite sex?

"Pretty good, I guess. How are you?" She had been raised polite, if nothing else.

"I'm fine. Thank you for asking." I stopped for a minute and wondered how to begin. If Carl was telling the truth—as I believed he was—this was a troubled girl. I had no way of predicting what her reaction might be to my questioning her about her relationship with her biology teacher. Would she freak out? Cause a scene? Spit at me? You never know with teenagers these days. Man, I'm starting to sound like my dad.

"Mr. Patrick, did you want something? Why are you pulling me away from class?" Smart, too.

I sighed. "Okay," I began. "I need to talk to you about one of your teachers. Mr. Turbot."

Any pretense Trish had been displaying had been false. My bringing up Carl's name had the effect of sucker punching her. Her eyes grew to twice the size they had been just seconds before, and it took nearly a minute before she was able to respond.

"What about him?" she finally managed.

"Well, I...he's your biology teacher, correct?"

"That's right."

"And, Tricia, would you say you and Mr. Turbot get along all right?"

"Holy shit!" she blurted. "He told you."

"He told me what?"

"Cut the bullshit, Mr. Patrick. It's obvious why you're talking to me about Carl." She used his first name like it was something she did everyday.

"Carl? You refer to Mr. Turbot as Carl?"

"He told you about us."

"What is it you think he told me, Trish? Why don't you tell me about you and...'Carl'?"

She suddenly took me by the arm and led me through the gym's exit

27

doors into the hallway beyond. Given the circumstances, I was leery about being alone with Tricia without any witnesses, but if I wanted her to continue our conversation, I might have to work on her terms.

"You know about our relationship, Mr. Patrick?" she asked when we were out of sight of the rest of the class.

"I know what Mr. Turbot has told me. I'd like to hear your perspective."

"Why? What's it to you?" Her soft demeanour had begun to crack around the edges.

Sometimes honesty is the best policy, and from a legal standpoint, I knew I would eventually have to disclose the nature of my relationship with Carl. "Mr. Turbot has retained me, Tricia."

"Retained you?"

"Yes. I'm still a member of the bar. I'm still a lawyer. Mr. Turbot has hired me to represent him should issues arise out of your allegations of unprofessional conduct."

"Why would he hire a lawyer? I don't understand this. What's the matter with him?" Trish's voice was beginning to rise.

"Tricia," I said as soothingly as possible, "according to Mr. Turbot, you have threatened to report a sexual relationship to the principal. He's having a difficult time trying to figure out why you're trying to destroy his career and his professional reputation."

"After what he's done to me, he can't figure out why I'm angry? What a prick. I can't believe I've loved him as long as I have."

I tried to let that pass for the moment. "What do you mean 'after all he's done to you,' What exactly did Mr. Turbot do? I need to know if I'm going to be able to help either one of you."

Tricia looked at me with anger flaring in her eyes. "He broke up with me."

Five

Thank God it was Tuesday. With a day like the one I had just had, it wasn't that I was looking forward to three more, only that there were just three days before the weekend. I had a feeling I wasn't going to get a whole lot of relaxation time.

I couldn't bring myself to face Carl again that afternoon. As soon as the bell rang at the end of the day, I made my best effort to get out of the school fast. That itself is no small feat. When I was young and in school, when the bell rang at the end of the day, those of us cool enough to have jobs at gas stations or Beaver Lumber could afford our own cars to take us home or to the homes of the many friends that could be acquired through the joy of car ownership. It didn't matter if the car was a beat up, 1966 Ford Fairlane; wheels were wheels. Those without cars started walking, at least as far as the nearest bus stop.

Not so today. Not even a Chrysler dealership can produce the volume of mini-vans that appear in front of a school in the immediate aftermath of last period dismissal. Oh, sure, there are a few station wagons, SUVs and sedans, and even the occasional compact, but hell hath no highway like the mini-van strewn driveway of the public school at eight thirty a.m. and three p.m., Monday to Friday.

By three forty-five, I was home. There were a few lifestyle changes I was not willing to make with my change of profession. One of those was my home. In my first three years as a lawyer, I had socked away most of my salary and lived comfortably off the avails of my in-laws' wealth. My ex-wife Sandi and I had a large, comfortable-bordering-on-luxurious condominium apartment in

Vancouver's Kitsilano neighbourhood. Though now divorced and employed in the public service, I couldn't bring myself to leave the proximity to the beach. Of course, on my income, I'd had to drop from a three bedroom to a small, 'one plus den,' but I could see ocean from the living room and could have my foot in the water in less than a block. Also, Starbucks was about eight hundred feet from the lobby.

The rest of my conversation with Tricia Bellamy had left my head swimming. Tricia had detailed for me her relationship with Carl as it had transpired over the past year. Shortly after the start of second semester, according to Trish, she and Carl had begun to spend time together after school when she was experiencing academic difficulty with Biology Eleven's categorization of basically everything organic into fila, strata and other arcane scientific terms. It was during this time that she alleged a romantic relationship had begun.

The night before a mid-term exam, Tricia and a small group of students had stayed late after school to go over material they knew would cause them difficulty on the exam. As time ticked by in the impromptu tutorials, the number of students decreased gradually until Trish found herself alone with Carl. At his suggestion, they ordered a pizza and continued to discuss the practical portion of the laboratory exam for the next day.

Tricia said she had always thought Carl was attractive; she also felt that Carl had always treated her differently, that he had some special interest in her. When they had finished their pizza and had exhausted every possible area of study for the test, Carl had finally suggested it was time to call it quits. It was after seven. When Trish realized how long they had spent together, and how much of his own time Carl had spent helping her, she says she was overwhelmed by a sense of being really important to Carl.

"We stopped by the door to the lab," she had told me, "and I turned to say thank you. Just to really say, you know, thank you for taking all of this time to help me. He was so close and so kind, and I had always liked him, and the next thing I knew I was kissing him. It was just that simple and that fast."

There had been no secret courting, no sending of notes, no surreptitious meetings, no long history of flirting. According to Tricia Bellamy, it just happened. And more importantly, it hadn't stopped. Both Tricia and Carl had been shocked at first. Neither had been planning or expecting it to happen. But once it had, she said it was like a floodgate of feelings had opened, and it seemed that things had become very intense very quickly.

The relationship hadn't become sexual right away. That was why Tricia had never felt she was being exploited or that the relationship was in any way wrong. She was seventeen years old and involved in a relationship with a teacher fifteen years her senior, but she also knew that he loved her. In fact, it had been nearly two months before she and Carl had "made love," as she had put it. They had been together ever since, until last week, when Carl had told Trish he could no longer see her and felt it was best if they kept their distance from one another outside of the classroom.

Of course, none of this jibed with the version of events Carl had given me earlier in the day. In fact, in his story, there were no events to corroborate: Tricia was his student, plain and simple. Her threat to report him to the principal was so far out of left field that Carl was literally in a state of shock. Furthermore, he had convinced me, and I believed him, or at least I had until I had met up with Tricia.

First impressions are often impetuous, but Tricia too had seemed truly genuine, a love-struck girl whose heart had just been broken by what she had thought was a long-term, loving relationship. She admitted she had threatened Carl in anger and that her preference was to continue their relationship. In fact, she was desperately seeking to reconcile with him. I had certainly met my share of sociopathic defendants who could concoct stories with imaginative detail, but it was difficult to believe that this girl could be dreaming up this entire history of her romance with Carl.

Which left me at this point, drinking red wine, staring out my living room window watching the sun disappear before even the five o'clock news could begin, wondering whose story had the most credibility and what the hell I could do about it.

After an hour of thinking and two glasses of wine, I was no closer to determining whose version of events I believed. I was also feeling a bit light-headed; at nearly six feet tall, I may look big, but without food, two glasses of wine most definitely can make me woozy. I decided to clarify my thoughts by heading up to Chianti, my favourite little Italian eatery, a few blocks away on Fourth Avenue.

Another advantage to living in the Kitsilano neighbourhood was its proximity to no small number of great restaurants. Fourth Avenue alone housed Italian, Indian, Vietnamese and Mexican restaurants, along with specialty stores that sold food from small countries I wasn't sure I had heard of.

If I actually felt like cooking, which I admit was rare, I could also walk easily to Granville Island Public Market, an island oasis of fresh produce, meat, bakeries and coffee. The island is also a cultural mecca in the urban centre of Vancouver, with four live theatres, renowned quaint bookstores, galleries and craft stores, all placed under the steel girders of the Granville Street Bridge.

"Good evening, Professor." Teri, my favourite server, greeted me as I walked down the sloped entrance to the restaurant. "Will you be joining us this evening, or are you taking our wares home with you?"

"And miss your company?" I replied. "Home equals work. Here equals pasta. Here wins." Teri led me to a table near the window, which wasn't my first choice, but considering the lineup that nearly always greets one at this restaurant, I couldn't complain. "Don't need the menu," I told her as I sat down. "I'll just have the special and a glass of Cab."

"To go with the..." she sniffed the air around me, "Merlot you downed before arrival? Tsk. Mixing Merlot and Cabernet. Shame." She walked away to place my order, leaving me wondering how she could always detect even the faintest hint of whatever I'd been eating or drinking throughout the day. While I waited, I planned my strategy for dealing with Carl and Tricia the next morning. A side of me wanted desperately to believe Tricia. As the younger party and, by general definition, the more vulnerable of the two, I felt I had a duty to ensure she was looked after. On the other hand, I had agreed to represent Carl, and I couldn't in good faith fail to do so. I knew I would have to reveal the details of my conversation with Tricia to him and get his response, which I imagined would be fierce denial.

Within a few minutes, my salad, wine and queen of sarcasm had arrived. "You look deep in thought, Win," she began. "Tough day saving the minds of our city's youth?"

"Oh yeah," I told her.

"What happened? Someone not do their homework, or was it an adolescent crisis like 'Oh my Gawd, graduation's only eight months away, and I don't have a dress yet'?"

"More along the lines of the latter, but on a somewhat grander scale."

"Yeah?"

"Yeah. Unfortunately, it's an actual legal matter, so I can't go into it."

"You just can't give up, can you?"

"I know. I kind of just opened my mouth and said 'yes' before I realized what was happening."

She smiled knowingly at me. "Look. Cheer up. You've never had a problem doing the right thing before. I can list all kinds of right things you've done: defending the defenceless, entering the teaching profession, dumping the Dragon Lady..."

"She dumped me, " I corrected.

"Details. Eat your dinner. Finish your wine. Go for your walk and listen to your heart. You'll figure out what to do." Teri walked away to serve the less glum pasta diners.

But she was right. I'd already decided that tomorrow I'd tell Carl I would defend him as best as I could. But if Tricia's story was true, I wouldn't try to get him off, only see he received due process.

That much I felt I could offer in clear conscience.

Six

The cold, crisp, sunny November morning of the previous day did not repeat itself. That's not unusual. I couldn't say how infrequent sunny November days are—I'm not a weatherman—but I know how much I celebrate the few we have.

Wednesday morning, I did not need my alarm clock to wake me. The sound of sheets of rain slapping against the sliding glass patio door was enough to jolt me awake. Unfortunately, it was only 3:47 am. One of my many flaws, according to my ex-wife, is my remarkable inability to return to slumber once the gods of awakedom have shown even the slightest interest in me. I've tried reading, late night/early morning TV, praying, cursing. It doesn't matter. Once I'm up, I'm up.

When you get up that early, not even the newspaper is there to keep you company. Despite contributing to the demise of my marriage, insomnia did do me some physical good. For a lack of anything better to do, my long-term lack of slumber had led me to a nearly six-year career of early morning running. The previous year, I had celebrated the finality of my divorce by running my first marathon. I hadn't won, but it hadn't killed me either. It also hadn't helped me sleep any better.

The bitter, icy rain this November morning effectively countered the sweat I built up as I finished my traipse out past the Jericho yacht club, along Spanish Banks to the edge of the university lands and back. There was almost no need to shower after the wicked pre-dawn downpour, but I still had all this time to kill. Generally, after showering and dressing, I read the two daily newspapers to fill the hours before a teacher can reasonably be expected to arrive at school in the morning.

One of the many advantages of living down by the beach and working at Sir John A. was that my morning commute was against traffic. In Vancouver's Lower Mainland, the bulk of traffic traditionally heads west from the outer suburbs into the downtown core. When you already live West, at least getting to work in the morning isn't inordinately stressful.

Of course, it also doesn't afford you much time to prepare mentally for unpleasant tasks on your to-do lists, like asking your colleague if he's been sleeping with his seventeen-year-old biology student. Unfortunately, reporting back to Carl was job number one of the day.

It may have potentially made it more difficult for Carl to start his day with an unpleasant visit from me, but I knew I would probably be ineffective in the classroom if I didn't get this off my chest. Coincidentally, it was on my lesson plan to discuss the criminal definition of sexual harassment with my Law Twelve class, but I was planning to steer the conversation away from relationships between students and their teachers as an example of what could be classed as a criminally inappropriate relationship.

In my three months of teaching experience, I had found that arriving at the school around seven thirty in the morning afforded me some quiet time to mentally prepare for the day. I admire those teachers who can run in at the last minute as the bell is ringing and begin their day without any panic kicking in. I need to coast into my teaching duties. Get a feel for the room. Anticipate what might lie ahead. I was always like that in court too, which wasn't easy as a Legal Aid lawyer: I had spent as much of my time travelling between courtrooms as I had inside them. At least as a high school teacher, I pretty much got to stay in the same room all day. For less pay. With fewer breaks.

By the time I reached the entrance closest to the staff parking lot, I was already nearly soaked through. No sooner did I pass through the doorway than I literally crashed into Carl. Damn the proximity of the science wing. It was going to be that kind of day.

"Winston!" he practically shouted as I entered dripping through the doorway.

"Good morning, Carl. Beautiful day, isn't it?" I am a master of small talk.

"Listen, what's happening?" he asked a little too loudly. Though we were alone, one lesson I had quickly learned in a high school was that the walls have ears. I had learned that in my second week, when I had called the photocopier a piece of shit while I thought I was alone with it. I'm now known as a technophobe with a hot temper.

"Not much. Let's go into your classroom." I gave my best surreptitious nod towards the door to remind him we needed privacy.

"Right." Unlocking the classroom door—if it isn't locked down, it won't be there in the morning is a general rule— Carl ushered me inside the science lab.

I had managed to avoid taking a single science class since eleventh grade biology myself. By the last month of school, when it became apparent that even if I scored 100% on the final exam, I could not possibly hope to pass the course, I had left the class, dumping my textbook and notebook in the garbage can by the door, vowing never to return. Thus far, I had been successful. Completing my undergraduate degree at a university that did not require science for admission, I had managed to go from the age of seventeen right through university and law school without ever having to light another Bunsen burner. Being in Carl's classroom was bringing it all back.

Sir John A. Macdonald isn't the oldest school in Vancouver, not by a long shot, but despite being Canada's third largest city, Vancouver has built a new high school for years, probably decades. J. Mac, as the school was known throughout the district, was really beginning to show its age. The room was long and narrow, with counters running along three walls. In the middle of the room, students would sit at banged up old pairs of tables, joined in the middle by a counter with a sink and one of those ridiculously long, tall faucets that were suddenly in fashion with studio loft apartment builders. It was depressing to think we were training future cancer researchers in this decrepit old facility.

"How you holding up this morning?" I asked him, looking for a stool on which to park my butt.

"I'm fine," he replied. "How did it go with Trish yesterday? You talked to her, right?"

"Yeah. I did." I could barely raise my head to look him in the eye. Carl wasn't helping by being unexpectedly cheerful.

"And? Did she come clean? Did she tell you why she's suddenly trying to wreck my life?"

"Not exactly, no." Bracing myself for the storm that was no doubt to follow, I put myself into lawyer mode and pressed on. "Basically, she confirmed for me the...uh...the story she came to you with."

"What? I don't understand."

"Carl." I paused long enough to let out a sigh. It can have good dramatic impact. If I wore glasses, this would be when I would take them off to rub the bridge of my nose. "There is no easy way to tell you this, but Tricia did not recant her story when I confronted her with your version of events. In fact, she filled in a fair number of details."

"What are you saying, Win?"

"I'm saying either Tricia Bellamy lies with the skill of a sociopath or that a physical relationship actually took place between the two of you."

"Jesus Christ, Win! I can't believe what I'm hearing!" Carl exploded, as I had expected he would. But even I didn't like the tone and the intensity of his voice.

"Would you calm down?"

"How the hell can I calm down?" he demanded. "This kid, this obviously disturbed, psychotic girl is trying to ruin me!"

Mustering up my courtroom bravado, I rose to face him as close to eye-to-eye as possible. "If you don't calm down," I hissed at him quietly, "Tricia won't even have to ruin you. You'll do it yourself." Carl glared at me, his eyes two small circles of ice. "People are starting to arrive in the building, Carl. If you don't keep your voice down, any hope of confidentiality is out the window."

After a small eternity, he turned away from me and walked towards his desk at the front of the classroom. He sat down behind the teacher's lab counter and became engrossed in a flint lighter used to light Bunsen burners. Also, if I remembered correctly, they could be used to torment people you didn't like by lighting their hair on fire. Flick. Flick. Flick.

"Did you tell her you were my lawyer?" Flick. Flick. Flick.

"Yes. I did."

"And that didn't get her to change her story?"

"Is that what you were hoping would happen?" Flick. Flick. Fli...

"Well, yeah."

"Why did you think telling her I was your lawyer would make her change her claim? Did you send me there to scare her?"

"Yeah, Win. I hoped that once she realized the seriousness of what she was saying, she would drop whatever she's doing to me, and we could just go back to school without having to worry about being fired."

"Or worse."

"Worse?"

"Tricia is legally a child. If you had a relationship with her..."

"She's seventeen!"

"And according to her, the relationship has been going on for over a year. That means not only was she a minor, but she was unable to form consent, since you were in a position of authority over her. That means this isn't just a civil matter. It's criminal. We're talking the potential for jail time."

"But she's lying! It's not true!" Carl nearly yelled again.

"Carl." I held up my hands. "Calm down." He paused long enough to resume his role of flint flicker. Flick. Flick. Flick. "I said I would help you, and I will. I gave you my word, and I am now your legal counsel. If you had a relationship with Tricia Bellamy, you showed extremely poor judgment, and I certainly wouldn't be proud of being your friend right now. But regardless, you have retained me as counsel, and I will see you through this."

"Okay. Thank you."

"Don't thank me yet. There's a 'but' in there."

"Okay...but?"

"But, if you aren't telling me the truth, if you are or were sleeping with Tricia, I will not try to defend your actions. I will only see to it that you are treated with due process. You understand?"

"Okay."

"And it would be really helpful if you would tell me up front the absolute truth."

"Win, I'm telling you now. As God is my witness, Trish is making this up. I don't know why, but she is going to destroy me. If she goes to the principal, it is inevitable that my wife will find out, and it will just create unnecessary stress. I did not sleep with Trish or any other student."

Damned if I didn't believe him. "Okay, Carl. That's all I wanted to hear."

"That's it?"

"That's it."

"What do we do now?"

"There's really nothing we can do. Now, we wait."

"But..." I could feel his anxiety rising again.

"There's nothing we can do. I talked to Tricia. I interviewed her. It's possible she believes this story she's telling. But even if she doesn't, in my capacity as your lawyer, there is nothing I can do to prevent her from going to the principal with this story. All I can do is defend you against her allegations once she makes them."

"But that's insane," he protested. "All it will take is for her to make a complaint, and I'm ruined."

"There are things we can do if or when this gets into the legal arena. Discredit her story. Ensure reliable alibis. I'll look after that. But we can't tie her down and stop her from talking to Don."

"Shit, it doesn't matter whether or not you can get me off, Win. All she has to do is talk to Don and make an accusation, and I'm history."

"Not necessarily," I tried to reassure him, though I knew he was basically correct.

"Yes. I'm completely innocent, but every student, every other teacher, every principal, every parent is going to be looking at me like I'm some kind of sex fiend."

"Just calm down, Carl."

"No. I'll end up having to transfer schools. And my wife will want to know why I'm leaving the school I love, and I'll have to tell her some kid is claiming I banged her!"

"Carl."

"No, Win. I can't just sit back and wait for Trish to fuck up my life." He got up and headed for the door.

"Where are you going?"

"I've got to try to stop her."

I took two steps after him to try to block his exit. "Wait. Do not go and talk to Tricia."

He whirled and faced me, eyes blazing. "Why the hell not?"

"Because obviously, previous conversations you've had with her have not gone well. Getting confrontational with her is likely going to make her more angry."

"I'm just going to talk to her."

"Trust me. If I'm going to be your counsel, you're going to have to listen to me." I stepped between him and the door.

"Win, move." Carl stepped back and put his hand to his forehead.

"Carl, listen to me. Just listen for a minute, okay?" I used my best soothing voice.

"Win, just get the hell out of my way, okay? I need to talk to Trish. I will not sit here and watch my life go to shit because of her." His voice was steely cold. I actually felt just a little threatened, at least enough to step aside from the door.

"Okay."

"I'm just going to talk to her, all right? Maybe I can fix this." Almost as quickly as his rage had come, it was gone.

"All right," I told him. It wasn't.

He put his hand on my shoulder momentarily, then walked out the door.

*   *   *

Days like that rarely get better, and this day was no exception. The kids were kids, not wonderful, but no one went out of their way to make the day difficult for me either. Carl had largely taken that task on himself.

The most disturbing part of the day came at lunch. When teaching days are going poorly, there are basically two approaches to lunchtime. The first is that you lock yourself away in your classroom and catch up on marking or maybe read the paper. I had already read two newspapers before arriving, and the thought of reading my law class's assignments, in which they discussed— probably quite poorly—'sexual harassment in the workplace laws', seemed a little too much to bear on this day. So I went to option two, which was to join my colleagues in the faculty lounge for empty chit-chat, bitching shop talk and plans for Christmas vacations. I can only spend so much time with adolescents before I need a bit of adult face time.

Walking into the staff room, I bumped headlong into Carl. It was as though he didn't see me. Without so much as an "excuse me," he shrugged by me and headed back towards the science wing.

"That was odd, don't you think?" asked Christine, a petite English teacher who had walked in with me.

"Yeah," I replied nonchalantly, "he must be having a bad day."

"That's just not like Carl. He's always so friendly."

"Yeah. That's always been my impression of him too." I let it drop at that, not wanting to get drawn into a conversation in which I pretended to speculate on the cause of Carl's surly disposition.

For the second time in as many days, I made myself scarce after school, but not before looking in on Carl. To my surprise, he wasn't in his biology lab, where you could almost guarantee he would have students in after school getting extra help on frog gutting and pig fetus dissecting assignments, but I couldn't tell if he had gone for the day, and I didn't really want to know. I knew he needed to blow off steam, and after the way we had parted before school, I didn't want to get in his face until he had time to cool off and reflect overnight.

I had to admit it didn't look good. His unexpected outburst aside, I still couldn't shake my gut instinct that Carl was telling me the truth. That being the case, I totally understood why he was so angry at the thought of Tricia going to the principal. He was right. He and I would know, but to everyone else around the school, Carl Turbot would be damaged goods once this got out. Even the innocent are usually believed to have done something to warrant this kind of accusation from a student.

By ten that night, I was outright tired not only of mulling over Carl's legal problems, but also of marking the aforementioned law class papers, so I surrendered to my Wednesday night weakness for *Law and Order*. Ten minutes into the program, and ten seconds into one of Fontana's complaints about dirt on his Italian leather shoes, I put down my wine glass as the phone rang.

"Hello?" I asked on the third ring. Damn, I wished I had set up the VCR to tape the show.

"Winston? Winston Patrick?"

"Speaking. Who is this?"

"Hey, Winston. It's Ralph Bremner. From school," came the gruff voice of the school's P.E. department head.

"Ralph, what's up?" I asked, not realizing that our meeting yesterday had cemented a friendship that warranted post ten p.m. phone calls.

"Sorry to call you so late. It's kind of official. The principal called and asked me to take a few names on the phone list. We're having an emergency staff meeting tomorrow morning. I'm just helping to spread the word."

"Oh, all right. Any idea what it's about?"

"Yeah, unfortunately I do. It's a bit of a doozy. It's actually about that kid you were talking to in my gym class yesterday. Tricia Bellamy."

"What about her?" I asked, alarm rising in my throat like floodwaters.

"Jeez, Win, did you get to know her at all yesterday?" Ralph asked tentatively.

"Did I get to know her? Ralph, what's going on?"

"I'm sorry to have to tell you this, Win. She's dead."

Seven

The boyish, peach-fuzzed police officer shook his head. "Some sort of emergency?" he asked.

"An emergency meeting. I really need to be there."

"Yeah. Best if you get there in one piece, counsellor," he replied, handing me back my driver's licence.

"Thank you, officer," I sighed, reluctantly signing the traffic citation. I'm generally hesitant to inform a traffic cop of my profession—albeit in the past tense—as a member of the bar. Like most of the population, cops consider lawyers one of the lower species on the food chain. Trying to talk your way out of a radar trap on the basis of being a lawyer usually just makes them mad. But this one looked young enough that I thought I might be able to bluff my way out of the ticket. I was wrong.

As a lawyer, I should have known better. As a teacher, I should have been going slower. I was clocked speeding through a school zone.

I was operating on less than two hours sleep. Since Bremner had called with the news of Tricia's death, I had paced a path in my living room carpet not even the vacuum would get out. Going to bed had been no use either. Despite my use of many of the devices various therapists and doctors have suggested, sleep had been an elusive beast that night. I had read an entire novel in hopeful anticipation of bringing on shut-eye. But no matter how hard I had tried, each time I had closed my eyes, my previous images of Carl romantically involved with Tricia Bellamy were replaced with images of Carl killing her.

I had no idea how she'd died, where she'd been found or any other relevant details. Who knew how much more information the principal would be able to provide? It was even possible the two events were coincidental. If Tricia was the kind of student who could concoct wildly believable stories in order to wreak revenge for some imagined wrong, she may very well have been the kind of person who was engaged in extracurricular activities that would endanger her life. In fact, if she was making up the story she had told me about her and Carl, this kid was probably into all kinds of hallucinogens and was running with the type of crowd that could provide them for her. She also could simply have been hit by a car.

Still, I couldn't help thinking that Carl should have called me. He had to know if Tricia's story had gone any further than the three of us, sooner or later the police would be looking at him as a suspect in her death. I had made it clear that I was his lawyer now; the fact he hadn't called me to express concern threw all kinds of new doubts into my opinion of his credibility.

An eerie gloom hung over Sir John A. Macdonald Secondary School when I pulled into the parking lot. Usually one of the earliest to arrive at school in the morning, I could see that today most of the faculty was already present. Seeing a Vancouver Police squad car at the front of the building wasn't an entirely unusual sight for an East Vancouver high school. Seeing five of them was.

The administrative office of the school was the only place where activity was raging. Phones were ringing off the hook as hapless secretaries confirmed to anxious parents what they had already heard on their morning news shows: "Yes, there has been a student killed. No, we're not releasing the name of the student yet. Yes, there will be school today. No, students do not have to come if they are too distraught. Yes, grief counsellors will be available to anyone who needs them."

I walked in and, as a reflex habit checked my mailbox for messages. There were four from parents informing me they were keeping their kids at home for the day. I couldn't blame them. Today was going to suck.

"Good morning, Winston," said Fiona, the school's matronly head secretary and unofficial surrogate grandmother to students and staff.

"Good morning," I returned glumly. "How are you doing?"

"I'm okay. I have to be. Students will be in here all day. How about you?"

"I'm all right. This is going to be pretty horrible, I'm betting."

"Yes. It will. You didn't teach her?" It wasn't really a question. Like most public schools, there was always one secretary who held the fabric of the institution together and knew what was happening. Fiona was ours. She would already have known not only that I hadn't taught Tricia, but also everyone who had. Those teachers would get special acknowledgment from Fiona when or if they arrived.

"No," I replied, "I didn't."

"Lovely girl. Good family. Her mother is on the parent advisory council. She's...she was a terrific young lady." Fiona did her stoic best to maintain her always present poise.

"That's what I hear."

"Staff meeting's in the library," Fiona said, snapping back to attention.

"Thanks," I said, gathering the stash of messages, memos and assorted school paperwork and turning for the door.

The staff assembled in the library was not the normal, chipper group of colleagues who traded bullshit, gossip and grievances in the lounge. You would think a group of people who work with teenagers day in and day out would be used to the idea that at some point something bad would happen to one of them. The school had not escaped its share of tragedy in the past. There had been students killed in car crashes, and one or two had suffered an untimely end due to illness. But from the muffled conversations around the room, I gathered that no J. Mac kid had been killed during the school year for many years.

I looked around the room for Carl but didn't see him. Within a few minutes of my arrival, nearly the entire faculty and support staff were gathered, and still there was no sign of my colleague-turned-client. I was about to slip out the door to phone him at home when Don McFadden, Sir John A. Macdonald's bland and generally considered inept principal, arrived to start the meeting.

There was no effort to arrange tables in the room for people to sit in any sort of formal fashion. It was enough just to give Don attention for a few moments so he could begin the proceedings.

"Good morning," Don began. "Thank you everyone for coming in early this morning. This is one of those things they don't prepare you for in principal school." Murmurs of acknowledgment emanated from the gathered staff. As Don resumed speaking, I looked up with some relief to see Carl slip quietly into the library. He took a seat on an easy chair next to the rotating rack of pulp fiction by the window.

"As you know, I've assembled us here this morning to discuss some tragic news that was given to me last night." Don paused. I can't say I was a fan of my new boss, but at this moment at least, he seemed much more human than he had since I'd first met him during my interview. "By now, you are all aware one of our Grade Twelve students, Tricia Bellamy, was killed yesterday. There is no easy way for me to say this, so I'm just going to come right out and say it. According to the police, Tricia was murdered."

The expected gasps, murmurs and sounds of disbelief flowed out of the collected staff. A slight buzz travelled around the room as some teachers had their speculations confirmed while others reacted with disbelief that one of our own could have found her end through murder. Don raised his hands to the staff to regain the room's attention, while I glanced over to Carl to gauge his reaction. He caught my eye, and in his I detected genuine sadness.

"People, please," Don continued, "students will be here shortly, and I really want to get through this." The buzz of quiet conversations began to diminish as people returned their focus to the principal.

"Don, what happened?" asked George Kyle, the head of the math department.

"I don't have a whole lot of information for you. And that's important, because there will be lots of speculation among the kids, and I don't want to start any kind of false rumours floating around out there."

"What *do* you know?" came a second question. This one came from Carl.

Don paused and looked slowly and carefully at Carl for a moment before responding. "The police contacted me at home about nine last night. Tricia's body was found in the middle of a soccer field at a park close to her home. A neighbour walking her dog caught sight of her and called the police. She...umm...she had her student card and driver's licence with her, so...identification was made very quickly. The police got in touch with me only about five or ten minutes after the body was found."

A teacher towards the back of the room was no longer able to contain herself and broke down in tears. She was quickly comforted by colleagues around her, plunging the room into an uncomfortable silence. I eventually broke it.

"Don," I asked, perhaps a bit too clinically, "do we know how she was killed?"

"Yes. We do. And we should be as clear as we possibly can when students ask, without traumatizing them any more than absolutely necessary." He paused a moment to check the notes on paper he held in his slightly quaking hands. "The coroner's preliminary examination indicates the cause of death was strangulation."

"Oh, God," came the voice of another teacher who couldn't contain her emotions and joined the first teacher in tears.

"And, because it is likely to come up from scared students, there is, as yet, no indication of...umm....sexual assault," he continued.

"At least she didn't suffer that," one of the school's senior teachers of home economics added to the discussion.

"Have the police made any arrests?" I pressed further, trying to focus the conversation away from details of the crime.

"No," Don replied. In that moment, for a very brief second, Don flashed a glance towards Carl. The look was so fleeting, I wondered if I had imagined it. "They have not arrested anyone. But, from what I have been told, they do not believe this was the act of a random killer. They do have suspects."

"It's not anyone at the school, is it?" one of the counsellors asked.

Don left an uncomfortable pause, seemingly unsure of how to respond. "I'm afraid I can't really say at the moment," he finally managed.

"What?" Christine from the English department demanded. "What the hell does that mean? Are you saying the police think Tricia was murdered by someone at the school?"

"I'm not saying anything like that," Don countered. "I'm saying the police have instructed me not to say anything at all about suspects. That's all I can tell you."

"Don," Christine protested further, "if there is a student in the school who may be dangerous to other students or to ourselves, we deserve to know. How am I supposed to teach my classes when I'm worrying about one of my kids being a killer?"

Similar comments of outrage followed Christine's. "People," Don cried out. "People, please! Listen to me." The room quieted down again, and he continued slowly. "I don't have any reason to believe that one of our students is a threat to anyone in the building. The police do not believe this is a random act. They will be here today. They will likely conduct interviews with all of Tricia's teachers." This time it was unmistakable, as Don shot another furtive glance towards Carl. "They will also probably be talking to her friends. So if a police officer comes to your door and wants to speak to anyone, please, just cooperate."

No protest came from the group this time as the magnitude of the day to come was beginning to sink in. "Most importantly," Don resumed, "please remember the most important thing is that we are all here for the kids. There are going to be some very upset kids today. The district will have extra counsellors here for any student who wants to come down and talk. They will set up here in the library. If you see any student who is responding particularly badly, whatever that may mean, feel free to quietly suggest to that student that they can come down here to talk to a counsellor. And," he paused for a moment, "that offer goes to all staff as well, especially those of you who taught her. Don't take this on yourself. These counsellors will be happy to talk with you, too."

The bell to signal five minutes to first period rang and broke the silence that had fallen on the room. "Okay," Don said. "Let's go out there and do our best. If anyone needs anything from us, get a hold of me or anyone in the office."

Teachers began shuffling reluctantly towards the door. This was not something I ever thought I would have to face as a teacher. Carl, I noticed, appeared to be making a conscious effort to avoid making eye contact with me. The lawyer side of me had doubts about the story he had been telling me. The teacher side of me knew that if Carl was telling the truth—if Trish had essentially been seeking revenge for some perceived wrong—Carl could very well simply be hurting from the loss of a student he'd taught and cared about.

I had just about reached the door to the library when I noticed the principal step beside Carl and take him gently by the arm, whispering into his ear. Once that happened, I had no choice but to abandon my plans to head to first period class and intervene in the conversation taking place between Don and Carl.

"Hey Carl," I began, sauntering casually up to the two men. "What's up?"

"Sorry, Winston," Don interrupted before Carl could reply. "You'll have to excuse us. We're just about to go have a little meeting."

I looked at Carl, carefully sending a question with my eyes. "You have a first period class, don't you, Carl?"

"Yes," he replied uneasily.

"There's a substitute coming in who's going to look after the class for a few minutes," Don said with contrived casualness.

"What do you want to see me about, Don?" Carl asked.

"Listen, I'd rather not talk about it right here. Just come to my office so we can talk about this...this unfortunate situation."

"No," I interjected. "No, Carl, that wouldn't be appropriate."

Don looked at me incredulously. I couldn't really blame him. Who was this upstart teacher with less than three months of tenure to tell the principal what is and is not appropriate? He took a few seconds to couch his response, which told me his meeting with Carl most definitely was not coincidental; somehow he knew something about Carl and Tricia, and he was planning to talk to Carl about it.

Finally, he recovered his composure enough to put on a stern principal's look. "Winston, I'm not sure what you mean. Carl and I are just going to have a little talk."

"Great. I'll come with you," I replied calmly and quietly, not wanting to draw the attention of the remaining staff to our little hubbub in the corner.

"Okay," Carl said, "that would be great. Why don't you come with me, Win?"

"Hold on," Don objected. "Winston, this is a private matter between Carl and me." Don leaned just slightly towards me, attempting to use his size to intimidate. Why do so many ex-football players end up as high school principals?

"There are no strictly private matters between teacher and principal, Don. We both know that. I'm coming with Carl, or he isn't coming." I talk tough for a skinny guy. But I can also run fast.

"Since when are you the staff's union representative?"

Bringing my voice to barely above a whisper, I replied, "I'm not. I'm his lawyer."

Don froze like deer in a headlight. Unfortunately, I had just given Don a whole lot of information long before I wanted to. But now it was out there, at least between the three of us.

"My office," he eventually said. "Let's talk."

Eight

The interior of Don's office was decorated in 1970s-era fake wood panelling. As an educator—and taxpayer for that matter—I found the principal's lack of stylish updating in his office comforting. It indicated at least some budget priorities.

After stopping at my classroom and putting the kids on temporary autopilot with the teacher next door checking in on them, we had walked the short journey from the library to Don's office without talking. He seemed to be wavering between fury at one of his teachers having retained legal counsel—from one of his other teachers, no less—to utter confusion as to why he would need to and how this all came to be. As we entered the office, Don closed the door slowly, then retreated behind the administrative barrier that was his fake oak desk. It took him more than a full minute to collect his thoughts sufficiently to begin the conversation. "What the hell is going on?" was the masterpiece he composed during his moment of silence.

Carl leaned forward and began to speak. I stopped him. "Why don't we begin with you telling me why it is you want to have a private meeting with Carl?" I proposed, quite reasonably I thought, to Don.

"Let me make something clear here, Winston. It is not generally accepted practice within the school system that teachers bring lawyers with them when meeting with the principal." He sounded pissed.

"I need to suggest to you that the events of today are leading me to the conclusion that 'generally accepted practice' will probably not be the order of the day. Let's go back again to why you want to speak to Carl."

Don sighed and leaned back in his chair before turning his

attention directly to Carl. "Mr. Turbot, I need to confirm something with you here. Do you want me to speak freely in front of Mr. Patrick? I am going to say some things here that I consider to be confidential."

"Yeah," Carl answered glumly. "Winston is a friend, and he is formally my lawyer, so yeah, you can talk in front of him."

"Okay," Don surrendered. "I guess I would like to start by asking why it is you've suddenly retained a lawyer, at least a former one, to deal with me?" The principal shot me a dirty look while saying "former one."

Carl began to speak again. I interrupted him again. "Why Carl has retained counsel is a matter of solicitor-client privilege. You need not concern yourself with that. You need only realize that until you hear otherwise from Carl or myself, your conversations with my client will be vetted through me. And I assure you there is no need to include the prefix 'former' in front of my title of lawyer. I am still a member of the bar." Not much of a comeback, I admit.

"Sorry," Don mumbled awkwardly. "I didn't mean to offend you."

"No offense taken. Now that we're all on the same page, let's get back to the issue at hand."

"Carl," Don began, "yesterday after school, Tricia Bellamy came to me, and she informed me that you and she were having a—a relationship of sorts that extended beyond teacher-student."

"She told you she and Carl were having an affair," I clarified for him.

"Yes. That's why I wanted to talk to him."

"I see," Carl replied. There was a brief, highly uncomfortable pause as Don tried to decide how to respond. I could practically smell the smoke burning.

"Is it true?" he began.

"What do you think?" Carl demanded with a snarl. He sounded ferocious. I had to admire his ability to come out swinging.

"I don't want to answer that right now. I would like to hear your side of the story," he replied.

"Carl's side of the story is quite simple: Tricia Bellamy's

allegations of sexual misconduct are unfounded and untrue. There was no relationship between Carl Turbot and Tricia Bellamy outside of a professional one," I interjected as firmly as possible. I have often found in legal practice that if you speak with enough gruff in your voice in an initial meeting, it often has the non-legal practitioner ducking for cover from the get-go. It sounds bullish and unsophisticated, but so were a lot of the people I dealt with in the criminal courts.

"I can't believe Tricia came to you," Carl moaned softly from the chair next to me.

"So, if I'm to understand this correctly, Tricia Bellamy, for reasons unknown, elected to come to me and inform me of a relationship that was not, in fact, taking place." Don was a quick study.

"That is correct," I told him.

"Well then, Carl, if you and Tricia were not having a sexual relationship, why did you feel it necessary to hire a lawyer?" Don asked.

"Tricia came to Carl, for reasons unknown, and threatened to expose this so-called relationship that was not, in fact, taking place. When Tricia made this threat, he came to me to seek my advice about what action he should take to prevent unnecessary hardship either to himself or the student, who was obviously troubled emotionally or perhaps psychologically or both. When Carl informed me he had a relationship issue with a student, he needed to retain me as counsel in order that what he told me would remain between the two of us. If he had not retained me as counsel, as a teacher, I would have had to take a different course of action."

"Is he paying you?" Don asked.

"That's privileged," I replied.

"What happened after he told you about Tricia's threat?"

"I spoke with Tricia to see if she would recant her story."

"Did she?"

"No," I replied.

"And you believe Tricia was lying, and Carl is telling the truth?"

"That's correct," I told him.

"And why is it you believe that?"

"Because I'm his lawyer."

"That's it? You don't have some other kind of, I don't know, evidence or something?"

"Don, I've been teaching here for seven years," Carl interrupted. "Has there ever been even the suggestion from anyone that I'm anything but a good teacher? Have you ever had a single complaint from a student? A parent? A suspicious teacher?"

"No, I haven't," Don admitted.

"Is there anything else you need from us?" I asked Don, rising to indicate we were terminating further conversation.

"You understand I had to follow up on this. There was no way I could ignore this. As much as I didn't want to believe it was true, when a student comes to me with something like this, I have an obligation to take necessary measures."

"What measures have you taken?" I asked Don.

"The police already talked to me about Tricia last night. They asked if I knew of anything unusual in her life. I had to tell them about Tricia's allegations."

"Shit!" Carl nearly exploded. "You told the police I was screwing Tricia?"

"Carl!" I reprimanded, laying my hand gently on his arm. "I think we should go now."

"Jesus, Winston! This guy has practically accused me himself!"

"Think of my position," Don pleaded. "A student comes to me saying her teacher was sleeping with her, and the same day she ends up murdered. I had to tell the police about Tricia's claims."

"And what did they say?" Carl wanted to know.

"Don't worry about that right now," I told him. "The police are going to want to talk to you. But it's okay. I'll be with you, and we will make sure you are okay."

"Carl," Don said, attempting to regain his authoritative posture. "Look me in the eye and tell me there was absolutely nothing improper going on between you and Tricia Bellamy."

"We're done here," I said. "You don't have to answer his questions. He has no legal authority to compel you to answer questions about a criminal investigation."

"No," Carl demanded. "It's okay. I want to answer that." He finally rose from the tacky, plaid covered chair to face Don. "Tricia was my student. A very good student, who worked hard, and who received my help. I never, ever, slept with or had an 'affair,' or any other improper relationship with her. And I sure as hell didn't kill her."

"Okay. Thank you." Don looked visibly relieved as a knock came on the door and Fiona poked her head in.

"Don," Fiona said gently. "I'm sorry to interrupt, but there's a detective here."

"Tell him I'll be right with him," Don said.

"He doesn't want to see you," Fiona said. "He wants to see Carl Turbot."

"Here we go," I told Carl. "It'll be all right."

* * *

Detectives Furlo and Smythe were plainclothes police officers from Vancouver's detective division. I had met them both briefly in previous encounters with the criminal justice system, but knew them more by their reputation among lawyers. Mostly bad. Furlo, in particular, like most cops, was not a huge fan of defence counsel. To him and cops like him, defence lawyers stood in the way of them doing their righteous duty. On some days, I didn't entirely disagree with him.

Furlo and Smythe had set up temporary shop in the small conference room off the main office, used for department meetings and small gatherings. When we arrived, Furlo was standing in the corner. Furlo was in his early forties and still looked like a full-time gym monkey. Despite police department dress codes, he wore a casual sports jacket over a black mock turtleneck shirt. He looked like the stereotypical tough guy in a 1970s cop show like *Charlie's Angels* or *Starsky and Hutch*. In fact, he kind of looked like Hutch. Or Starsky. Whichever one was the blond cop. He looked up when we entered, a bit confused by the fact that there were two of us. He didn't seem particularly displeased to see me, which indicated he didn't yet know why I was there.

Detective Jasmine Smythe was a fortyish, stylish woman who had fought and struggled her way up through the police ranks, facing opposition not only as a woman but as one of a very small black community in Vancouver. I had had very little contact with her in my short period in Legal Aid, but no defence lawyer I knew was thrilled to find Smythe was an investigating officer against a client. You could count on the fact that not only would the evidence be pretty solid, but every form would be carefully filled out, every "t" crossed and "i" dotted so that no evidence she presented to Crown prosecutors would be tossed out for procedural bungling. She had recently become one of the detective world's increasing number of techno geeks and sat at the conference room table with a laptop in front of her. A Blackberry lay next to the computer. By contrast, Furlo was reviewing notes on a $1.29 spiral notepad.

Smythe rose out of her chair as I entered the room with Carl in tow. "Mr. Turbot?" she asked.

"Mr. Patrick. Winston Patrick. I'm a teacher here."

"You're Carl Turbot?" Furlo asked, stepping towards Carl from his spot along the side wall.

"Yes," Carl replied quietly. "I understand you wanted to see me?"

"That's correct, Mr. Turbot," Smythe told him soothingly. "We just have a few questions we need to ask you. Please. Have a seat."

"Who are you?" Furlo demanded. Classic bad cop.

"Winston Patrick," I introduced myself a second time.

"I heard the first time," he growled. "Why are you here?"

"I think what my partner is asking," interjected Smythe with a genuine smile, "is if there is something you would like from us. We don't have you on our list of people to speak to specifically this morning." Classic good cop running interference for bad cop.

"I am counsel for Mr. Turbot," I stated neutrally.

Furlo's body visibly tensed, leaning forward with one hand on the battered conference table. "I thought you said you were a teacher here."

"I did. I teach law. I also practice it."

Smythe tilted her lovely head and smiled again. "Winston Patrick. You used to work with Legal Aid. Pre-trial centre duty counsel at Main Street. I thought the name sounded familiar."

"You mean you didn't recognize me from my handsome

visage?" I returned her smile.

"You would think I would remember that," Smythe said, returning my pre-serious conversation, casual flirtation. She played the game well.

"Could we get back to what the hell you are doing here with Mr. Turbot? Why has he got a lawyer with him?" Furlo groused.

"Come on, Detective," I put back at him. "You know better. Mr. Turbot has a lawyer because he is about to be interrogated by the police about a homicide. Were you not planning to inform him of his rights?"

"We're questioning all of Tricia Bellamy's teachers about her. We're looking to see if anyone noticed anything unusual about her in the last little while. That's it. Nobody's being interrogated here. Are you planning to legally represent all of her teachers, Mr. Patrick?" I could tell Furlo and I had definitely started out on the right foot.

"Why don't you cut the hostility and the bullshit, Detective Furlo," I replied, doing my very best to ensure I spoke with as little condescension as possible to avoid inflaming Furlo's obvious short fuse. "You know full well why I'm here with my client. You have selected him for questioning based on information provided to you by the principal about allegations of sexual misconduct, allegations, I might add, which are without merit, evidence or any corroboration. Mr. Turbot is not Tricia's first period teacher, or even first alphabetically among her eight teachers, so let's just be honest about the fact that this is a formal questioning. Or would you prefer that my client and I leave here now without answering your questions?"

"Patrick, you have a strange way of thinking that you're helping your client by opening your mouth and..."

"Mike," Smythe interrupted, "Mr. Patrick has a legitimate presence here. Let's get on with what we're trying to achieve."

"Whatever," he sighed, tossing his spiral notebook onto the table and flopping into a chair.

"Mr. Turbot, I know this is uncomfortable, so let's start over. Please. Have a seat." Smythe smiled again and seemed to warm the room, delicately waving her hand to the chair across the table.

Carl reluctantly sat down, never completely taking his eyes off Furlo. After our short verbal battle, it was beginning to sink in just how much shit he was in. I could actually physically feel his discomfort and anxiety. Facing two police detectives in a homicide investigation is discomfiting, even when you have nothing to hide. It was one of the reasons I was originally drawn to defence work. Over the years at the Vancouver law courts, I had seen many a petty criminal, and many an innocent bystander, nearly crumble under the investigatory prowess of cops and prosecutors determined to see conviction. Even the innocent will occasionally get talked into admitting to inappropriate or illegal conduct just by the sheer fear of the people across the table.

"Mr. Turbot, let's just cut to the chase so we can get on with the investigation," Smythe began. "According to the principal, Tricia came to him with allegations of a sexual relationship between her and you. Is there any truth to her complaints?"

Carl looked warily at me for permission to respond. I nodded my assent. He spoke quietly, nervously. "It is absolutely untrue. I have never had a physical relationship with Tricia or any other student. I'm a married man."

"So was I," interjected Furlo. "Three times. It rarely slowed me down."

Smythe rolled her eyeballs at her partner's display of testosterone-driven bravado. "Mr. Turbot, why would Tricia say those things if they weren't true?"

"How can he know that, Detective Smythe?" I asked.

"We're not in court here, Mr. Patrick. Can't we just ask him to speculate?"

"Go ahead, Carl," I conceded.

"I don't know. For some reason she was mad at me. She came to me and threatened to go..."

I interrupted. "What Mr. Turbot is referring to is that Tricia indicated to him she was planning to complain about a relationship that did not exist. It wasn't expressed as a threat in exchange for some favour or quid pro quo arrangement."

"Is that right?" Furlo asked Carl.

"That's right," Carl confirmed. At least he was following my lead, more than a lot of my clients had been able to.

"Was she struggling in the course, looking for some leverage to help her through the program?" Smythe soothingly inquired of my client.

Carl looked carefully at me again for approval, which I granted with a very slight nod. "Tricia is—was..." he corrected himself, "a very capable, bright student. She was having some trouble with a few assignments and concepts lately, but that's not uncommon in senior biology. It's very demanding."

"When you say she was having trouble, how much trouble? Was she failing?" Smythe pressed.

"Well, no. That's just it. Trouble for Tricia was slipping slightly below an 'A'. I mean slightly. I could show you her standings."

"That's okay. What else can you tell me about why she would have made this accusation?"

"I just don't understand. Look, I can tell you that Tricia was a very driven student. She set high standards and was a perfectionist. I understand she felt the same way about athletics. She could be stubborn about learning a concept. If she didn't understand, she would stay and get help and beat herself up until she understood. But she was never a problem. She never had disciplinary issues. I never had to reprimand her or throw her out of class. I can't tell you just how shocking it was to have her throw this threat from out of left field." Carl's voice had begun to rise to a level approaching frantic.

"Okay, Mr. Turbot. That's fine for now." Smythe pulled a business card out of her leather carry case. "If you think of anything else, anything at all that strikes you about her recent behaviour, please give us a call."

"That's it? I can go?" Carl asked.

"Sure. Thank you for speaking with us. I know this must be a very hard day for you and all of Tricia's teachers today." She pushed her chair back from the table and rose.

"Yes," Carl replied with a sigh of relief. "Thank you." He and I both rose from our seats. I had turned to shepherd my client to the door when Furlo broke his self-imposed silence one last time.

"Hey, Turbot. Look. Just between us, okay?" He actually winked conspiratorially. "Even if you were bangin' her, it doesn't mean you killed her. It would just help us rule out any loose ends if we were sure you were being straight with us. It doesn't have to leave this room. Were you and she going at it?"

Carl was horrified, and as he opened his mouth to speak, I jumped in. "Don't dignify that juvenile outburst with a response. You asked my client that question already, and it was answered." I pushed him out the door and turned to face Furlo. "Not only are we talking about a teenager here, Detective, in schools we tend to frown on discussions of 'banging' students. If that's the best you can do, I don't hold a whole lot of hope about you actually apprehending her killer. Detective Smythe," I nodded towards Smythe, who looked positively embarrassed by her partner.

I could feel Furlo's stare burning into the back of my skull as I left the conference room. I heard him mutter something about asshole lawyers as I shut the door.

Nine

The rest of the day was exactly how it looked on the television news. And television news was everywhere. Unlike many lawyers, I had never developed any special love for cameras and press conferences. My cases had generally been low profile, attracting little interest from the broadcast media. So many of my clients were among the downtrodden that they didn't present a lovely image on camera. If it ain't pretty, let's not put it on air. On the flip side, I had never particularly disliked the media either, as many of my prosecutorial colleagues and many cops did. Reporters just had a job to do, though they often did it in as superficial a manner as they could. But generally if they wanted a quote, I gave them a quote. If they didn't, I didn't go looking for them. Today I didn't have to look far. People often comment about how crass and insensitive it is for television news cameras to show up during a time of grief, particularly when there are kids involved.

It wasn't a productive day. Many more kids came to school than I thought would. Even those who were most upset could get the comfort they needed by being around the people closest to them in their lives. Often, those people were their friends at school or even their teachers, rather than their families.

Don McFadden had gone on the P.A. system to make the gruesome announcement just after we had finished speaking with him. By then, most of the kids had already heard; dozens had been interviewed by reporters outside the building. If there was any plan of breaking it to them gently, the throngs of police and media personnel greeting them upon arrival pretty much spoiled it.

Classes were limited to "seat work", having kids do limited brain activity by "read this and answer the question" type assignments. Even at that, big chunks of class time were consumed with me asking how everyone was feeling, which was usually followed by a fresh round of flowing tears. I like to think I'm a terrifically sensitive guy. Apparently either I'm not, or I haven't figured out how to allow my sensitivity to manifest itself appropriately. New teachers have it drilled into their heads that they need to keep an enormous professional and especially physical chasm between teacher and student. Accusations like Tricia's are pretty much evidence of the reason why those practices are so drilled into us, but it's almost impossible when a student collapses into your arms grieving the loss of a friend to step back and say "Whoa! You're not supposed to make physical contact with me."

But I tried. I thought it would be best if I could keep my distance and direct my students into working on actual curricular objectives. It just made me come across as cold. As many times as I tried to go over the homework, or assign a new task, I was met with "Mr. Patrick, how can you expect us to think about school?" I couldn't really. But hanging out all day with grieving kids was making me so uncomfortable and awkward that I felt a need to attempt to redirect their emotions into something productive. It didn't work.

The staff room was a quiet, numb space at lunch. It wasn't a place I really wanted to be, but I had an ulterior motive: I wanted to find out if word of Carl's alleged transgressions had travelled through the school. As his lawyer, I might have to attempt some damage control if rumours had begun to fly. Though conversation was relatively subdued, no one appeared, at least, to be discussing Carl or any other staff member as potential suspects in Tricia's death.

It took all the energy I could muster to make it through the afternoon. The tears began to dry up somewhat as the day progressed, but the entire school was cloaked in a blanket of emotional exhaustion by the end of the day. The principal commanded a brief meeting at the end of the day to discuss means by which we could attempt to bring the place back to relatively normal operations the next day.

"As much as possible, we need to get kids back into the school routine so they are not focused on these issues," Don stated to the assembled faculty. "We need to let kids know that we're still here if they need support, but that school needs to carry on." Even he didn't sound very convinced.

At the end of the meeting, I caught up with Carl in the hallway as he headed for the door. "How are you holding up?" I asked him.

"I'm all right, I think," he replied quietly.

He didn't seem so. I stopped him and looked him directly in the eye. "Carl? Are you sure you're okay?"

He looked slowly at me. "I don't know if I can tell you this."

"Yes, you can, Carl. You can tell me whatever you want. It's privileged."

"No," he countered. "It's nothing legally damaging, I don't think. It's just that..." his voice trailed off.

"What is it?"

"I guess this morning I was so caught up in defending myself against Don's accusations, that it didn't really strike me until later."

"What didn't strike you?" I asked, worried.

"I'm just...as the day went on, I realized how upset I am at Tricia's murder. I just, I can't believe it. I didn't want to say anything in case it aroused more suspicion of me." Carl's eyes were actually welling up with tears.

I took him by the arm. "No, Carl. It doesn't. It tells me you're a hell of a teacher. Go home. Don't do any marking. Don't do any work. Just take an evening to look after yourself."

"All right," he replied glumly.

"Are you going to be all right? Do you want some company?"

"No," he smiled lightly. "I'll be all right. My wife's at home. Thanks, Win, for everything."

"It's okay. Everything will be okay. We'll look after this. Just call me if you need anything, even just to talk, okay?"

"Okay. Goodnight." Carl turned and walked out the door.

*   *   *

A weird thing about my chronic insomnia is that I sometimes have the ability to sleep in the afternoon. Not always, but just enough to screw up my ability to sleep again at night. Since it had been a particularly bad week for sleep, I could not wait to get home to my comfortable Kitsilano condo and crash on the couch for a couple of hours. I knew I would pay for it in the middle of the night, but my body was giving me the signal that the sleep deficit was getting bigger than I could expect to cope with.

I was so tired that I approached my apartment building as though I were approaching the gates of Heaven. Unfortunately, St. Peter was at the gates: my ex-wife stood guard outside the front entrance to the building. After having my car broken into on numerous occasions, I had abandoned parking in the building's underground "secure" parking garage and now parked on the street. Since that necessitated my entering through the building's front door—currently blocked by my ex-wife—I sensed a need to rethink that decision.

Sandi Cuffling, formerly Patrick, is a very attractive woman. Not the cover of *Glamour* magazine kind of attractive, but a woman who has the ability to turn heads when she walks into a room. Over our years together, she had come to cherish that ability and wore it like a merit badge. Some days I still missed her. Today wasn't one of those days.

"Look who's here. Did we change the shape of future generations today?" Sandi was fluent in a different dialect of the English language. Sarcasm. In the past four years, I'm not sure I'd heard her speak without it.

"Hello, Sands," I said, doing my best to seem relatively interested to see her. In Sandi's world, the fact we were divorced was no reason we ought not to be part of each other's lives. Hostility between ex's was so nineties. It's much more sophisticated to still be friends. I was about as interested in continuing a friendship with my ex-wife as I was in re-marrying her, but I was raised as a polite gentleman and couldn't bring myself to tell her to go piss up a rope.

"I've been waiting for you," she said. Her tone held just a hint of accusation.

"And here I am."

She looked at her expensive watch. "It's almost four thirty."

"You and the general population are under the mistaken impression that the working day of a teacher ends when the three o'clock bell rings. There is slightly more to it than that, but until such time as you become a teacher, which would entail mixing with the rabble that is the teenagers of the world, you would not understand."

"You are a bitter one today."

"It's been one of those days." I opened the front door and headed into the lobby. It was tempting to close the door, knowing Sandi didn't have a key to the building. But again, I was raised polite. Sandi followed me into the artificially ornate entrance hallway, looking over my shoulder as I checked my mail box. Sandi could never stand it when I received mail addressed only to me. I thought she would be over it now that we were not living together any more, but apparently not. Not satisfied simply with reviewing the contents of my mailbox, she proceeded to follow me up to my apartment.

"So how have you been?" she asked as we travelled down the hall.

"Fine."

"That's it? Fine?"

"What were you looking for?"

"A little detail about how your life is going. Do you know how long it's been since you called me just to chat and say hi?"

"No." Reaching the door to my suite, I unlocked it and paused long enough to throw Sandi a question with my eyes. My question was: what the hell do you want? She interpreted the look as: do you want to come in?

"It's been a long time," she informed me, following me into my apartment.

"I'm not sure. Do you think it could have anything to do with the fact we're divorced?"

"You know I still care about you, Win." She stopped and looked at a painting I had recently hung on the wall. "Hey! That's new."

"Yes."

"That's weird. You buying art."

"I like art."

"Well, I know, but it's just strange, you know? It was the kind of thing we used to do together."

I gave her a sideways glance as I kicked off my shoes. "Actually, it was the kind of thing you did for us. My job was to hang up what you purchased." Sandi walked slowly around my apartment, stopping in front of the large glass patio door to take in the view. Admittedly, it was a good view, but Sandi seemed out of sorts, even for her, and it was clear she wanted to talk to me about something but didn't seem to know how to begin. I decided not to say anything and see what would happen. In the classroom, we call it "wait time", the period between when the teacher asks a question and someone volunteers an answer. It's often awkward, but sooner or later someone will speak just to break the uncomfortable silence.

Sandi continued to stare out at the rain beating down against the patio door. Her long blonde hair, dampened by the rain, hung past her shoulders. Her strong shoulders, sculpted in the gym through dedication bordering on fanaticism, sagged with the weight of whatever she wanted to tell me. In fact, it wasn't like her to allow rain to affect her appearance. I'm not proud to admit that a large part of the power Sandi held over me for so long was her physical strength and strong beauty.

"Aren't you going to ask how I am?" she finally asked.

"How are you?" I supplied her with what she apparently wanted to hear.

"Fine," she answered coolly.

"Good. I'm glad we cleared that up." Sandi's sarcasm could be contagious.

Another of Sandi's amazing arsenal of talents was her ability to pout, which she did in the classic "stick out your lower lip" fashion often favoured by ramp-walking fashion models. To be fair, Sandi had, in fact, worked as a model, principally when she was twelve years old, displaying training bras and adolescent undergarments for the Eaton's catalogue. Somehow, Sandi's modelling career had stalled at the ripe old age of fourteen. But she could pout. She was putting it into use now as the unwritten signal I remembered from the tumultuous end to our marriage. It still worked on me now as it did then. I'm nothing if not pathetic.

"Okay," I sighed. "Sandi, I'm sorry. Obviously something is upsetting you and you want to talk to me about it. Although why you continue to choose me as your confessor in lieu of one of your numerous confidants at the spa never ceases to baffle me."

"Because I know I can always count on you to listen to me. You don't judge me."

"Sands, I always judge you. Often disparagingly, sometimes even to your face. Do you not remember our marriage at all?" Sandi waited patiently for the signal that I would be quiet and let her speak. Eventually, I always did. It's part of her charm and her power that she manages to wield over me to this day. "I'm sorry. Carry on."

Sandi finally turned from her post at the window to face me. "I hardly know where to begin."

"I generally find things go best when you just blurt out whatever's on your mind," I offered helpfully.

"I'm pregnant." Her admission hit me in the solar plexus, which I've been led to believe is a fancy way of saying my stomach. I tried to keep a poker face, though historically I've always been a terrible poker player. Sandi looked at me and nearly laughed. I guess I wasn't so good at hiding my shock.

Finally, I managed what I often do when I'm faced with a socially uncomfortable situation: I made an inappropriate joke. "I was thinking you looked a little heavy."

Sandi's smile dropped dead away. "That was cruel even by your standards," she informed me frostily.

"I'm sorry," I said for the third time in as many minutes. My ex-wife always brought the apologies out in me. "Reflex reaction to shocking news, I guess. I've had that kind of a week." We stood across a five foot divide and stared silently at each other a while more. We communicated about this well during our marriage too. "Why are you telling me this?" I finally asked her.

"I thought it was important that you know," she replied, returning to her business-like disposition.

"Why? It's not mine."

"Winston! Why would you even say such a thing?" she demanded.

"Because it's been nearly two years since we separated, in case you've forgotten."

She smiled coyly. "But it hasn't been two years since we've been together. You may never be able to resist me."

She had me there. But I wasn't about to allow her the upper hand in this conversation, whatever this conversation was about. "It doesn't count when you're drunk. Besides, it's been long enough that medically I know my original proclamation is true."

Sandi smiled again. She had a way of pre-emptive smiling that told me she was about to deliver an "I told you so" moment. I really didn't need her to say it; I knew exactly what it would be. She said anyway. "See? You never should have given up law. You instinctively went into paternity suit protection mode." Throughout most of our marriage, particularly the latter half, Sandi had generally proved herself the stronger advocate of our union. Why she hadn't entered the practice of law herself is a puzzle. It might have been the requirement to show up at work each day which would have interfered with her spa exercise and facials.

"Is that why you're here?" I tossed out desperately. "Are you trying to find some warped means of obtaining child support?" It did not appear there was any way I could restore my dignity in whatever this debate was about. With most people I didn't care. I'm a gracious loser with plenty of practice. But somehow with Sandi I could never bring myself to concede.

"I thought you might want to know. That's all." She put on her genuine hurt look. I knew how contrived it was, but I fell for it every time.

"I'm sorry." I restated my "talking with my ex-wife" mantra, deciding to play nice for the remainder of our chat. "That was thoughtful of you." I paused momentarily. "Do you know who the father is?" Whoops.

She brushed past me towards the door. "That's it. We're done." This was the part of the conversation I knew I didn't have to respond to. Sandi never left the room without a parting shot. Sure enough, she got as far as having her hand on the doorknob when she turned around to face me. "You are a little, little man," she proclaimed, staring obviously below my waist as she pronounced the second "little." It was almost disappointing. I'd heard that one before, but it still left a new scar each time.

"Thanks for stopping by," I threw in the last word as she headed out the door. "I'm sure you'll let me know where you're registered for shower gifts." Not bad, considering how little time for prep I'd had.

"Prick," she hissed, sticking her head back in the doorway. With that, she turned and left. Always the last insult.

With Sandi out of my life—at least for the evening—I took to the task that I spent most of my evenings on: marking and preparing for class. After last night's failed attempt to complete my marking, I knew I had some catching up to do. If there's one thing I had learned in my long teaching career, it was the necessity of keeping up to date with marking student work. If you turn your back on it for a moment, it multiplies and grows at an alarming rate. As a rule of thumb, I believed it was good practice not to collect any new work from students until I had returned the previous assignment. However, in my nearly three months of teaching, it was one of the first rules of thumb that had fallen by the wayside. Besides, I had other issues clouding my mind. As if Carl's situation wasn't enough, I could not yet quite digest the load Sandi had just dumped on me. I didn't think I was upset per se; I had harboured no real desire for children before, during or since our marriage, but her obvious entrance to the next chapter of her life was discomfiting to say the least.

But one of the biggest obstacles to productive marking was the fact that it was November. For those who aren't couch potatoes, November is sweeps month on American network television, which means that is when all of the best TV shows have on all of their best episodes. It really got in the way of my marking: I didn't care how much I needed this job to pay the mortgage—and my alimony to Sandi—nothing stood in the way of watching *CSI*.

Around ten fifteen, I was well into a strong episode of *Without a Trace,* and partially into ninth grade discussions of the French Revolution's impact on the development of democratic systems when the phone rang. Under normal circumstances, I wouldn't even answer the phone on a Thursday night. All of my friends know better than to interrupt the most important night of TV viewing. So far though, nothing about the week had been normal, so I felt like I'd better answer. I found Carl on the other end of the line.

"Hey," I answered his greeting. "Is everything okay?"

"No," he answered, "not really." Carl sounded not only down but also afraid.

"Carl," I implored him, "what's wrong? Are you all right? Are you hurt?"

"No, I'm not hurt," Carl returned uncomfortably. "It's just that…I didn't know who else to call. I'm really sorry to call you so late, Win."

"It's okay. I'm here for you. Do you want to get together and talk? We could meet someplace."

"Umm, no," he countered. "I don't think they'll let me."

Suddenly I realized what he was trying to tell me. "You don't think who will let you?" I demanded sternly.

"The police," Carl finally admitted. "They've picked me up."

Ten

In recent years, the Vancouver Police Department had moved the bulk of its operations to a swanky new building just below the Cambie Street Bridge that leads into the downtown core of the city and the business sector. As the city's population and volume of crime had grown, the police force had grown with it, making their previous digs on Main Street, at the entrance to the city's renowned Chinatown district, too small to house the accoutrements of modern crime fighting. Parts of the police department still operated out of the old Main Street offices, which were conveniently located adjacent to one of the two downtown criminal courts.

The detective division of the VPD was in the new glass and brick building on 3rd Avenue. Even police officers had marvelled at their new headquarters when they'd first moved in. The new building had also received the requisite howls of protest from citizens and taxpayer watchdog groups, convinced that Vancouver's finest were not in need of such luxury facilities.

Personally, I liked the new headquarters. The offices actually had windows, in addition to the obnoxious fluorescent lighting always found in government buildings. If you were in the right office, you even had a view of False Creek's harbour, with its funky, upscale condominiums and townhouses, marinas and markets, and beyond to the Concorde Pacific residential towers at the foot of gentrified Yaletown. I suppose an argument could be made that the police station isn't really supposed to be a pleasant place: we certainly don't want to encourage people to be there, after all. On the flip side, for the hundreds of police officers and civilian personnel who had to make their living there, I could understand the desire to increase productivity by not making the place a hell hole to work in. What did taxpayer groups know anyway? Of course, the planners could have been a bit smarter and not had the state of the art gym easily visible through the floor to ceiling windows overlooking busy Second Avenue below. Experience tells me taxpayers hate to see their employees working out.

When Carl told me where he was, I was relieved. Being taken to the new police headquarters likely meant he had not, in fact, been formally charged with anything just yet. In that case, he would likely be booked and headed for pre-trial detention, a nice, comfortable way of describing the jails where prisoners are held until the system figures out what should happen to them next. Indeed, if charges had been formally sworn against Carl, we would likely have already been preparing for arraignment proceedings. Since I had not heard from Crown Counsel and likely wouldn't at this time of night, it was more likely the police had picked him up for further questioning. That they had done so without first notifying me irritated me immensely. The detectives of record on the case knew full well that Carl had retained me as his counsel, and as such they ought to have made efforts to contact me. At least Carl had it together enough to call me before they could launch into further interrogations.

It was clear to me that the altercation earlier in the day had made a lasting impact on Detective Furlo. Generally, legal counsel has little difficulty accessing the building. In fact, I had been there so many times, I was on a first name basis with the desk officer who hovered at the entrance to the building to keep out the unauthorized riff-raff. Police preferred to have only authorized riff-raff in the building.

When I arrived at headquarters, there somehow was no longer any record of me as regular defence counsel. True, I had not been in the building in that capacity for over a year. I had, however, been in the building a month before meeting my cop friend Andrea Pearson for lunch. No doubt Detective Furlo wanted to make sure I knew I was on his turf, and he would be calling the shots. Oooh. Big man keeps lawyer waiting, filling out forms at the front counter.

Finally, my identity and legal credentials verified and visitor's pass securely affixed to the lapel of my Adidas jacket, I headed towards the elevator, assuring the nighttime desk clerk that, yes, I knew my way. I entered the detective division on the fourth floor and immediately spotted Detective Smythe working away at her laptop at her work station. It was still amazing to me how little workspace was allotted to individual officers. I had spent most of my legal days doing Legal Aid work, and I'd had a bigger office. She looked up when I came in as though she had been waiting for me. Judging by the late hour, I guessed she couldn't really do much more until I arrived.

"No rest for the underpaid," I offered by way of greeting.

"Not that you would know. I thought taxpayer money flowed directly into the pockets of defence lawyers," she replied. I could grow to like her.

"There must be a hole in mine. Somehow whatever gets there still seems to get spent by my ex-wife."

"Ouch. Residual bitterness, thy name is Winston Patrick." Smythe paused to smile at me.

An obnoxious voice interrupted our peaceful moment. "Mr. Patrick. So glad you could make it. I hope you didn't having difficulty getting in to see us." I could hear Furlo's smug smile without even having to turn to see it. To her credit, his much more mature partner gave me the same roll of the eyeballs performance she had demonstrated at our last meeting. Clearly, she was a detective of a different calibre.

"Let me guess," she said to me. "Clerk had no idea who you were and insisted on checking all the credentials before he let you in. This despite the fact he was informed we would be waiting for you. Christ, Mike," she complained to her partner, "I have kids at home I wouldn't mind seeing eventually."

"So should we cut him loose now," I said, "and avoid all the needless wrangling, at the end of which I will end up taking my client home anyway, or do you have a masochistic notion of dragging this out all night? I do have classes in the morning that I would rather be preparing for."

"Absolutely," Smythe assured me. She had a smooth quality in her voice that made me think she could probably sing jazz. I'd bet she sang a lot to her kids when they were little. She maybe even still did.

"Oh?" Furlo feigned surprise. "Was your client under the

impression that he was being held? We just wanted to ask him a few more questions is all."

"This despite the fact you were fully aware he had retained counsel. Did you read him his rights, or did you not bother with the police academy at all?" My insomnia was catching up to me, and I was getting testy.

"And in case you've forgotten, your client was given the chance to call you, which brought you here. I don't think that we've done anything wrong here, counsellor, so can the sanctimonious bullshit." Furlo may also be an insomniac.

"Sanctimonious? Someone got a thesaurus for his birthday?"

"God," Smythe complained. "Why couldn't he have had a woman lawyer? Like I don't have to wade through enough testosterone during the day around here? Can you two little boys behave, and let's get through what we have to do so we can all go home?" Her exasperation was completely unfeigned, and I thought we might really be in trouble.

Furlo and I looked at each other like two sons caught quarrelling in church. For the moment, I thought it was best to behave. "Okay," I conceded. "Do you have something new that we didn't cover earlier today, or is this exploratory drilling?"

"We *have* something new, Counsellor," Furlo explained calmly, apparently also agreeing to a temporary cease fire.

"Winston," Smythe faced me, "how well do you know your client?"

"You know I can't go into the specifics of our relationship. He's my client and colleague."

"I know you're focusing more on a teaching career than a legal one now," she continued. "I just thought you might want to reconsider working with Mr. Turbot, since you're planning to spend more time in schools."

"What are you telling me, Detective Smythe? What did you find?"

"Fingerprints," Furlo announced with no small amount of pleasure, "on the body."

"Take me to my client," I said calmly, masking the emotions that were tugging beneath the surface.

Detective Smythe rose from her desk and headed down a hallway at the end of the room. Furlo gestured grandly, even bowing slightly at the waist, for me to follow Smythe down the hall. He was enjoying his perceived advantage. It wasn't unusual for the police to pick up a suspect for further questioning with evidence as strong as fingerprints. That at least placed Carl in close contact with Tricia. It certainly wouldn't be enough to lay criminal charges, but it did call into question the veracity of Carl's insistence that no physical relationship had taken place between him and Tricia Bellamy. If he was physically involved with her—and his fingerprints on her body certainly lent credence to her accusations—it provided the police with a motive in her killing. What's worse, from a personal perspective, it made me question the client and my desire to represent him. I was now wishing that I hadn't been in my classroom when Carl had come to see me.

We found Carl sitting in a desolate room, at a particle board-and-veneer table with a half-empty cup of cold coffee in front of him. Despite the fancy new police headquarters, it was well known among employees and regular visitors to the police station that one area the new facilities had failed to address was the abysmal quality of the coffee provided. It was even worse than the brew found in teacher faculty lounges in public schools. Carl had wisely given up drinking the police department standard issue swill.

"Winston!" Carl jumped to his feet, suddenly reinvigorated when I entered the room.

"Hi, Carl," I responded. "How are you doing?"

"I'm okay, I guess," he replied. He seemed happy to see me, which was understandable. Somehow my students haven't yet begun to feel quite the same way.

"Good." I turned to face the two detectives. "So what's the story, Detectives? Are you going to lay a charge, or do we go home?"

"We still have nearly twenty-three hours, you know that," Smythe gently reminded me. Under Canadian law, Furlo and Smythe could detain Carl for twenty-four hours without laying a charge. At that point, he would need to be charged with a crime or released.

"If you think you have enough evidence to charge him, what are you waiting for? I have class in the morning." Sometimes being brash and up front was the best defence.

"Why don't you ask your client how his fingerprints got onto

Tricia Bellamy?" Furlo challenged.

"I told you," Carl began.

"Carl! Just wait a moment," I admonished him. "Exactly where were the fingerprints found?"

"Where?" Furlo asked.

"Yes, where. Where on the body were my client's prints allegedly found?" Carl visibly flinched as I began referring to Tricia as "the body." It couldn't be helped. It was important to distance myself from the victim if I was going to mount a decent defence to what was looking like a stronger case.

"Your client's prints were found on the victim's watch and a partial print that looks very close to your client's was also found on both of the victim's hands," Smythe responded to my question.

"That's it?" I tried to sound confident. Homicide wasn't my specialty.

"What more do you need?" Furlo sneered.

"Well, for starters, I understand Tricia Bellamy was strangled. How about fingerprints around her neck? Find any of those?" Carl was visibly paling by the syllable.

"No," Smythe admitted, "we did not."

"Ever heard of gloves, Counsellor? I refer you to U.S. v. O.J. Simpson," Furlo quipped.

"I've heard of it, yes. Though it was a state, not a federal case, which makes it State of California v. Simpson. Your point being that you found no prints whatsoever on the victim's neck?"

"That's correct," Smythe returned. "At this point, no prints of any kind, even partials, have been found directly on the victim's neck."

I turned to face Furlo, since he was the more aggressive of the two. I couldn't even get a rise out of Smythe, which meant the likelihood of flustering her into a mistake was much less than with Furlo. "I suppose you have a scientific theory about the prevalence of prints located anywhere except on the one part of the body where death would have been caused?"

"Yeah, smartass, he put the gloves on so he could strangle her without leaving prints."

"And the victim stood there calmly watching her assailant putting gloves on so she could be strangled? This is what you've got?"

"Or maybe, he felt remorse after he offed her, and while weeping over her body, removed his gloves to wipe his eyes."

"Then ran his fingerprints all over the hands and her wristwatch. This, after having the foresight to bring gloves to avoid the detection of prints in the first place." I stood up from the table next to Carl. "I guess it really is time to go."

"Doesn't it bother you, Patrick, that your client's prints could be found on the body at all?" Furlo demanded angrily.

"What bothers me is that you've failed to even consider the myriad means by which a teacher's prints could be found on a student. Classrooms are not big places. People make inadvertent contact all the time. A caring hand laid on a student's arm to offer encouragement. A touch on the elbow as you say 'excuse me' in the stairway."

"And on her hands," Smythe reminded me, suddenly rejoining the conversation.

"Mr. Turbot told you during your earlier questioning that Tricia Bellamy had expressed some difficulty with the subject matter and had come in for tutoring. They were in a biology lab conducting science experiments. That a 'partial' print could be left on her hands is hardly grounds for detaining my client." I was bluffing.

"It is when you consider the fact they were sleeping together," Furlo sneered.

"And that, Detective, is the last I want to hear of those unfounded allegations. This was a troubled student who for reasons unknown alleged an inappropriate relationship. Until such times as you have some kind of corroborating evidence of such a relationship, you would be well advised to refrain from making any statements in that regard, or you may find yourself and your department staring down the business end of a civil defamation suit."

Furlo, for once, was quieted by my threat. Smythe did not come to his aid.

"And furthermore," I continued, "just how in hell did you get my client's fingerprints for comparison?"

"He offered them when we brought him in," Smythe explained calmly.

I looked at Carl in disbelief. His eyes turned pleadingly to me. "I didn't know what to do. They said they wanted my fingerprints, so I gave them to them."

"You brought my client in here because you found 'some' prints on the body?"

"Prints that turned out to be his," Furlo demanded.

"Talk to Crown Counsel. Even assuming you can gather enough evidence to build a credible charge, I'll have those prints thrown out as being collected improperly, without the advice of counsel, without an arrest warrant being sworn out." I practically pulled Carl from his chair. "Carl, it's time to go home." Smythe and Furlo made no effort to stop me. "Goodnight, Detectives."

"Good night, Mr. Patrick," Smythe offered. Despite my staged hostility and indignity, she still had class enough to offer polite, closing niceties.

"Hey, Patrick!" Furlo sneered. "Why doesn't your client give us a DNA sample, and we'll speed things up immensely?"

"Not going to happen. Not now. Not ever," I replied, though I knew if any more damning evidence came our way, obtaining a court order for Carl's DNA would be relatively routine.

Outside the room, I hurried Carl down the hallway, past the detectives' work area to the elevator. While we waited for the car to take us down and into Vancouver's drizzling night air, I turned to face him. "Let's get this clear. Do not offer anything—*anything*—to the police unless I'm with you. Not fingerprints, not answers to questions, not DNA samples, nothing. They know you have defence counsel. They know better."

"I'm sorry," he responded. "I panicked. I don't get picked up by the police very often."

"And you won't again. If they come to see you, if they phone you, if they so much as send you an invitation to the police ball, you call me first, okay?"

"Okay," he said. "Is that true, what you said about getting my fingerprints thrown out?"

"Hell, I don't know. I was making it up," I confessed.

"Well, you sounded convincing to me." He forced a smile.

"Terrific," I said. "I should have been an actor."

Eleven

By the time I had taken Carl to his home and me to my mine, it was well past midnight. And still I had not completed my marking.

I had managed to convince Carl it would be a good idea not to come to work on Thursday morning. In fact, I had called our "teacher-on-call" service even prior to going to the police station to ensure Carl's classes would at least be looked after. Somewhere down the line since I had been a high school student, substitute teachers had changed their moniker to teachers-on-call in a bid to get more respect from students and colleagues alike. As far as I know, students still figured it was holiday time whenever their regular teacher was away. The only time I had ever been thrown out of high school during my own adolescent years was over the grief I had caused a "sub" during a Social Studies class. Back in the eighties, schools had no sense of humour. You told one substitute teacher to fuck off and you were outta there.

Fortunately, Carl was meticulously organized, and his lesson plans were prepared for someone to take over for him. It would have been hard for him to be prepared for the circus at the front of the school when I arrived on Friday morning. If news of Tricia's death had brought out the best of Vancouver's media machine, news of Carl's questioning by the police had brought out the rest of them. How they even knew he had been picked up for further questioning was a mystery that wasn't too difficult to solve. Detective Furlo would be going out of his way to make sure I had a difficult job defending the man he had already decided was guilty. He had even let it slip that a certain former lawyer turned teacher was acting in Carl's defence. The moment I stepped out of my car,

Cameron Dhillon, a local television reporter, was headed my way. I'd never met him, but he knew just who he was looking for.

"Mr. Patrick?" he began, cameraman in tow. "Are you defending Carl Turbot?"

"Yes, I am," I replied lamely. I felt as ill-prepared as I had been during my first trial—which I had lost. Working with legal aid clients, it had been rare that the media took interest in any of my defendants.

"Has Mr. Turbot pleaded not guilty?" he pressed on. By now, a handful of other reporters had noticed the activity near the staff parking lot and were hurrying over to get in their two bits before I could make it to the doorway.

"Mr. Turbot has not and will not be pleading guilty or not guilty because he has not been arrested or charged with any crime. A plea would be premature at this time." I used my snotty lawyer tone.

"Sir, why has Carl Turbot hired a lawyer if he isn't guilty?" came a question from a print reporter. You could always tell. They still carried notebooks.

"I have no comment on Mr. Turbot's decision to retain counsel. That is information that is privileged between solicitor and client."

"Aren't you a teacher at Sir John A. Macdonald high school?" Cameron Dhillon continued.

"I am, and I have classes to teach, so if you'll excuse me." I pressed forward through the gathering throng of media hounds and did my best not to hear the questions they shouted at me as I went by. It's a curious phenomenon, the media scrum. What we often see on television is the tail end where reporters figure that the subject of their scrum leaving is a cue to start shouting as loudly as possible. How they figure that would help to hear their questions and respond to them any better is an enigma. I suppose when their bosses see the tape back at the studio, reporters want to be seen at least trying to get the all-important quote from their source.

Once I reached the doorway of the school, the press backed off. It is an unwritten rule—it may even be written for all I know—that schools are somehow sacred ground onto which reporters shall not tread without an engraved invitation. As a general rule, school administrators are all about avoiding negative publicity, so I was fairly confident Don would not be inviting the press in to ask questions. But of course, Don was waiting for me inside the doorway, just past the line of sight of the press. I pretended not to see him, despite his position in the middle of the hallway. That was pretty immature, I admit, but immaturity is an occasional unintended side effect of working with teenagers all day. Don didn't look happy to see me.

"I see your client is not coming to work today," Don began, foregoing a polite "good morning." Don said the word "client" with a sneer, as though he found the word personally distasteful. I suppose from his perspective as the person in the school at whom the buck purportedly stopped, the word could be distasteful.

"I believe he was feeling a bit under the weather," I reported to my supervisor. "And good morning." I continued walking away from him, down the hallway towards the main office.

Don nearly snarled at me. "He was under the weather, or he couldn't bring himself to show his face around here."

I turned. "Are you asking a question or making an editorial comment?"

"I'm asking you. Is he sick? Is he quitting? What's going on?" Sweat was forming on his nearly bald head.

"I don't represent Carl with regard to his teaching duties. From what I understand, he called in sick, he has arranged for his classes to be covered. End of story. If you have questions about his health or the appropriateness of his sick leave, I suggest you take it up with the union representative."

Don stepped in front of me to bring me to a halt. "You know something, Winston? I used to like you."

"Thank you," I interrupted. "That's very nice to know."

"You have an impressive resumé, you had a very good interview, I hear good things about you from the students," Don continued.

"I feel a 'but' coming."

"You're damned right there's a 'but' coming. 'But' you're a smart ass. 'But' representing a teacher who may have been sleeping with and killed a student is a really odd way of endearing yourself to me.

'But' going out of your way to alienate yourself from me is not a good way to ensure a continuing appointment to this school or even this school district." He was on a roll.

"Are you out of 'buts' yet?" I posed calmly.

"Don't push me," he hissed quietly, since a couple of teachers had rounded the corner and were doing a poor job of pretending not to listen to our exchange. I decided to take advantage of the audience to ensure the line was clearly drawn in the sand.

"I have no desire to push you. But endearing myself to you is not only not paramount on my list of immediate or long term goals, it would likely 'unendear' me to the rest of the staff, who are frankly more useful to me personally and professionally than you are. Since you're bringing up my status as teacher, let me remind you of my continued status as litigator, and if you think you've got bad PR now, wait until you see what happens when I sue you, personally and the school board corporately should I not secure tenure because I failed to 'endear' myself to you. Have a nice day."

I walked away in a self-righteous huff. After spending time with both Sandi and Furlo, I had a pressing need to ensure that the last word in a conversation was mine for a change. It took only thirty seconds for me to feel guilty about snapping at Don. Having all of this go down couldn't be easy for him. I also knew I was going to face a very tough class first period: Law Twelve.

Law Twelve class is intended to serve as a general introduction to legal principles and perhaps interest senior students in a career in the practice of law or law enforcement. The class has the potential to be very interesting, intellectual and enlightening, unless, of course, school counsellors use it as a dumping ground for any student who needs a Grade Twelve credit. My three law classes contained an eclectic mixture of students, some of whom were generally interested in law and how the legal system worked, some who reluctantly did the minimal amount of work in order to get through the course, and a small spattering whose interest in law class was directly related to their perceived need to beat some kind of Youth Criminal Justice Act prosecution hanging over their heads. This morning, I knew one hundred per cent of my budding legal practitioners would have only one case on their mind.

Reaching into my letter box in the office, I pulled out a stack of those little pink-coloured "while you were out" message slips. Not only had every major and minor media outlet attempted to contact me at school that morning, but it seemed a fair chunk of my students' parents had also tried. I have 214 students. Maybe I should have called in sick. Carefully sorting the messages from parents from the messages from reporters—and promptly depositing reporters' requests for interviews in the garbage—I caught the stare of Fiona Bertrand, the head secretary. She was not pleased.

"Good morning," I tried.

"Perhaps for those of you who aren't charged with having to answer phone calls non-stop for the same teacher," she huffed.

"Sorry. I'm certainly not pleased the media is hounding you at school. They were not invited."

"I guess it can hardly be surprising when you take on a case like this one, can it?" She continued. "I thought you gave up law so you could work for the benefit of young people?"

Mental note. Ensure Fiona Bertrand never makes it onto a jury should Carl ever be brought to trial. Since I could think of nothing better to say, I turned and headed for my classroom. Fiona did not seem the type who would permit me to have the last word, even if I tried.

Walking down the stairs to my classroom, I was astounded as I rounded the corner and saw a most unusual sight: students, a whole bunch of them, waiting outside my classroom. This was unusual, because class didn't start for nearly ten minutes. By November I had grown accustomed to having kids wander in at the last minute—or several minutes after the last minute. As of yet, my magnetic personality had never drawn an early crowd.

"Good morning," I said, unlocking the classroom door and trying to sound non-plussed. I'm not entirely sure what plussed sounds like, mind you. They weren't buying it. The group of about fifteen students poured into the room after me.

"Hi, Mr. Patrick. How are you doing today?" began Elizabeth Lawson, a brighter student on whom I could usually count to participate and lead discussion and debate about legal issues.

"Hi, Liz," I replied calmly. "You're all here early." Even as the words came out of my mouth, other students in the class began to trickle in. I was heading towards perfect attendance.

"So?" Jillian Ballantyne had a penchant for understatement.

"So?" I responded. I imitate understatement when the need arises.

"So, what's happening?" Liz pressed on. "With Mr. Turbot?"

"Liz, Jillian, everyone, look. We may have only been together for a few months, but I have to believe there are a few sacred things you've learned during our time." They looked at me, then each other, then back at me. Doesn't anyone study any more?

Virtually the entire class had entered by the time Sarah Kolinsky spoke up from her desk, where she had moved away from the growing crowd around mine. "Solicitor-client privilege." The bell rang to punctuate her assessment of where I was attempting to lead them in the conversation.

"What?" Jillian asked.

"Solicitor-client privilege," Sarah responded. "He can't say anything about it because, as Mr. Turbot's legal counsel, any information he has is strictly confidential."

"Thank you, Sarah. Thank God someone's been listening to me." The class began to settle unusually quickly this morning. As much as I wanted to focus their attention away from Carl's troubles, I had to remind myself that they had just lost a classmate, and a trusted teacher was suspected of killing her. They had to be going through all kinds of confusing emotions. As was I.

"We can't talk about it at all?" Scott Harton demanded. Scott could be a bit of whiner when it came to doing his work, but he was also very bright and occasionally very funny.

I sighed. Why had it taken a tragedy to get the rapt attention of my law class? "I guess we can talk about it in very general terms. I'll make you a deal. I'll fill you in as much as I can. You can ask questions, but I reserve the right to decline to answer. Fair enough?"

"But don't we have a right to know what's going on, since it's happening in our own school with one of our own teachers?" another student, Jessica, asked. I noted that Tricia had described Jessica McWilliams as her best friend. I was surprised to find her there—she should have been grieving at home.

"How much information the school releases to you is really up to the principal. You need to understand that I'm talking here not just as your teacher but also as a lawyer. I'm wearing two hats. I'll tell you what I can, but I'm also retained as defence counsel. I have to protect the integrity of the case. I'm required to by law."

A silence fell on the room as they considered their next move. I felt for them. I couldn't help but lament that this "teachable moment" was essentially out of my reach because of my solicitor-client restrictions on speaking freely. Any other teacher in the school would have had much more freedom to pursue this line of conversation.

Finally, Gurpreet Jewal, a beautiful, intelligent student who rarely spoke in class discussion, raised her hand tentatively from the back of the room. "Mr. Patrick?"

"Yes, Gurpreet?"

"Are you able to tell us if Mr. Turbot will likely go to jail?" she asked with genuine concern.

"I can tell you that at this point the police have not sworn out an information or sought an arrest warrant. That means they do not have evidence to support the allegations you're hearing in the media this morning." I noticed one student had the front section of this morning's *Vancouver Sun* on her desk. It was disturbing how much conjecture there already was. On the other hand, it was refreshing to see high school students reading the newspaper.

"But do you think they're going to arrest him?" Scott interrupted, pressing harder for my opinion.

"At this point, I honestly couldn't say. Mr. Turbot is under suspicion for what I believe to be inaccurate, untruthful and irresponsible reasons. I do not believe there is any evidence linking him to this horrible crime other than the fact that he was, in fact, her teacher." So there. I wished Furlo and McFadden were there.

Sarah spoke up with her usual sarcasm. "You sound like you're holding a press conference."

"Maybe I'm seeing you as good practice."

"Why do they suspect him at all?" Gurpreet asked again.

"That's one I can't go into details about. I'm sorry."

"Surely they must have some kind of evidence if they're thinking about him as a killer?" another student chimed in. "Man, this is just unbelievable. I have him for biology."

"Again, I don't know what kind of evidence the police think they have. Why is that?" I asked, making an effort to at least get some usable teaching time out of this interrogation.

The class looked at me, stunned for a moment. Jessica popped open her law textbook and began thumbing through the pages. She seemed particularly interested, understandably. "Why is it," I continued, "that I don't know all of the evidence the police believe they have?"

"Because they don't have to tell you?" Scott offered.

"Why not?" I insisted. Hmm. There could be an assignment in there somewhere.

"He hasn't been charged yet," Sarah responded. "They don't have to release their information until after a charge is laid."

"Good," I confirmed. "And why would they tell me about their evidence even after a charge is laid? Wouldn't they be just giving away their case to me?"

"Disclosure laws," Jessica offered, looking up from her textbook. "The Crown is required to disclose its evidence, so the accused has a full understanding of the Crown's case and can prepare a defence," she continued, reading straight from the text.

"Right. So until such time as the Crown decides to lay charges and build and prepare a prosecution, which I don't think is going to happen, I won't necessarily know what evidence is available. This case is a little unusual, since it involves a young person. The police have been pretty good about sharing information with me, because more than anything, they want to catch the person responsible. The longer they focus on the wrong person, the harder it will be to find the real killer. That's why I also try to be as helpful as possible." Fortunately, the students would have no way of knowing how much I was going out of my way to be a smartass with Furlo. But the gist of what I said was true. "But again," I attempted to conclude, "all of this concern about evidence and disclosure is essentially moot, because it is extremely unlikely the Crown will even decide to lay charges."

"How can you be so sure?" Scott pressed.

I paused for a moment then sighed. "Because, Scott, Mr. Turbot is innocent. He did not kill Tricia Bellamy." I realized how much influence I was having over class opinion. They seemed to accept my assertion of Carl's innocence.

I wished I believed me as much as they did.

The other law class I taught that day went much like the first one, with students clamouring for as much information as they could wring out of me. Some of them were on the road to being pretty fine litigators. By and large, my students seemed at least to have satisfied their curiosity, but also some of their fears had been alleviated; most would feel pretty comfortable about going back into Carl's science classroom when he returned to school.

It is often noted by those in the educational field that kids are much more resilient, forgiving and understanding than adults are. I noticed throughout the remainder of the day the nearly evenly divided response of the teaching faculty I encountered. For the most part, I aimed to keep away from them; they were understandably uncomfortable. Of the half of the staff that seemed to be on Carl's side, about half of those were supporters because they knew, liked and respected Carl and could not or would not believe he could be responsible for Tricia's strangulation. They at least made me feel like I wasn't alone. The rest supported him just because he was a teacher; die-hard unionists, professional supporters and the like. Their thinking seemed to be that even if Carl was guilty, he deserved our support. Even they helped to keep my morale going.

The other half of the faculty was wary of my very presence. It seemed incomprehensible that a teacher could devote energy to defending someone who was accused of such heinous acts. It truly went against everything we were supposed to believe in about the sanctity of the teacher-student relationship and our primary objective of ensuring that students were safe with us at all times. By the end of the day, I was determined to bring Carl Turbot's involvement in the death of Tricia Bellamy to a close.

Twelve

Detective Andrea Pearson was a detective with the Vancouver Police department. And a good friend of mine. In fact, Andy and I had been been friends since before high school. For as long as I could remember, Andy had wanted to be a cop. As kids, playing cops and robbers was always predictable when she was around; I would be the bad guy because there was simply no way she could portray that part when in her heart she knew her reason for being on this earth was to stop crime. Not an episode of *Baretta, Hawaii Five-O, Police Story* or a host of other seventies and eighties cop shows was not committed to her memory. She even watched *Charlie's Angels* religiously, not the least because it showed women in the lead crime busting roles. This, of course, was a plus for me, since it justified my having the famous Farrah Fawcett in the red bathing suit poster in my room: swimsuit model for me, semi-role model for Andrea.

From the moment we left high school, Andrea Pearson had gone straight to the University of British Columbia to study a double major in criminology and psychology, her two passions. Four years and an Honours Bachelor of Arts degree later, she had gone straight to the Vancouver Police Academy, where she'd finished at the top of her class. That's right, the top of her class. Above the other women candidates. Above the men. Above everyone. That fact never went unnoticed, not only among her fellow police officers, but also her superiors. At thirty-five years old, she had been a detective for nearly six years, making her one of the more senior members of her squad.

Much to my mother's chagrin, Andy had never married. More to the point, she had never married me. Andy had everything going for her. Her family was Irish—good Irish, my mother would make

88

the distinction—in heritage, though they had been in Canada even longer than my family had. Her family were practicing Catholic, another of the many failed prerequisites of my Jewish ex-wife that my mother could never overlook. Of course, now that I was divorced, I was an "improper Catholic." All of which only goes to show I should have married Andy in the first place, and everyone would have been happy. Everyone, that is, except Andy and me.

Andrea and I had never dated. Never. Ever. When you grow up with a girl who for all intents and purposes was essentially a boy to you, it's difficult to think of that person as anyone you plan to hop into a matrimonial bed with. Or even just into bed with.

It certainly wasn't that Andy wasn't attractive. From a strictly objective point of view, I could see why any man would make efforts to win her favour. The reason she had never truly hooked up, it seemed to me, was probably because she intimidated the hell out of just about every man she met. A lifelong fitness fanatic—it was Andrea who convinced me to take up late night running as a potential cure for insomnia—she was buff enough to lead new recruits at the academy in hand to hand combat drilling. No one, not even the gym monkeys with bodies that looked like someone stuck an air compressor hose up their bums, could outdo Andy in physical health. It's entirely possible that most men were afraid to date her because they worried if they ever broke up, she'd kick the shit out of them.

Andrea wasn't officially working Tricia's murder. But I knew she would be in the loop, given her seniority and highly respected status among her colleagues. Despite the fact that many of her cop friends knew me, no one would keep Andy in the dark. No one would dare. She met me at the Thai Palace restaurant on Burrard Street, which served Vancouver's best heart attack inducing, spicy Thai food. It was also a good place to talk without fear of being overheard by the patrons, most of whom patiently waited their turn at the karaoke machine. Andy was already in "our" booth when I arrived.

"How well do you know this guy?" she started as I slunk onto the faux velvet bench.

"Fine thanks, how are you?" I replied. We had the kind of relationship where opening pleasantries were optional and most often ignored.

"Don't get pissy on me, Win. I thought we could cut to the chase." Andy was the only person I allowed to call me "Winnie." What could I do? She could kick my ass too.

"How do you know I invited you out to talk about legal matters? Why do you think I might not have something else to talk about?"

"Because nothing exciting happens in your life," she reminded me. "You have no other news."

"Sandi's pregnant," I blurted out. I have so few opportunities to scoop Andy on anything. Somehow, she would have found out within a few days, and I wasn't about to let this rare moment pass.

"The she-beast is preggo?" she exclaimed. "Holy shit. I would have thought her yoghurt expired a long time ago."

"She's only two years older than us."

"Still." She paused and took a sip of her Corona beer straight from the bottle. She looked across the table as she gulped half the lemon-yellow liquid. "Have you two been at it again?"

"No! Shame on you for even thinking that. You have a dirty mind."

"And a healthy soul. They go together," she told me. "She come and tell you?"

"Yeah," I told her. "Last night. She dropped by to share her happy news."

"Why'd she tell you? She want something from ya?"

That gave me pause. My mind had been so focused on Carl and Tricia that I really hadn't given enough thought to just why Sandi had made the trek to my place to inform me. Why the hell did I need that info?

"I don't know," I confessed. "I pissed her off, and she left before she could tell me."

"Typical. You always piss her off good."

"Well. I piss her off well."

"Don't start." The waitress arrived with appetizers. Despite my inherited propensity for bland British food, I could also get hot and messy with spicy food. The difference between Andy and me was that I would pay dearly for it later with heartburn and indigestion. She always tried to convince me to order separately so I could get food with less spice, but it seemed like a test of my manhood so I always refused. I hated it when her manhood was stronger than mine. Andy dove into the finger foods.

"So are you in a funk about this?" she continued, hot sauce poking out from the corner of her delicate mouth.

"About Sandi?" I asked. "Hardly. I really hadn't given it much thought."

"Then why bring it up?"

"I thought you might want to know," I told her.

"In case my biological clock went into jealousy overdrive?"

"It's not beyond the scope of possibility. You're not getting any younger."

Andrea considered that for a moment. That was not a good sign, because it usually meant she was preparing a verbal assault. She cocked her head slightly to the left, peering with curiosity at the top of my head. Finally, she said, "Your hair's thinning."

"Okay. You win," I conceded. "You're starting to hit below the belt."

She smiled coquettishly. "I wasn't talking about hair below the belt."

"And I wish you wouldn't. This is a family restaurant."

The waitress arrived again to take our orders as we were winding down on the fiery hot appetizers Andy had ordered prior to my arrival. Over her shoulder, a young couple cheerfully sang a duet of Britney Spears' bubblegum hit "Oops I Did it Again" in Cantonese. It didn't sound any better in Chinese. It also didn't sound any worse. Andy ordered a Thai chicken dish that showed three red hot peppers beside it on the menu. Not to be outdone, I said I would have the same.

"Are you insane?" she said. "You can't handle those types of spices."

"Thanks, Mom," I countered.

"Someone has to mother you. You don't listen to the natural one, and you divorced the second one to come along."

"Please. You're killing my appetite."

"You're too skinny. We should have gone out for cheeseburgers. You're starting to look like a camp survivor."

"My mother's Catholic guilt, not Jewish guilt."

"Seriously, I think you need to eat more. This teaching thing is making you waste away."

"No," I told her. "The food level is probably fine. I need to sleep more and run less."

Andy tilted her head again, this time just slightly to the right. This was her signal to me that she was no longer bullshitting and was genuinely concerned for my well being. It made her angry when I brushed off these attempts at trying to improve my state of being.

"Seriously, have you seen anyone?" she asked.

"I see you," I said. "And not nearly often enough."

"Shut up," she replied. Andy had a way of saying "shut up" that was not mean spirited. She was probably the only person I knew who could say "shut up" in a caring, compassionate manner. "Don't get cute on me," she warned.

"I'm not already cute?" I tried to continue a line of conversation away from my physical and emotional health.

"I'm talking about going to your doctor."

"Here we go," I began to protest.

"Win," she insisted, "you haven't slept properly in, like, three years. Sooner or later you're going to have to acknowledge that it's not normal to live on less than three hours of sleep each day and find out what the hell's wrong with you."

"Thank you for putting it so gently. What if I find out I'm nuts or something?"

"At least we'd know medically what we've believed all along." She paused long enough to cause me to to wonder what had happened and look back up from my food. When my eyes came level, I found her staring at me.

"What?" I demanded. She didn't respond, only continued to give me a commanding stare. In many ways, Andy and I communicated non-verbally like an old married couple. She didn't really need to say anything else, because I knew she has reached her end of the conversation. I now had two choices: accept what she was trying to tell me to do, or start a lengthy argument.

"Okay," I eventually acquiesced. "You win. I will go to the doctor as soon as I have time."

"Thank you," she said with just a hint of smugness in her voice.

"Of course, he'll tell me to avoid stressful situations like dinner with you."

"I'll survive eating dinner alone." She paused. "Are we done with avoiding the real reason you wanted to have dinner with me?"

"Yes," I confessed, "I have exhausted all other avenues of conversation for the time being."

"In that case, I return to my original question: how well do you know this guy?"

I could tell by the tone of her voice she had found out something she knew she was not supposed to tell me because it wasn't yet public information.

"Not all that well," I admitted. "He's basically just a guy I work with, but we've been friendly. He definitely helped me to get acquainted with the oh-so-subtle nuances of surviving in a public high school." I paused and thought about one of my earlier encounters with Carl. "When I was bumbling through my first conflict with a student, he stepped in and helped. It kind of forged a friendship."

"It doesn't look good, Win," she told me, then paused as the waitress returned with our dinners.

She thanked the waitress and, unbelievably, actually added hot sauce to what I'm sure was already a flaming hot, spicy meal. I had to draw the line somewhere; I opted to eat my dinner as was. I watched her in awe as she picked up a steaming bunch of noodles and sucked them indelicately into her mouth without even flinching. Gingerly, I pulled apart one tawny noodle and placed it daintily on my tongue. Immediately, I began to choke as my soft palate was suddenly aflame. At that moment I reached the panicked conclusion that I could actually die in a small Thai restaurant. How humiliating.

Andy was nearly beside herself with laughter. "Here," she said, pushing my glass of water towards me, "take a drink, you dumbass!" I gulped water like a camel on its ninth day as perspiration broke out and began flowing down my forehead. "I told you not to order that," she told me. "You don't have to show off for me, remember?"

After a full minute of chugging water, dabbing my head with a napkin and loosening most of my clothing, I managed to recover sufficiently to sputter out a few syllables. "Tasty," I gurgled out at her.

Andrea, meanwhile, had taken advantage of this medically necessary lapse in conversation to wolf down more than half of her dinner. I knew before the evening was done she would consume a fair portion of mine as well. The way Andy eats, the woman should be huge, but constant body-abusing exercise has fat cells scared to go near her.

"Are you all right?" she asked, giggling like the teenaged girl I remembered.

"I'm fine," I gasped, my pulse slowly returning to normal. I signalled to the waitress, who found her way over to our table. "I'd like to just have some kind of house salad please. No dressing." The waitress took my order and turned towards the kitchen. I turned back to Andrea. "You were saying it doesn't look good?"

"No," she replied, turning serious.

"Why?"

She gave me a look that reminded me I was receiving extremely privileged information. "There's some pretty strong evidence."

"The fingerprints? I thought we had pretty much debunked any significance those prints had. Those illegally obtained prints, I might add."

"There's more, Win. DNA. They got some preliminary results back today."

"DNA? Where the hell did Furlo and Smythe get a DNA sample from?"

"The coffee cup in the interview room. A pencil in his biology lab with his teeth marks on it, and apparently a few other assorted odds and ends they found in the classroom."

"Jesus Christ," I complained, "what kind of detectives have you got working down there? I'll move to strike all of that as illegal searches. You can't go taking samples from coffee cops in the police station."

"But you can from a public school classroom. He doesn't have any guarantees of DNA privacy there," she countered.

"We'll see," I threatened. "I don't think the Charter of Rights and Freedoms will permit DNA sampling simply because my client is a public employee." By then I was fuming as much from the tactics of Furlo and Smythe as I was from the Thai noodles. I thought we had established some parameters of how my client would be treated during the remainder of the investigation.

"Hey, Win!" Andy ordered. "I'm not opposing counsel here, remember? Don't shoot the messenger. I'm only telling you what I've found out about your case."

"You're right," I told her, exhaling heavily. "I'm sorry. It just pisses me off. Not so much that I'm going to have to file suppression motions, more that they're wasting time with Carl that they could be using following other leads."

"There are no other leads, Win," she told me gently. "This is the direction they're focusing on."

"That's bullshit. There are any number of ways that strands of hair, or fingerprints or whatever they've found on Tricia could have innocently come from my client. And I'll fight them over using that as evidence anyway."

"I don't think you want to do that, Win. They'll just get a court-ordered DNA sample from Turbot anyway. We're not talking about a stray hair on the body."

I looked at her quizzically. I could sense she was worried about telling me the next part, not only because a murder case is generally out of my purview of experience, but also because it involved a friend and colleague.

"What are you talking about?" I asked as the waitress returned with my very plain looking salad.

Andrea waited until the waitress had left the table, then looked at me and said bluntly, "Seminal fluid."

I felt as though someone had punched me in the stomach. For a moment I found it difficult to breathe as I digested this new information. If the forensic scientists had found semen from Carl on Tricia, it pretty much blew away the notion that she had been concocting a scheme to hold over Carl's head for whatever twisted reason we believed she had invented.

After a small eternity, I recovered enough to continue. "I thought there was no evidence of sexual assault?"

"There wasn't," Andy told me. She had finished her dinner. "There was no indication the body had been assaulted. They went to her house. They found trace semen evidence on a pair of underwear in her laundry hamper. They figure it was relatively, umm, fresh." She said the last word uncomfortably.

"Holy shit," I proclaimed, lacking any more suitable legal term for the turn my case had suddenly taken. "And it matches the samples they took?"

"Apparently enough that they're not worried about you fighting the collection of those samples. They figure Tricia's story is enough to get them a court order for a sample, and then they'll have him."

"That's impossible. It can't be right," I protested feebly.

"Only if you refuse to believe it. Win," she said, reaching across the table and taking my hand, "it looks pretty clear your guy was at least having sex with the girl. That's going to give him proximity, motive. You sure you're gonna be up for this?"

"I pretty much have to be. I wouldn't be much of a lawyer if I suddenly bailed because I didn't like the look of the evidence."

"You don't have to be much of a lawyer," Andrea reminded me. "You're a teacher now, remember? You could probably get a judge to excuse you from defending him."

My cell phone rang from inside my jacket pocket. Extricating my hand from Andy's, I reached into my pocket.

"Hello?" I asked. I listened quietly to the voice on the other end of the line give me information I knew was destined to come, having heard Andrea's information and interpretation of the case. I just hadn't thought it would come so quickly. After a moment or two, I thanked the caller and hung up the phone, simultaneously signalling the waitress to bring the bill.

Detective Andrea Pearson looked at me expectantly. "Well?" she asked. "You don't look good."

"That was Jasmine Smythe," I tell her. "They would like me to meet them at Carl's house. They've got a warrant, and they're going to arrest him."

Thirteen

Carl and Bonnie Turbot lived in an East Vancouver house architects anachronistically refer to as a "Vancouver Special". Vancouver Specials began to appear on the local architectural scene in the 1960s, mostly in the eastern parts of the city.

It was in the East End towards the Vancouver suburb of Burnaby. Scarcity of land and its ever increasing price had led city planners to permit, if not smaller lots, at least narrower ones. Thus, home designers were faced with the difficult task of developing profitable homes that everyday, working class people could afford and that would somehow fit this new, thin slice of land zoning that was unique to Vancouver.

The result is an often-mocked long shoebox of a house that looks a lot like a two storey version of a mobile home, without the trailer park and rental pad. There are literally hundreds, if not thousands, of these Vancouver Specials dotted throughout the city, and while designers and "artistes" scoff at their boxy image, for many years it was the home of choice for people anxious to break into the home-owning segment of society. In recent years, architecture students have begun a kind of a love affair with the homes, attempting to develop selected Vancouver Specials into a respectable genre of home building. Largely, it hasn't worked.

Carl and Bonnie's house was white—as almost all of them are—with green trim around the windows and front doorway. Their shoe box abode was sandwiched between two houses of obviously different vintage: 1930s hard stucco bungalows. In the front yard, if you could call it that, stood two willow trees whose drooping branches hung well out onto the quiet street. When I arrived, Furlo and Smythe were already waiting outside in their unmarked Crown Victoria police cruiser.

"Good evening, Mr. Patrick." Detective Smythe smiled at me as she opened the driver's side door of the car. It struck me as odd that Smythe would be the driver and Furlo the passenger. He seemed the macho type who would have a hard time letting a woman drive. Come to think of it, he seemed the macho type who would have a hard time just working with a woman partner, particularly one senior to him.

"Keeping you up late?" I asked by way of reply.

"The life of the weary flatfoot," she replied. Smythe had the look of someone who knew for herself the job she was doing was important, just and honourable, but a little distasteful at times. To her credit—and I gave the credit to her because I was convinced Furlo had nothing to do with it—there was no need for them to include me in their plans to arrest Carl. The phone call could as easily have come from Carl after he arrived at central booking.

"No doubt. I had forgotten how much fun it can be when you're on call. At least with teaching you don't generally get called out to work in the middle of the night."

"Maybe you should stick to teaching then," Furlo snarled as he rose up from out of the passenger seat. And the testosterone battles began anew.

The three of us stared across the car at each other for a moment that was more awkward than tense. Furlo and Smythe at least both appeared to recognize how uncomfortable a situation we'd all found ourselves in. The murder of a child, even one who was nearly embracing adulthood, is about the worst type of case anyone can be assigned to. Given that the prime, about to be apprehended, suspect was in a role we all like to believe is relatively sacred just made working anywhere near this case all the more unpalatable. Though I had given up law to move into teaching, over the past year of my teaching practicum I had still consulted on a number of cases and picked up the odd bit of pre-litigation work for friends' firms just to keep myself in legal shape. But we all seemed to know, standing around in the cold November air, that this was not the type of extra-curricular moonlighting I would have taken on had I known where it was going.

Finally, Smythe broke the uncomfortable silence. "Would you like a few minutes alone?" she asked, gesturing towards the house.

"Yes," I replied graciously. "Thank you." I turned towards the elongated homestead before pausing. "Does he know you're here?"

"We've been quiet as a mouse," Smythe replied, smiling. "Two mice actually."

"What, no S.W.A.T. teams?"

"You've been watching too much TV," Furlo condescended to me. "We call them E.R.T.'s here." He was making reference to Vancouver's elite Emergency Response Team, generally dispatched to assist in the apprehension of violent criminals or in hostage scenarios. Taking down a mild-mannered biology teacher was likely below them.

"Ten minutes?" Smythe asked, as though we were making an appointment to meet for lattes after I picked up the dry-cleaning.

"Sure, that will do," I replied as I began to make my way towards Carl's front door. Because I am who I am, I couldn't resist suggesting to Furlo, "You wanna watch the back door?" I nodded my head towards the side of the house.

Furlo's top lip curled up in a lop-sided grin-come-sneer. "You're not out in ten minutes, we're coming in. Anyone's missing, I shoot you first." Generally, once fire arms are mentioned, I find it best to surrender the last word. I'd had to do that a lot that week. I wondered if Furlo would like to meet my ex-wife.

By that time, I was convinced that not only Carl and his wife but also all of his neighbours must have been aware of our presence. How often do people stand in the rain chatting outside grey sedans at ten thirty at night? Apparently, often enough that as I tentatively rang the doorbell, the people in Carl's neighbourhood continued to take no notice.

It was nearly two minutes before a dishevelled and sleepy looking Carl opened his front door behind a safety chain.

"Yeah?" he asked groggily. Through the small crack he had permitted in the doorway, I was already aware of the distinctive odour of alcohol.

"Carl, it's me, Winston Patrick," I told him. "Open the door. I need to come in."

"Winston?" He considered this carefully, squinting through the barely open doorway at my now soaking wet visage on his doorstep. "What are you doing here?"

"It's important. I need to talk to you. Come on. Open up. Now." As a rule, semi-drunk people are about the only people I ever have success with talking forcefully to. I turned towards the street and waved and smiled at the two detectives, both still standing against their car. I wondered if they were going to stand in the rain for the full ten minutes I'd been allotted, or if they'd seek refuge in the car. Smythe gave me a bendy fingertip wave back. It almost looked like flirting, but then it was late, and I do have a vivid imagination.

The door closed momentarily, and I could hear Carl wrestling with the front door safety chain. I figure those are more for show than anything else; it doesn't really take much to push through cheap chain link.

Carl opened the door and, seemingly recovering the good manners I had always seen him demonstrate at school, waved me into the entrance hallway. "Come in. Come in. Sorry to keep you standing in the rain." He was oblivious to the two detectives at the curb.

As I entered Carl's house, I couldn't help but come to the conclusion that most of what my ex-wife had suggested about the earning potential of a teacher was apparently true. Looking into Carl's modest home, I sheepishly felt the teensiest bit grateful that my previous profession, coupled with some relatively savvy investing, had permitted me to live with a lifestyle a few degrees higher than what Carl and Bonnie Turbot appeared to be living. Clearly, no one becomes a teacher as a get rich quick scheme.

From the front hallway, Carl led me immediately up a flight of stairs to the main living room area. As we reached the top of the stairs, Carl gestured into the narrow living room at the front of the house. The Turbots had done a pleasant job of decorating the shoe box. It at least looked homey. "You want something to drink?" he offered.

"No, thank you," I replied. It was hard to know where to begin. How do you explain to your friend that he's busted? I forced myself to refocus my mind to think of Carl just as a client. Keeping my distance was becoming increasingly necessary if I was going to give him an adequate defence. I looked quietly around the room, then gestured with my head towards the long hallway that trails off into darkness along one side of the house. "Is your wife sleeping?" I asked Carl.

"No," he responded, looking away down the same darkened passage. "She's not here."

"Oh." That's the best I could conjure up for the time being.

"She...umm...Bonnie has gone to stay with her parents for a little while," he managed to confess.

"I see."

"It was, I guess you could say, a little tense here after the media broke the news that I was a suspect in Tricia's death."

"I can see how that could create some conflict in the household."

"Yes."

There was a long pause during which both of us stood looking mostly anywhere but at each other. Finally, I sat down on the edge of the couch and invited him to do the same.

"Carl, I wish you had told me the truth about Tricia." Though I meant our conversation to be about legal strategy, somehow I managed to make the statement be all about me and immediately regretted it. The last thing I needed from my client was to have him feel like I was against him. The truth was I was slowly beginning to lean that way.

"What are you talking about?" he demanded. From the sound of his voice, I could tell that whatever alcohol he'd consumed following his fight with his wife, its effects had not completely worn off. His voice was unsteady, no doubt partially from emotional turmoil, but there was also the slightest slur to his consonants. This wasn't a good time for him to undergo any further questioning.

"Your relationship with Tricia was much more than teacher and student. I don't know how serious it was. I don't know if it was romance or love or lust, and I don't care. What I do care about is the fact you were having sex with her, and you denied it to my face. That doesn't help me, and it doesn't help you."

"That's not true!" he blasted indignantly. "I told you that she was making it up. She's trying to get me in shit!"

"Enough! No more bullshit. I know about you and Tricia." His eyes were wild again, and I saw the flash of wild anger he had shown me two days earlier at the school. I had a momentary flash of Carl's rage exploding and him wrapping his big hands around Tricia's neck, choking the life out of her in a darkened park.

"Carl," I continued, lowering my voice in an attempt to calm him, "I know about it. The police know about it. They have evidence that can and will prove it."

Another pregnant pause passed between us as the anger flowed out of him nearly as quickly as it had appeared. Finally, he looked up and nearly whimpered, "How did you find out?"

"I didn't," I told him. "They did. They found some soiled garments when they searched her bedroom. Preliminary DNA tests indicate a match to you."

"They have my DNA?" he asked. As a scientist, he certainly understood how it works. I sensed his confusion and imminent panic at the thought of what other information about him might be on file.

"Evidently we leave all kinds of DNA kicking around our classrooms. It wasn't difficult to find something with your DNA signature."

"Holy shit," he mustered.

"Yeah. That was about my reaction." I paused for a moment, afraid to ask the next question. "Why didn't you tell me about your relationship with Tricia?"

He looked at me pleadingly. "It's not what you're thinking, Win."

"What I'm thinking isn't really the issue here. More important is what the police who are in front of your house are thinking. Not to mention the thoughts of the judge who they managed to convince to sign a warrant for your arrest."

"The police are here? Now?"

"Yes. That's why I'm here. You're about to be arrested."

Carl, I was quickly learning, was a frequent rider on the pendulum of mood swings. The confusion I had seen give way to anger was now replaced with a veritable wave of fear. He leaped to his feet and actually ran to the front window, parting the curtains to see his anticipated captors below.

"They're out there?" he asked. He suddenly sounded very

young, like an adolescent who has just been informed the school bully has shown up to punch his lights out. "I don't understand," he continued, his breath coming faster as real panic set in. "I thought you said their evidence was no good. I thought it was going to be all right?" He had begun to pace. I hoped Furlo and Smythe couldn't see his shadow dancing back and forth in front of the window. They might think he was planning to run.

"I thought everything was going to be okay. I also thought you weren't sleeping with one of your students, Carl. This sort of changes the perspective of the police, and quite frankly, I can understand why they're looking at you very carefully."

He continued to pace, his breathing growing shallower to the point I thought he was beginning to hyperventilate. All the while he was muttering "Oh, Jesus. Oh, God. Oh, Jesus. Oh, God."

Finally, I stood up, grabbing him by the shoulders to brace him and guide him back to the chair. "Carl, there isn't a lot of time. I need you to sit down and talk to me for a few minutes while we can still be reasonably assured of our privacy." He sank down and looked up at me for salvation, as though by simply listening to me he might be free of whatever demons were tearing up his insides.

"Okay," he gasped out, recovering at least some of his composure. "What do we need to do?"

I slumped back down on the couch, looking at Carl across the coffee table. "For starters," I began, "you can explain to me why you didn't tell me right away about you and Tricia."

Carl looked across the room directly into my eyes, looking for some confirmation that he ought to break his own silence and reveal the details of what had been happening.

"You're going to need to trust someone now," I told him gently. "It may as well be me. Your wife sounds like she's gone, I can't imagine anyone at school is going to come near this. Tell me the truth. Were you having sex with Tricia?"

"Yes," he said. "I was."

At least that much was out in the open. Glancing at my watch, I realized that in mere moments Smythe would not be able to restrain her partner any longer, and Carl would be led out in cuffs.

"Was this a one time thing, or was it a relationship like Tricia described?"

Carl stared at me, his eyes pleading for me to understand. "It isn't what you think, Win. It really isn't. I, we were in love."

"You loved her?"

"And she loved me. My God, it was so wonderful but so wrong at the same time. I've been making this constant trip between heaven and hell for over a year."

"What do you mean?"

"Look. It wasn't some perverted thing, as much as it sounds that way because of her age and the fact that I'm her teacher. I don't know if she's very mature for her age or I'm immature, but she is just the most wonderful woman in the world." Carl continued to refer to Tricia in the present tense. Denial, perhaps? Or was this still the liquor talking?

"It started out very innocently. She was in my Grade Eleven biology class. Of course I noticed her physical appearance. She's a beautiful girl, and objectively I could see that. But I never set out to seduce her or anything."

"Tricia told me you first got, uh, together one night working late on a biology lab," I interjected, trying to move it along.

"That's right. We'd had lots of conversations, she would just hang around and chat and then one night, it just happened. I don't know how to explain it except to say that we kind of looked into each other's eyes, and the next thing you know we were kissing madly. It was right out of some teenage romance movie."

"And no one ever suspected anything? You kept it hidden for nearly a year?" I asked incredulously. In the nearly three months I had been at J. Mac, I had most definitely learned that schools are a hotbed of gossip. Even I knew about which teenager was dating which teenager. It seemed impossible to believe a teacher and student could be romantically involved for so long without word getting out, no matter how hard they tried to conceal it.

"No. At least I don't think so. We were very discreet. We used to meet in the evenings. Sometimes on the weekends. It was like dating. We talked about everything. She is the most understanding, giving person I have ever met." Tricia had resumed the present tense again.

"Then why did you 'break up' with her?"

Carl looked down at his hands. I couldn't be sure, but he seemed to be examining his left hand, where his wedding ring would be sitting were he wearing one. "I don't know. Somehow Bonnie, my wife, suspected that something was going on. I don't know if she knew anything for sure, but she hinted around that she thought I was spending so much time away from home that something must be going on."

"So just like that, you were able to dump Tricia?"

"God, no," he protested. "It was the hardest thing I ever had to do. I even spoke to my priest about it. He's the only other person who knows this, Win. He's the one who insisted I break up with Tricia. He said I owed it to God to honour my wedding vows."

I could relate to that one. Having made the decision to forego my wedding vows, my priest, and the entire organization of the Roman Catholic Church, had essentially told me where to go.

"So?" I prodded.

"So I made the decision that it would be best for both of us to call it off. I've never been so depressed."

"And Tricia?"

"She was crushed at first. She sobbed and cried, but she didn't seem angry. She never asked me to change my mind. She never demanded anything of me. She was entirely mature about it."

"Until she threatened to expose you."

He looked up at me again. "That's just it. It was well over a week since we had broken up. She was pleasant and everything in class. I thought things were going to be fine. It's like she suddenly snapped."

I sighed. I hated to have to ask the next part. "What happened next?"

He looked back at me with what appeared to be genuine surprise. "What happened when?"

"On Wednesday. The day Tricia was killed."

Carl's face broke into a pained, near horrified expression. "Winston!" he proclaimed. "You don't think that..." He couldn't bring himself to finish the question.

"I told you, what I think isn't important. You have to understand the police have even more good reason to think you killed her."

"But I didn't!" he wailed. "I love Trish. I would never do anything to hurt her." With that, the damn burst, and Carl slumped over in the chair, painful sobs flowing from him. I had no way to comfort him, so I just sat back to let him cry himself out.

While I was waiting, my cellular phone beeped again in my pocket. Reaching in, I popped it open and answered, knowing full well who it would be.

"Time's up, Counsellor. Should we come in?" Smythe asked me politely.

I knew I had no right to ask, but I did anyway. "Five more minutes, and I'll bring him out myself."

"I'll give you two," she replied and hung up before I could respond. Even good cops have their limits.

"Come on, Carl," I told him soothingly. "It's time."

He sat up and began wiping away at his face. "I'm sorry, Win. I really am. I'm just so lost. I can't believe she's gone." I hated myself for it; I could feel myself being dragged into his emotional response, starting to believe what he was saying to me. There was just one piece that didn't fit.

"Carl," I asked him as he rose to his feet, "the police found Tricia's underwear with your DNA on it in her laundry basket. When was the last time the two of you were together?"

He looked at me wounded, caught like a kid skipping classes. "When I went to try to talk to her after you did. We talked and things were going okay, and all of a sudden—it just happened."

"Where?" I demanded.

"At school," he said, hanging his head again to avoid my incredulous stare. "It was the only time that ever happened."

"So you and Tricia had sex the day she was killed?" He flinched when I used the term "had sex."

"Yes. And then I went home. And that was the last time I ever saw her. I swear to God."

He looked so pathetic, standing there pleading with me to

believe his version of events. It was going to take an enormous amount of debunking of the police's theories about my client.

"I'll let the police in," I told him, heading back towards the stairs as the front doorbell rang.

I headed down the stairs to meet Furlo and Smythe as Carl waited at the top of the stairs. I opened the door once again to the blustering rain. Furlo stood leaning against the doorjamb, handcuffs swaying from his raised hand.

"Okay, Teach," he said, smiling smugly. "Detention time!"

I knew he had been dying to use that the whole time I'd left him out in the cold, fierce rain.

Fourteen

So far, most of my week had been taken up in some way, shape or form by the legal problems of Carl Turbot. It seemed only appropriate that my Friday evening should be wrecked as well. I sensed Furlo was deriving perverse satisfaction from eating into my weekend. I don't know if he slapped the cuffs on extra loud, or it was just my imagination, but his smug grin told me, at least, that he felt I was some kind of lowlife for defending Carl. He was going to take as much time as possible while I escorted my client through the booking process. Even if my Friday night plans just involved going to bed early to catch up on sleep, Furlo was determined to sabotage that. Ha, I thought. Little does Furlo know that insomniacs don't sleep any better just because it's the weekend. I wasn't going to sleep anyway. One grabs self-righteousness wherever one can find it.

Of course, Providence would have it that all those neighbours who had been seemingly oblivious to Furlo, Smythe and myself out talking on the sidewalk suddenly appeared in their doorways just in time to see Furlo's dramatic display of patting down and cuffing Carl. Smythe looked apologetic, knowing full well I wouldn't have brought Carl out armed and that Furlo's dramatic displays were intended to embarrass his suspect in front of his neighbours. Unfortunately, there was nothing she could do about it; searching the suspect before placing him under arrest was proper procedure.

Once one neighbour stuck his head out, porch lights came on up and down the street, and despite the bitter, near winter rain, a number of busybody neighbours braved the downpour with umbrellas and cups of hot chocolate in hand to watch the proceedings. Certainly, this would not have been completely unexpected for them, given the enormous coverage that had been given to Tricia's murder and Carl's subsequent questioning. Some were likely planning their comments to the media, who would surely arrive once word of his arrest was leaked out. I was fairly confident that by now a local resident was probably telephoning the newsroom of one of Vancouver's TV stations, hoping to catch their fifteen minutes of fame.

"We can't believe it," they'd say. "He was always such a pleasant neighbour. Quiet. Kept to himself. Never bothered anyone, but always gave you a pleasant wave and good morning. We're completely shocked." In the entire history of television and homicide, has there never been a murderer whom neighbours thought was kooky all along? Don't loud and obnoxious neighbours ever kill people?

Once Carl was securely tucked away in the back seat of the Crown Victoria, I hopped into my car to follow the two detectives to the pre-trial holding centre, where Carl would be processed and placed into formal custody. Once behind the wheel and in the late Friday evening traffic, my adrenaline began to subside, and I had time to process the events.

Much was beginning to bother me about Carl's case. Apart from its inherent unpleasantness, little legal alarm bells were sounding in my head's attaché case. The first element of concern was the speed at which the investigation had progressed. It was only yesterday morning that Carl and I had been interviewed at the school; a few hours later, he had been picked up for questioning, and within twenty-four hours he was under arrest. Certainly, Furlo and Smythe looked completely haggard, and I had no doubt they had been working around the clock since Tricia's body had been found early on Wednesday evening. Vancouver doesn't have a great number of homicides, so every one of them is taken very seriously, but the death of a young person would definitely see all of the stops pulled out to catch her killer. While Furlo and Smythe were the lead detectives—and likely their energy had been focused almost exclusively on Carl over the last thirty-six hours—there must also have been dozens of officers working different angles and gathering evidence for an arrest to happen so quickly.

Even the evidence itself was troublesome, essentially because there didn't seem to be a lot of it. On the surface, Carl's DNA found on Tricia's undergarments looked extremely bad, but only insofar as it potentially gave Carl a motive for wanting to see Tricia dead—if she was dead, she couldn't report on their inappropriate and illegal relationship. But motive usually isn't enough for Crown counsel to advise an arrest be made. The DNA finding only proved Carl had had sex with Tricia, not that he had killed her. Indeed, since the underwear wasn't even found at the crime scene, as far as I could tell, they had very little to directly suggest his involvement in her death.

The high profile nature of this particular case would have had any good police chief wanting to see an arrest made quickly, but by the same token, the very fact this case had garnered so much media attention should have made the Crown extra careful to ensure they had a rock-solid case before making an arrest. The justice department would look much worse if they focused their investigative efforts on one suspect, only to have the case against that suspect collapse due to a premature arrest or a lack of solid evidence.

The DNA sample itself was also troublesome, and not just because it positively identified Carl. How had the police come to make that positive identification in less than twenty-four hours? I had had very little legal experience with homicide, but what I did know was that forensic analysis, apart from being expensive to conduct, was also notoriously slow. Advances in DNA testing and myriad other crime scene technology meant forensic evidence was used not just in murder cases, but in almost any crime where human DNA evidence could be gathered. Consequently, there was always a huge backlog of DNA sampling that prosecutors and defence counsel were anxiously awaiting.

Carl's DNA had been collected, tested and reported to the police in what must have been a matter of hours. True, a case like Tricia's would be considered important, but not that important. Somehow, Furlo and Smythe had pushed the DNA analysis to the very front of the line and had clearly kept technicians working overtime to make the identification of Carl Turbot. For that kind of pressure to be applied to the forensic team, someone much higher up than Furlo and Smythe must have had a hand in speeding up the process.

That, of course, smelled of politics and pressure that had nothing to do with the fact that the prime suspect was Tricia's teacher. Even the apparently heinous nature of Carl's romantic—a term I was forcing myself to use—relationship with Tricia wasn't enough to justify the kind of pressure that must surely have been exerted to get that kind of speed and commitment from everyone involved. Tricia, or more likely, someone in Tricia's family, was connected to the powers that be in a way that warranted faster than normal action on everyone's part. Of course, the police came out winners too: they got to show the world they'd caught the killer, and fast.

The last key problem that kept tugging at me was that despite Carl's sleeping with Tricia, despite his trying to use me as his legal protector should that relationship be discovered by administration, despite what looked like a rather obvious motive for wanting Tricia dead, something about him kept bringing me back to a belief in his innocence. I don't consider myself to be a gullible person by nature, and I admit to having been burned on occasion by trusting people I should not have, but for the most part my experience at determining whom I can and cannot trust has proven pretty successful. And however naïve I hoped I didn't turn out to be, driving behind Furlo and Smythe as they delivered my client to lockup, I just couldn't accept that the man who had held my hand through my introduction to high school teaching, the same man who worked tirelessly with students, the very same emotional wreck who broke down sobbing in grief at the death of someone he claimed to love, could have killed her in cold blood. No, I just couldn't accept that.

It was clear that I had a considerable amount of work to do. Whether or not I believed wholly in Carl's version of events was no longer relevant. If Carl was going to get a fair and aggressive defence, I had to believe in his claims, at least to the degree that I could give him the best defence money could buy. Which was the first point I put down on my legal to-do list. Once a lawyer, always a lawyer, I suppose, but Carl and I were going to have to sit down really quickly and start figuring out what kind of fee I was going to be paid. Call me shallow, call me uncaring, but I was not about to undertake the massive amount of work that preparing a murder defence entails completely free of charge, especially considering I had this other full-time job that was extremely demanding of my time.

Item number two on my mental checklist was figuring out a way by which I could somehow do both of my jobs simultaneously. I don't think it's overstatement, especially to anyone who's been a teacher, but by the end of a day of working with kids, I had barely enough energy to scrape together some kind of dinner, mark the work the kids did one day, plan something for the next day and get enough sleep to function. Fortunately for me, that last part is a task I have been avoiding for a number of years.

The larger problem was scheduling court appearances. Not to appear a complainer, but judges are not especially forgiving when it comes to trying to schedule around other commitments. Similarly, I'm pretty sure the school's management would not be too keen on letting me postpone my classes until evening, when court lets out.

Being so new to the profession also made it quite unlikely the Vancouver School Board would grant me a temporary leave of absence to fight the case. Given the negative publicity and numerous phone calls from irate parents they were likely already receiving, the school board would not take kindly to another of their teachers seeking time off to defend the one charged with Tricia's murder. Even once the trial was over, it was pretty much guaranteed that Carl would be fired from teaching and have his credentials removed, if not be prosecuted for having a sexual relationship with a minor in a position of trust, the original charge Carl had come to me about. That was a legal challenge that would have to wait.

The more I thought about it, the more I realized our best course of action was to make sure Carl never went to trial. It just seemed impossible that I could adequately defend him, and I didn't really feel I was ready to bail out of the teaching profession just yet. One of the first things we would have to do was make every effort to nail down Tricia's exact time of death, details of which had not yet been released to me as quickly as Carl's DNA test results had been. Then Carl and I had to make sure he was able to come up with a very good alibi that proved he couldn't have done it. On the face of it, it seemed like pretty sloppy police work that the detectives had apparently done very little to confirm Carl's whereabouts during Tricia's murder. Of course, that perception of sloppy detecting was based on my growing conviction that Carl had been wrongly arrested.

The Vancouver pre-trial detention centre is located at the poorest, most drug-addict ridden corner in Canada's poorest neighbourhood. Hastings Street is considered an arterial route and becomes a highway a little further east, taking the driver who chooses its traffic light-congested lanes from close to Stanley Park in the west to the eastern edge of the suburban city of Burnaby, just east of Vancouver. The entire stretch of roadway from end to end is littered with all manner of pawn shops, rundown fast food joints, a sprinkling of car dealerships and the Pacific National Exhibition fair grounds, historically a major agricultural trading ground that evolved into an amusement park and now is slated for permanent destruction and restoration to park space. Some attempts have been made to gentrify the neighbourhoods that Hastings passes through, but somehow, those attempts never seem to take in a meaningful way. It doesn't matter how much a city council spends on improvements, it's as though Hastings refuses to allow new buildings, sidewalks and hanging baskets to penetrate its aura of washed out, rundown dowdiness. Some claim that's its charm.

One block north of Hastings, Main Street meets Cordova at the outer edge of Vancouver's renowned Chinatown. Strangely, small merchants, largely "mom and pop" Asian family operations, have not only survived, but thrived amidst the largest collection of homeless people and strung-out addicts the country has to offer. It's no secret why so many homeless people and junkies end up in Vancouver: compared to other major Canadian cities like Montreal, Toronto or Winnipeg, Vancouver's wet winters are practically tropical. It has long been a grievance of B.C. politicians that our province foots the bill for the derelicts, the neglected and the addicted of the other nine.

It's at the intersection of Main and Cordova that the forbidding pre-trial detention centre sits kitty corner from the old Vancouver Police Department headquarters. Definitely an equality-based institution, the centre houses those awaiting their day in court for crimes as small as minor break and enter to capital offences like rape or homicide. Even Canada's only real terrorists, charged with the bombing of an Air India flight that killed over three hundred passengers and crew, had spent their pre-trial months preparing with their counsel in the facility at which Carl was just now arriving.

The gaping garage door at the end of the driveway off of Cordova yawned open as Furlo and Smythe delivered their cargo for processing. Not being an official of the police or the courts, I was left to park my car on the dark, rain-soaked streets. Most people would not feel comfortable leaving their car, especially if it were an expensive one, parked outside in this neighbourhood. But the reality of the area surrounding the courts was that car theft was relatively uncommon. For most of the people for whom the streets of Vancouver's downtown East side was home, a car really isn't a prized theft item. Where would they go? The supply of drugs, food handouts and even temporary shelter for those trying to break their street existence is all located in this neighbourhood. Why would they want to leave?

I was buzzed through the front entrance doors by a night security guard who looked surprised to see me. "Winston Patrick," he proclaimed boisterously. "I thought you'd given up this game." Meinhard Werner was officially part of the Sheriff's department, which is responsible only for the operation of our court system, including the transportation of criminals from prisons for court appearances. Meinhard, however, presented an image far from that which we equate with law enforcement. Nearing sixty, with a belly that protruded well beyond the capacity of his belt, Meinhard's principal responsibilities were the signing in of visitors and the completion of the daily crossword puzzle in the *Province* newspaper. Oddly, though the *Province* is the "dummed down" tabloid paper in the city, its crossword puzzle is much more difficult than the one in the *Vancouver Sun*, its main competitor. One of life's little mysteries.

"Hey Meinie," I replied. "This is a temporary dalliance, I assure you."

"You probably just missed me," he joked jovially. How anyone working the evening shift on a Friday night in the worst part of town could consistently remain so happy is another of life's little mysteries.

"That must be it."

"So they bringing your boy in back now?" he asked, glancing down at video monitors showing the various entrances to the facility. It was hardly surprising Meinhard would know who my client was. If I flipped over his *Province* newspaper, I'm sure Tricia's murder figured prominently on the front page. By the weekend editions of the two dailies, my picture from this morning's media scrum at the school would make me instantly recognizable.

"Yeah, I guess so," I offered glumly. There was little I could do for Carl right now except see to it that he was processed properly and given an appropriate place to bunk down. Unlike what is often portrayed in fiction, I knew Furlo and Smythe would make sure their prisoner was safe and sound and not locked up with a violent offender. The police generally have little interest in allowing their prime suspect to sustain any harm prior to going to trial. After sentencing however, anything goes.

Meinhard looked me over, his joviality sliding just slightly. People often view law enforcement personnel and defence counsel as enemies. It isn't always the case. As much as Meinhard got to see the lowest of the low come through his watch, he always showed tremendous respect for the process and the principle of innocent until proven guilty. He had never made me feel like I was a lesser citizen for defending those charged with a crime, even the guilty ones.

"A bit of a tough one for ya, I imagine?" he asked, trying to give me some comradely support.

"It isn't the most comfortable position to be in, that's for sure."

"He work with you, this one? Is that how you came to be his counsel?" He hooked his thumb towards a video monitor to his right, where a grainy image of Carl and the two detectives could be seen getting out of the car and heading towards a freight-like elevator in the underground parking lot.

"Yeah," I replied. "We teach at the same high school. He approached me to ask for some legal advice, and next thing you know, I had a client."

"Yeah, well, it's going to be an ugly one, if the media dogs are right. You hang in there, and you'll do right by him, one way or the other."

"Thanks. I'll do what I do."

He gestured towards the doorway at the end of the hallway. "You remember the way, or would you like an escort?" Meinhard knew visitors weren't really supposed to wander the innards of the building, but most practicing legal counsel were unofficially permitted to make their way to meet with clients without the aid of a sheriff escort. It was another of his subtle ways of saying "welcome back."

"I think I still remember," I told him.

"All right then. Go get him," he said, passing me a plastic encased visitor's badge and unlocking the hallway door with a loud, electronic buzz.

The interior hallways of the pre-trial centre are painted institutional cream, not quite blinding white, but also devoid of colour, warmth or personality, three elements generally not permissible in publicly funded buildings. The only decoration on the walls was the occasional "No Smoking" sign and a variety of scuff marks, where reluctant prisoners dragged and slid their bodies and handcuffs and wary new lawyers bumped their briefcases. I wound my way through a short maze of hallways to the central processing areas, where Carl would be getting fingerprinted, searched, given prisoner's garb and assigned a cell until his first court appearance. I found Furlo and Smythe standing aside as a fingerprint technician worked Carl through the process.

Ambling up to the two detectives, I decided that for the time being I might try a less adversarial approach. It might prove to be more useful in gathering information.

"Coffee, Winston?" Detective Jasmine Smythe offered. I noticed Furlo was working his way through a Styrofoam cup of what must surely have been his twentieth cup of the day. Smythe carried with her a bottle of water she sipped from periodically. I also noticed she called me by my first name.

"No, thank you. It will only keep me awake all night."

"You mean you're not going to camp out here to tell bedtime

stories to your client?" Furlo asked. He had already resumed punctuating the word "client" with a sarcastic drawl. For the time being, I refused to be drawn into a verbal pissing match with the bleary-eyed detective. I wondered how long my resolve would last.

"You two didn't waste any time solving the case, Detective Smythe. You must be very confident." I was on my non-combative best behaviour, just passing the time of night with my two VPD friends.

"Maybe we're just that good," she replied with a smile. "And why don't we drop the formality? It's Jasmine. Call me Jazz."

"I like that. Jazz. It has a very smooth sound to it."

"Winston," Jazz smiled again at me in mock embarrassment, "are you flirting with me?"

"Would that be a good idea?" I smiled back coyly. At least, I was trying to be coy.

"Gosh," she adopted a southern belle persona. "Why I'm old enough to be your mother."

"No one would believe it for a moment. If anything, they'd accuse me of being your sugar-daddy."

"Jesus Christ," Furlo blurted out, "are you two finished fucking around here? I wouldn't mind dumping the perv over there and going home. Some of us haven't slept in a long time."

"Well, at least you haven't tired yourself out actually gathering sufficient evidence," I retorted. It was embarrassing how quickly my resolve not to fight with Furlo had fizzled.

Furlo put his Styrofoam coffee cup down on a nearby table and walked towards me, slowly, menacingly. His lack of sleep and abundance of caffeine had heightened his already aggressive personality to the near breaking point. I wasn't helping. Rationally, I recognized his approach for what it likely was: Furlo was drawing a line in the sand to see whether or not I would flinch. This was a good time to be the bigger man—at least in terms of maturity— and apologize for my snide comments and walk away. Secretly, I was starting to enjoy how quickly I could get under Furlo's skin.

"Don't kid yourself," he hissed, pushing his considerably wide frame into my personal space. "This is the worst type of crime. No one wants to see a kid—a kid—murdered. But when you have a kid who was being abused by her teacher, a man who should have been a person she could turn to for help, someone she could trust, and he not only takes advantage of her so he can get his own rocks off, then whacks her when she's no longer interesting to him or she threatens to expose him for the pig that he is, you can bet your ass that I'm going to work around the clock and do everything I can to put your piece of shit client in the shit can for as long as our pathetic Criminal Code will let me. Your client is the worst kind of asshole we deal with. And as a parent of a daughter especially, he makes me sick. So don't you worry, Winnie, we have and will continue to gather all the evidence we need."

He paused a moment to breathe his stale coffee breath directly into my nostrils. I felt like I was getting CPR at a Starbucks. Then he continued. "You're in the big leagues now, teacher-boy. No more little Legal Aid penny-ante stuff. You're just feeling like such a shit because you recognize what a lowlife you're defending."

Two choices again. Walk away. Or. I cocked my head slightly to the right. "Did you pick that up reading pop psychology books when you were supposed to be catching the real killer?"

My chest pounded as Furlo's hand pushed me back against the wall behind me. "You listen to me, you little fuck..."

"Michael!" Smythe burst sharply, suddenly reminding us of her quiet presence throughout the exchange. "Step back, now!" she commanded. Amazingly, Furlo did exactly as he was told. It was as though acting tough with me was perfectly acceptable, but crossing his partner was not something that would even enter his mind. Immediately, he backed away, turned around and crossed the room, picking up his coffee cup and walking back towards Carl and the sheriff's employee, who were watching the exchange in wide-eyed wonder.

Smythe turned her sharp glare to me, softening it ever so little. "Why?" was all she asked, with a deep sigh.

"I don't know. I can't help myself?" I tried.

She gave me a caring look. "He's right, though, Winston. This is going to be a big, ugly case. From the point of view of your teaching career, which I respect greatly, by the way, think carefully about whether you want to continue representing your client. This might be a good juncture at which to pass this off to other counsel."

"I can't do that," I replied. "That would not be right."

Detective Smythe took my right hand in both of hers. "I know," she said. "I thought I would try. Let's try to be good, okay?"

"Okay," I said. "Scout's honour."

"Good," she said, releasing my hand and picking up her purse. "Goodnight, Winston."

"Goodnight, Jasmine." Then, because Jasmine had such a disarming way about her, I called across the room to her partner. "Goodnight, Detective Furlo. I apologize for upsetting you." It was the best I could offer.

"Whatever," he grumbled, not bothering to counter with an apology of his own for tossing me against the wall. He turned to leave, then paused and walked back over to me. I prepared for a firm handshake. Instead, he stopped to stare me down again. "One more thing. Stop flirting with my partner. You do it again, I'm going to give her husband your home address. That's former B.C. Lions defensive tackle Warren Smythe, in case you've forgotten." With that he turned and left, accurately tossing his coffee cup into the waste basket from a distance of nearly twenty feet. Impressive.

Catching my breath for a moment, I turned and walked over to where Carl was removing his belt and emptying his pockets. He watched me carefully as I sauntered over, trying to gauge my impression of the state of his situation.

"Jeez, Win," Carl began shakily. "He seemed really pissed off at you."

"Yeah," I admitted a little sheepishly. "I have that ability to alienate people. My ex-wife would confirm that for you," I added, trying to inject some much needed levity into the room. As is often the case, I recognized immediately my timing was ill-placed. Looking at Carl, I could see that the gravity of his situation had sunk in, and he looked more terrified than I had seen him to date.

"Look," I continued gamely, "don't worry about my relationship with the police. He's pretty much not our concern any more. It is not at all uncommon for the police not to get along with defence lawyers.

Cops like Furlo, if they had their way, would shoot first and ask questions later." Of course that was an unfair characterization of Furlo. He was going to extraordinary lengths to ensure he had a rock-solid case against Carl. There was no way he wanted to see this case fail due to some minor procedural flaw. He was going to be doing this one by the book, but Carl didn't need to hear that right now.

"Okay," he said, a little dejectedly. He raised his lowered head to meet my eyes, like a beaten puppy, looking to his master for some kind of explanation for the torment he was going through. I wished I could tell him that everything would be fine, but I didn't feel right making that assurance until I had more information to work with.

"Did you want to go into one of the conference rooms?" the helpful young sheriff's officer asked. He looked about nineteen, much too young to have actually completed the Justice Institute training course now required for virtually all courthouse positions.

"Thank you," I told him. "We'll just take a few minutes."

"That's all right," he replied. "Believe it or not, it's actually a slow night." He was right. For a Friday night, I would have expected to see all manner of minor arrests coming through central processing around this time. Thus far, we had been entirely alone.

The sheriff took us down yet another narrow hallway and ushered us through a plain door into a small room, holding only a cheap, standard, government-issue table with three stacking chairs around it. I pointed to a chair. As he lowered himself wearily into a chair, the sheriff closed the door and left us alone, though I knew he would be standing immediately outside the door. His guardianship in the hallway was pretty much a formality. The door could not be opened from the inside without a special key device inserted into a latch key slot where the doorknob would normally be.

After a silent time, during which I tried to think of comforting words for my client, Carl finally asked, "Is this it? Am I going to jail, Win?"

"Yes. You are. In a manner of speaking."

"What manner of speaking? What does that mean?"

I sighed. Briefly my Law Twelve class flashed before me. I wondered if any of them would be able to explain Carl's present circumstances and what was about to happen to him. I suspected that less than half the class could.

"For starters, though it's going to feel like it, this isn't technically 'jail'," I began. "This is pretty much just a holding place until we can get you before a judge. When that happens, we argue for getting you released pending trial, and we go from there."

"Is that like bail?" he asked plaintively.

"Yes. If we're lucky, the court will release you without bail, but because it's a murder case, and it is getting a fair bit of media attention, we will likely have to try to post bond. It's called a 'surety', and it's the court's way of having you guarantee that you'll show up for trial."

"I don't have much money," he began to protest. I recognized that any legal fees I could expect to collect, just like in the olden days, were likely to be picked up by Legal Aid. So much for hiring an investigator and assistant. At Legal Aid rates, I would be lucky if I could recoup my photocopy costs. My ex-wife would be so proud.

"You don't generally have to put up too much money. We won't have to worry about that for a while," I told him, easing into the bad news.

"When will I be bailed out? How long do I have to stay here?"

"Under the Criminal Code, you're generally entitled to a first court appearance within twenty-four hours or as soon as possible. But it's Friday night. That means the likelihood of us finding a sitting judge on the weekend is pretty slim. I think it's one of the reasons they arrested you so quickly. They buy a couple more days of investigative time while you have to wait for your first court appearance."

"But that's not fair," he protested. He was beginning to sound like one of his own students, complaining about an upcoming exam or major assignment that infringed on their teenage social life.

"Legally, it is fair. There's really nothing I can do about that. The good news is that it will also buy me a couple of days to start preparing to get you out of here. Look, the police know you're not some hardened, career criminal. But they believe you killed Tricia."

"But I didn't." He slammed his open palm down on the table. "I didn't kill her. Winston, I loved Trish." Clearly, he had sobered up from his alcoholic haze of earlier in the evening. He had resumed speaking of his lover in the past tense.

"Right now, believe it or not, that doesn't really matter. The detectives, and probably the Crown Counsel who has been assigned to this case, believe they've caught their man. They also figure that since this was some kind of crime of passion, by arresting you tonight and leaving you to cool your heels over the weekend, you'll be scared into making some kind of plea by the time we get into your first appearance on Monday."

"They think that I'm going to plead guilty?" he asked indignantly. "I didn't kill her."

"That's not what they believe, and they're hoping they can avoid a messy trial by having you cop a plea."

"I'm not pleading guilty to killing the woman I loved," he insisted vehemently.

"Let's not worry about that right now. And for the time being, I don't want you referring to Tricia as 'the woman you loved'. In fact, I don't want you referring to anyone or to anything about your case. Have you got that? Not a word. Not to a guard, not to a detective, not to a Crown prosecutor. No one. You don't say anything about the murder or your relationship with Tricia unless I'm present. You understand?"

"Okay," he relented. "I won't say anything."

That dispensed with, I figured our time was just about up. There was nothing more I could do for my friend right now. "Good," I said, rising from the table. Walking around to his side, I placed my hand on his shoulder. "This is going to be a really tough time, Carl. It will be worse than anything you've been through, but we've got some time on our hands. My first job will be to get you out of here on Monday. Then, we're going to work on ensuring there's no way this ever gets to trial. But it isn't going to be easy. We'll have lots of work to do."

He looked up at me, placing his hand across mine, still on his shoulder. "I don't know how I'm going to thank you. I don't have much, but I'll pay you as my lawyer, I promise you that."

"We'll take care of that later." I walked towards the door to notify the sheriff's officer that we were done. Then I turned to face Carl again.

"I'm going to ask you something one more time. It's not a question defence counsel generally get into. It isn't technically relevant, but I'm not just a lawyer any more. I'm a servant to two loyalties, so I'm going to ask you anyway. Whatever your answer is, I'm still going to be your lawyer, and I'm going to defend you. But for my own state of mind, I have to know the absolute, honest truth. Did you kill her?"

Carl's eyes filled with tears. I knew and—damn it—believed the answer before he even spoke it. "No. I told you. I loved her. I would have given my life for her. I did not kill her."

"Okay." Running my hand through my hair with exhaustion, I regarded him one last time. "I'm very relieved to hear that. Is there someone you want me to call?"

He looked absolutely lost. His wife had already taken off to her parents'. It didn't seem likely she was going to want to come visit him in jail. "I don't think so."

I knocked on the door. "I'll check in with you tomorrow. Try to get some rest, all right?"

"All right," was all he could muster. The door hummed as an electronic pass card key buzzed the lock and the sheriff's officer poked his head in.

"We're done," I told him. "Goodnight, Carl."

He was slumped at the table as the sheriff came to escort him to his first-ever jail cell. I turned and headed down the hallway towards the front entrance, unable to watch.

Fifteen

A funny thing happened when I returned to my apartment after leaving Carl: I slept. Almost immediately upon closing my door, a wave of tiredness hit me. It was like walking into a big wall of exhaustion. In fact, I was so tired, I actually felt nauseous.

I'm no scientist, but when I feel that way, it is a sign I should go to sleep. Simple as it sounds, for those of us for whom sleep is a constant battle, just the notion of going to bed can fill you with anxiety. The bags under my eyes add at least five years to my age.

It was nearly two a.m. as I undressed, carefully picking up my clothes and placing them in the laundry hamper next to the ensuite bathroom door. Sandi was always amazed at what she deemed my obsessive need for tidiness and order around the house. We would come home from a party or family gathering—and with her family, there was always a wide assortment of social responsibilities—and Sandi would simply dump her clothes on the floor, only to wait in bed while I went around picking them up and hanging them in the closet where they belonged, or placing them in their assigned spot in the laundry room.

In the past week, I had accumulated probably around eight hours of sleep. Sleep deficit often catches up with me at the strangest times. No doubt many lawyers taking on a murder case, especially when it was the kind of case likely to be difficult, long and very public, would sit up all night worrying about the case and beginning a mental to-do list of briefs to prepare, witnesses to interview, and assorted menial startup tasks ad infinitum.

I found myself remarkably calm. It was as though returning to my original calling had brought about an inner peace. That worried me. Fortunately, it didn't worry me enough to lose sleep. I literally collapsed into bed and crashed.

The phone rang minutes later. Actually, it was hours later, but the phone's interruption of my sleep made it seem as if I had just lain down. The only thing worse than the phone ringing and waking you up is when it gives two short rings instead of just one. As nearly every apartment dweller knows, the double ring is an indicator someone is standing outside the front door of the building waiting to see you.

I grumbled into the receiver. "You better not be selling something."

"Get up," came a much-too-perky voice. "I have fresh raisin scones and coffee."

"That's not good enough," I replied.

"I have a gun, and I can shoot my way in."

"That's better," I said, pressing the number six to admit Detective Andrea Pearson.

Glancing at the clock, I saw it was nearly ten a.m. I had slept for almost seven and a half hours, some kind of record for me. Maybe things were getting better. Then Carl flashed into my barely conscious memory, and I realized things were likely to get worse long before they got any better. Stumbling out of the bedroom, I managed to make my way to the front hallway just as Andrea began to pound on the door. Fists of steel, that one.

"Good morning, sunshine!" she beamed as I opened the door.

"Hmmph," was my reply, walking away from the door in the general vicinity of the bathroom. "I gotta whizz."

"Lovely. Maybe you could find some pants in your travels. This is how you greet me? In your boxers?"

"I don't remember inviting you," I growled, closing the bathroom door behind me. A quick glance in the mirror confirmed the vast amount of sleep had done little to improve my overall visage.

For informal clothing, I managed to find an old pair of warm-up pants. I rarely wore them, because they were those annoying plastic type that make swishing sounds when you walk. I hate announcing my pending presence. But for Andrea, they would just have to do.

When I resurfaced from the bedroom, Andy had already placed scones in the toaster oven and was scanning the fridge for jam.

"You need to shop," she complained. "Don't you have jam?"

"In the cupboard," I replied wearily.

"Who keeps jam in the cupboard?"

"I do."

"You're supposed to refrigerate it."

"Only after it's opened."

"How are you going to enjoy your jam if you never open it?"

"This conversation is already wearing me out," I groaned.

Reaching into the cupboard above the sink, Andy let out a little cry of victory upon discovering a jar of Smucker's Grape Jelly. I think I got it as part of my divorce settlement. With a slight grunt, she popped open the jar's lid, pausing first to blow off the accumulated dust.

"So?" she asked.

"So what?" Sometimes we play beat around the bush games like this.

"Well, you were sleeping at nearly ten in the morning, which for you is some kind of miracle. That means, I guess, that the remainder of the evening—after the point you blew me off and left me alone in a restaurant, I might add—must have been particularly tiring, meaning you were kept busy for some time with your client. Correct?"

"I can see why you're a detective," I said, slowly beginning to wake up. Just the smell of coffee in the morning has that effect on me.

"How'd it go?"

"About as well as I could have expected. They had a warrant, they were determined to pick him up and hold him over the weekend while they gather more evidence."

Andrea frowned at this. In her mind, you didn't make the arrest until you had ample evidence—and to her way of thinking, ample generally was meant to include more evidence than the prosecution could ever need. There is nothing worse than putting your heart and soul into an investigation and still finding you don't have enough to get a conviction. I could tell Andy wasn't pleased with the way this investigation was going, but there was little she could do without being accused of interfering with her fellow detectives' work. This was especially true considering Furlo and Smythe would know full well about Andy's friendship with me. Even if she had caught the case, she likely would have been forced to recuse herself as the lead detective because of my involvement.

The toaster oven bell chimed, and Andy reached in, placed the four scone halves onto two plates and began applying large amounts of grape jelly to them.

"Is the intent to completely disguise the taste of the baking?" I asked.

"I told you. You're too skinny. We'll start with jam, then I'll find something really fattening to feed you."

Placing the two plates at the small pass-through bar between my kitchen and dining area, she dragged a stool from the dining room side back to the kitchen so she could face me while we ate. "How's your client?" she asked.

"He's lost. This is a man who probably hasn't even driven through the neighbourhood the jail's in, let alone set foot inside one. I hope he survives the weekend."

"You gonna see him today?"

"Yeah, at some point." I took a bite of the still-hot scone she had provided. "You still haven't told me what brings you here, other than your ulterior motive of fattening me up for the slaughter."

Andy studied me a moment. "I'm here to help you solve the crime."

"What?"

I waited while she wolfed down half a scone. "You really convinced that your boy didn't do it?"

"Yes. I am. I know it sounds ridiculous, especially considering he admitted to me last night that he did, in fact, have a sexual relationship with her, but I don't believe he killed her."

"Good enough for me," she said. "Your best defense on this one is going to be finding someone else to pin it on."

I scowled at her. "I'm not looking to pin a homicide on anyone."

"You know what I mean, Winnie," she said with aggravation.

"There's something going on with this case that it's being rushed through so quickly. Furlo and Smythe are both good cops. This is rushed even for them. There's pressure, big pressure to get this solved, and the big 'they' may push ahead for prosecution with what little evidence, albeit pretty damning evidence, they've got."

"You know, that's what I was thinking last night. Even if we stipulated to the sexual relationship, that sort of gives them circumstantial, but not much else." I waited a moment. "Unless you know something I don't."

"Even if I did, I couldn't tell you, though you know I would. It's locked up pretty tightly, 'eyes only' kind of stuff. A fellow can't even do a little snooping out of interest on this one."

"That's weird."

"Yeah, it is," she agreed.

I finished off the last of my scone. Andy, well ahead of me as always in the food department, had already crossed the kitchen floor to put two more scones in the toaster oven.

"I think I'm fine with this one," I told her.

"We'll see," she replied. "So. What's the first order of business?"

"Well," I told her, sipping my coffee, "Carl's going to have to face bail hearings on Monday. And I've got to teach. So I'm going to have to call in some reinforcements. I'll get on that today."

"You going to get a co-chair or something?"

"At least someone who can pinch hit for me when I have to be in the classroom."

"Who you gonna get?" she asked.

I smiled at her. "You don't want to know."

Andy shook her head seriously. "Oh, shit, Winnie. You've got to be kidding."

"I'm not," I replied as the toaster oven chimed.

*　　*　　*

Derek Cuffling, barrister and solicitor, practices a wide variety of law. He began his career as a junior crown counsel, prosecuting minor cases for the Attorney General's ministry. He soon found the draw of greater billing hours and greater billing rates of private practice much too compelling to continue in the direct employ of Her Majesty, so he set up a small practice close to the downtown law courts.

Mostly through Providence, but also through the assistance of his high society-minded parents, Derek had drawn a couple of very high profile cases, particularly one involving insider trading allegations against a former provincial cabinet minister, one of many former and current government officials with whom Derek's legal career would bring him into legal contact. Those early successes garnered the attention of one of Vancouver's largest law firms, McAllister, Willson, McAllister and Dupere, who had recently bought out Derek's practice, making him a junior and one of the youngest partners in their firm. Derek is also the older brother of my ex-wife, Sandi.

Though Derek and I had met through Sandi, we'd really become friends while I was at law school. Three years my senior, Derek was active in the U.B.C. Law faculty long after his graduation as an alumni advisor to students nearing completion of their law degrees. As an immediately successful graduate, at the time leaping ahead in the Crown Counsel's office faster than any of his peers, he was inspirational to young associates-to-be trying to forge a career despite what was seen then as Vancouver's relatively limited legal opportunities.

By the time I had graduated, the legal career opportunities seemed much more vast, with Derek helping his U.B.C. peers wade through the widening areas of law springing up. Recently, in addition to his successful criminal defence practice, Derek had ventured into the entertainment and intellectual property law field as Vancouver's burgeoning film and television industry grew to eclipse all other locations save Los Angeles and New York. If there was an area of law in which to make a buck, Derek was there. In that regard, he was very much like his sister. In all others, he was quite different. For starters, he still liked me.

McAllister, Willson, McAllister and Dupere occupied four floors of a building on Georgia Street, kitty-corner to the renowned Vancouver Art Gallery and directly across from the historic Hotel Vancouver. The building was pretty much chock full of law firms.

From the outside, like many downtown offices of the late eighties and early nineties, it was rather ugly, though the architects had adorned the building with lady of mercy nursing statues on the four pillars. On the inside, however, Derek's employers had spared no expense in bringing opulence to their workplace. It's an odd legal principle that the grander your office is, the more confidence your high-end clients will have in the firm. Never having been a high-end client, I can't pretend to know how they think. I would think, however, that the more ostentatious my lawyer's office was, the more I would want to scrutinize my legal bills to ensure I wasn't being bilked any more than necessary.

Although it was Saturday, I knew Derek would be in the office, along with most of the other junior partners and associates who aspired to be one. Contrary to the popular perception of those outside the legal profession, lawyers, even high-priced, successful ones, often put in ridiculously long hours, working six day weeks in order to maintain their client load and an acceptable number of billable hours. For lawyers like Derek, financial necessity wasn't so much the reason he worked on the weekend, because his family was wealthy long before he went to law school. Derek loved to work.

Rather than calling ahead to announce my pending visit, I opted instead simply to show up at the firm's headquarters. Though it was unlikely Derek's team of secretarial staff would be present on the weekend to intercept calls for him, it also meant there would be no one answering the phones. If there should be a secretary there, he or she would likely run interference for Derek also. Throughout last summer, in between finishing classes to prepare for my teaching career, I had managed at least once a week to drag Derek away from precious billable time to engage in such fruitless pursuits as running Stanley Park's seawall or rollerblading in Mount Seymour's demonstration forest on the North Shore. Not exactly serious lawyerly behaviour.

The security guard at the front desk of the building knew well enough by now to grant me access. When I arrived in the reception area of, there was no one at the front desk, though the main office doors were unlocked. Who would attempt to rob a law firm?

Making my way past the floor-to-ceiling picture window with a spectacular view towards the port and North Shore mountains, I wound through the maze of hallways to the northwest corner of the building, where I could see Derek through the open door of his office, dressed casually in a golf shirt I knew was more expensive than the suits worn by some of the legal assistants on his staff.

"And I gave up all of this for teaching?" I announced as I approached his office doorway.

Derek looked up from the laptop at which he was busy hacking away. The modern day lawyer frequently does his own typing. "No, you gave up a scrubby little run-down office, where you invited society's riff-raff not to pay you for your services," he replied. Derek has a terribly disarming smile, nothing smarmy about it. But it was powerful enough to charm clients, juries, opposing counsel, even the occasional judge. At thirty-eight years old, Derek stands at over six feet tall and is a bit of a health fanatic. He runs about as much as I do, but whereas running has made me skinny to the point of concern, it has contributed to his muscular physique and all round "Adonis-ness". It occasionally pisses me off.

"Yeah, but work, work, work. It's all you ever do."

"As if you're here to try to take me away from all that."

"What makes you think I'm not here to invite you to a rousing defeat in racquetball?" I asked him, though I was fully cognizant that by now Derek would be fully apprised of my legal relationship with Carl. Anyone who read a newspaper would be.

"Two things, really," he replied, cautiously hitting ctrl-s on the keyboard to save whatever it was that had brought him to the office on a Saturday. I wondered why he didn't just take it home with him. "One: you haven't defeated me in racquetball in nearly two years and two: you've really plucked a ripe apple this time."

"It was more like the apple fell onto my head as I was walking by."

"People are wondering if you went into teaching to tap into a market of educators needing legal counsel."

"People?"

He turned to face me again and smiled. "Okay, Sandi's

wondering that." My continuing friendship with Derek since our divorce was a constant strain on the sibling relationship. Sandi believed her brother showed a profound sense of disloyalty by remaining a friend of her ex-husband. Derek thought it was terribly amusing to see his little society sister get so immensely pissed off. I wondered if our friendship hinged on Sandi's lack of acceptance of it. "What's up?" he asked.

I flopped into the chair opposite his desk. The chair caught me in a soft embrace, its distressed leather gently distributing my weight into the luxurious padding beneath. This lone chair was more expensive than my previous budget for my entire office. "I need favours."

"Of course." Derek hit a few more keys on his computer. I knew he was bringing up his calendar to determine just where my legal career was going to coincide with his. "What do you need? First appearance?"

"Yep." It was amazing how much he seemed to know about where my case stood. I knew part of it was due to the media coverage; the rest was simply based on his instincts as a trial lawyer.

"Paper said he was arrested yesterday," he continued, already formulating a plan in his head. "Couldn't find a late night judge?"

"Nope," I replied. At least some of the anxiety that had been building since Carl first came to me was beginning to ebb, knowing that Derek was taking an interest in the case. For a fleeting moment, I toyed with the idea of asking him simply to take over the defence altogether. Carl would certainly be in more capable hands than mine. I also knew I would be pushing the boundaries of both friendships if I were to attempt to offload my client now that he faced a murder trial.

"First appearance on Monday?" Derek was almost muttering to himself as he stared at the laptop's screen, alternately clicking with the mouse and typing in a few quick strokes on the keyboard. I knew he was clearing things out of the way to devote a few hours of time to my case. I didn't try to express it, but I really did appreciate it. We knew each other well enough that I didn't have to say it.

"Eleven a.m." Carl's appearance had been arranged before I even got out of the pre-trial centre's doors the previous night.

"Can't go getting all 'Chartery' on this one," Derek murmured. Canada's overarching Charter of Rights and Freedoms pretty much spelled out that an arrested person gets his or her first court appearance within twenty-four hours of arrest, unless it is unreasonable for that to happen. The word "reasonable" in the Charter has been the cause of much difficulty in legal proceedings because of its subjectivity: one man's reasonable is another's utterly ridiculous. It was generally held though that a person arrested late in the evening—especially on a Friday and especially when the charge involved homicide—could scarcely make an argument for a weekend delay in first appearance somehow depriving the person of fair process.

"I suspect not," was all I could think of to say in agreement. In most of our endeavours, Derek and I operated on an equal footing. Sitting here with my first—and hopefully last—really difficult murder case had me feeling somewhat inferior.

"Okay," he said, typing the finishing touches on his keyboard. I knew that before he left the office today, his computer calendar would be linked up to his secretary's, and she would be aware of his schedule for Monday morning and would make the requisite changes to his appointments. "First appearance should be fairly straightforward. What exactly do you want me to do?"

"Hmm, go to it for me."

He looked up at me quizzically. "What do you mean? You're not coming?"

"I have to teach classes," I lamely explained. "The principal is already not too pleased he has a teacher on staff accused of the crime. He is even less pleased that another teacher on staff is representing the first."

Derek leaned back in his chair and glanced up at the high ceiling in his office. "Yeah, I guess I can see how that might not look so good for a principal. He must really be losing sleep. How's he handling things?"

"Not well. He's not talking to me much."

"I guess not." Derek leaned forward and began to laugh gently at my predicament. "Man. You still know how to get yourself in shit, don't you?"

"It's a character trait."

"Or flaw, depending on your perspective." We both smiled. We considered my habit of getting myself stuck with odd cases to be rather amusing and perhaps a measure of my belief in seeing that all people get a fair trial, not, as my ex-wife attested, a symptom of my poor judgment and character.

"So you just need me to handle his bail application?" Derek asked, almost a little sadly. I could tell this case had started to pique his interest, and he was looking to stay involved. It is little known to members of the general public that many lawyers, even the high-priced ones, often take on cases that offer little or no compensation, simply because they believe strongly in the legal principle at stake or because they feel a challenge in the case. Other times, major law firms require their associates, sometimes even their partners, to take on some pro bono cases each year, just to ensure their legal and courtroom instincts and ethics stay intact. I can recall a number of times in drug court where I would see high-powered talent from major firms doing Legal Aid defence cases. It's a way of giving something back.

I smiled inwardly. "Well," I told him. "I'm pretty sure I could use some litigation muscle. With some of the big-time losers you've defended, I can't think of anyone better to turn to for assistance."

"So your client is a big-time loser too?" Try though I might, it was virtually not possible to insult Derek. He has such thick skin that he takes nothing personally.

"Only in the ever-impartial eyes of the media," I retorted.

"Okay." He confirmed his attachment to the case with a slight slap on his glass topped desk. "What have you got so far?"

That gave me yet another moment for pause. I didn't "got" much of anything. In terms of Carl's defence, I was basically operating on my own conviction that his version of events was true. I had no evidence to back up that conviction, and I told Derek so.

"So you have a whole hell of a lot of work to do this weekend," he stated the obvious.

"Yeah," I admitted. "I'm going to drop by to visit Carl and then begin doing some research."

"Library here is open if you need it," he offered, granting me access to his law firm's extensive legal reference library. This was essentially a no-no, but the firm was so pleased it had acquired Derek that he pretty much had the run of the place. "I take it then, you don't have much of a strategy developed yet?"

"No. Andrea seems to think there is some kind of pressure from on high. Our best defence at this point might be a good offence. She's decided she believes in me believing in my client and figures the best way to clear him might just be to find the actual perp."

Derek gave me a careful look. Without saying it, Derek was giving me a basic law school caution. My job as Carl's defence counsel was not to solve the crime for the police. It isn't a good defence strategy to act as investigator and prosecutor of someone other than the client.

"I agree that would make life easier—" he began.

"But I'm going to work first of all on looking into his alibi at the time of death, something the police were largely quiet about," I interrupted.

"Good a place as any to start," he agreed. "Email what you have sometime tomorrow afternoon, and we'll talk Sunday night before I go into court. You gonna be okay to get time for trial?"

"I'm hoping it doesn't come to that."

"Better make plans in case wishful thinking doesn't hold true."

"Okay. Thanks, Derek. I'll be in touch," I said, standing to let him get back to his paying work.

"Just a minute," he said, standing also and looking at me awkwardly. "Have you talked to Sandi recently?"

"Yeah. The other day."

"Did she talk to you about anything in particular?" he asked cautiously.

I had nearly forgotten Sandi's news. "Yeah. She told me she was pregnant."

I could feel Derek searching my face for some kind of reaction. "And?"

"And? And I didn't know she was even dating anyone in particular."

"Neither did anyone else."

"Ahh."

"You're okay with it?"

"Why wouldn't I be?"

He laughed and shook his head. "Because for reasons known only to you and her, my sister has long before, during and after your marriage to her, managed to hold a bizarre, captivating spell over you, and news of her pending maternity may just affect you in matters that will cause you to sleep even less than you already do."

"Man," I told him, shaking my head in mock condescension. "You need to let go. It's over between your sister and me. I've moved on. It's time you did, too."

"Right," he told me. "Just don't do anything stupider than usual."

"Like re-marry your sister to make an honest woman of her?"

"Don't think it hasn't crossed my mind."

"It hasn't crossed mine. I'm happy for her."

"We'll see," he cautioned. With that foreboding message, I turned and left Derek to defend the upper echelons of society from their brushes with the law.

Sixteen

Carl looked like hell. Incarceration, even for the very short term, does not agree with most people. This is especially true for first timers and the wrongfully accused who have no real business being in a jail cell. An old television documentary called *Scared Straight* placed young people into the prison system for a period of time in order to show them what they could expect from a life of crime. Though the pre-trial jail certainly was much more humane and safer all around than the maximum security prison in which Carl could expect to do time if convicted, spending the night behind bars had made a lasting impression on him.

He was brought to a small room much like the one we had spoken in last night, although a bit bigger, including a longish conference-style table designed to permit lawyers to spread out the reams of paperwork in front of their clients, to show them the product for which they were being ridiculously overcharged. While I knew he would have been safe and free from harassment from some of the rougher criminal elements—at least in the short term—Carl looked as though he'd sat all night with his back to the wall, terrified of what might befall him, while he awaited my return.

"How are you holding up?" I asked him as he sat down.

"I'm okay," he tried to assure me unconvincingly. "I'm fine."

I sat down next to him at the table and laid a hand on his shoulder. "I'm sure this has been the absolutely shittiest night of your life. It's okay to have been scared by it. It's totally normal."

He looked around the room, as though checking to make sure we were alone. "Yeah. It wasn't so bad. What happens now?"

I sat back and explained to him our current situation, what would happen when he appeared in court on Monday, and that I had the services of Derek Cuffling, one of the best defence lawyers in the city on our side. At that he perked up a little, until he found out I wouldn't be next to him in the courtroom for his first appearance.

"What are you talking about?" he pleaded. "You're not going to be there?"

"I can't."

"Winston, you're my lawyer. I want you to be there."

"You'll be in good hands with Derek. I'm telling you, you'll be in even better hands."

Carl had a panicked, pleading look in his eyes. "Winston," he continued. "I know this guy is good. He may be the best even, but I don't know him. I know you."

Gently laying one hand against his shoulder again, I took his hand in my other. "Listen to me. I told you this was going to be difficult. It is particularly difficult for me, not just because of the fact that it involves you having an affair with a student. It is difficult because I do not practice law full time any more. I'm a teacher. There are times when I need to call in some help. This is one of those times. If we're lucky, we may not need to worry about court time after this, but if we do, I'm not sure how we're going to work around it. That's why I need Derek to work with me. If anyone can find a way to clear this before it even gets to trial, it's him."

He sighed and settled back down in his chair. "Okay. Whatever you think is best."

"Trust me. This is the only way it can work."

A moment passed during which neither of us quite knew where to go next. Finally, he turned to me and asked "How much is going to be, you know, out there, about me and Trish?"

"What do you mean?"

He hesitated a moment. "I mean, will people have to know about our relationship? Do we have to reveal that?"

"Carl, the police pretty much are locking up the physical evidence that the sexual relationship took place." Again he flinched at my description of their relationship as "sexual". Clearly, in his head it was something beyond just the physical. I was defending a hopelessly romantic biology teacher. "At this point, I have no plans to contest that point in our defence. I think it would be best simply to admit to that part of the relationship and move on. If we try to hide it or get that information quashed and it comes out, we'll just look worse. I'm sorry. There's just no way we can get around that."

The defeated look returned to his face. "I guess I can pretty much forget about teaching again when this is over." He looked so forlorn it was painful to look at. Carl may have loved Tricia Bellamy, but it was clear he loved teaching. He would soon be grieving the loss of both loves. I wondered where love of his wife and grief at what was surely the demise of that relationship fit into his emotions.

"I won't sugar coat this in any way. You had a sexual relationship with a student. Yeah. You won't be teaching again when the trial is over. Right now, I need to concentrate on keeping you out of prison for Tricia's murder."

"I didn't kill her," he protested.

"I know, but the reality of the presumption of innocence isn't as cut and dried as it sounds. Yes, the prosecution has to prove beyond a reasonable doubt that you're guilty, but the single best defence we can give is to prove beyond a reasonable doubt that you're not."

"How are we gonna do that?" he asked. Hmm. Legitimate question. I reached into the battered leather attaché case I had carried since I was an undergraduate student and pulled out a yellow legal pad.

"Let's start with Wednesday. Three nights ago, when Tricia was murdered. Where were you?"

"Where was I?"

"My first line of defence for you would be to place you definitively in a location where you could not have killed Trish. What did you do on Wednesday night?"

He thought for a moment. I couldn't expect and didn't want his response to come too easily. If it did, it would appear he had given it a lot of thought, as though planning his alibi. Having him stop to try to remember helped to cover over those still lingering doubts I might have about his involvement.

"Well," he began, "I worked fairly late at school."

"Until what time?" I pushed him, jotting down his ambiguous response, starting what would surely amount to many pages of notes. It occurred to me that with an arrest coming so quickly, I had not even been informed if an accurate time of death had been determined by the coroner. Note to self: better start finding out the facts of this case—quickly.

Carl stared momentarily into space, searching the recesses of his memory for what he felt was the appropriate response. "I guess it was around eight or eight thirty," he finally offered tentatively.

"Are you sure about the time?"

"Well, no. But I know it was quite late. With all that had been happening with Tricia, the breakup and our fighting, our..." he paused momentarily. Finally he began again. "Our making up. I had just let work fall behind. I had labs to mark from the previous week that I hadn't even gotten to yet, and there was a lab scheduled for Thursday morning that I had to set up. Frog dissection. It takes a lot of work to have everything ready."

"I can imagine." I reflected queasily on the image of Carl wandering his biology lab preparing a whole host of dead frogs for his kids to carve into. No wonder I had ailed nearly every science course I ever took.

From my own memory, I recalled that Ralph Bremner, the P.E. teacher had called me during *Law and Order*, which meant it was after ten p.m. How sad was my life that television was so important, I could figure out what I was doing and even schedule events around my favourite shows? Another note to self: get a social life.

But knowing the call had come in after ten o'clock also told me that probably a couple of hours had transpired between the discovery of Tricia's body and Bremner's phone call to me. Assuming Tricia was found relatively soon after her murder— another detail I needed to pin down post haste—that would place her time of death around eight o'clock, or sometime just before. If Carl's timing was correct—and if we could find a way to verify it— he was working at the school while Tricia was being murdered. All of a sudden my first truly high profile murder case didn't look quite so bad any more.

Jotting down the details of timelines running through my head, I turned back to Carl. "Did you talk to anyone while you were working at the school?"

He suddenly seemed to clue in to what I was attempting to do. His dour expression slowly began to lighten. "I guess I must have spoken to someone."

"Who?" I demanded. With the scent of an alibi for my client, I was getting anxious. I admit I already had visions of tossing Carl's alibi in Furlo's face and watching him try to squirm out of it.

"Well," he began, "I had a couple of students with me for a while. The school has a budget for lab assistants, and we're given a certain amount of time to have them help us."

"Who were they?" I asked, masking my disappointment. Given I was planning to stipulate that Carl had had a relationship with a student who regularly stayed after school with him, I would rather not have needed to rely on the testimony of other students alone in a science lab with Carl as his alibi. But given that they might prove to be credible witnesses, I jotted down their names just the same.

"Does that help?" Carl wondered.

"It may," I offered noncommittally. "What time did these two students leave?"

Again he paused to think. "I don't remember exactly. It wasn't too late. One of them had a chemistry exam the next day, and I didn't want to take away from her study time."

"Think, Carl. Getting as close to the exact time is important."

His face brightened suddenly. "Wait a minute," he proclaimed. "The lab assistants carry time sheets. I would have signed them with the hours they put in. We can check the exact time with the office."

"Good," I told him, putting it on the side of my legal pad under the subheading "to do."

"But I think it was about six o'clock when they left." That didn't please me immensely. If my suspicions about Tricia's time of death were correct, that would still have provided Carl with plenty of time to meet with her and kill her. It was possible the police already knew that.

"What about other people in the building? Adults, preferably."

Carl peered off into space, no doubt conjuring up images of the night he lost Tricia. It was helpful for me to think of Carl as a grieving lover. The more sympathetic he appeared, the better. "Did you run into any other teachers working late that night?"

He chuckled. "No. I think a lot of my colleagues think I'm some kind of a workaholic because I'm often at school so late." Actually, a lot of his colleagues now had their own ideas about Carl's reasons for hanging around the school so late. I was certain I was going to hear from many of them at school come Monday.

"What about janitors? Cleaning staff? Doesn't our school have night school classes?"

"Tuesday and Thursday," he replied. "They wouldn't have been in on Wednesday night." He thought a moment longer. "I'm sure at some point I talked to Jurgen. I always see him when I work late."

"Who's Jurgen?"

"He's one of the night cleaning janitors. He cleans the science wing of the building. I'm sure you've met him at some point." He was right. A large high school has so many staff, it's hard to keep track. Thinking about it, although I had said hello on any number of occasions since joining the staff, I could not recall the name of the janitor who came and cleaned my classroom and wing of the building every day. I wondered if he thought I was a snob. I wondered if I was a snob.

"Do you know what time that would have been?"

"No. Not exactly. But he definitely came in to empty the waste baskets and sweep the floors. And I know it was after the kids left, because he had popped his head in a couple of times while they were still there and said he would come back later. The last time I saw him, he did come in, and I was there when he cleaned my room. We talked."

"What about?"

"Oh, the usual. How his family was doing. The Canucks. That kind of thing."

"Okay. I'll talk to him too," I told him, writing down Jurgen's name on my growing list of things to look into. I wondered how much of this it might be possible to do on the weekend. It seemed to me the school had provided me with a list of all of the staff's phone numbers. Of course, it also seemed to me that it was in my desk in my classroom. Wouldn't do me a whole lot of good there.

"All right," I continued, "I think this could be helpful. I'm going to talk to these people and anyone else who might have been there and can verify your whereabouts."

"So they may be able to help?" he asked hopefully.

"Let's keep our fingers crossed. A lot will depend on finding out Tricia's time of death. Once we have something definitive, we can start asking people if they can confirm your presence away from the crime scene." I decided to take one last stab at jogging his memory before leaving. "Are you sure there wasn't anyone else you talked to?"

He looked at me hesitantly.

"What?" I demanded. "What is it? This is no time to hold out on me, Carl. If there's someone you're thinking of, you need to let me know."

"Bonnie," he said quietly. "My wife."

"Oh," I replied gently, "what about her? Was she at the school with you?"

"Well, no," he began, "but I did call her at one point, I think just before I left the school."

"Is it possible she would remember the time of your call, or for that matter, when you got home?"

"I suppose it's possible," he confirmed. "But, given what's going to come out about me and Trish, I don't know how helpful she's going to be."

"Surely she'll tell the truth?" I asked hopefully, though I couldn't necessarily believe she would either. It was one thing to defend your spouse against spurious allegations, but when the spouse you thought you knew and loved so well was sleeping with an eighteen-year-old high school student, it would surely turn your world upside down. I knew Bonnie Turbot could prove to be a very unreliable witness for Carl's defence. Still, it had to be checked out.

"I guess she will," Carl said. "But who knows how much she remembers? I don't know if she'll remember exactly what time I called home. Isn't it possible to check the school's phone records?"

"I don't know. I doubt it," I told him. Unlike what you see on television cop shows, even the good ones like *Law and Order*, getting a computerized printout of all of a phone line's activities is no simple matter. I knew it could be done, but it would probably take a court order to get the phone company to comply. I put that on my list under the subheading of "ask Derek."

"Wait a minute," Carl blurted out. "We have one of those boxes!"

"What boxes?"

"You know, for the phone. It shows the numbers coming in so you can decide whether or not to answer the phone."

"You mean call display?"

"Yeah. That's it. We just got it, in fact."

"When?"

He searched his memory again, then looked at me gloomily. "Sunday afternoon. We had gotten some hang-up phone calls during the past couple of weeks, so on Sunday we went to the phone store in the mall and picked up the call display. I had just hooked it up."

"Did you find out who was making the calls?"

"No. The caller had blocked their number, but I had a pretty good idea."

"Tricia."

"Yeah. I think she was planning to tell Bonnie about us."

I started doing the math in my head. "You told me you and Tricia had been broken up for over a week, right?"

"Yeah," he confirmed sadly. "It was on a Thursday. She came to me on the Monday of this last week with her threats to go to the principal. So that makes it ten or eleven days since we had broken up."

"Were the calls coming before you broke up?"

He thought about that for a moment. "Yeah, I think so."

"Think carefully. This could be important. You started receiving hang-up calls before you and Tricia broke up?"

"Yeah. Yeah." He was nodding his head to his own inner dialogue now. "We did. It was definitely before Tricia and I broke up."

"So why would Tricia have been calling to tell Bonnie about your relationship before you even broke up with her?"

That seemed to stymie him for a moment. Finally, he looked at me and said "I don't know."

"All right," I said, making a few more notes. "But in the meantime, your call display unit should be able to tell us the date and time you called from the school. Have you erased it since Wednesday night?"

"No, I don't think so."

"Okay then. I will definitely look into that." I closed my legal pad and plopped it into the battered attaché case. "Is there anything else I can do for you today? Is there someone you'd like me to call?"

Carl looked freshly dejected. Looking down at his hands, he shook his head slowly. "No. I think the fewer people who are involved the better."

I stood up but put my hand on his shoulder one more time momentarily before leaving. "Okay. We'll try to keep this as low-key as possible. But I'm going to have to start going out and beating the bushes a little for information."

"All right," he told me. "Do what you have to do." It broke my heart to leave my friend sitting there, but there was nothing I could do about it until Derek got him through his bail hearing on Monday. For now, I was more useful to him outside the pre-trial centre, trying to gather information.

"Winston?" He looked up at me. "What's going to happen to my classes?" I had to admire his dedication. With all he was going through, his mind was still on the wellbeing of his students.

"I arranged for a substitute for you for yesterday. For the time being, I imagine she'll continue to teach your classes."

"Is she good?" he asked.

I really didn't know. I had given much less thought to Carl's students than he obviously had. I thought I should probably try to find out a little about the students he taught on a daily basis. Some of them might prove to be helpful in his defence, though I knew I had to be very careful about that line between my role as Carl's lawyer and my role as a teacher in the school. Carl was my first concern, but as a teacher I still needed to safeguard the wellbeing of any student in the building.

"I guess she's good enough," I told him.

I have found that people who truly are innocent of a crime tend to believe there is no possible way they can be convicted of it. "If I didn't do it, I can't go to jail" seems to be the logic. I have also found it to be a naïve view. The good news was that with many of the clients I had defended, if they weren't responsible for the crime they were convicted of, they were likely responsible for some other act for which they had yet to be caught. It's an entirely wrong-headed point of view for a defence lawyer, but it was how I managed to achieve some peace—if not sleep—when I lost a case that I knew I should have won.

An idea dawned on me. "Look," I told Carl, "I know you have a lot on your mind, but there is not a whole lot you can do for your case right now until I find out some more of the facts. So why don't you make yourself useful while you're in here?"

"Okay," he said.

"The school is going to assume you're away for the long term. But this new teacher isn't permanent yet. Why don't you spend a few of your hours in here preparing some really detailed lesson plans for her? At least you'll have the peace of mind of knowing your classes are well looked after." I didn't add that it would be something I could bring up later to demonstrate some of his redeeming character traits.

He seemed to brighten at the thought of doing some work for school. Strange. I had been teaching only three months, yet I didn't feel that much enthusiasm about preparing lessons for class. Of course, I hadn't been sitting in a jail cell all weekend either.

"That's a great idea," he said. "I could plan lessons for the next week at least. I could even prepare notes for labs."

"Excellent." I smiled at him. I would feel a little bit easier with Carl in jail until Monday knowing he was at least actively engaged in something. "What do you need?"

He thought for a moment. "Something to write on, for starters." I reached into my attaché case and pulled out a separate yellow legal pad, plopping it down on the table in front of him. I also dropped a couple of pens on the table. "My textbooks would be useful, but I think I can basically go from memory."

"Do you have copies of the textbooks at home?"

"Yes."

"I'm going to go by your house to look at a few things, especially your call display unit. If you can make do for today, I'll make sure I drop them by tomorrow."

Carl looked much more relaxed than when I had arrived. For some people, vacations are the most debilitating part of the year. Work is the relaxation they need. Carl seemed to be one of those. I already knew he'd taught summer school each year he'd been a teacher.

"Thanks, Winston. You've been such a good friend."

"I'm here to be a good lawyer, more importantly. I'll see you tomorrow."

We said our goodbyes, and I left him inside the interview room, indicating to the guard outside we were done and Carl could be returned to his cell.

Leaving the pre-trial centre, I turned left on Hastings Street and walked the two blocks to my parked car. It was late afternoon, but I wasn't yet headed for home.

I had plenty of work to do.

Seventeen

When you try to explain Canada to Americans who haven't been here, the comparison is often made between Seattle and Vancouver. Most Americans know that Seattle is legendary for its rain, a reputation Vancouver shares. Many Americans—particularly those who view Canada as a snow-covered, dog-mushing wilderness—are surprised to find out that Vancouver gets even less snow than Seattle.

The South Granville area, running the roughly seven or eight blocks from Broadway to 16th Avenue, is an upscale shopping area paling in price and variety to the trendier Robson Street downtown, but still pricey enough to be beyond the reach of average Vancouverites. The area includes designer clothing stores, salons and recently a garish big box bookstore chain, which, despite its monumental size and rather tacky appearance, has done much to bring needed foot traffic into the area.

Of course, one of the other key characteristics shared between Seattle and Vancouver is their passion and near obsession for coffee. Both cities are overrun with Starbucks and myriad other coffee houses, from the chain stores to the mom and pop operations. Despite the wealth of choices, one of my perennial favourites was none other than Seattle's Best Coffee, a brand name sold in many private coffee houses, but also with its own café on Granville at 11th.

After meeting—or waking me—for breakfast that morning, Andrea and I had arranged to meet at Seattle's Best at four thirty to figure out what we each had learned about Tricia's death. Andrea was likely to have the most information, since her plan for the day included going to the office to find out surreptitiously as much as she could about the murder investigation from the perspective of the detectives assigned to the case. Of course, she also took the greatest risk, professionally anyway. Though police files were not officially locked away and kept secret from other detectives, it is considered bad form to poke around someone else's investigation. Detectives are notoriously territorial, and the thought that another cop might take an unhealthy interest in one of their cases is enough to start a departmental feud. Furthermore, Andrea's friendship with me was well known in her department; snooping through Furlo and Smythe's notes would not win her any friends. The last thing I wanted on my conscience was my contribution to the destruction of my best friend's career. I hoped she would be very careful. I also wasn't expecting she would have found out much.

I sat alone in the front corner of the café. The booth was recessed and provided at least some semblance of privacy. Andrea walked in as I nursed my latte, a decaf, in hopeful anticipation of repeating my successful previous night's slumber. As usual, a few heads turned as she walked up to the counter to place her order for what I knew would not include any low fat or decaf product. Andy's metabolism burned at a rate that required no special restrictions on her intake of calories.

As she waited for her order to be filled, Andy opted to stand and gaze around the room, checking out products on the shelf and potential partners in the store. She was disappointed by both. Though she attracted the attention of a few patrons, none would live up to her exacting standards. No one in the room looked like they could consistently run a seven-minute mile in a ten-kilometre race.

When her order arrived, she ambled over to my table as though spotting me for the first time.

"Nothing too promising?" I asked her as she sat down.

"The whole world isn't a smorgasbord," she replied. "That would be too easy."

"And so would you be."

"Sleep has not made you any less a smartass," she observed. Nothing short of surgery was likely to do that. It was how I kept myself at a distance from anyone I didn't want too near. Of course, it also kept at a distance some of those I might want to have near. "How has your day been?" she added.

"Well, I spent a chunk of it at the local jail."

"You used to spend half your life at the local jail. One afternoon there is a step up."

"True."

"How's your client?" she asked with real concern.

"About as good as he can be, I suppose. A first taste of incarceration usually convinces people they do not want to be there. If we get him out of there, I'm not worried that he's ever going to do anything to put himself back again."

She nodded thoughtfully as she took a sip of her latte. There are two kinds of people in the world: those who like their drinks absolutely piping, smoking hot and the rest of us. Andrea always orders her drinks extra hot, what she describes as "lawsuit temperature." She has lips of steel. My bland, sensitive British stomach pretty much required the cooling of my caffeine to somewhere between lukewarm and kind of hot.

"Derek on board?" she asked nonchalantly. I knew Andy was not at all happy at my choice of co-counsel, at least from a personal perspective. Anyone who might in some way reconnect me with my ex-wife was essentially persona non grata in her eyes. Andy also suspected, as did I, that Derek carried if not an Olympic-size torch, at least a camping-size one for her. Most would consider Derek an ideal catch. Andy couldn't get past his connection to Sandi. Her disdain for my choice of first marriage knew no bounds.

"Yep. He's going to handle Carl's first appearance on Monday." I filled her in on the details of our conversation and laid out my initial plans for how Derek might handle some of the work my teaching might prevent me from getting to. She nodded her consent, though I wasn't particularly looking for it.

"That's good," she sighed, sitting back and taking another sip of her latte. "That's good," she repeated, nodding as though deep in thought. "I think you're going to need the help on this one."

"Thank you," I countered. I knew full well Andrea did not mean her comment as disparaging in any way. Still, it's sometimes useful to make her feel guilty.

"Don't be a shit," she scolded. This was obviously not one of those times. "You already knew this case was bigger than what you're used to. I'm telling you, it's got big and complicated written all over it." This was her way of segueing into telling me she had found out something important during her afternoon of snooping.

"What have we learned?" I asked, not wanting to beat around the bush any longer.

She reached into her backpack and pulled out her notebook. She is a meticulous note keeper, writing down things that everyday people take for granted. I knew she would not have been able to take notes while she was hunting for information on Tricia's case; she would have had to sneak out her data quickly, then find a quiet place to quickly record all of the information she had learned. This she did in a typical, spiral bound police notebook that every cop on television and in real life carried.

"For starters," she began, "this is big."

"You said that already," I intoned.

She looked up from her notes to scowl at me. "I thought it was big enough to merit repeating the cautionary note." I loved it when she talked official.

"My apologies. Please continue."

"Detectives Furlo and Smythe were out of the office, I think finally taking a few hours of downtime and to catch a little bit of sleep. They've pretty much been going around the clock since the discovery of the body."

"So I gathered. Furlo made a point of telling me how hard he's been working to lock up my client," I told her.

"Furlo is the kind of cop that would like you to know how hard he is working. He would be telling you that even if the case fell into his lap, which in some ways, this one did." She paused, ostensibly for dramatic effect. She wanted me to prompt her along. I obliged.

"What do you mean it 'fell into his lap'? You think the case is bogus?"

"No," she was quick to clarify, not wanting to cast any inaccurate aspersions on the professionalism of her colleagues, even one she wasn't particularly fond of like Michael Furlo. "Furlo is the kind of cop who is looking for advancement, but he's not going to risk his chance of promotion by busting someone he doesn't believe is guilty. If Carl is behind bars, it's at least in part because Furlo believes him to be guilty. Also, there's no way in hell Jasmine Smythe would be part of any plot to arrest someone for political reasons. She is too straight-up for that. But the politics are huge."

"There's interdepartmental squabbling on this one?" I asked, assuming personalities within the police command structure were coming into play in the investigation. While this could make individual officers a bit pissy to work with, it didn't really concern me that much, at least in its impact on my defence.

"The politics extend way beyond the detective division," Andy continued solemnly. "The case file is still pretty preliminary at this point, since Furlo and Smythe are still working hard to gather evidence and haven't had much time to complete a lot of the paperwork. But there are a few really interesting notations in the file."

My heart rate kicked it up a notch. "You actually went through the case file?" I nearly shrieked at her. "Jesus, Andy! I wanted your help, but you're going to get yourself fired! I can't take on a wrongful dismissal suit while I'm in the middle of a murder defence."

"Relax," she told me and took a sip of hot liquid. "There was no one around, and I just took a few quick peeks. If anyone knew I had been in there, I would have known about it by now. There's nothing I'm going to tell you that wouldn't be disclosed to you during discovery anyway."

"All right, give it to me. I mean no disrespect to the victim here—I met her once, and she seemed like a hell of a kid—but what is so all hell-fired that her death is getting everything into an uproar? And *who's* in an uproar?"

"For starters, there are notations of a couple of very interesting phone messages coming into the inspector of the homicide division. The first message came from his excellency's office."

"The mayor?"

"None other. It appears that by sometime mid-morning on Thursday, the mayor had put in calls to the chief, who had

152

forwarded inquiries to the inspector," she confirmed.

"The mayor is required by provincial statute not to be involved in police investigations," I informed her as though talking to a Grade Twelve law student.

"Correct," she confirmed, "but he is chair of the police board, which oversees operations. It doesn't give him the right to direct investigations, and to his credit, he doesn't normally try. But evidently he's not the only one. Smythe made notes that calls have come into the department from the A.G. in Victoria."

The Attorney General is essentially the top lawyer in the province. Appointed by the Premier as a member of cabinet, he or she is usually also an elected member of the Legislature, though that is not officially required. The Vancouver Police Department, like the R.C.M.P., operates at arm's length from the legislative branch of the government, guided by the Policing Act and the Criminal Code of Canada. Though the Attorney General has a significant amount of clout in determining what types of actions may be pursued in the courts, he almost always remains completely neutral and uninvolved in criminal cases. The very fact he had made a phone call to the police department had taken the "simple" case of homicide into the political arena. It could also prove to be useful in my preparation of Carl's defence, though I didn't share that thought with Andrea. She had put her ass on the line for me, after all.

"Did she note what the A.G. said or wanted?" I pressed.

"Not really. Like I said, they haven't done a great deal of paperwork yet, and I'm sure she didn't talk to him herself. It's probably more of a mental note that there is pretty significant pressure to clear the case."

"Have you ever heard of the Attorney General taking a personal interest in an ongoing investigation?"

"Not since I've been there," she confirmed. "And he's not the only one so keen on seeing it cleared."

"Other than the mayor?"

"Other than the mayor, rumour has it around the station that a call came from Ottawa." She let that one sink in for a moment.

"The Prime Minister's office wants a progress report on the

status of a teenager killed in a park in Vancouver?" I was beginning to break out into a small sweat. I knew it wasn't from the coffee. It was dropping below the lukewarm level.

"Not quite. But definitely from the federal cabinet. Specifically Foreign Affairs." She referred again briefly to her notes.

"This was in their file?"

"No. The Foreign Affairs angle is just rumour at this point, because I haven't talked to Smythe and Furlo about it and don't really intend to unless it becomes necessary."

"Probably a good plan." I had made myself sufficiently unpopular with at least half of the detective duo in charge of gathering evidence against my client. Even if Andy's career were immune to the repercussions stemming from such a conversation, Furlo in particular was not likely to be forthcoming with any information prior to official discovery procedures. "So why Foreign Affairs?"

"Turns out Tricia Bellamy was the niece of the consul general of Serbia in Vancouver. Evidently, he is making all kinds of noises in diplomatic circles about getting Carl convicted sooner rather than later."

"Federal government has no jurisdiction over how the courts plan trials," I informed Andrea of the obvious.

"In a perfect world," she countered. "What crown prosecutor do you know would be immune to pressure from a federal cabinet minister about getting a high profile case before the courts as soon as possible? The police, the Justice Department, everybody is gonna want to try to avoid looking bad in diplomatic circles when the relative of a diplomat is killed."

I thought about that for a moment. We have all kinds of checks and balances in our legal system to ensure political influence has no part in the administration of the courts. But it was hopelessly naïve to think a few well-placed phone calls wouldn't have some impact on how things got done. I had seen that already by the speed at which the forensic evidence in the case had been processed thus far.

"Bellamy doesn't sound particularly Serbian," I mused aloud.

"It isn't. That's the step-dad's name, and he's long since gone. Mom's a widow, twice, I'm led to believe. Her maiden name is

Dantolovec; she's the sister of the consul general, whose name, by the way, is also Dantolovec."

"That sounds a little more Balkan," I replied. A relatively straightforward homicide case—if there is such a thing as a straightforward homicide case—now had the potential for "international incident" written all over it.

A flurry of thoughts went through my head. What impact did this political pressure have on the potential for prosecution to go forward? Would my efforts to mount a credible defence be hampered by my own local, provincial or federal government? What kinds of ramifications would there be should I be successful in getting an acquittal for Carl? Should we really worry about diplomatic retribution from Serbia? Could Canada take Serbia in a fight?

I realized I had stopped listening to Andrea. She realized it too. "Where'd you go there, big guy?" she asked.

"Oh, just thinking about defence lawyer things," I responded, evading her question to avoid revealing that my feeling of inferiority was surfacing again. The last thing I wanted for me or for Carl was for his case to become fodder for not only local but also national and international media.

"Yeah well, I hope you've got some good tricks up your sleeve, 'cause I think you're going to need them. You know the Crown will put one of their big guns on this."

"Bigger than me?"

She didn't even bother to dignify my smart-assed rhetorical question with more than raised eyebrows above the rim of her coffee cup, which she drained with one backward toss of her head. The next comment would have to come from me, and I knew it had better not be snide.

"Furlo and Smythe don't strike me as the types to be intimidated by political pressure to make an arrest, especially Smythe. Furlo talks big, but Smythe seems to be the brains of the operation. She wouldn't bust Carl unless she was pretty sure, don't ya think?" I asked.

"I like to think so, but the pressure would come from the inspector or even the chief. They're the ones who would feel the heat from the politicos. And don't kid yourself about Furlo. He's a lot brighter than he lets on."

I thought some more, because I wasn't quite sure what else to say. Then I stumbled on an important point. "I know people hide behind their locked doors at night, especially on a cold winter night, but I just don't understand how someone can be strangled in a neighbourhood park, and no one notices."

"That's another thing I found out. Crime Scene says she wasn't strangled there. No signs of disturbance around the body to indicate any kind of struggle. They figure she was killed somewhere else and dumped in the park."

"They got that based on the crime scene?" I asked suspiciously.

"Yeah, why?"

"It's winter. It rains. There was probably all manner of people around the park and the body when she was found. Any indications of a struggle were probably wiped out by cops' feet or the weather."

"Yeah, well, save it for the courtroom, Counsellor. That's the theory the investigators are working from. They're going to search Carl's house top to bottom to see if they can find any indication she was killed there before being transported."

"In front of his wife? They figure it was a family affair?"

"It's a place to start. I'm sure they won't limit themselves to his house."

"What about time of death?" I asked, remembering the single most important point I had put at the top of my to do list.

Andy consulted her notebook once again, flipping back a page to find the item that was obviously at the top of her list as well. "Coroner's office puts time of death between seven fifteen and eight p.m. The 911 call was made at 8:07. Assuming time of death was towards the latter end of the coroner's window, the perp may well have been nearby when the call came in."

"Who called it in?" I wanted to know.

"Mr. A. Nonymous," she said.

"Shit."

"Yep. No interviewing the caller to see how much he actually saw."

"And naturally the theory has the perp as the caller?"

"Naturally."

"Which makes the detectives want even more to point the finger at my client," I speculated.

"Figuring he was truly a lovelorn murderer who couldn't bear to see his dead lover lying alone in the park after he dumped her there, so he called it in himself in order to ensure a speedy response," Andy finished my thought for me.

I sat back in the now uncomfortable booth, seeking some inspiration, which wasn't coming. "Carl was at the school until after eight o'clock."

"Says who?" she asked.

"According to Carl," I continued, "he didn't leave the school until well after eight, maybe even eight thirty."

"Anyone vouch for that?" she demanded.

"Whose side are you on?"

"His word is gonna be worth shit here, Win. You have to know that. Can anyone definitively place him at the school throughout the evening, or at least between seven fifteen and eight?"

"I have a list of names of night custodial staff, including one who talked to Carl sometime that night. I'll start there." I sighed. My good sleep of the night before may have helped to catch up on my sleep deficit, but it was wearing off. I just wanted to go home. Actually I wanted to go home and drink red wine, but I didn't see it happening for a while.

"Start with those and see where you get."

"Yep." I started to rise. "I'll get on that."

"I'll come by your place later with pizza, and we can see where we're at."

I cocked my head at her. "If you're helping me out on this, how come you're buying all the refreshments?"

She smiled at me. "I said I'd bring the pizza. I didn't say I'd pay for it."

*   *   *

On an impulse, I decided to drive out to the school to access the phone list I knew was back at my regular place of employ. I had always viewed schools as a nine-to-five operation, Monday to Friday. But many schools—Sir John A. Macdonald Secondary included—often act as hubs of the community, with various different groups, clubs and teams making use of the facility on a regular basis.

In addition, our school also housed the Vancouver Distance Education Centre, a small wing of the building dedicated to servicing the needs of students, both teenaged and adult, who opted to do their learning from home rather than in the building itself. Often times, the Distance Ed centre was open weekends for tutorial sessions so those students trying to obtain their high school diploma while working at the same time could come by and receive the tutorial assistance they needed. It was, however, late in the day and I wasn't sure anyone would still be around the centre, someone who could let me sneak through into the main building to retrieve what I needed.

When I pulled into the side parking lot, just off 41st Avenue, I did find that the other individual you could usually count on being at the school at the strangest of times was there: the basketball coach. Unlike our American counterparts, coaching in Canadian schools is a strictly volunteer activity, with teachers receiving no extra pay for the hours they put in on the field or in the gym. That didn't stop the tireless few from working nights and weekends to help their athletes hone their skills and work towards that all-important athletic scholarship. Though Canada's national game is allegedly hockey, you wouldn't know it from the emphasis placed on basketball at the high school level. This is especially odd for a city like Vancouver, whose brief foray into the world of professional basketball was a disaster known as the Grizzlies, who had uprooted and moved to Memphis, Tennessee, where they'd continued to suck until recently. Nonetheless, high school basketball season was the longest and most involved of all of the extracurricular activities, and sure enough, an early Saturday evening tournament was conveniently for me, being held at the school.

It seemed bad form to simply march through the gymnasium

without showing at least some passing interest—which I admittedly had little—especially since our team was currently playing against a team from Coquitlam, a neighbouring city about twenty-five kilometres from Vancouver. Not only that, in the third quarter, we appeared to be winning, a rarity for our school, so I felt I had better hit the bleachers for at least a few minutes. Big mistake.

Though I had travelled around downtown Vancouver and the trendy South Granville shopping district undetected by the masses, it really had not occurred to me how much my Saturday morning front-page coverage would have been absorbed by parents and students of my own high school. Players, fans and parents seemed to lock their stares on me as I crossed from the orange, double exit doors to the bleachers closest to the home team. The heretofore cheering crowd hushed as I took a few steps up into the stands and sat down near the end wall of the gymnasium. I was concerned that even the game itself might come to a close as players on the court paused to see what had drawn the attention of their cheering supporters.

I smiled casually at the nearest adults and turned my attention to the action on the court, hoping my nonchalance would direct their focus back to their teenaged sons playing on the court. Within a few moments, most present had recovered a semblance of manners and had at least stopped staring at me. I could tell from the muted mutterings, however, that I had become the principal topic of conversation while they half-heartedly applauded for their team of choice.

Though the direct staring had abated, I felt flushed from the attention I knew I was getting. I also figured I would only make matters worse by getting up right away and leaving, so I was doomed to see this basketball game through for the time being, at least until something spectacular enough happened to draw everyone's attention long enough for me to make an escape.

I hadn't thought I would be so pleased to see a high school student, but shortly after I sat down, Sarah Kolinsky, one of my brighter than average law students, plunked herself down next to me on the bench. She was joined by Jillian Ballantyne, one of her law classmates.

"Hey, Mr. Patrick," Sarah opened amiably.

"Hi, Sarah. Hi, Jill. What are you doing here?" I asked the incredibly lame question. I'm sure I've mentioned that I've never been good at small talk with members of the opposite sex, even when they're teenaged high school girls, and I'm a sophisticated legal professional.

They stole glances at one another, then studied me carefully. Jill finally spoke. "We're watching a basketball game." It was a statement, but as was the habit of many teenaged girls, the intonation at the end of the sentence made it sound like a question.

"You seem to have gathered more than your fair share of attention," Sarah observed wryly. I wasn't really in the mood for wry just then, but the two girls didn't seem openly hostile towards me—unlike the rest of the gymnasium—so I didn't want to alienate them.

"It was that obvious?" I asked.

"Oh, yeah," Jill noted.

They weren't sitting next to me solely because of my obvious charm. It had also been rare for girls to sit next to me when I was in high school, unless they needed something. Sarah, who had demonstrated her bluntness both inside and outside of class, brought up the subject that had obviously taken them over to sit near me.

"How's the case going?" she asked, as though we were part of the same law firm.

"It's going," I told her. "Nothing new to report since yesterday, really."

"Except that Mr. Turbot has been arrested," she countered.

"Yes. Except that." A lull in our conversation followed, during which both girls looked at me rather expectantly. I didn't respond to their not-so-subtle hints.

When they could wait no longer, Jillian finally spoke. "Well?" she demanded.

I turned to face my interrogators. "Well?" I repeated.

"What's happening today?" Jill insisted on knowing.

"Not much. I'm just watching a basketball game."

"Bullshit," Sarah suddenly blurted out.

"Excuse me?" I asked. Three months on the job, and this was the first time a student had actually sworn directly at me. Sarah knew I was being indirect with them, which I respected. Still, her choice of admonition seemed to warrant some kind of response.

"I said bullshit," she repeated, oblivious to my role as teacher and hers as student. Or she didn't care. "You haven't been to a basketball game this year."

"How do you know?" I threw back at her. Man. Hanging around teenagers can make you pretty juvenile.

Jillian chimed in, pointing to one of the players on the court. "See the centre? She's dating him. She's been at every game. You haven't."

"Which brings me back to my original assertion that you're obviously here to do something for Mr. Turbot's defence," Sarah continued. "Otherwise, you wouldn't drive all the way out here on a Saturday evening. Not even you can have that boring a social life." She was wrong on that account, but I had to credit her deductive reasoning skills.

"You know there's little I can tell you," I told her, resorting to my teacher voice.

"Solicitor-client privilege, I know," she replied. "But as far as I know, you wouldn't be violating privilege by telling us if Mr. Turbot has made bail yet." It was uncomfortable being at the receiving end of Sarah's persistence, but I couldn't help but feel a small sense of satisfaction at her understanding of the concepts we had covered in class. At least it made me feel I might have some hope as a teacher.

"No, you're right. That wouldn't be a violation and no, he has not made bail."

"Why not?" Sarah wanted to know. "I assume he's an alleged first-time offender. He shouldn't be considered a flight risk or a danger to anyone else." I smiled slightly. She'd even remembered to use the adjective "alleged."

"A technicality, really," I told them. "Court won't proceed with a hearing until Monday."

Their next question I was sure was going to be about whether or not I believed Carl was guilty and the chances I had of achieving an

161

acquittal. They seemed to be searching for the best way to phrase the question when one of my other students, Liz Lawson, and a woman I assumed was her mother, ambled over and stood down on the bleacher in front of me. Mom didn't look happy to see me.

"Mr. Patrick?" she demanded.

I looked up and tried to smile neutrally. "Yes?"

"I'm Carol Lawson, Liz's mother."

I did the gallant thing and stood up as my mother had taught me to do in the presence of a lady. "Pleased to meet you," I said, putting out my hand. She didn't shake it. Me and women.

"I understand you are representing the biology teacher accused of killing Tricia Bellamy." It too wasn't a question.

"That's correct," was all I could think of in response.

She continued, building up steam for the speech she had likely been rehearsing in her head since I'd walked in. "I could not in good conscience sit over there without telling you how entirely inappropriate I think it is that you would be defending that man, especially considering your position as a teacher in this school." Her obviously dyed blonde hair caught the glare from the overhead gymnasium lights. I was almost blinded.

"I understand," I told her calmly, hoping to bring a quick end to this conversation that was already beginning to attract the attention of those seated immediately around us.

"No," she told me sternly, "I don't think you do."

"Mom!" Liz protested in that manner only a teenager can. They have an uncanny ability to turn a single syllable world like "Mom" into a two syllable whine. In this case it was appropriate. At seventeen years old, it was obviously mortifying for Liz to have her mother come over and complain to her teacher in front of her classmates. For their part, Jillian and Sarah seemed to shrink from the hostile stare of Liz's mother.

Carol Lawson shushed her daughter with a glare then turned her attention back to me. "Do you think it's acceptable that a teacher was having sex with a student?" she demanded.

"I wouldn't ever think that's acceptable, Ms. Lawson," I explained to her. "And that is not the matter for which I have been retained. At this point, I am really not at liberty to discuss the details of my client's case with you."

"A girl is dead," she hissed at me. "The man deserves to be locked up."

"If he had, in fact, killed her, I would agree with you. The man is entitled to a defence." I wanted to be as vague as possible about Carl's innocence. I sensed she didn't want to hear it anyway.

"A defence?" she cried loudly. "What if he is the one who murdered that poor girl?"

"What if he isn't?" Sarah suddenly burst in. "I don't think I would feel any better knowing we'd locked up someone who didn't kill Tricia."

Carol Lawson paused only long enough to consider Sarah briefly before continuing her attack on me. "There are plenty of lawyers out there, Mr. Patrick. You're supposed to be a role model for kids here. Defending lowlifes like Mr. Turbot is not how you go about being a role model."

"Thank you for your input," I replied as calmly as I could muster. "I respectfully disagree. I'm defending the principles of justice and working within the strict parameters of the law I teach to these students. I'm not sure how much more of a role model I could be." Of course, I didn't really feel that way, but the woman was starting to piss me off. A healthy dose of self-righteousness felt a propos to the moment. She was about to respond when a mostly bald head appeared on the floor below her bleacher, stepping up to join us. Don McFadden, principal.

"Hi, Mr. McFadden," Jillian announced in a voice that seemed designed as a warning to me. I was starting to think some of my students actually liked me.

"Hi Jill, Sarah, Liz," he responded before turning to me. "I see you've met Ms Lawson, Mr. Patrick?"

"I've just had the pleasure, yes," I replied. Don looked a little more uptight than usual.

"Ms Lawson is on our parent advisory council," Don informed me. Every school has its own parent advisory council, or P.A.C. As the name suggests, the P.A.C.'s job is to bring to the attention of the school issues or ideas parents feel need to be addressed. In my short teaching career, I'd had no encounters with the P.A.C., either individually or corporately, but I knew our P.A.C. was very involved in the running of the school. At least that was the polite term tactful teachers used. It was also commonly believed among teachers that whatsoever the P.A.C. shall want, the principal shall make so, in order to avoid discomfort for our administrators. The unspoken message in Don's introduction was that I was supposed to be nice to Mrs. Lawson and do nothing to make her angry. It appeared he was too late.

"We were just discussing Mr. Patrick's defending of your Mr. Turbot," Carol Lawson continued in her shrill, louder than necessary voice. Her daughter was shrinking in humiliation as the attention of more and more people in the stands was diverted from the basketball game to the conversation in the bleachers.

"I see," said Don. He was beginning to sweat.

"We were also discussing his role at the school," Lawson carried on, "and how he probably should choose whether he wants to be a teacher or a lawyer."

"Odd," I broke in, "I don't remember that part of the conversation."

Don threw me a vicious warning glance. How someone who was such a wuss in front of a parent could think he had any credibility in the "I'll scare the employees with dirty looks" department was beyond my comprehension. If I pushed this parent's buttons any more, I honestly thought Don might begin to cry.

"Mr. McFadden?" Sarah broke in suddenly. "I personally think from a law class perspective, there couldn't be a better object lesson. Even if Mr. Turbot is guilty..."

"Which is doubtful," Jillian interrupted.

"Which is doubtful," Sarah continued, "he is entitled to a fair, honest and aggressive defence. That's what Mr. Patrick is doing."

Don was caught in a difficult position, I had to admit. As much as he worried about offending a prominent parent, he also didn't want to be seen unfavourably in the eyes of the students.

"Thank you, Sarah," he told her. "I'm sure Mr. Patrick appreciates your support. This will probably make for some valuable instruction in your class, too." Both Sarah and Jillian smiled at that. It sounded like they had won their point. Only their classmate Liz didn't smile. She obviously knew her mother better and knew that the discussion wasn't over.

"Mr. McFadden," Mrs. Lawson proclaimed further, "I have to tell you I think it is entirely inappropriate that he be here teaching in the school while defending an accused child murderer." She spoke as though I was no longer in the room. Several parents who were seated nearby nodded in agreement. I subtly glanced around the immediate vicinity for another adult who might be on my side. I didn't see any.

Since it appeared no one would be jumping to my defence any time soon, I went on the attack. "I have to tell you, Ms Lawson, I think it is entirely inappropriate for you to attempt to persuade Mr. McFadden to take action against the tenure of my employment. I tell you this from the point of view not only of a teacher who is well aware of his rights, but also as a litigator who is well versed in the School Act, the Teaching Profession's Act and the Criminal Code. In short, Ms Lawson, you're out of line."

Tossing around the names of laws and the odd legal term is something we lawyers like to do, often because it has the perverse effect of throwing people into panic mode. In this case, I had inadvertently hit two targets: wanting to throw Ms Lawson off track, I had caught my hapless principal in the crossfire, sending his pulse rate soaring and paling his skin to an unhealthy, skim milk tone. He lurched forward, grabbing my arm and pivoting me on my precarious spot in the bleachers.

Sensing the urgency of the situation too late, Don tried to steady me, to no avail. He had succeeded only in spinning me counterclockwise, causing me to lose my balance and sending me crashing into the wall behind me. Had I been more together—I was used to being verbally, not physically shoved around—I would have been able to right myself using the solid gym wall as a brace.

Arms flailing, I reeled over on my left ankle for just seconds, before it too, perched perilously on the very edge of the thin bench, slid off the bleacher and down to the seat below. Tragically, that seat was occupied by parents and a few students who had come to cheer on their basketball team. Drinks flew, voices bellowed as the newest member of the J. Mac teaching faculty crashed noisily onto the waiting laps, shoulders and heads below. Despite the action on the court, all eyes turned to the far end of the gym where I now lay with my ass and legs tangled among those of the family upon whom I had landed, with my head pointed down yet another level of the bleachers, nearly touching the gym floor.

Though I wasn't aware of the referee blowing the whistle to stop play, stop it did. Even the players on the court were now looking my way. This I could tell without seeing, since the gym had fallen eerily quiet. No one seemed to know exactly what to do. I felt it was my duty to take the first action. Unfortunately, it was going to take me several moments to accomplish that. The adrenaline that had kicked in as I started to fall was completely used up, along with all of the air from my lungs and diaphragm, when my lower back had hit the knees of the kid I had landed on. As I lay there, I went through a body checklist, mentally checking to see which parts of my being I was still aware of and over which I could exercise control.

It seemed a very long, very quiet time before anyone spoke, but I suddenly became aware of my three students—Sarah, Jill and Elizabeth—crouching next to me and repeatedly asking me if I was okay. I was also aware of suddenly feeling really old. I wondered if I had broken a hip.

"Mr. Patrick!" Jillian was nearly shouting at me. "Can you hear me?"

Finally, my checklist got as far as my voice, and I tested it out. "I can hear you," I told her. "I'm okay."

"Are you sure?" Liz demanded, the tone of her voice telling me she was more than just a little mortified by what she was no doubt perceiving as her role in my crash. "Maybe we should call an ambulance."

"No, no. I'm okay," I said, beginning the long struggle to get up. The family upon whom I had fallen reached down to lend me their assistance. They appeared to be no worse for wear for having had me drop into their evening activities. Don was suddenly beside me also.

"My God, Winston! Are you all right?"

"Yeah. Yeah. Only my dignity is crushed," I tried hard to be jovial. I wasn't kidding though. In a high school, this kind of embarrassing incident stays with you for a long time. I'd had plenty of them when I was a clumsy teenager, and I knew that it usually took something pretty monumentally cool to make people forget a show-stopping performance like the one I'd just had.

Don and I both expressed our apologies to the family who'd provided the break for my freefall. By then I was standing at ground level, and Don wisely suggested we step out of the gymnasium so the game could resume. I thanked my three students and would have tossed one last parting shot at Mrs. Lawson had she not conveniently disappeared. I guess as a P.A.C. parent, she had a reputation to uphold; she didn't want to be seen with a lousy gymnast like me. To my utter amazement, however, as Don and I headed for the door, a small spattering of applause broke out, which quickly grew to rousing, enthusiastic clapping throughout the gym, including from the players on the court. I could not discern if the accolades were in appreciation of my surviving my plunge, the way the crowd cheers the injured hockey player as he is escorted off the ice, or if I was being collectively mocked for my idiocy. I preferred to think the former, but knew it was much more likely the latter.

When we reached the hallway outside the gym, Don turned to me. "Geez, Winston. I am so incredibly sorry. I had no intention of pushing you."

"I know you didn't, Don."

"I mean really. Are you sure you're okay? Do you want me to take you to get checked out?" His concern was genuine.

"I'm fine. Really."

"I'm so sorry. Oh my God. Nothing like this has ever happened."

"I know, Don. It's okay," I comforted him. "It was an accident. No permanent harm done."

He sighed, rubbing his hand over his sweaty, near hairless head. For a moment, neither of us spoke. Don eventually raised his head, and with sad eyes told me, "You know, this hasn't been an easy week for me either." His tone was that of a confidante, as if we might enjoy commiserating in each other's misery, some of which for him was being caused by me.

"I'm sure it hasn't," I said. "You know, this was never my intention when I got into teaching either. But you have to understand. I am Carl's lawyer now. That's not going to change. Maybe the sooner I can get through his defence, the sooner this will be over and life around here can go back to some semblance of normalcy."

He looked pleased at the prospect. "What are you doing here anyway?" he asked, smiling at me.

Since we were getting along so famously now, probably because he was afraid I was going to sue him, I thought I would answer honestly. "I was planning to get hold of a staff phone list and check out who was working the night Tricia died. Carl worked late here that night, and if someone saw him here and can verify the time, his defence gets a whole lot stronger."

Don looked back towards the open gym door, where a few spectators could still see us in the not so private hallway. "What do you need?" he asked.

I thought for a moment. "Staff phone list and the names of everyone who was working, including janitors, secretaries, anyone, on Wednesday night."

"You got a fax machine?" he asked.

"Yep."

"Why don't you let me go get that in the office and send it to you at home?" he offered.

It sounded like a reasonable compromise. I gave him my fax number and headed out the door with my head held as high as my now aching neck would permit.

Eighteen

As I walked down the interior hallway of my apartment building, the scent of pizza wafted towards me, which told me Andrea had not only beat me to my apartment, she had followed through on her promise of pizza.

Andrea and I had keys to each other's apartments. I had her key ostensibly because I would periodically go in to feed her cat if she was away or if the job kept her late. Why exactly she had my key, given I had no pets or even live plants to look after, was bit of a mystery. But she carried a gun, and when she had suggested she ought to have a key to my place, I had gone along with it.

My humiliating escapade at the school had worked up a robust appetite. I knew we would have to spend a few minutes rehashing where I was on Carl's defence, and what Andy was planning and able to do to help me. But after that, I just wanted to eat pizza, drink wine and watch a movie. A lot of people think you're supposed to eat pizza, drink beer and watch a movie. I am of the belief that you can drink red wine with pizza as long as the wine is Italian.

Unlocking my apartment door, I stepped inside as the aroma of mozzarella and what would surely be ample amounts of pepperoni greeted my anticipating taste buds. "Honey, I'm home!" I called out.

"Funny you should mention that," came Andrea's reply. Something in the tone of her voice told me all was not copacetic in the Patrick household. I hung my coat up in the entrance hallway closet then entered the great room of the apartment—at least that's what I liked to call it. Really, it was just the living room, dining room and kitchen pretty much all together in one space, save for a half wall between kitchen and "dining room". As I looked into the

169

living room, I discovered the source of Andrea's tension sitting on my leather sofa.

"Did you have a good day at work, dear?" Sandi asked sarcastically. As much as I really did not want to spend any time with my ex-wife after the experience I had just had, I was still momentarily bemused at the thought of Sandi and Andy sitting alone in my apartment trying to make small talk until I returned. Not only did the two of them not like each other, their mutual distaste was no secret one to the other. To their credit, they seemed to be behaving civilly towards.

"Should you be drinking wine in your condition?" I asked my former spouse, pointing to the wine glass in her hand, not knowing or caring whether I was revealing a secret in front of my oldest and closest friend.

"It's non-alcoholic," she informed me.

"Sacrilege."

"And I don't have a 'condition,' Winnie. I'm pregnant. You make it sound like I have a disease." From the corner of my consciousness, I could just make out Andy's chuckle, hearing my ex-wife refer to me as "Winnie." I have never confessed to her that Sandi also used to finish the moniker with "the Pooh."

"Maybe you do have a disease."

Andrea made a short, whistling sound between her teeth. "Five yards! Hitting below the belt!"

"I think someone already took care of that action," I retorted. Shit, I was in a pissy mood.

"Jesus, Win," Sandi protested. "What did I do to deserve this?"

"Don't you mean 'who' did you do?" You ever get the feeling your evening is going to degenerate into a shouting match?

"Time out!" Andy declared. "In your corners!" She pointed to a seat opposite where Sandi was sitting. "Far be it from me to take up sides with the She-Demon here...no offense," she said to Sandi.

"No worries. He's offending me enough already."

"But I gotta tell you, Mr. Patrick. You're being a bit of a shit since you walked through that door."

"My door," I corrected her. "My door, which was locked, and I entered to find two intruders. I should have you two arrested."

Andrea raised and lowered her eyebrows simultaneously in classic Groucho Marx style. "Would you like I should cuff the two of us?"

"Ooohh," Sandi chimed in with a faulty Marilyn Monroe. "I'm game if you are."

Between the two of them, they were managing to dissipate the tension in what seemed like my now crowded apartment. But I couldn't be nice again without one more rant. "And another thing: I am not at all comfortable with you two getting along! You are throwing my world into even more disarray! You!" I pointed mock-angrily at Andy. "You have a standing order not to admit my ex-wife into the building without my approval!"

"Hey! Don't blame me," Andrea threw up her arms in defeat. "She rang the door buzzer. I thought it was the pizza guy. No offence," she said again to Sandi.

"None taken," Sandi assured her. "Speaking of which, I'm starving, and I'm eating for two."

I looked pleadingly at Andrea. "What do you want me to do, shoot her?" she asked.

"Would you?" I asked.

Somehow, no matter how hard I tried, I couldn't seem to upset Sandi. And yet just a few days ago, I had sent her storming out of there without even trying. She was just impossible to figure out.

"Besides which," Sandi continued as she headed towards my kitchen, "I came over here so you could apologize for your rude behaviour on Thursday night. If you keep this up, I'll have to come back again, so you can apologize for tonight's rudeness. But if I stay for pizza, all will be forgiven."

"Oh, joy," I surrendered, as is virtually always the case in my conversations with Sandi. We made our way over to the dining room table. Sandi took plates out of the cupboard, guessing the correct cupboard on the first try. Andrea and I sat down at the table as Sandi placed the large pizza box on the centre of the table. "This is pretty much what you considered 'eating at home' when we were married, too," I commented.

"Enough already," Sandi stated firmly. "You're pissed that I'm here. I get it."

"Seriously, Win," Andrea added. "Move on. Why don't you start by bringing us up to speed?"

"Yes!" Sandi declared. "I've been dying to talk to you all day after I woke up and saw your picture splattered over the *Sun* this morning. You even made the front section of the *Post*. They barely know the west coast exists." Andy had shown me the front page of the *Vancouver Sun* when she'd arrived in the morning. I was unaware the Toronto-produced *National Post* had carried the story as well. I was quickly becoming coast-to-coast infamous.

While we ate, I gave Sandi the background on Carl's case, since it helped me to get it back out in the open and hear out loud as many details as I had. She listened intently, only interrupting once to express her dismay at her big brother again getting involved in my life. As we talked, Andrea interjected with additional information she had picked up since our coffee meeting earlier in the afternoon, including that Carl had two arrests for assault as a juvenile, a fact that would have been sealed in court records once he became an adult, but by pulling the right strings, Andrea had been able to find out. She was also confident that if she knew about violence in Carl's past, Furlo and Smythe would know about it too.

By the time I got around to explaining the events at the basketball game, we had finished eating and had moved into the living room to finish our wine; real wine for Andy and me. We began by laughing—okay, they were laughing—but as I filled in the details, both Andrea and Sandi's looks turned to genuine concern.

"So he pushed you off the bleachers?" Andrea asked incredulously.

"I'm sure it was an accident," I replied. "There's no way the principal really planned to get into a physical altercation with me in front of a gymnasium full of spectators."

"Still," Andy persisted, "maybe I should pay him a little police visit, just to make his life miserable."

"You don't think his life is already pretty shitty this week?"

"Are you sure you're not hurt?" Sandi asked for about the fourth time. She had never shown this much concern for me when we co-habitated.

"I told you, I'm fine. My back hurts. My neck hurts. My ankle hurts. But I managed to get out of there on my own steam, so I'm sure I'm okay."

"Stand up. Let me see," Andrea commanded. As usual, I obeyed her. Both Andrea and Sandi stood behind me.

Andy reached out and put her hand in the middle of my back. "Does it hurt to the touch?" she asked. I let out a yelp when she applied even a small amount of pressure to the area. Of course, that doesn't really mean much. I have a pathetically low threshold for pain. I cry if I have to pop a zit. "Take your shirt off and lie down on your bed," she demanded, walking over to my bedroom doorway. "I want to take a look."

"Since when do you know anything about backs?" I protested.

"For God sake's, just do it!" Sandi joined in. Double teaming. Taking my shirt off, I headed into the bedroom and lay face down on the queen size bed I hadn't bothered to make that morning, unusual for me. The two most prominent women in my life leaned over me, examining my naked torso for obvious signs of damage.

"Holy shit, Winnie!" Sandi exclaimed. "Your back is going black and blue."

"It goes with my moods," I replied half-heartedly. It was required of me to be a smartass but I'm not a big fan of my own injuries.

"Winston," Andy added, "I'm a little worried. It's possible you may have fractured a couple of ribs or something."

"I didn't fracture a rib."

"How do you know?" Andy asked. "Are you breathing normally?"

"Not really, no."

"How come? Does breathing hurt?" Sandi wanted to know.

"No. It's because you've got me lying face down in a pillow."

"Goddamn it Winston!" Sandi shouted, picking up a pillow and whacking me with it. As she did, white light flashed before my eyes, and I contorted my body as bolts of pain pulsed through my entire torso. I think I yelled, or maybe whimpered.

Both Andy and Sandi stood back in alarm at my outburst and obvious agony, then approached the bed cautiously. With my head turned towards one side, I felt Sandi sit down gingerly beside me, where she apologized for hitting me with the pillow.

"It's okay," I told her. "It just took me by surprise for a minute, that's all."

I felt Andrea flop down beside me on the opposite side of the bed. Beads of sweat had broken out on my forehead and across my shoulders. Shit. I really was hurt. Both women gently laid their hands on my back, delicately stroking my unclothed upper body. It was soothing and relaxing and momentarily dulled the pain. So much so, I couldn't resist voicing the brief, indecent thought that flashed through my brain.

"That's nice," I told them. "You know, there's no reason for this to stop. You're both welcome to join me."

Andrea's hostility was obvious, though she refrained from physically assaulting me. "Christ, Win! What is it about men and their perverse threesome fantasies?" she protested, though she knew I was mostly kidding.

"Foursome," I corrected, nodding towards Sandi's side of the bed. "She's pregnant."

"Okay, now you're just being sick!" Sandi opined, getting up off the bed.

"Medical check's over. Suffer solo. Get up!" For some strange reason, I never tired of being ordered around by Andrea.

Wincing as I got up, I pulled my shirt back on over my battered body and followed the two women out into the living room. Andrea was already reaching for her coat. "I'm gonna go. I'll talk to you tomorrow. Need anything else?"

"Nothing I can think of. You're leaving already? We haven't even watched a bad movie yet."

Andrea turned and paused with her hand on the doorknob as I followed her into the entrance hallway. "Raincheck," she said, then nodded her head back towards the living room, where Sandi had once again taken a seat on the couch. "I think she has things to talk about."

I stole a glance at Sandi then turned back to Andrea in panic.

"Like what?"

"I don't know," she insisted. "But she did come here unannounced for the second time this week. She's pregnant. I'm thinking she's got things on her mind."

"Oh shit," I complained. "I have to be her confidante? Why can't you do it? Wouldn't she be better off talking to another woman? Even if it's you?"

"I'll ignore that for now. Besides, she and I called a temporary truce for tonight. I'm hardly girlfriend material. I'm afraid that will have to be your job. Have fun." She kissed me on the cheek, opened the door and was gone.

Closing the door behind me, I walked back into the living room, where Sandi sat sipping fake wine on the couch. Where the hell did she find fake wine? Certainly not in my house.

I noticed then that Sandi, so casual during the earlier parts of the evening with Andrea present, now had taken on an air of expectation, as though there were things she was just itching to talk about with me. I wondered for a moment if she and Andrea had conspired the latter's early departure. I retired the thought quickly; no matter what Sandi's needs were and how sympathetic Andrea might be, there was no way they would work together on personal issues.

"So?" I began for openers as I walked back into the living room.

My admittedly beautiful ex-wife looked up from her comfortable position on the sofa and addressed me with what appeared to be genuine concern. "Are you sure you're all right?"

It was probably not very kind of me to feel this way, but I did. The more concern Sandi showed for me, the more my "spider sense" was tingling. Something about sympathy or empathy coming from her told me not to drink any more wine: staying alert was an imperative. She might be after the deed to my condo. "I really am fine. I just bruise easily. Monday will be the real test. That's when we see how thick-skinned I am after everyone at the school comes up with any number of ways to ridicule my fall from grace."

"It won't be that bad," she tried to assure me.

"Have you forgotten high school?" I asked.

"I went to an all-girls school, remember?" She paused for a

moment. "Come to think of it, that's probably worse."

We looked at each other silently across the small void of living space that a Kitsilano neighbourhood apartment affords for such awkward moments. The track lighting above the fireplace was slightly dimmed, as was the overhead light over the dining area table, creating a low glow off the off-white walls. The gas fire was lit, but as is the case with gas fireplaces, the flames were too small and too blue to do much dancing on the walls.

"So?" I finally said, making sure my one syllable was inflected into a question.

"So?" Sandi repeated.

"You're still here, which indicates you want to talk about something. In fact, you've never actually stated why you came here tonight."

"Always the lawyer," she chided.

"Teacher," I corrected.

"Tell that to your client." She was turning snippy, which was a habit we easily fell into whenever we were alone in a room. She sighed and flopped her head back against the sofa before continuing. "Sorry."

"No problem." Pause. "Did you want to start by telling me about being pregnant?"

Her head sprang forward again. "What do you want to know?"

It was my turn to sigh. "Sandi, I don't particularly want to know anything. Your love life is your business, but the fact you've made two unannounced visits, and you're still sitting here in my living room has led me to believe you want to talk to me. You being pregnant, I assume, is about the biggest thing in your life, so I've put two and two together and determined that is the subject which you wish to discuss."

She looked across at me with something I had not seen from her in a long time: sad eyes. I was accustomed to Sandi looking angrily at me, or even with enthusiasm, generally when discussing items she was planning to purchase. But sadness was not something I'd often seen in her. I think she equated sadness with weakness, and she didn't like me to have the upper hand.

176

"Yes," she finally admitted. "I came here to talk to you about being pregnant."

"I'm listening."

"Well, for starters, the father and I are no longer together." She let that one drop to see what shock value it had. I kept my poker face on so as not to show any incredulity.

"I see."

"It turns out we didn't have as much in common as I thought. We were together for about four months." She made little swirlies with her fake wine in the wine glass. For some reason it bothered me that she was drinking fake wine from my good wine glasses. I felt like she should be drinking it from a plastic cup. "But it didn't work out."

Since I felt like she had left a gap so I would say something, I did. "Does he know?"

"About the pregnancy? Yeah. He knows."

"How did he take it?"

"I don't date horrible people. He took it well. He was surprised, shocked, of course. But he was gentlemanly about it. He asked what I planned to do."

"What do you plan to do?"

She looked directly at me again, with the old sparkle in her eyes. "I'm drinking fake wine, aren't I?"

"That much is clear. What do you plan to do about Dad? Or more appropriately, no dad?"

Her face spoke a challenge to me. "Hundreds of thousands of women raise children on their own, Winston. I have the means. I'm going to raise this baby without its dad. If he wants to be part of the baby's life, so be it. But make no mistake about it. With or without him, I'm going to keep this baby."

"Fair enough," I told her, hands held up in mock surrender. "I'm not questioning your maternal instincts." At least not out loud. Sandi was about the least maternal woman I could think of off the top of my head. Inside I worried she might view a child as some sort of possession she had not yet managed to acquire with her family's wealth and influence. But I wasn't about to say that to her.

Even fake red wine stains when thrown from across the room.

Sandi was quiet again for what must have been at least a full three or four minutes. Since I could think of nothing to say, I let her have the quiet time to think about whatever she wanted to say to me next. I spent the time alternately looking at her and the fireplace, hoping that all of this deep, pensive conversation might help me to sleep through the night. Mr. Sensitive.

After a small eternity, Sandi was ready to resume conversing. "Winston," she began, and I knew she was serious because she didn't refer to me as Win or Winnie. "Do you ever think that maybe we made a mistake?"

Dangerous territory this. "Many times," I replied ambiguously, hoping I could get her to continue without having to commit to anything too deep.

"Really?" Her eyes lit up in surprise, or maybe it was delight. It was hard to tell. Either way, I could tell immediately she had misinterpreted my ambiguity.

"Didn't both our parents tell us that right from the beginning?" I added, trying to clarify without hurting feelings any more than necessary.

She seemed a little angry. "I don't mean about getting married. I mean getting divorced. Doesn't it seem to you we kind of rushed it?"

"Sandi, you walked out on me, remember? There wasn't a whole lot of 'we' in the decision process. You left."

"Because you were abandoning everything you had worked so hard for," she insisted.

"No, because I wasn't happy doing what I was doing, and I needed to make a change. You delivered an ultimatum: you and the law or teaching."

"And you chose teaching over me." She was starting to pout. Her mood swings in this short conversation were amazing. Could pregnancy hormones be kicking in that quickly?

"No. That's not true. I chose not to be dictated to by an ultimatum that was unreasonable. You determined you couldn't live with my not being a lawyer and left. Period. End of story." I stood up and paced towards the front window. As usual, the late November night was delivering a cold, icy rain. From my window, the rain puddles on the sidewalk below appeared to be glowing as the incandescent light from the street lamp spilled onto them.

I whirled and faced Sandi again. "Why are we even having this conversation? We've had it a hundred times."

"Don't you wish we could be...I don't know, a family?"

A-ha! There it was. For a change, I decided I would be gentle with my ex. As much as she was showing determination and reserves of strength in keeping her baby, the pieces of the puzzle were falling into place, and I could sense her real fear. "Sandi," I began, sitting down next to her on the sofa, "you're not making sense. You want to start a family with me? And some other guy's kid?"

She was no idiot. She knew how ridiculous it sounded. It occurred to me Sandi and I had once been really close, and maybe she didn't have anyone with whom she could feel that close again. "I don't know," she answered my question. "It just would seem so...so..."

"Familiar?" I offered. "That's a hell of a reason to get married again." I put my arm around her and she willingly laid her blonde head on my chest. Fortunately, she was on my good side; the bruising from my bleacher fall was gently placed against a couch cushion.

"Shit," she said, returning to the Sandi I knew.

"Yeah, shit. You're scared. That's normal."

For the first time in a very long time, she began to cry quietly in front of me. And for the first time in an equally long time, I didn't mind having her there in my arms, just being held.

Nineteen

Sandi left around midnight. Before going to bed, I spent about an hour on the computer, preparing a brief of what I had learned so far about Carl, his relationship with Tricia, his whereabouts the night she was murdered and Andy's recent discovery of his semi-violent criminal past. Seeing all the information down on the screen in front of me did not fill me with a great deal of comfort. In fact, it looked pretty skimpy. Still, since I had needed to prepare something, this was as good a way as any to proceed. When I had outlined everything I thought I knew, I copied the document into an email message and sent it off to Derek. Hopefully he would be able to mount a credible position from the document that would at least enable Carl to go home on bail. I was pretty confident the Crown prosecutor would argue that Carl was a flight risk and indeed, might be a danger to other students and would want him remanded pending trial. If nothing else, I was hopeful Derek would at least win Carl some temporary reprieve from incarceration.

By about four forty-five a.m., I gave up pretending I was going to get any more than the two or so hours of sleep I had already achieved, got out of bed and prepared for my running ritual.

Though winter doesn't officially start until December 21st, I have always believed November is the coldest, dreariest month in Vancouver. I don't like to dissuade myself with statistics, but I know for a meteorological fact, at least in my own mind, that in November it rains more often, more coldly and with more gusty winds than in any other month. It brings a special magic to the early morning—or middle of the night, depending on your perspective—outdoor aerobic workout.

Donning runners, toque—a most necessary item, since a great deal of body temperature is lost through the head—long sleeved running shirt, rain proof—supposedly—running jacket and yes, even spandex-lycra running pants, I headed out the door. As ridiculous an outfit as it was, it was necessary for survival as a runner in winter.

I warmed up by doing a light jog for couple of blocks east to Cypress Street, where I turned down towards the water, passing Vancouver's more expensive single family homes. Old money lived there, including a city councillor who had been unfortunate enough to have his address published, making his home the site of numerous protesters over the years. As I reached Vanier Park, backdrop to the Vancouver Museum, known to locals as the Planetarium, I turned west again, joining the seawall as far as it would take me before crossing back up to Cornwall Avenue again.

It usually took me until just about the Vancouver Yacht Club before I got my pace up, something around a six and a half minute mile most mornings. Not super speedy, but consistent. From the Yacht Club, I re-joined the ocean front trail that would carry me all the way to Spanish Banks at the foot of the U.B.C. endowment lands. The ocean at this time of morning was barely recognizable, especially with the dark, overcast sky. If you peered carefully in between raindrops falling onto the eyelids, you could just make out container ships in the harbour, waiting their turn to pass under the famed Lions Gate Bridge into Burrard Inlet, where they would unload their wares.

Though this was pretty much my regular route, I never tired of my waterfront runs. At this time of the morning, the city felt as if it belonged to me, with the twinkling lights of the downtown core beckoning from across the water. Why so many lights are on in so many buildings throughout the night was a mystery. But it was one that I got to ponder alone on my pre-dawn treks. On a really good morning, or bad one depending on your perspective, I often ran well past Spanish Banks and up the road to the university, occasionally completing a full circuit of the university lands before trekking back home along West 4th Avenue. Those mornings were good, because I truly pushed my endurance; they were bad because it generally meant I was out even earlier because I had been able to sleep even less. It was an odd paradox that the less I slept, the more I was able to run.

Morning runs were also where I got much of my thinking and planning done, and this morning was no exception. Though it was Sunday, there was a lot to do before I returned to the classroom on Monday. By the time I made it back to my apartment, it was nearly five forty-five, enough time to enjoy a hearty breakfast at a local café that opened early on Sunday mornings.

Shortly after seven thirty, I had showered, shaved, dressed, had breakfast at Molly's Cafe on 4th Avenue and returned home, already finding two messages waiting on my voicemail at home. The first was from Andrea. So was the second. That she had called me twice that early in the morning told me she really wanted to talk to me. It wasn't the early hour that was so telling; Andy is a perennial early riser, even on her days off. It was the double phone call. Of course, I knew she wanted the details of the remainder of my evening last night, and I toyed with the idea of not giving her the information until much later so she could be tortured all morning. But I knew I would end up paying for that, so I dialed her number right away.

"Where the hell did you run to? Alberta?" she asked immediately upon picking up the phone.

"It's Sunday," I protested. "It's the one day I spoil myself with a good, fatty breakfast."

"I saw you shirtless last night, remember? Believe me. You can stand a few more fatty breakfasts in your week."

"I am not too skinny," I told her pointlessly, since we'd had this argument numerous times in the past.

"Not in the concentration camp survivor sense, no, but you're getting close. So," she forged ahead, "was breakfast a solo affair or what?"

"What are you talking about?" I feigned indignation, though I knew she worried obsessively that Sandi's wiles would somehow rope me in. To Andy's eyes, it was only a matter of time.

Andy took my evasive response as confirmation of her inquiry. "For God's sake, Win, you slept with her, didn't you? Man, you are so predictable."

I smiled, despite the fact I should have been insulted. "No," I told her, "I did not sleep with Sandi."

At least one statement of disbelief was required. "Bullshit." There it was.

"Why would you even think that?"

"She drops by unannounced, acting like she gives a damn about how you're doing, all vulnerable and pregnant. It's what you do."

"It is not what I do," I protested. "It's over."

"That hasn't stopped you in the past," Andy accused. She alluded, of course, to one of two mistakes I had made since Sandi and I had initially separated. The first being that during an evening of arguing and confusion over where we stood, we had ended up in bed. The second mistake had been, of course, that I had told Andy about it.

"That was once. It was a long time ago. I'll have you know that last night she only wanted someone to talk to and a shoulder to cry on, and as bitter as I generally am towards her, I decided to provide both. And, after I talked her out of wanting to remarry me, she went home."

This was one of those times when I wished the age of everyone having video phones had actually arrived, because at the moment I could almost see Andy doing a *Three's Company* spit-take with her coffee. "She wants to get back to together? As in permanently?"

"Relax," I replied. "She's thinking with her pregnant hormones, and she's a bit scared. Daddy will buy her something expensive, and she'll feel better."

A silence filled the telephone receiver. "Are you coming this morning?" she finally asked.

"Yeah," I told her. "But I have a few things I want to do first. I'll meet you there."

"All right. I'll see ya," she told me, then hung up the phone.

"There" was Fairview Presbyterian Church on Fir Street, not far from where I lived. After committing the indiscretion of not only marrying a Jew, but then divorcing her, the welcome mat outside the same Catholic Church I had attended with my parents all my life had quickly been metaphorically whisked away. Still, liturgical habits died hard, and I had found myself at the steps of the local Presbytery quite

183

by accident. Literally. While out running very early one morning, I had come across the minister of the church out exercising his physical side, which he assured me helped stimulate his spiritual side. The following Sunday, I had found myself on the old building's doorstep, looking for somewhere that might permit me to practice my faith.

Remarkably loyal friend that she is, upon discovering that I had rediscovered a church life, Andrea had begun attending with me, herself having given up attending the same Catholic church both our families had attended. When I told her about this welcoming new place I had found, Andy felt a yearning to return to some sort of structured environment that wasn't nearly so judgmental nor passionately evangelistic. In fact, we were among the youngest Presbyterians in the building.

I agreed I would meet Andrea in time for Sunday service, or as close to the start time as possible, but I had a couple of things I wanted to do while it was still early.

The neighbourhood around J. Mac is best described as working class. It is neither terribly run-down nor particularly upscale. Houses, because it is Vancouver, are probably out of the price range of the average first-time homeowner, but many of the families in the area had purchased their homes before prices in even East Vancouver had skyrocketed in the late 1980s. Neighbourhoods like this were far less transient and more stable than some of the tonier abodes on the west side, where the wealth of the owners was often a fleeting thing.

By around eight thirty, I had made my way back across town to the site where Tricia Bellamy's body had been found. Tricia had been discovered in a park about four blocks from our high school and just a few blocks north of where she had lived with her apparently diplomatically-connected family. Those connections in themselves made me wonder why Tricia's family wasn't living in a more affluent part of town. Though most people did not go into the diplomatic profession to get rich, one assumed that rank and privilege might extend to immediate family members.

The park itself was on 43rd Avenue and, for the most part, was just a large patch of long grass in the middle of suburbia. There was no sign to indicate the park had been named. There were no formal playing fields, though an area was set aside at the far end that included swings, see-saws and a climbing apparatus with hanging ropes and old tires attached to the sides. The park looked as though it had not been tended for some time. It was winter, but the grass had grown to a height that indicated it had not been cut since long before its growing season had ended. It was one of those blank land patches the city felt it was supposed to install out of some sense of obligation rather than real public service.

The park was surrounded on its east and west sides by lanes which adjoined the back sides of typical East Vancouver houses, including Vancouver Specials just like Carl's. On the south side was 44th Avenue, I sat in my car on the north boundary of the park, 43rd Avenue. Across the street and facing the park was Meadows Manor apartments, which looked to be an old folks' home. It seemed completely incomprehensible to me that in all of these houses that looked out onto the park, not a single individual had seen or heard anything the night of Tricia's murder, especially the seniors, rumoured as a group to be even worse sleepers than I. Especially considering she was definitely found prior to eight thirty in the evening. According to Andrea, Furlo and Smythe and the other detectives and patrol officers who investigated that night could find no witnesses from the surrounding area. I found myself doubting the efforts put into the neighbourhood interviews, especially once the lead detectives had spoken to Don McFadden, then met my client the next morning. How hard were they really looking to find witnesses?

Getting out of my car I headed into the centre of the grassy parkland, much of which had been flattened by what was surely a small army of police and crime scene investigators a few nights previously. The rain that had so pounded me during my pre-dawn run had happily let up, though after several days of rain, the field in which Tricia's body had been dumped was still a soupy mess. It made me envision trenches and battlefields in Europe, probably because I was supposed to be preparing to teach about the First World War in my Social Studies class the next morning.

The police were largely finished with the site, and the crime scene was now just part of the field. It was clear from the number of impressions left in the mud where the body had been and where the bulk of police personnel had spent their Wednesday night. I couldn't be sure, but the spot where I estimated Tricia's body had been found seemed to be geographically in the very centre of the nearly perfectly square plot of park land. It was almost as though her killer had viewed the centre of the park as some sort of bullseye; placing her outside the centre would have been, what? Less of a statement? Looking around the park, it was difficult to imagine the placement had been accidental, though I realized I was making the supposition based on no more than eyeballing the scene. Still, it told me the killer was trying to tell Tricia's eventual discoverers something: "Look. I'm not trying to hide what I did. I want you to find her." Of course, Furlo could and probably had made the argument that that kind of thinking pointed the finger even more so at my client, who was so lovelorn he wanted her to be found right away.

But that didn't make sense either, and I had to believe Smythe would be thinking about that angle. Assuming Carl had killed his lover because she was about to expose the relationship, would it not make much more practical sense to try to hide the body? I've never killed anyone, but that's what I would do.

I walked around the site of the body several times in slow circles that grew wider in circumference as I walked. I don't know what I was looking for. Rationally, I knew the likelihood I would stumble upon something as useful as a "clue" was pretty remote; the police had most surely been all over the park. Still, it seemed kind of rude to go knocking on doors before nine a.m., so I continued my circle walking until I had done a complete perimeter of the park more than once. As expected, I found nothing of interest.

Finally, the big hand on my watch told me it was approaching a respectable hour, even for a Sunday morning. I chose the line of houses on the northeast corner of the park and headed around the corner to their fronts, not wanting to seem too presumptuous by arriving via their backyards and kitchen doors.

Standing in front of the first house, I paused to consider my task. I sort of wished Andrea were with me. Of course, I knew she could not come and interview potential witnesses with the prime suspect's defence counsel, but I wished I had at least thought to consult her about the questions I should ask these homeowners. Facing the large number of houses down the side street, I was starting to recognize the futility of my plan. "Oh well," I said aloud. I was there anyway.

I walked up through the wrought-iron decorated gateway and rang the intercom next to the front door. A few moments passed before scuffling and chain un-bolting could be heard through the doorway. I could understand how residents might be extra security conscious after a victim had been discovered virtually in their backyards. On the other hand, a chain doesn't do a whole lot of good if you unlock it the minute someone rings the doorbell. A Chinese woman at least in her sixties opened the door and stared at me without speaking.

"Good morning," I began with a smile. "I'm sorry to disturb you at this early time. I wondered if I could ask you a couple of questions about the incident that took place here the other night?" I pointed towards the rear of her house, indicating the spot where surely she had been aware of the police presence.

The woman responded by staring at me some more.

"You see," I tried further, "I am a lawyer, and I am looking into the investigation. I was wondering if you could tell me anything you might have seen or heard out of the ordinary." Sometimes silence can motivate someone to answer your question, so I let one hang in the air for a few seconds. When that didn't seem to generate any communication, I tried on my best, albeit not terribly impressive pronunciation of the one Mandarin word that I knew. *"Nee-hou?"* I said, attempting to engage the quiet woman somehow.

Hearing my feeble attempt at Chinese, the woman's eyes lit up momentarily, and she fired off what was probably several sentences at me in either Mandarin or Cantonese. I knew one word. I couldn't even tell which dialect she was speaking. When her alien barrage ended it was my turn to stare wordlessly at her for a moment. I wished I had an old 1940s fedora to tip gallantly at her with a bow.

Since I didn't, I just looked at her, smiled, said "Thank you" and turned away. My first potential witness interview of the case. Wow.

Enthusiasm dampened but still determined, I plodded next door, noting from the corner of my vision that the Chinese woman continued to watch me through her open door. I smiled again at her, even giving a slight bow as I walked down her next door neighbour's pathway. I found my right hand gesturing as though lifting an imaginary chapeau. Man. I was born in the wrong decade.

A long time passed between my ringing of the second house's doorbell and the door opening. When it did, a man of about forty-five stood in a maroon coloured, velvet bathrobe. He looked as though he hadn't shaved in several days, and the crusties around his eyes told me I had woken him up. His breath told me he was probably hung over.

"Good morning," I began with a smile, minus the bow. He didn't appear to be from the far east.

"I ain't interested," he told me gruffly.

"You're not interested in a 'good morning'?" My sarcasm doesn't take weekends off.

"I'm Catholic," he told me inexplicably.

"So was I," I replied. He was opening up to me early on in our relationship.

"Look," he grumbled before I could go any further, "I don't want to talk about my beliefs with a stranger. Besides. It's Sunday. Shouldn't you be in church?"

"Shouldn't you be?" I asked. "You said you were Catholic."

"Yeah, well, I had a late night. But I still don't want your magazine." He began to close the door.

"Sir, I'm sorry," I said, putting the palm of my hand against the closing door. "I don't know what you're talking about."

"You J.W.'s and your magazines."

"Jehovah's Witnesses?" I asked.

"Yeah," he answered. We both seemed thoroughly confused.

"I'm not a Jehovah's Witness," I told him.

"You're wearing a suit," he stated.

"Yes," I admitted. I had wanted to look presentable. "But I'm not trying to convert you. I'm a lawyer."

"Oh, shit," he complained. "Even worse." And Sandi wondered why I had wanted out of the legal profession. "Whadda ya want?"

"I'm investigating the homicide discovery that took place in the park behind your house."

"Why?" he wanted to know. "They already caught the guy." On the face of it, that was a perfectly reasonable question.

"I am aware of that. The 'guy' they caught is my client."

That piece of information seemed to immediately anger him. "And you want me to help you?" he demanded. "You've got a fuckin' nerve! I have a daughter almost that age myself. Your 'client' should have his balls cut off!"

"Very eloquently put," I countered. "I'm really just trying to find out what people may have seen that night."

"You know what?" he shouted. "Fuck you!" This time there was no stopping him from slamming the door in my face. I looked down the street at the remaining houses. Two down.

At the third house in the row abutting the park, the scene at house number one was repeated almost entirely, though this time the woman who answered the door was Indo-Canadian, rather than Chinese. She wore the most beautifully ornate silk *sari*, as though planning some elaborate ceremony. I wondered if Sikhs—or was she a Hindu?—went to temple on Sundays. It's amazing how culturally unknowledgeable a person can be. She seemed to know about as much English as her Chinese neighbour two doors up, and I did not know a single syllable in Hindi, Punjabi or whatever language she spoke, so I did my smile and nod thing and walked away.

Three major language and ethnic groupings in three houses. How did these people hold block parties?

By the time I had reached the end of the block and was headed into the street whose houses faced the small park land, I was beginning to feel a bit discouraged. Of the remaining three houses I had visited on the row, two appeared to have no one home, the third, which had a person actually willing talk to me without cursing, was not home the night Tricia was discovered and thus had no new information to offer. A half hour on a cold morning had not gotten me far, but I was still determined.

Bracing myself for rejection, I sauntered up to the first house that would have had a plain view of the park. When I rang the doorbell, I heard the sound of feet pounding heavily down the stairs leading to the front entrance. In my head, I was visualizing a very large person opening the door, but then the detective instincts in me kicked in, and I realized the footsteps were moving too quickly. When it struck me who would be opening the door, I actually turned to leave, but before I could get away, I heard the locks on the door coming undone. I turned back to face the inevitable. Something moving that quickly and pounding that heavily on the stairs could only mean one thing: a teenager. And given the neighbourhood I was in, it was going to be a student from my school.

I said a silent prayer it wouldn't be someone I knew, and maybe wouldn't even know me. The door opened, and I knew God was busy listening to everyone else in churches all over the city that morning.

"Mr. Patrick?" Scott Harton from my Law Twelve class asked me with no small amount of confusion. He was dressed in sweat pants and a T-shirt. In fact, I didn't think I had ever seen Scott in anything other than sweat pants or track suit bottoms. Why should the weekend be any different?

"Good morning, Scott." I tried to sound casual, but it would have freaked me out too if one of my high school teachers had shown up at my door.

He stared at me for a moment before asking, "What are you doing here?"

"I was checking to see if you've done your homework. Have you?"

He looked confused again. He was good at that look. "No."

"Why not?"

"I was going to do it later."

"Hasn't anyone ever taught you it's better to do your homework early in the weekend and get it out of the way?" He didn't quite know how to answer that one, quite rightly. There wasn't really a good answer for it. I decided to let him off the hook. "Actually, that's not why I'm here."

"Oh."

"I'm here because I'm canvassing the neighbourhood. As I'm sure you're aware, the park here is where Tricia Bellamy was found last Wednesday night." I waved my arm backwards, loosely gesturing towards the park.

"Oh. Yeah. I did know that," he replied softly. I did not know how well, if at all, Scott knew Tricia. I realized I not only did not know a great deal about Tricia, I didn't know much about any of my students. With seven classes, I had over two hundred kids I was trying to get to know. I had the distinct feeling that by the time I did get to know even just a little about all of them, it would be June, and I'd be awaiting my next new set of classes.

"In class the other day, you didn't mention you lived so close to the..." I stopped myself to seek out the right word. "So close to the park."

"No." Scott's lowered tone and his downcast eyes told me that if Tricia wasn't at least a friend, her death in such close proximity to his house had made a significant impact on him.

"Scott," I said gently, "were you and Tricia friends?"

He waited a moment before responding. I was his teacher, but I certainly hadn't developed the kind of relationship where he automatically felt he should open up to me about his feelings. I hadn't sought that kind of relationship any more than he had.

"We've known each other a long time. We went through a lot of elementary school together and all through high school." He stopped either to clarify his thoughts or to make sure he wasn't about to break down and cry in front of me. Or both. "We weren't best friends or anything, but we were friends."

"I'm sorry," was all I could think of to say. Not much of a comfort I'm sure, but it was what I had to work with on short notice.

Scott shook himself out of his moment of grief, as though just remembering I was there. He seemed to break free of whatever more pleasant memories he was having of his slain friend. For a flash of a moment, my mind sent me spiralling down a path I didn't want to go, one in which I saw my student at the end of it as a potential alternative suspect to Carl. I shook myself free of the image and silently chastised myself for it. That I was already grasping at my students as suspects was telling me I was getting desperate and a little out of my league in the defence arena. It didn't say a whole lot about me as a teacher either.

In an effort to assuage my guilt, I tried to slide back into teacher mode. "Scott, did you talk to one of the counsellors at the school? There are people there to help you through the shock of this, especially people who are Tricia's friends." I made sure to refer to his friendship status in the present tense. I didn't know what I would do if I suddenly caused him to have an emotional breakdown on his front stoop.

"No. I'm fine, really," he assured me. "But thanks for asking."

"Okay. Just let me know if you need anything, all right?"

"Yeah." I started to turn to leave when Scott stopped me. "Mr. Patrick? You never did say exactly what you wanted."

"No, you're right. I didn't. Look, it's all right. I was just trying to find out what people around the park might have heard or seen that night. But it's okay."

"I didn't see or hear anything. My little sister was in the house, but she was watching TV. I was listening to music in my room."

"As opposed to doing your homework?" I tried to lighten the moment.

"In addition to," he replied, then smiled a little awkwardly. "But you know what? One of my neighbours has been pissed off for the last couple of days because he says the police haven't listened to him."

"Listened to him about what?"

"I don't know. I didn't talk to him. My dad says that old Woo's raving that he tried to report something, and the cops wouldn't listen to him."

"Old Woo?" I asked.

Scott looked a little embarrassed. "Sorry. Mr. Woo. He lives over on the corner there. That's the back of his house." He pointed across to the backs of the row of houses that abutted the third side of the park.

"All right. I'll talk to him. Thanks, Scott."

"No problem. Mr. Patrick?" he asked one more time.

"Yeah."

"I like Mr. Turbot. I've had him for two years, so don't get me wrong or anything." He hesitated before continuing.

"It's okay, Scott. I'm his lawyer and your teacher, but that doesn't stop you from having an opinion."

"It's just that....it's just that you know he was...umm....screwing around with Trish?"

"What are you talking about?" I asked, playing naïve.

"He and Trish had been seeing each other, I mean as a couple, for like a year."

"She told you this?"

"She told Jessica."

"Who's Jessica?"

"Jessica McWilliams. My girlfriend. Trish's best friend. She's in our class."

"Oh. Okay, thanks. I'll definitely want to talk to her," I said.

"Look," he began to explain, "it doesn't mean he killed her."

"No," I agreed, "it doesn't."

"I don't think he did. I know him. I just can't see him killing someone, let alone one of his students. Let alone Trish."

"I don't think he did either, Scott. But thanks for telling me this."

"Okay," he told me. "I guess I'll see you tomorrow."

"Yeah. Thanks again." I gave my student a weak smile and left him standing watching me in the doorway as the November sky resumed its usual mode of operation and began to rain again. Given the rain, plus the likelihood I would run into more of my students, coupled with the new information I'd gotten from Scott, I opted to skip the rest of the houses on Scott Harton's row and head straight for Old Woo's house.

Twenty

Jian Woo, or Arthur, as I found out later he was known in Canada, lived in yet another Vancouver Special. Serious effort had been made, presumably by Mr. Woo, to beautify this basic, generic box-shaped house. I'm no horticultural expert—the plants I have in my apartment are silk, and I have killed those—but I know enough to know most people can't sustain floral displays in their yards during the winter. Mr. Woo was an exception. Whatever the brightly coloured flowers were, they added just the right spark of colour to an otherwise dreary pre-winter day in a bit of a dreary neighbourhood. And they were real. That much I knew, because I stopped and touched one on the way to his door. Take time to stop and touch the flowers, I always say.

The door to Mr. Woo's house opened before I'd even reached the end of the boxwood-lined sidewalk and had a chance to knock on the door. Clearly, my next interview, if not expecting me, was at least watchful of those who came and went on his little corner of the block. I stepped under the overhang of the sundeck off the living room—virtually identical to my client's—and into the gaze of Arthur Woo.

Mr. Woo looked to be in his seventies, or perhaps even eighties. It was hard to tell from his short, strong body, and his face, which belied his age despite its leathery skin, appeared to have spent a good deal of its years in the hot sun. I envisioned him a farmer in a faraway rice field, toiling away under Chairman Mao's regime, hoping for improvements from the Communist Leader's much heralded "Great Leap Forward".

"Good morning," I began my spiel.

"Good morning," Mr. Woo responded pleasantly. His "good" sounded a lot like "goooood". His accent was heavy, but he seemed to understand me better than his neighbours across the park.

"I wondered if I could ask you a couple of questions?"

"About the girl? The girl in the park?" He poked his short, stubby finger at me in an accusatory way, his voice resonating with excitement.

"Yes," I told him, "about the girl in the park."

"You come in. Come in," he commanded, his voice taking on a tone half-angry and half-instructive, as though he were accustomed to giving orders to underlings. Obligingly, I entered his house.

Mr. Woo nearly bounded up the stairs from the landing, his advanced years doing nothing to interfere with his ability to climb between floors. I followed him up the stairs, somewhat more slowly than my septuagenarian host, I'm embarrassed to admit.

The inside of the house lacked the same colour and brightness of the outside. Mr. Woo must have spent most of his days and his energy outside tending to the wide variety of flowers growing around his home. Inside, the carpet looked like it was the original that had been placed in the house when it was built, torn in the corners, with a well-worn path leading from the kitchen to the living room, where the carpet had sunk from the foot traffic. It looked like a foot highway.

"You sit," Mr. Woo ordered, pointing to an orange, fake velour-covered couch against one wall. As I sat down, Mr. Woo disappeared into the kitchen without a further word, leaving me to take in the few visuals his main living room had to offer. There were the requisite pictures of children, and I assumed grandchildren, on one wall. In the pictures, I noted a woman who looked to be in her sixties smiling and surrounded by small children posing for the camera. I didn't hear any conversation between Mr. Woo and anyone else, so I assumed Mrs. Woo was either out or was no longer among us. A few moments passed before Mr. Woo reappeared unannounced, carrying a wooden tray with a teapot and two very small teacups. He caught me looking at the picture on the side table.

"My family," he announced. Then he looked at me and said "Tea." It did not appear to be a question, so I simply said "Thank you."

"This is Mrs. Woo?" I asked.

"She is dead," he proclaimed firmly.

"I'm sorry," I said. If Asian families are known for taking in their elderly parents, particularly widowed ones, there was no sign of it in Mr. Woo's house. There was no indication anyone else shared the Woo abode. I forged ahead.

"You mentioned the girl in the park?"

"Yes, the girl," he said, delicately pouring tea into one of the small porcelain cups.

"Did you see or hear something the night she was found in the park?" I asked.

"Yes. I try to tell police, but they don't not want to hear it."

"They didn't want to hear what, sir?"

"That night, I was out on deck in the back, by the kitchen. You want to see?"

"Maybe later," I waved him on.

"Very big car, very big come down the alley. This is not normal. No big cars like this one live here."

"You're sure one of your neighours didn't get a new car, or maybe had someone visiting?"

"No," he insisted. "The car does not stay. It drive around and around the park, then it stop." He made a circling gesture with his arm, showing me how the car appeared to be searching the park for the right place to stop.

"Why were you outside in the rain?" it suddenly struck me to ask.

"It start to rain very heavy. I go outside to get some of my flowers I have been trying to make grow in cold weather. I keep them under the picnic table when it rains heavy."

"Did you see who was in the car?"

He stopped for a moment, as though disappointed in the question. "No," he told me. "I do not see, but I know the car stopped. I see car circling and circling, like he was lost. Then I pick up my plants and move them under picnic table. I was going to come back

196

into the kitchen, and I hear noise like bell, coming from the alley." He did an imitation of the sound that had caught his attention and based on his impression, I surmised he was referring to a car's warning tone if you open the door while the keys are still in the ignition or the headlights are on.

"I look down into alley, man was getting in the big car and closing the door so I could not see his face." Mr. Woo looked disappointed in his failure to be able to identify the car's driver, especially since he now figured the car was related to the discovery of Tricia some time later.

"What time was this, do you remember."

"7:55," he said with authority. "I write it down."

"I don't suppose you got the licence plate of the car?"

"No," he said, again disappointed. "All I could see in the dark was the flag."

"The flag?"

"On the licence plate. The Maple Leaf." British Columbia licence plates do not have a Canadian flag on them, which told me that whatever car was in the alley around the time Tricia's body was placed in the park, was not from this province.

I decided to take a shot in the dark. "Do you happen to know what kind of car it was, Mr. Woo?"

"Big," he told me again. "Very long. Like Oscar car."

"Oscar car?"

"Like with the movie stars. At Oscars. Very long car."

That narrowed my search down to limousines with Canadian flags on the licence plates. There's only three million cars in the Lower Mainland. How hard could that be to find?

"And the police didn't take this information from you?"

"I try to tell them. There were many police outside, and I keep going up to the police to try to tell them, but they all say they are busy and telling me go home." I pictured patrol officers securing the scene on a cold, blustery night and an old Chinese man frantically waving his arms and talking about big cars and plants that get rained on. Someone missed out on an important opportunity to talk to a potential witness.

I couldn't think of anything else to ask Mr. Woo so, taking my last sip of tea, which was surprisingly tasty, I thanked him for inviting me and helping me.

"Are you going to catch him?" he asked me. "The one who kill the girl?"

I smiled at him. "I hope so."

Mr. Woo looked at me gravely. "You be very careful. You don't want to get hurt."

"No," I agreed. "I don't. But I have people who will help and who will look out for me." I wondered how he, with his old fashioned values, would feel if he knew that my help and protector was a woman who I would stand behind while she kicked the butt of any bad guys. I reached into my pocket and pulled out one of my old business cards. I had already crossed out "Lawyer" and my office phone number and written my home number in their place. "If you think of anything else, please call me," I said, handing him the low budget card.

He looked a little disappointed to see me go. I got the impression he didn't get a whole lot of company. "You will let me know when you catch him." It too wasn't a question.

I decided I would, and I told him so.

Looking at the piece of paper I had given him with my name and number, he looked at me, puzzled. "You are not a policeman?"

"No," I told him.

"Then why you want to know about girl in the park?" he asked as he opened his front door to see me out.

Judging from the reaction I'd been getting as Carl's lawyer, I decided to bend the truth just a little. "I'm her teacher," I told him. "I want to catch her killer."

He smiled slyly then delivered a line he must have picked up from TV. "Go get him."

I left to do just that.

*　　*　　*

I probably would have made a lousy detective. By the time I had finished chatting with Arthur Woo, I was feeling a little victorious and thus did not bother trying to visit the remaining houses—which were in the majority—whose residents I had not yet interviewed. Buoyed by what I viewed as a critical new piece of information, I didn't want to face any more rejection or even possible language barriers.

Furthermore, I knew Andrea was waiting for me at Fairview Presbyterian. Not only did I not like to keep her waiting, but I also wanted to tell her about my chat with the elderly horticulturist and see if she could find a way to start tracking down the limousine Mr. Woo had seen the night Tricia's body was dumped in his community backyard.

The service had already begun by the time I made it back to the Kitsilano neighbourhood where I lived, slid in the back of the sanctuary and took the seat Andy had reserved for me on the aisle near the back. I was hardly the most devout of followers. Truth be told, going to church was mostly a habit I'd had a difficult time breaking after my years of attending Mass with my parents, but I benefitted from or at least enjoyed the time of quiet reflection and music.

That morning I was positively jumpy, and Andy was not the only one who noticed. Throughout the sermon, I fidgeted constantly to the point of distraction. I should have been sent off to Sunday school with the kids before the sermon began.

It's a funny thing about churches. People hardly knew us at all—we tended to be Sunday attendees only—so they had a hard time trying to establish exactly what our relationship might be. Older people, who made up the bulk of the Fairview flock, gave us knowing nods and smiles, as though it was only a matter of time before we realized how much we were in love and would soon marry.

By the time the service was over, I practically pushed Andrea outside, despite several attempts by people in the church's lobby to engage us in small talk.

Andy took me by the arm and pulled me aside from the departing crowd of worshippers. "Could you make any more of a spectacle of yourself?" she accused. "You come in late and you sit and fidget like an eight-year-old."

"I have a lot on my mind," I told her.

"Obviously you found out something that has gotten you all aflutter."

"Aflutter?"

"I talked to my mother earlier. It's her kind of terminology."

"Could have been worse. You could have had to talk to *my* mother."

We walked up next to her car, which was parked about a half block down the rain-soaked street from the old stone and brick church. "So what have you got?" she asked.

"A potential witness," I said smilingly.

"Placing Carl at the school?"

"Placing someone else at the crime scene." I said it with confidence mixed with just a hint of bravado. Even to myself, I sounded like I had solved the crime already.

"Who?" she asked forcefully.

"Mr. Woo."

"Who's he?"

"An old man who lives near the park."

"Who does he place at the crime scene?"

"I don't know."

Andrea looked at me the way a mother looks at a child who is trying to convince his mom he has no homework. "What exactly did your Mr. Woo see?" Her tone was stern, but I wasn't defeated yet.

"A car. A limousine to be exact."

"A limousine. Did he get the plates?"

"No. But it did have a Canadian flag on the plate." I smiled as though that would tell her everything.

"Wow. I'll find a judge and get a warrant to arrest every limousine owner in the city."

"You're beautiful when you're sarcastic."

She was all business now. "So this Mr. Woo sees someone get out of a limousine and dump Tricia's body, but he doesn't think to get the licence plate."

"It was dark. And he didn't actually see anyone dump a body."

Detective Andrea Pearson let out a deep sigh. "So you have an old man, in the dark, see a limousine pass through his neighbourhood on the same night the kid's body is found, and you figure this will spring your client?"

"Not when you put it like that, no."

"Did you get anything from the rest of the neighbours?"

"No."

She cocked an eyebrow at me. "Why not?"

I hung my head. Now I really was the kid who hadn't started his homework. "I gave up after talking to Mr. Woo."

"Why?" she accused.

"Because it seemed like..." I let my voice trail off, too embarrassed to complete the thought.

"A clue?" Leave it to Andy to finish my embarrassing thought for me.

"I'm new at this," I protested too loudly. A couple of church ladies with dainty winter hats turned and smiled at us as they walked by. I smiled back. I wondered how many of them had seen the Sunday morning paper before they'd left for church, and if my face and Carl's were plastered on the front page of the morning tabloid.

"So what you actually have is 'bupkiss'," my friend informed me.

"Is that the technical term you detectives use? Because I still prefer the term 'clue'."

"Which isn't a term most people who aren't playing the board game use. And even if it was, you haven't actually provided us with one."

"It's better than what we had when I woke up this morning."

"Barely."

"What about the limousine in a middle class, working class neighbourhood, conveniently stopping moments before the discovery of Tricia's body was phoned in? Why the hell weren't your little uniformed comrades willing to consider evidence from Mr. Woo? And aren't they supposed to canvass the neighbourhood after something like this? Nobody even came to his door." I felt a little self-righteous indignation was called for.

Andy's a good friend. She put aside her professional disgust for a moment and thought about what I'd told her. "You said there was a Canadian flag on the licence plate?"

"Yeah," I told her.

"Which B.C. plates don't have. I don't think any provincial plates have the maple leaf on them," she continued more to herself than to me. "Except…" she added without finishing.

"Except for what?" I asked, sensing Andrea's brain clicking into high gear.

"Except for diplomatic plates." She smiled.

"As in cars driven by consular staff?" She nodded. "Jesus!" I proclaimed, again a little too loudly as two more elderly members of the congregation timed their passing by. I just smiled at the elderly man and woman and bid them a nice afternoon.

"Don't get too excited. That doesn't mean much yet. But it is an interesting coincidence that the department has been getting calls from the Serbian consulate, and we potentially have a diplomatic vehicle at or near the scene of the crime." Andrea was staring off into space, probably wondering how she could go about making use of this information on a case she was not connected to, at least not officially.

"I don't suppose you can go question the ambassador, or whatever they call him?" I asked, though I was pretty sure I knew the answer. You didn't need to be a lawyer to understand diplomatic immunity. What most people believed from having seen movie plotlines developed around the concept, was that diplomats could, and routinely did, get away with criminal acts in the host country. The opposite was true, at least in Canada's case. Indeed, it was the practice of most governments to seek the expulsion of diplomatic personnel who broke the host country's laws, as Canada had recently done with a Russian diplomat who had killed a pedestrian in Ontario while under the influence. It might not be the kind of justice one hoped for, but at least the offending party was removed from the country.

I knew what Andrea was thinking. If Serbia's diplomatic officers were in any way involved in a crime, they would most certainly be removed from the country. Canada could ask Serbia to waive diplomatic immunity to permit prosecution within our legal system, but such waivers were rarely given. In this case, however, which would be considered particularly heinous due to the nature of the crime, it was not beyond the scope of possibility. But I realized, as Andrea must have been thinking too, that before one could even begin to think about questioning diplomats, an act sure to create a national and international stir, one must be pretty damned sure of his facts.

"All we have is a Canadian flag on a licence plate," Andy said, voicing what we both knew was a resounding lack of evidence. "Even that is sketchy. Considering how dark it was, the rain, the age of your old witness and the requisite deteriorating eyesight, we still have bupkiss."

"You looked enthused a few moments ago," I reminded her. I didn't want her excitement to wane.

"Winston," she finally returned to focus. "It's possible that we're on to something here. But this isn't my case. I can't go to Smythe and tell her some old man may have seen a limousine with diplomatic tags, so can you drop your investigation of Turbot? We need to have something more."

"Can we at least go by the Serbian consulate and check out their cars?"

"For what? To see if they have diplomatic tags? Of course they will."

"To see if they have a limousine," I tried.

"Which is also quite likely. Look, from what you've told me, you don't even have a description of the car, other than it was very big. Even if we find a limousine with a flag on the plate, which is virtually guaranteed, we've got nothing to say that car was at the scene. We'll need to go back to the remaining houses to see if anyone saw a limousine that night, and maybe a licence plate."

"We?" I asked.

"Okay, me." I was surprised by her answer. I was thinking she really meant I would have to go back door to door.

"Andy, you can't do that. It's not your case, and if someone finds you out, you're in deep shit. I appreciate your help, but between Derek and me, we can handle it."

"Bullshit," she told me forcefully. I looked around, expecting to see some other church lady standing beside us at the wrong time.

This time, we lucked out. "You're too slow, and you're getting to be too public. You already told me your visit to the neighbourhood generated hostility. Derek makes too much money to visit East Van. I can flash my badge, ask a couple of pertinent questions and be gone. People don't generally check to see if you are listed as the official investigating officer. I ask, they answer."

She had a point. Most people when confronted by a police officer will dutifully answer questions because they feel they don't have a choice. It was a point of law that often had pissed me off as a defence counsel, but in this instance it seemed to be working in my favour, so I was quickly tossing my principles aside. Hmmm. Just like a lawyer.

"What should I do then?" I asked, feeling a bit left out of my own investigation.

"You should go back to doing what you set out to do in the first place: get Carl's alibi locked up tight. Got any plans to do that?"

I explained to her how Carl had telephoned his house on the night of the murder and that the call should still be showing on his call display box at his house.

"You know the police will have been in there?" she asked.

"Yeah, but it's not a crime scene, and he is my client, so I should be able to get in. I'm sure they wouldn't have erased the call display unit, and if they did, they would have written down any numbers, right?"

"If they're good, and they are. You got a key?"

Another flaw in my plan. I hadn't thought about how I was going to get into Carl's house. "I'll stop by and check in with Carl, then pick up his house key from his personal effects at the jail."

"Good. Dinner at my place tonight?"

"You're cooking for me?"

"No. You're bringing take-out. I just don't want to risk meeting at your place and having the 'ex' show up again unannounced."

She got into her car and closed the door without saying goodbye.

Twenty-One

Carl looked much better than when I had left him on Saturday afternoon. In fact, if it were possible for it to be so, he was almost chipper; focusing on preparing his classes seemed to give him a new purpose and energy to do more than mope around in his cell. It had definitely been one of my better ideas, and I gave myself a metaphoric pat on the back. My visit was brief, and after he elicited a renewed promise from me to return with his beloved biology textbooks, I obtained his house keys and headed back to East Vancouver for the second time that day to check out the Turbot residence.

Crime scene tape, if there had been any, had already been removed, and in the various cars lining the quiet street, I could see no indication anyone had been posted to block entry. Whatever the police might have wanted to find, they had either left already disappointed or had found what they'd wanted and moved on. I wondered if they had found anything with potentially probative value I'd have to try to explain away, much like Carl's romantic relationship with Tricia. I really had no way of knowing until discovery, when Crown would be obligated to share their evidence with me, so I tried to put it out of my mind for the time being.

The house seemed very quiet as I stood inside the doorway. I couldn't think of a reason it shouldn't be, but the stillness already struck me as strange and made the hairs on my arms stand up in eerie alarm. Before going further, I turned and locked the front door. I didn't want to be the victim of a crime in someone else's home.

Heading up the stairs, I took in the scene in the living room. I was certain police had been through, but there was no evidence of it. Detectives have become very careful about homes and businesses they search; it is bad PR for the department when the media shows a residence has been summarily tossed by the cops.

A long, narrow hallway to the left of the kitchen led away from the living room, in a floor plan identical to Mr. Woo's, except in reverse. The first room on the left seemed to be Carl's study. A corner-fitting desk held a computer and printer, both of which looked to be a couple of years old. I flicked on the Hewlett-Packard and thought I'd see if I could find anything of interest.

Two bookshelves took up a large portion of the opposite wall. I scanned the titles, bracing myself for *Lolita,* but not finding it. There were no books I figured the police would be able to identify as showing that Carl had a propensity towards violence or pedophilia. In fact, Carl's reading interests did not appear to extend any further than science books and the occasional journal on science education. Dedicated. I flipped open my list of prescribed texts he had given me, found them and laid them out on the desk to take with me on the way out.

I wasn't sure what else to look for. In retrospect, I might have been better off having Andrea do the house search while I continued with the neighbourhood canvass, but I knew I could not have asked her to do that. I also figured it would be easy to search a house to find evidence of a person's guilt, but more skill and critical thought was required to search a house for evidence of a person's innocence.

I could find nothing of value to our case in Carl's little study, but I also couldn't think of anything useful I might find in any other room. And I especially didn't want to go poking around the Turbots' master bedroom. I was about to give up and leave when I remembered the computer, now fully booted and waiting to do my bidding. I pulled up the rolling office chair and sat down to peruse the hard drive's contents. It is usually pretty easy to determine a person's level of sophistication in computer skills. Those with fewer skills seem to have the simplest filing system. In Carl's case, a folder sat on the desktop simply titled "Carl". Another sat just above it titled "Bonnie". Since Carl was my primary concern, I decided I would begin my invasive search with his files.

Some would argue—and my ex-wife certainly has—that I'm an obsessive compulsive. I prefer to think of myself as neat and orderly. It's a character trait—a positive one I believe—that extends to my personal computer. It irritates me to no end when other people cannot manage their computer files in an orderly fashion. I had to resist a powerful urge to re-organize Carl's computer life. Inside the "Carl" folder—it was practically a miracle he'd even managed that small piece of techno wizardry—were probably hundreds of documents with titles ranging from "Doc1", clearly one his earlier efforts, to "BI12examphilo". Anything and everything Carl did on his computer, from teaching notes and assignments, to letters and report card information, was summarily dumped into one folder. How did he ever find anything? My mind began racing, creating a system through which I could establish some order, then I stopped myself. Carl was not paying me as a computer consultant. Come to think of it, he wasn't paying me at all. All the more reason to limit my efforts to that which would help his defence.

A fairly quick browse through his files did not turn up anything so obvious as "IloveTrish.doc". Adjusting the display to list the folder's contents by date, I began reading through items in the last month. Nothing was there to indicate correspondence to Tricia that would establish the date they had broken up or detailing the prank phone calls he'd been receiving. The most recent files in the folder primarily dealt with school matters, including a host of letters to parents dated just days before, to accompany report cards scheduled to be sent home on the following Tuesday. There was a letter for each of Carl's students—something teachers at my school did not generally do. I had already learned to select "canned" comments from a database list; by selecting a number, a one sentence comment appeared on the report card. Carl obviously didn't feel that was sufficient. Dedication. Again.

I closed Carl's folder and stole a quick peek at Bonnie's. Her folder seemed equally devoid of systematic organization and even less used than Carl's. Clearly, Bonnie had not much use for the home computer. Maybe she used one at work all day and couldn't face any more screen time when she got home at night. I had no idea what Bonnie did for a living, or for that matter, where Bonnie had been the night Tricia was killed. I put that thought aside for the time being.

I closed up Bonnie's file and launched the Turbots' email program. Judging by what appeared to be a fairly limited use of the computer's abilities, I wasn't expecting to find Carl was a real net hound, but it was an almost unheard of thing for people not to be at least moderately connected. It was here I found the first nugget of interest. Carl had so much to learn about his computer. In the "preferences" section of the program, Carl's program was set to keep a copy of sent email on the hard drive. Come to think of it, my own personal computer was set to do the same thing, though I had set mine that way because, as a lawyer, I had fostered the habit of keeping virtually every document and email I had had anything to do with. Of course, I wasn't trying to conceal an illicit affair with a teenaged girl.

And that's where I found it. Carl had written to Tricia using his home computer and had actually saved the emails. True, Tricia had a Hotmail address with a pseudonym which did not specifically identify her, but it didn't take me long to figure it out either. There were seven messages sent to Tricia, all of which appeared to be replies to messages the late student had sent to her teacher/lover. It wasn't graphic; there were no steamy, erotic passages between torrid lovers, but the more recent of the communiqués expressed my client's desire to see Tricia do well and in the second to last email he'd sent her, the magic word appeared: love.

Carl was not only bad with computers, he was hopelessly ineffective at cheating on his wife. Morally, I knew it wasn't a skill I should even concern myself with helping him to improve, but it was painful to see—for lack of a better justification—a fellow guy so hopelessly inept at covering his philandering trail. True, in high school, I had been dumb enough to date two girls at the same time, but I had taken great pains to keep the two relationships hidden. My problem had been my mouth—no big surprise there.

Carl had told me his wife had been suspicious nearly a week earlier and had moved out shortly thereafter. Logically, that told me whatever suspicions Bonnie had had, something had happened to confirm those feelings. It seemed quite likely she had uncovered Carl's affair through the same emails I was reading.

"Who the hell are you?" a woman's voice practically screamed.

I quickly hit ctrl + q to exit the email program and turned to face my accuser. Bonnie Turbot, I presumed, stood briefly in the doorway to the study, and panic was just beginning to set in. She turned to flee.

"Bonnie! Wait!" I cried out. "It's okay! I'm Carl's lawyer!" She reappeared in the doorway, ashen-faced and breathing heavily. I noticed my own pulse was racing. Her green eyes seemed now to focus on me, and recognition flashed across her face.

"Winston Patrick," she said through slightly quickened breath. "You've become quite the celebrity," she added dryly.

"So far the paparazzi pretty much lets me live my life." I paused for a moment. "I didn't hear you come in." Locking the door behind me only worked as a security measure against those who did not have a key of their own.

"Find what you were looking for?" she pointed towards the computer on the desk behind me. Lawyer for her husband or no, I was still snooping. Though I had quit the email program, there was no escaping that I was the proverbial kid with my hand in the cookie jar.

"You're assuming I had any idea what I was looking for." I tried to downplay my electronic spying. "I was just reviewing some information that might be useful."

"And what did you find of use to my husband's defence?" she asked, and the tone of her question answered questions. She had even managed to paint quotation marks with her voice around the word "husband".

"Nothing really," I lied. She knew I was lying, and she knew I knew she knew. Bonnie Turbot had turned from scared homeowner victim to interrogator, prosecutor and judge. The transformation had taken seconds.

At first, second and even third glance, it was difficult to understand what had led Carl to cheat on his wife. Bonnie Turbot would not be found on the cover of a glamour magazine, but she had strong, lovely features that caught your eye. Her green eyes, which were steely to the point of viciousness at the moment, shone out from under dark brown, nearly black hair. At a distance, I would guess her ethnicity to be generically European. There's always much more to a relationship than meets the eye—I am practically a poster child for that concept. But on the surface, first impressions had me silently questioning what could have led Carl to a teenager instead of this woman before me—other than the obvious allure of Tricia's youth and perhaps the onset of a premature mid-life crisis on my client's part. I didn't figure asking Bonnie about it would have been productive at the moment.

"Maybe I can help you," Bonnie resumed questioning me. "Would you like to read his love emails to his young protégée or perhaps his terribly simplistic journal in which he laments what he's gotten himself into?"

"There's a journal?" I asked. I had searched Carl's files for that very item.

"There *was*," she confirmed. "Until I deleted it. I was angry."

"Understandably," I agreed with her, because I couldn't think of a reasonable way to scold her for deleting a document I wanted to read. We looked at each other for a time. Bonnie Turbot's breathing had slowed from panic pace to slow, deep breaths, as though she was sleeping while she stood staring me down. It was disconcerting.

"So he doesn't deny it then?" she asked.

"Excuse me?"

"The thing. The affair he was having with that..." She paused, no doubt wanting to hurl invective at the "other woman" but refraining considering the other woman had been, in essence, a kid and was now a dead kid. "His affair with his student," she managed to finish her sentence. "He's admitted it finally?"

I smiled awkwardly. "I really can't discuss that. It's privileged conversation between solicitor and client."

Her eyes flared fire at me. "Whatever," she declared and turned her back to march away, leaving me alone again in the study. I stood for a few moments wondering what to do next. It was one of those awkward situations. Do I leave? Go back to snooping? Given the first impression I had managed to make, I figured I should at least try to talk to her while I was there. Who knew if she'd let me in the next time I showed up? Of course, I had a key, but she could always have the locks changed.

After arguing with myself a few moments longer, I finally went in search of Bonnie. I found her in the kitchen, putting the kettle onto the stove.

"Tea?" she asked, not at all surprised I was still with her in the house, but talking to me as though I were a casual visitor. Maybe I was back on side.

"Please."

She went about pulling out two mugs from the dark brown, 1970s-era cabinets, placing a tea bag in each cup, without bothering to employ a teapot. My mother would be outraged. This behaviour ruled out Great Britain as a primary component of Bonnie's European ethnicity.

"You did find the emails?" she asked again. "I found those after I found his 'journal.'" She said "journal" with the same verbal scorn with which she'd used the word "husband" earlier. Given this information had not come directly from my client, I felt I could respond truthfully.

"Yes. I did."

"Idiot," she hissed. "I can't believe he would write to her from our own computer." She was in that stage of emotion where her hurt at her discovery of Carl's infidelity had at least temporarily been replaced by rage.

"I got the impression Carl is not the most savvy user of computers," I added, inadvertently adding fuel to her vitriol.

"You're not kidding," she growled. "It was painful for me to teach him what little he knows." The kettle boiled, and she poured steaming water into each of the mugs. Reaching in with a spoon, she tossed the tea bags down the sink but did not make any move to turn on the garbage disposal. It took all of my self control not to walk over and do it for her. Did she not know how tea bags can stain a sink? Okay. Maybe I am a little obsessive compulsive.

"Did you always make a habit of checking up on what Carl does on the computer?" I asked with just a little accusation in my voice.

Bonnie turned to face me. "Hey! He was the one cheating on me from our own computer. How do I know he wasn't fucking her in our own bed?"

I didn't have an answer to that and would not have proffered one if I had. She had hot tea within throwing distance, and judging from the tea bags in the sink, she wasn't afraid to make a mess.

"I had sent something from work to our home email address," she continued calmly. Her emotions ran from raging hot to serene at the changing of the second hands on the wall-mounted clock. She took a sip of her piping hot tea. "I logged onto our computer here at home to download the email I'd sent from the office. Along with my message came one from her." Dead or no, the thought of Tricia still naturally brought up harsh feelings in this spurned spouse.

"What is it you do?" I asked.

"I'm a social worker. Ministry of Children and Families, Child Protection Branch. Ironic, huh?" Ouch. Even if she were planning to forgive and forget her husband's transgressions, she was duty-bound by her profession to see to the safekeeping of the child. As though reading my thoughts, Bonnie continued. "So not only is my husband cheating on me, he's cheating on me with a woman so young that I have to report his conduct. So much for not airing your dirty laundry." As quickly as it had disappeared, her anger had resurfaced.

"And did you?"

"Did I what?" she snapped.

"Did you report your husband to your supervisor or to another case worker?" I wondered how large the web of people who knew about Carl's romantic liaisons was.

Bonnie walked slowly over to the refrigerator, momentarily lost in thought. The refrigerator was of the harvest gold variety, much like the one I had grown up with in my parents' kitchen. "No."

"Why not?"

"I wasn't thinking," Bonnie said, reaching inside the fridge. "Milk?"

"Thank you," I replied and stood by the counter as she brought it over to me. She simply handed me the four litre plastic jug the milk came in.

"Sugar?"

"No, thank you. Milk is just fine." Bonnie continued to sip at her scalding tea, to which she had added neither milk nor sugar. Strong tea. Strong woman. She leaned her backside against the counter, staring at me or perhaps through me.

"I'm sorry," she said at last. "What were we talking about?"

"You were telling me why you didn't do something social worker-esque about Carl's involvement with one of his students."

She looked at me seriously, another wave of anger rising. It seemed it didn't matter what I said, she simply went from calm to anger in a kind of rhythmic pattern. "Why do you think?" she demanded rhetorically. "It isn't bad enough what he's doing to me and what he's doing to her? You figure I wanted to share that around the office?"

"You couldn't have shared it with another office?"

"What's your point, Mr. Patrick? You figure if I had done something official, the kid might not have been killed?"

"I'm not entirely certain I have a point, Ms. Turbot. I'm kind of grasping at straws here." She considered that for a minute. Since I could see the anger wave receding, and I hadn't quite measured the wavelengths yet, I sensed this might be the opportune time to hit her with a few of the heavy questions. "Do you think your husband killed Tricia Bellamy, Ms Turbot?"

She took an enormous breath, held it for about thirty seconds then let it out before answering. "The police already asked me," she said ambiguously.

"And now I'm asking you. Putting aside whatever facts the police think they've given you, do you think your husband is capable of having killed a student, even one who was threatening to expose their relationship?"

For the first time since I met her, Bonnie's eyes began to soften and even moisten to near tears. "No," she whispered. She was fighting back her tears now, so I waited until she could give me her full response. "I half-wanted to believe he killed her, I was so mad at him. You have no idea what it's like to find out you're being cheated on."

"No, I don't," I agreed.

213

"And then when she was murdered, I'll actually admit to you I was scared for a while. I was scared for him, and then when it hit me he might have actually strangled a girl to death, I was a little scared of him."

"You thought he might hurt you?"

"No. I don't know," she sighed, exasperated. She put down her tea cup. "When everything started pointing at him, yeah, I did think maybe he did it. He's got a temper, maybe it could have been him. But the more I've thought about it over the last few days since I left, the more I realized Carl just didn't have it in him to do something like that. I just can't believe he did." This was sounding a little bit better to me, or at least a bit more useful in terms of using Bonnie Turbot as a defence witness. I had to get one thing out of the way first.

"Ms Turbot," I began, then opted for a gentler touch. "Bonnie. I want to ask you something that is going to sound truly awful considering I'm defending your husband, but I'm going to ask it anyway."

She looked up at me, eyes dry again, and I could sense that the calm wave might have ebbed, and the anger behind it was on its way. "What?"

Full steam ahead. "Where were you the night Tricia was killed?"

"You fucker!" she hissed. "You break into my house, snoop through my things and now you try to blame me to get my cheating husband off?"

"Bonnie!" I protested. "I am merely trying to ascertain where you were, because Carl said he talked to you that night on the phone, from school. If that's true, if you remember talking to him, it may just prove Carl could not have been committing the murder."

"Unless he had someone do it." That was a turn I had not expected the conversation to take, especially coming from his wife.

"Let's leave that possibility aside for now. Do you remember talking to Carl that night?"

She thought about it for a moment. "I don't know. Probably. He usually calls me at some point or another if he stays at school late."

"But you don't know for sure if he called you?" I prodded at her memory.

She seemed to search the recesses of her memory. "Yeah. He did. He always does. I'm sure he called me."

"Do you remember what time?"

She thought about that too. "Around seven thirty or so?"

"Carl mentioned you have a call display unit on your telephone. Where is it?"

"It's over here," she replied, walking out of the kitchen and back into the living room. She pointed to the small, reclining box next to the telephone on an end table next to a very well worn recliner type chair. Looking down at the box, I noticed the screen was blank. I pressed the scroll key to review the last numbers displayed. There were none.

"Bonnie," I turned to my reluctant hostess, "when did you leave to go stay at your parents'?"

"Thursday afternoon. Why?"

"And you haven't been back here until tonight?"

"No. I only came back tonight because I needed some more things to wear to the office. What's wrong?"

"If Carl phoned home on Wednesday night from the school, the school's telephone number should be in the call display's memory. It isn't. You didn't erase the numbers before you left?"

She looked at me quizzically. "We've only just gotten the thing. I don't even know how to erase the numbers. I hadn't really even looked at it." It seemed strange to me that the police would go to the effort of erasing the numbers from the unit, if they'd looked at it at all and I told her so. I would have to check with Furlo and Smythe.

"That's odd. I can't imagine why they would have erased it. Standard procedure would be to leave everything as close as possible to the way it was, especially considering this wasn't the crime scene. But someone must have erased Wednesday night's calls."

"And every call since then," Bonnie added. I hadn't thought of that.

"It isn't possible that you haven't had any calls since Wednesday night either. I called here on Thursday and Friday to check up on Carl."

"So you mean someone has come in and deliberately erased the messages?"

"That's what it looks like," I confirmed. "I just don't know who, why or for that matter when."

"It had to be recently," Bonnie informed me. "I called here this afternoon to check messages."

The hairs on my arms began to stand up on end again as I glanced over towards the stairs down to the front door. "So somebody cleared the messages today," I said, half-asking a question. Bonnie looked at me, and the anger she had shown earlier gave way to discomfort. "Were you planning to stay here tonight?" I asked.

"Not now," she replied.

"Good. I'll wait with you while you get your things." For the next fifteen minutes, I waited, picking up Carl's textbooks from the study and keeping watch out the living room window. When Bonnie Turbot had collected enough things to get her through another couple of days at her parents' place, we left together.

Twenty-Two

Once Bonnie was safely on her way to her parents' place for the night, I dropped Carl's biology textbooks off with the security guard at the pre-trial centre then met with Andrea at her place to compare notes on what we'd learned. On the face of it, not a whole hell of a lot more, despite the hours we had been putting in. On the plus side, after canvassing more than a dozen individuals, Andrea had found one person who thought they maybe, kinda saw a limousine in the neighbourhood the day of Tricia's death. Outside of that, her canvass had turned up nothing.

It hadn't taken long once we got together before I was completely exhausted. Andy might interview and investigate for a living, but even when I was practicing law, there were pretty severe limits on how much footwork I was responsible for. In my practice, going out and collecting evidence was hardly something that took up my time. To make matters worse, the first thing I noticed when I returned to my apartment was a file folder on my dining room table. I had left it there when I'd come home on Friday night, and it had sat there unopened all weekend. It contained assignments that had to be marked before I returned to school on Monday morning. I made a half-hearted effort to do some marking, but by the time I'd skimmed through even the first assignment at the top of the stack, my heart wasn't in it. I went to bed.

As usual, sleep escaped me. Sunday night sleeplessness was a phenomenon I had experienced since I'd graduated from law school. There was something daunting about a whole work week ahead of me that made it nearly impossible to wind down. Consequently, while I know very few people who look forward to a

Monday morning, my first days of the week always seemed especially bad. And this one promised to be a doozy. By four o'clock, when I'd slept all I knew I would, I got up and began my running ritual. I made it only a block before my right calf began to cramp fearfully. Sunday morning's run had been long enough that my body had simply decided it would run no more until I was well-rested. Given that I wasn't sleeping, I couldn't even give my body an estimate when that rest might happen. It was a vicious cycle.

If there was one bright spot to the start of my week, it was that there was no press corps waiting upon my arrival at Sir John A. Macdonald Secondary. That was hardly surprising, since I arrived at school around six thirty, both sleeping and running having been ruled out. In fact, I arrived at the exact same moment as the daytime caretaker, who was just unlocking the side entrance door nearest the staff parking lot.

Rudy Herndier had been the janitor at the school since before I was in high school. Now well into his fifties, he showed few signs of slowing down or aging at all, save for what was probably significantly less hair than he had begun his janitorial career with. Though I had spoken with him only briefly, he always had a friendly hello for me, as I suspected he had for anyone who came across his path.

"Good morning, Winston," he said with surprise. "This is early even by your standards. You keep this up, they're going to make you principal."

"Good morning, Rudy," I replied. "It seems highly unlikely early promotion is in the cards at this point."

He nodded knowingly. He probably knew more about what went on in the school than anyone else. "Yeah," he said a little sadly, "I suspect you're probably number one on the boss's shit list."

I smiled and nearly laughed at that. As unpleasant as I knew the day was probably going to be, fielding question after question about the case—most of which I would be unable to answer—it was amusing at least that Don McFadden's obvious disdain for me was apparent to others. "I'm not expecting a Christmas card, no," I agreed.

Rudy finished unlocking the door and stepped inside. "Gotta run," he told me. With that he took off on a brisk trot towards the main office where, I suspect, he was hurrying to shut off the school's burglar alarm. A few moments later, I too arrived at the main office door, where Rudy was closing and locking an electrical panel with one of an enormous number of keys attached to one of those chain pulley key rings. How a janitor ever kept that number of keys straight in his head was baffling. I had two keys for the school, and I was constantly attempting the wrong one every time I went to open my classroom door. "How's our boy doing?" Rudy asked me.

"Carl?"

"The very one," he confirmed. "I imagine he must be awfully frightened in jail there."

"It isn't pleasant, but he's holding it together," I confirmed.

Rudy looked at me seriously. "Any realistic hope of him getting out of there?"

"He should be out later this morning."

"Really?" he sounded surprised.

"Bail," I told him. "We're nowhere near trial yet, but I have a good friend who is a very good lawyer who will be working on Carl's interim release. I expect he'll be home by noon."

He smiled at that. "Well. That's good news." It was? I wasn't really expecting a whole lot of moral support from school employees, but it was nice to have someone on side. "There's just no way he killed that poor girl."

"I don't think so either." I headed towards my mailbox to see what kind of superfluous paper work I would find in there this morning. Fortunately, I was there ahead of everyone, so no one would have had a chance to dump in my box more junk for me to fill out.

"I know so." He said it with such conviction I actually stopped and turned around.

"You sound pretty sure of yourself," I said to him casually. "Do you know Carl well?"

"Well enough to know he wasn't capable of strangling a student. That man practically lives for working with those kids. There's just no way he could bring harm to one of them." I wondered if Rudy knew about Carl and Tricia's extracurricular activities and how that might have impacted his assessment of Carl's homicidal capabilities.

"I've only known him a short while," I agreed, "but I'd have to say he is definitely not the murderous type."

"That and the fact he was here that night. I don't know how the police have even arrested him. How could he be working in the lab and killing the poor girl at the same time?"

"What was that?" I blurted out.

Rudy looked baffled. "What was what?"

"You said Carl was here the night of the murder."

"Yes."

"How do you know? Were you still here late in the evening?"

Rudy let out a laugh. "Oh God, no. I'm an hourly man. Strictly by the book, or the union'd be all over my arse. No. No. But Jurgen remembers clear as day he talked to Carl around eight or eight fifteen that night. He had just come back from supper break."

I reached into my coat pocket and pulled out my notebook. Flipping it open to a page, I asked "Jurgen Pathe? From the night crew?"

Rudy looked surprised. "Yeah. Jurgen. You haven't talked to him?"

"No. I haven't."

"Well, shit, no wonder poor Carl is still locked up. I'll have him come by and see you when he gets on shift this afternoon."

I looked at Rudy warmly. "Thank you, Rudy. I appreciate it."

With a shrug, he turned to leave. "No problem."

The day was looking up, so much so that I went to my classroom with a file folder full of student assignments and spent an hour and a half catching up on my teacher work. It was too soon to be popping out the victory champagne, but knowing Derek would soon be working on Carl's release and that I had what sounded like a good alibi witness about to blow a hole in Furlo's investigation, I was feeling somewhat less distracted in my teaching duties that morning. About ten minutes before classes were scheduled to begin, I heard a slight rapping at my open classroom door. Looking up, I saw Christine Wilson from the English department. Outside of Carl, Christine was the closest approximation to a friend I had on staff. She looked worried.

"Hey, Christine," I said in greeting.

"Hi, Winston," she replied a little formally. "Sorry to interrupt you while you're working."

"No problem. Peace and quiet time has long since expired," I told her, noting the growing volume of teenager noise in the hallway as the first period was drawing near. "What's up?"

Christine looked a little uncomfortable, which was unusual. Since I'd been at the school, I had been drawn to Christine's upfront, occasionally blunt perspective on things. In faculty meetings, she could be counted on to be the first teacher to call "bullshit" when presented with a particularly inane piece of bureaucracy by the administration. For her to approach me tentatively was unusual given her nature, but considering the events of the past week, understandable. She walked into the classroom and closed the door behind her.

"Have you talked to anyone this morning?"

It was almost a rhetorical question, but in the interest of speeding up the conversation, I answered anyway. "Not really. I chatted with Rudy briefly when I got here. I came in pretty early, and I've been catching up on marking I had planned to do over the weekend. I kind of got sidetracked by other things the last couple of days." I smiled at her to break the tension.

"So I guess you haven't been to the staff room?" she suggested.

"No. Why? What's up?"

She looked around uneasily, as though others might be listening in. "There's a lot of not too friendly chat going on among the staff."

"Like what?"

"There are people who are not too pleased with the fact Carl is scheduled for a bail hearing today. There's a kind of lynch mob mentality among some of our colleagues."

"Some of them?"

"Not all of them. Definitely not. But some very unpleasant, umm, details seem to be emerging in the discussion."

"Such as?" I was using a lot of verb-less sentences, allowing Christine to fill in the appropriate parts of speech. When people were uncomfortable with what they had to say, the less you interrupted them the better.

Christine sank into the student desk, which, given her size, was actually easier for her to do than it was for many of my Grade Twelve students. Whenever holding forth to my students too long in class, I tried to remember how comfortable those one piece, desk-and-chair-combined seats were. Though she physically fit into the torturous apparatus, she still looked uneasy.

"Christine, it's okay. Just tell me," I tried to encourage her to continue.

She took in and let out a deep breath before continuing. "The rumour mill has it that Carl and Tricia Bellamy were sleeping together." She said it while staring down at the desk, like a student unsure of the appropriate response when called upon in class. She felt the pause hanging between us and finally looked up for my reaction.

"I see," was all I gave her. That was a detail that had not yet made it to the media; having had time to scan two dailies this morning, I was sure of that. Though some of the media coverage hinted at the topic when searching for a possible motive, none of the outlets as far as I could tell had come right out and suggested it. They were rightfully concerned about the possibility of a lawsuit should they allege that impropriety without solid supporting evidence. Even Furlo would not have allowed that information to leak out among our teaching staff lest it hinder the investigation. That told me the information had probably been shared in confidence between the principal and a teacher he trusted—though even Don didn't know for sure if the relationship had happened as Trish reported it—or that teachers were simply speculating on their own. I wasn't really surprised. If I were not directly involved in Carl's defence, I'm sure a romantic liaison would be the kind of motive I would suspect too.

Christine looked at me as though anticipating some further explanation. "So?" she asked.

"So?" I parroted.

I think she recognized I was ethically bound not to say much, but she needed some reassurances in her own mind. "So what are you going to do?" she asked.

"About the rumours? Nothing," I told her. "Look, this is nothing unusual. It happens in any high profile legal case. People talk about it and offer hypotheses about what may have happened. It's natural, doubly so because people here know both the victim and the accused. I can't stop them from talking."

"So you're not going to, I don't know, go in there and refute the allegations?"

"I'm going to do no such thing. It may sound sanctimonious, but my sideline job right now is to defend Carl in the courts, not in the media, not in the faculty lounge, not in the classroom. I will share what information about his defence is appropriate to whatever setting I happen to be in. Suffice to say I am confident this matter will be resolved quite shortly," I told her, thinking to myself that once I confirmed Carl's alibi with Jurgen Pathe, the police would pretty much be forced to refocus their investigation in another direction. Christine, however, looked a little disappointed.

"Oh," she said flatly.

"I really don't have any choice."

"It's just that, I'm worried about you too, Win," she told me. "Among the lynch mob side of the staff, there is growing discontent about your involvement in Carl's defence."

"That's to be expected. Defence lawyers are rarely winners of popularity contests." She didn't look convinced. "Look, I'll focus on mending any fences once Carl's case is cleared. And I feel pretty confident in assuring you it will be."

That seemed to brighten her a little. She let out a sigh. "That's good. It doesn't make any of this any easier thinking one of our own colleagues—no, one of our friends may have been involved." The warning bell rang to let kids know they had five minutes to get to their first class. "I'd better let you go," she said, rising from the desk.

"Thank you for telling me how people were feeling. I appreciate it."

She smiled a lovely, warm smile at me as she approached the door. "You may just want to avoid large gatherings in the staff room for a while. Especially if there's rope around."

"I'll do that."

"And you can always eat lunch in my room with me," she said playfully. I detected flirtatiousness in the suggestion, but having a disastrous track record with the opposite sex, I didn't want to presume too much.

"I might just do that, too." With that she opened the door and disappeared into the throng of Grade Nine social studies students pushing their way into the room.

Thank God I had ninth graders first period in the morning. That was a statement I am sure few teachers make very often, but in this case it was a good thing. Though Grade Nine students are at a human development stage often referred to by educators as "mentalpause", their energy can be contagious, and more importantly, their focus is often easily diverted in new directions. This was definitely true of my first period class. They approached me tentatively, as though they knew full well there was something amiss about their teacher's involvement in this very public affair, but they couldn't quite put their little fingers on it. Only one student actually had the temerity to ask about the events of the weekend and of what was happening to one of their science teachers. I was able to brush through a non-committal response fairly quickly and get the class focused on doing the work I had been meticulously planning. Okay, I hadn't been meticulously planning anything, but they were fourteen years old. Pushing their minds in another direction didn't require a great deal of meticulous planning. I knew it wouldn't be that easy with my senior law class I would see in the afternoon, but I had a few hours before I had to worry about them.

By lunchtime, I was admittedly hungry for a little bit of adult contact, but I was wary after Christine's cautionary note. I thought I would test the waters first by heading down to the main office to check for messages. As I walked down the hall, I felt like Moses parting the Red Sea, or at least like Charlton Heston in the movie version, since the path that cleared for me as I walked felt very artificial. Students were stepping aside not out of respect for their elders—thank God for that, really—but because kids were truly standing on the sides to gawk at me. I may have been teaching at the school for nearly three months, but many kids were seeing me for the first time. It was a little like being a rock star, except one who was leaving a courtroom after escaping some nefarious charges. A few fingers, whose owners clearly had forgotten their mothers' admonitions against such conduct, even pointed directly at me as I approached or passed, with their owners conversing in whispers about my identity.

Recognizing that if the kids—who as a general rule are more forgiving than adults—were displaying such obvious emotion about me, a trip to the faculty lounge to enjoy some mature conversation for the duration of the lunch period was most definitely not a good plan. If I wanted to sit through a meal surrounded by hostility, I could get an invite over to my ex-in-laws' for dinner. The food was at least better. On the other hand, having been at the school since the wee hours, I was nearing the point of starvation. I was even willing to trust my innards to the school's cafeteria. School cafeterias are break-even operations, meaning they have to sell enough of their wares to pay for themselves. Since the prevailing theory on teenage food consumption states only fried junk food will be eaten, many school cafeterias are pretty much a burger and fries operation. Still, I was hungry.

The school cafeteria can be a pretty unwelcoming place at the best of times for those who prefer to dine without shouting, kids running around and the occasional morsels of food being launched through the air. I am one of those people. Even in the cafeteria my infamy had preceded me, and a hush fell over the room. In my limited teaching experience, it was the quietest the cafeteria had even been, and I almost decided to stay in there to eat my lunch, but after purchasing my greasy cheeseburger, fries and chocolate milk—there had to be some nutrient value to the meal—I carried my tray back towards my room, stopping at the main office along the way for the dreaded messages.

And messages a-plenty there were. If half my students' parents had called last week after my name had first appeared in the local media, the other half had called this morning, with repeat calls from about a third of the first bunch. I didn't bother to sort through them all in the office. The hostile glances and outright glares I was receiving from most of the office staff told me this was not going to be the most welcoming crowd either. So piling my messages and assorted notes and bureau-glom onto my cafeteria tray, I went back to my classroom, closing and locking the door behind me. If anyone was planning to vent their feelings towards Carl, me, or the legal system in general, I wasn't about to permit them to do it on my time.

I began chomping on my limp cheeseburger while flipping through the stack of pink "While You Were Out" slips. It was a strange header for message pads in a school. Teachers rarely got to be out of the building during the day. I guess no office supply company has thought to print up "While You Were Trapped in an Unventilated Room with a Group of Teenagers" slips. Most were of the generic variety, with the little box that said "Please Call" ticked. It's a little known fact about teaching that calling parents back is not always a simple task, particularly in a large school like the one I taught in. The simple reason is that it is often impossible to find an available telephone, or if you can find a phone, to find an available outside line on which to make a call. Most schools, even large ones, have no more than five or six phone lines. When there are more than two thousand kids and well over a hundred teachers, counsellors, support staff and administrators in a building, five phone lines doesn't really offer many opportunities. Added to the fact that it was lunchtime, when any teacher who needed to contact parents was trying to do so, I had found it virtually impossible to make any telephone contact with parents.

Other messages had comments written in the "Message" portion of the slip. These seemed to be in the short form parlance of the secretaries who were burdened with answering my phone calls. The messages ranged from "you should be fired," to "why are you doing this?" to "tell him he's an asshole," though the secretary who transcribed the message was delicate enough to jot down "a-hole".

Among all of the messages and a memo from my union inviting me to a retirement benefits workshop—which seemed a bit premature, even considering the school population's current mood toward me—there was a sealed white envelope with my name carefully written in blue ink on the front. There was no return address to indicate from whom the letter had been sent and no stamp to indicate it had originated from outside the building. Tearing open the envelope from the top—it is a pet peeve of mine that some people insist on tearing envelopes down one side—I pulled out the single sheet of white paper. Computer printed about halfway down the page was a very short message that read: "I have information for you. Meet me after school today across the street by the mausoleum. I will find you." The message was unsigned, unsurprisingly, and was cryptic only in that the party who wrote it wanted to meet me in a graveyard. Given that I was defending a murder case, it didn't seem like a place I wanted to visit on a rainy November afternoon.

After finishing my lunch and the remainder of the marking I had neglected to complete over the weekend, I pulled out my cell phone. Derek's personal assistant picked up the phone when I dialed his direct line. I asked if Derek had returned from court. His assistant asked who I was. I identified myself, after which she replied coolly, "Oh. It's you." Me and the ladies. Reluctantly, I could tell, she put me through to Derek, who had returned only moments before.

"How'd it go?" I asked him.

"Please," he told me, "it was a bail hearing."

"So you were successful?" I said, though I could not imagine him not being. In response, I could hear him munching on a sandwich. "No problems?"

"Only that you now owe me for your client's cab fare to send him home," Derek replied.

"I'll pay you by spotting you five points in our next racquetball game. Then maybe you can finally win a bet."

"You think I need to be spotted?"

"I think you do." A muted voice could be heard in Derek's office, no doubt his personal assistant—secretaries are so passé in the legal profession nowadays—standing in his doorway, making sure I wasn't about to lead Derek off his carefully crafted schedule again.

"We'll see," he replied.

"So it went well?"

"Absolutely." He paused and then returned. "Gotta go. I'm getting the glare." I could picture his entire office staff attempting to pry him away from me.

"Thanks."

"Yep," was all he bothered to say in reply. The line went dead, and I shut off my cell phone. It was annoying enough when kids' phones rang in class; I didn't want mine to interrupt my own lesson. That was that. As quickly as it had all begun, Carl was now safely at home awaiting the outcome of the next round of legal maneuvering. Placing the phone back in my jacket pocket, I crossed the room and opened my classroom door. Unfortunately, today was not a day in which I had a preparation period, so there would be no sneaking out early to check up on Carl's wellbeing, or to go early to the cemetery across the street to await this mysterious information that was too sensitive to write in a sealed envelope.

The rest of the afternoon passed by with little to throw me off my pedagogical path, though last period was another of my law classes, so the topic of conversation naturally turned to Carl Turbot's case and my involvement in it. With senior students it is much more difficult to distract them from a topic upon which they wish to spend some time, but after several of their questions were rebuked with a standard "I can't discuss that because of solicitor-client privilege," most soon tired of trying to pry loose further information and settled in to working on the projects I had assigned in the previous week.

The kids had barely made their way out the door when an adult head poked its way in. "Winston?" he asked.

I looked up to see a familiar face whose name, had I not been expecting him, would not have been known to me. "Jurgen," I replied, "come on in."

Jurgen Pathe entered the classroom, leaving in the doorway a rolling janitorial cart. He looked to be about my age, hair slightly greying at the temples. He looked a little tentative, as though he were being asked to stay after school against his will. "Rudy said you wanted to see me?" he asked. "About Carl Turbot?"

"Yeah," I told him. "I understand you talked to Carl last Wednesday night when he was here working late?"

"Sure," he said without the slightest hesitation. "I often run into Carl in his lab. He always seems to be here later than anyone else." I realized "anyone else" included me, since clearly I could barely recognize Jurgen's face as part of the evening shift janitorial crew.

I pulled my notebook out of my open briefcase and began to take notes. "You're absolutely certain you saw Carl on Wednesday night, the night Tricia Bellamy was killed?" I wanted to make sure his statement was crystal clear and that no one could accuse me of twisting his words or making suppositions not based on fact.

"Sure, yeah," he told me. "Yeah, I came back off of my dinner break and headed straight for his room."

"Why did you specifically go to Carl's room after your break?"

"Because when I had come in earlier to empty the trash cans and to sweep up, he had a couple of kids in the lab working with him. I didn't want to disturb them in case it was an assignment they were working on." That jibed with what Carl had told me about the lab students who had been working with him. "When I came off of my dinner break, I went directly to Carl's lab, because it was the room I had skipped along the way."

"And he was there when you went into the room?"

"Oh, absolutely. We talked for a few minutes while I was cleaning up. He looked like he was getting ready to leave."

"What did you talk about? Do you remember?"

He searched his memory for a few seconds. "I don't know that I remember exactly, but it was probably the usual stuff. Hockey, the shitty weather, that kind of thing."

I took a deep breath that I hoped he wouldn't notice. "Jurgen. Do you know what time it was you saw Carl?"

"I can't say for sure, down to the minute or anything, but it must have been a little after eight o'clock since that's when I came off my break."

"You're sure? You didn't take dinner break at a different time or anything that day?"

"No. It's pretty much always then. We often toss the TV on during dinner break and watch *Jeopardy*, which is over at eight. That's pretty much how we time the end of dinner break: Final Jeopardy equals back to work." He smiled and chuckled lightly at this mundane routine, and I smiled with him.

"Have you told this to the police?"

"Sure," he replied matter of factly. "I talked to a guy on the phone."

"Detective Furlo?" I asked.

He looked a bit confused. "No, I don't think so. That doesn't sound familiar."

"Did the police officer identify himself?"

"Yeah, well, I called them. Some guy on the phone told me the detectives on the case weren't in. So I left my name and number, and the guy said they'd get back to me. Never did, so I figured they didn't need my information."

"But they definitely knew what you were calling about?" I pressed on. If this was yet another witness the police were dutifully ignoring, I was going to start getting pretty pissed off.

"Absolutely," Jurgen insisted. "I told the guy on the phone exactly what I told you. That I saw Carl here that night. I called them on Friday afternoon after I saw on the news Friday that Carl had been questioned. I called right away. That's why I was so surprised to hear Carl had been arrested Friday night. I mean, how could they arrest him if they knew he had been here?"

"That's an excellent question. Jurgen, thank you so much. I can't tell you how helpful you've been." That was the truth, since now Carl's alibi was becoming even clearer.

"Hey, no problem. I knew Carl couldn't 'a done it. He's not the type. He's really a great guy. Always chattin.' Always friendly. No way he killed anyone, least of all a student."

I thanked Jurgen again, and he headed out the door to begin his cleaning rounds at the other end of the building. I perused again the stack of phone messages to which I would need to respond, but my eyes kept going back to the two single lines of type on the plain white paper. In all likelihood, it was some teenager's idea of a joke, adding an extra bit of intrigue to what was already an uncomfortable situation. Still, even if that were the case, how much cooler would I look as a teacher if I showed up, unafraid? Sometimes being a teacher is as much about image as being a teenager is.

J. Mac is located directly across the street from Mountain View Cemetery, a city-owned and operated public cemetery, interning the city's working class and holding a sufficient number of early Vancouver settlers to make the graveyard of historical significance. If kids were spooked or superstitious about the graveyard, it mostly didn't show. I frequently saw students who used the park-like setting as a short cut to homes on the other side of the massive green and granite space. It wasn't unheard of for students to use the quiet anonymity of the cemetery as a place to meet when skipping out of classes, or to smoke a joint or down a few beers on a Friday night. I hadn't attended in my own school days, but I did have friends that had, and I had once partaken of similar experiences in my youth. Fortunately, my graveside partying ambitions, coupled with my Catholic fear of doing anything smacking of sacrilege, had rendered my partying with the dead a one-time experience.

I waited until close to four o'clock before venturing out for my rendezvous with the mysterious correspondent. Since he or she had neglected to mention a time other than "after school," I opted to wait not only for the bulk of the students to have departed but also in hopeful anticipation of a break in the inclement weather. Of the former, I was fortunate that most kids are as anxious to leave the school on a Monday afternoon, as they are reluctant to return to it on a Monday morning. There was enough rumour and innuendo floating around about me without adding "creepy graveyard skulker" to the litany of adjectives students and no doubt their parents were using to describe me. Of the latter, I would probably be waiting until April for better weather, and I wasn't sure my messenger would hang out in the graveyard until then.

Mountain View was understandably deserted, given the rain. Leaning my umbrella into the wind, I wandered slowly down the access road, looking for any signs of life among the grave markers. A concrete building with surrounding wrought iron fencing sat towards the rear centre of the property, and I presumed this was the structure at which I was to meet my shy communicator. Reaching the structure, I still saw no one and proceeded on a tour of the circumference of the mausoleum, hoping whoever wanted to talk to me about the case would show before I caught pneumonia. As I rounded the back corner, a voice gently called to me from behind, "Mr. Patrick?"

I turned, startled, and who wouldn't be given the location, expecting to see a student who would burst out laughing, able to tell his friends how he'd scared the shit out of the law teacher. Instead, two men in long, heavy winter coats stood with their backs to a large tree. One wore a black baseball cap, pulled fairly low down over this face, the brim protecting him from the rain. The cap held a Molson Canadian beer logo, along with the admonition from Canada's largest brewer to "take care." The other had nothing protecting his head nor face, but did at least, sensibly, have his heavy woollen collar turned up to stop the rain drips from the tree overhead from running down his back. Both appeared to be in their early to mid-twenties, too old to attend the school, too young to be dressed in expensive, stylish coats more common on the colder east coast than on the generally mild west. "Yes," I replied only slightly breathily. "You said you had information for me?"

In reply, Baseball Cap—as I had quickly named him in my own head—stepped forward and hissed, "You fucker." At that his right arm shot forward so quickly I was barely aware of any movement. His closed, leather-gloved fist struck me so hard in the stomach that any air in my body blasted out in a whoosh, and I instantly fell to my knees. Because I think stupid things at stupid times, I briefly agreed with Andrea that I was, in fact, too skinny, and had I had a little more fat around my middle, I might have absorbed the shock of the punch a little less painfully. As it was, I was only able to double over on my knees and fight for breath. "What kind of pig are you that you want to free a child fucker? A child killer?" Baseball Cap continued. Now that he had spoken more than three syllables, I could detect a slight accent, European of some kind, but as I've said, I suck at identifying ethnicities.

My lungs burning from the sharp intakes of cold November air my body was taking in faster than I was ready for, I started to raise my head to face my attackers with questions of my own. Baseball Cap's friend, whom I had not yet had time to establish a nickname for, belted me with a swift backhanded slap against the side of my ear which sent me off my knees sideways into a fetal position on the soaking wet ground. My breath was slowly returning to me. I managed to turn my head slightly to look up at the two, more to ready myself for the next blow than in any attempt to identify them. Baseball Cap was saying something to me, but one ear was burning and ringing from the blow to the head while the other ear was pressed into the mud. He appeared to be asking me a question, but I was unable to breathe enough to respond, even if I had been able to hear.

Baseball Cap stepped forward and let loose a kick with his right foot, which caught me on the right hand side of my chest, just above the pectoral muscle, of which I have very little anyway. This time I heard myself groan as the force of a steel-toed boot sent me rolling over backwards, where I slammed up against a marble tombstone. I tried to maneuver myself into a sitting position with my back against the grave marker, if only to see what the two messengers would do next. As if to punish me for my insolence, Baseball Cap reached down and grabbed me by the front of my own mud covered jacket and hauled me to my feet. I was so scared, he practically had to hold me, as my knees wanted to buckle and put me back on the ground. By now I could begin to make out what he was saying.

"The police have done their jobs. They have their man. That is all that you need to worry about," he told me. For a moment it occurred to me that these two might actually be cops who were trying to intimidate me, but I couldn't believe that what little I had found out would have Furlo send goons over to try to dissuade me from further investigation.

"Do you understand?" his partner asked from over Baseball Cap's shoulder, and I noted his European accent was even thicker.

Like an idiot, rather than at least pretending to agree with them, I foolishly gasped out a question. "Who are you?" I wheezed, which, on the surface, seemed a perfectly sound piece of information to want to obtain. Baseball Cap answered by clenching his gloved hand and punching me across my left jaw. As my head snapped to the right, he duplicated his partner's backhand and sent my head spinning in the other direction.

"Are you fucking stupid?" he demanded. I wanted to apologize and tell him that yes, clearly I was stupid, and if he would just stop hitting me I could begin the journey to getting smarter. Unfortunately, all I could muster was a slight whimper that only seemed to make him angrier. Before I could even turn to deflect it, Baseball Cap raised his knee sharply, making contact with my groin. What little air was left in my deflated lungs blasted out and Baseball Cap let go of the front of my jacket, allowing me to crumple onto some unfortunate stiff's gravesite. On the way down, I actually heard glass break, which must have belonged to a vase holding flowers in front of the tombstone.

"You will leave this alone," the unnamed assailant ordered. As if to punctuate his point, he stood over me and spat, though mixed with the falling rain, I was unable to discern what were raindrops and what was saliva hitting my face. I lifted my head slightly, just as his running-shoed foot slammed into the side of my head. I remember being thankful for just a moment that at least he wasn't wearing boots like Baseball Cap was. The last thing I noticed was my two attackers getting into their car, a long black limousine. Then my world went dark.

Twenty-Three

Andrea and Detective Jasmine Smythe both looked stern. On the back wall of the emergency room, Detective Michael Furlo had taken up the position in which I had grown accustomed to seeing him: arms folded across his chest, left leg crossed over his right at the ankles and leaning against the wall. He was the very picture of nonchalance, reluctantly brought into the hospital to find out what had happened to one of his least favourite defence lawyers.

I was having a hard time recalling all of the details myself, it had happened so quickly. In fact, I barely recalled waking up with my face pressed into the muddy grass in Mountain View graveyard. When I had looked up, a small group of students had gathered around me, obviously unsure of what exactly their next step should be on seeing one of their school's teachers lying prostrate in a graveyard. It was the fingers of one of the students, Cameron Graham, that had roused me out of unconsciousness when Cam had figured the least he could do was take my pulse to determine whether or not I was alive. By the time I had begun to focus and attempt to sit up, paramedics and fire department personnel had arrived, summoned by one of the many students who now routinely carry a cell phone. I had attempted to resist going to the hospital, but as I stood with the assistance of a paramedic, my body had disagreed with my decision, and I'd begun to slump back down to the ground. That had firmed the resolve of my rescuers to get me to hospital and, with a gaggle of high school students watching, I was carted off to Vancouver General, where less than an hour later I sat trying to explain myself to my friend and to the detectives.

"Why the hell did you go over there by yourself?" Andrea

demanded. Her voice was louder than usual, though that perception may have been the result of my pounding head.

"I figured it was a prank or something," I replied groggily.

"And this was a good reason to go out and meet pranksters in the cemetery?" Jasmine Smythe asked.

"I wasn't anticipating getting attacked."

Andrea shook her head in disgust. "Jesus, Win," she scolded. "A note says 'meet me in the graveyard', and you just wander over there?"

"Hey, they fooled me," I complained. "I'm not used to all of this cloak and dagger shit."

"Cloak and dagger?" Furlo suddenly opined from the back of the room. "It was an unsigned note! That's one step above a school kid tapping you on the shoulder and shouting 'boo'!"

"Thank you for your concern, Detective Furlo. I'm sorry my assault has taken you away from other important pursuits."

"That's it!" Furlo nearly shouted. "The little shit is obviously going to make it. I'm done here." He turned and headed out of the room, letting the door close behind him.

"You never miss a chance to piss him off, do you?" Smythe chided me gently.

"Sometimes I can't help myself."

"If it makes you feel any better, he made some snide comment about you when we heard about the attack. Something to the effect of: good, maybe they'll have to wire his mouth shut," Smythe told me with her warm smile.

"So you didn't recognize them at all?" Andrea asked, refocusing the conversation to the assault.

"No. I've never seen them before."

"But you said they had an accent," Smythe picked up. "European?"

"I think so," I admitted. "But I can't be sure. European was just a hunch. Czech. Hungarian. Russian."

"Serbian?" Andrea suggested just a little slyly.

"Definitely could have been from the Balkan region."

"Would you know the accent again if you heard it?" Smythe continued, oblivious to the message sent between Andrea and myself.

"I don't know," I admitted. "I think I could, but I'm no dialect expert." I paused for a moment. "I don't suppose this leads you to believe you've arrested the wrong man?"

"I think we'll need a little more than someone wanting to kick your ass."

"This doesn't seem a little out of the ordinary to you?" Andrea asked her colleague. Jasmine Smythe looked back at Andrea suspiciously, but Andrea continued. "I mean, how often does Joe Public go after defence attorneys simply because they think the crime is nasty?"

Jasmine thought about that a moment. "It is a little unusual," she conceded. "But this murder is getting a lot of attention. Shit, Winston, you've seen the coverage you've been getting. The media showed up at your school, for God's sake. It sure as hell wouldn't be difficult for someone to track you down. These goons didn't give you any indication of why they were so passionately interested in kicking the shit out of you?"

"No," I told her. "All they said was I should let the police do their jobs. As if I was the only thing stopping cops from earning an honest day's pay."

"Hey," she said, "my partner's gone. You don't have to keep up the insults."

"Sorry. Force of habit."

"Anyway. I'm going to chat with the secretaries at your school in the morning, see if we can't get any more information on your two Euro-friends. Pearson, you gonna look after your little buddy here?"

"I'm on it. Thanks for coming, Jazz," Andrea replied.

"Keep your head up," she told me then left the room to Andrea and me.

Andy sat down next to me on the bed, and I smiled up at her. "Black limousine, huh?" she asked.

"Yeah. I'm almost positive."

"There is one registered to the Serbian embassy in Vancouver. Diplomatic plates. Don't suppose you saw those through your swollen, puffed-up eyes."

"That would be too easy."

"Yes. It would. Still, I'll try to find a way to drop it into Jasmine's hands and see if they can't at least have a look in another direction. I wouldn't hold out too much hope though. Furlo's still convinced Carl's the man."

"That's what I figured. Are you gonna drive me home?" I asked.

"No. You're staying here."

"What? I'm fine. A little bruised, maybe. But I wanna go home. I've got classes in the morning."

"No. No you don't. That's been taken care of. Docs wanna keep you here overnight for observation, just to be on the safe side."

"An overnight stay? Such luxury in our overburdened health care system."

"Anything's possible when your best friend is the law."

I turned my head away from her and laughed. "The law? Geez, Sheriff. I hope you're gonna clean up this town."

"I aim to. Besides, while you're in here tonight, I'll have some time to find out a few more things. You stay." She held up her hand in a stop sign pose, as though talking to a German shepherd. Well, it was me, so maybe more like a cocker spaniel. Andy leaned over and kissed me on the cheek. "If you're really good, I won't tell your mother you're in the hospital."

My mother was already leaving twice-daily messages on my voice mail about how friends and family were talking in not too flattering terms about Carl's case. I'd briefly tried in a short call to defuse her interest, then just stopped returning her messages for the time being. My hospitalization would mean her at my bedside, and there's no way to hang up from that. "I promise. I'll be good. In the name of all that is sacred and holy, do not tell my mother I'm in the hospital."

"We've got a deal then. I'll see you in the morning." She got up and left the room. Whether it was the morphine or the adrenaline-charged fear that had affected me, for the second time that week, I actually slept.

*   *   *

Which is to say I slept in two hour stretches. Every two hours, a nurse would come in and ask me inane questions, to check me for signs of concussion. In my groggy state, I preferred to believe she wanted to know what day it was, my last name, if I knew where I lived, because she was harbouring secret romantic feelings for me. It must have been crushing for her to recognize that it was a violation of her nursing code of ethics to get involved with a patient in her care, otherwise I'm certain she would have asked me out. Instead, in the morning she asked me to leave. The bed would be needed by someone else. They gave me breakfast first, which is more than I can say for a couple of other overnight engagements I've had.

I tried to think about school as little as possible when I went home. I knew arrangements would have been made for a substitute to take over my classes, and though I had not been anticipating an absence, there was enough there for a replacement teacher to at least make their way through the day. I took a very long, very hot shower. After towelling myself off, I took a careful look at myself in the mirror. The bruising that had already been on the side of my torso from my bleacher fall was still evident, though it was beginning to turn a sickly, pale yellow colour. That bruising was joined by the damage Baseball Cap had done with his steel-toed boots to the right side of my chest. Doctors had taken an x-ray and told me that though it was painful, none of my ribs had been broken, apparently a good sign. The left side of my face was bulbous and puffy, already beginning the early stages of bruising, and I knew I would have to cancel my weekend dinner plans with my parents. If my mother saw me like this, she would probably move in, and I knew I couldn't survive that.

After getting dressed and putting coffee on, I placed a call to my client to find out how he was doing. When he realized I was calling him from home when I should have been at school, I had to confess what had happened to me. He was horrified, coupled with feelings of extreme guilt.

"Why would someone do that to you?" he demanded.

"I wish I knew. Your case has attracted a lot of attention. It was probably just some vigilante justice types sticking their noses in." Of course, I didn't believe that for a minute. My mind had begun to fill with conspiracy theories as to who exactly my attackers were and in whose employ they were acting. Neither of them had seemed to me to be the type of people who would have undertaken that action on their own. I also knew Andrea was thinking the same thing and, with or without the consent of the two detectives on Carl's case, she would be poking around trying to determine just who was responsible for my attack. That, at least, made me feel a little better. Once she found out who had wanted me beaten, she would also have a better idea of who was really responsible for Tricia's death.

Carl also told me that Bonnie had come home to stay with him. That struck me as strange, given the conversations I'd had with her on Sunday afternoon. Shortly after Carl had made it home from his bail hearing, he had put in a call to his estranged wife, and after sharing a lot of tears, Bonnie had decided she wanted the support of her husband, and she wanted to offer her support to him. I crossed my fingers and hoped they could somehow keep it together.

Late Tuesday evening, Andrea phoned to check in with me and find out if my prognosis showed I was going to survive. While I had been busy lying around my apartment feeling sorry for myself, she had been busy. "I think the reasonable doubt building for Carl is growing stronger," she told me confidently.

"How so?" I asked.

"I told you there is a black limo attached to the Serbian embassy," she went on. "I went back to the neighbours around the park where Tricia was found and caught up with a couple of the no-homers from my first time around."

"And someone else remembered seeing the car?"

"Better. He remembered seeing the driver."

I pulled myself up into a sitting position on the couch without letting out a major groan. God, I must be feeling better already, I thought. "How close was he to the car?"

"Close enough to ID the driver."

"Shit, that's perfect."

"Not quite perfect," she cautioned. "We didn't get so lucky that he saw the driver hauling a body out of the trunk or anything. But he definitely saw the driver just before he got back into the car. He says he thinks he made eye contact with him."

"Shit," I said again because that's mainly how I was feeling. "You think he's in danger?"

"From the driver? I don't know. Probably not."

"Why not? Someone came after me. If this driver is related at all to Tricia's death and to the attack on me, why not go after a witness he knows can put him at the scene?"

"Good point," Andrea conceded. "But why wouldn't he have gone after this witness right away? You'd think if he was going to make this witness disappear, that would have happened by now."

She had a point. I wasn't even a witness to any of the proceedings. Why attack the defence lawyer and not the man you know can place you at the scene? "I don't know. But you don't think he needs to be protected?"

"I think there are a lot of people who need to be protected, but at this point I can't exactly order surveillance. What I can do is talk to night shift patrol watch and see to it that cruisers go by there more often."

"Won't that piss off Furlo and Smythe?"

"I'll do it under the table. Nothing official, just a request to keep on eye on the neighbourhood in general. It's about all I can pull off for now." She didn't sound at all happy about it.

"Okay," I tried to reassure her. Suddenly the residual fog in my mind from my cemetery beating cleared and I blurted out, "Holy shit! I forgot. I have news for you."

"What's that?"

"I've locked up Carl's whereabouts for the time of Tricia's death." With all that had happened, I realized I had yet to tell her about Carl's alibi from the nighttime caretaker. I explained my conversation with Jurgen in as much detail as I could. By the time I finished, I was positively elated.

"You're just telling me this now?"

"It slipped my mind. That happens when you have people repeatedly pounding on your head."

"I imagine so."

"So this is great, right? This proves Carl didn't do it. He couldn't have."

"Not so fast," she replied. "What you've got is a statement from a person friendly with Carl who may or may not be reliable as a witness."

"Come on," I protested. "We can't write him off just because he knows Carl. They're not best friends. What's his incentive to lie?"

"Probably nothing. But it's not going to be enough to knock the case right off track. Keep in mind time of death isn't always down to the minute either. But this is good. It's really good."

"Do you want me to call Furlo and Smythe?"

"No, I definitely do not. No matter how the case is going, I sense you're not their favourite person right now, especially Furlo's. I'll have coffee with Jasmine and tell her what you've told me. I'll also see if I can't subtly suggest she re-canvass the neighbourhood."

"And what would you like me to do?" I asked.

"Get better. Rest. That kind of thing. And don't go back to school."

"I can't stay here forever," I told her. "Someone has to provide learning for the masses."

"Take at least another day, all right? There's no need to rush back."

Reluctantly, I agreed to extend my sick time for one more day. I was feeling better, though. Mostly I didn't feel prepared for the stares, the questions and the tilted-head inquiries about the state of my health I knew would follow upon my return to duty. Andrea bid me adieu, and I called the school board's substitute teacher dispatch system to book off sick for another day. At least that gave me something to do; I spent a couple of hours typing out meticulous lesson plans, which I faxed off to the school late in the evening. How nice it must be to have the kind of job where being sick doesn't require as much effort as going to work.

By early the next morning, it felt like life was getting back to normal. I had been awake by quarter to four, and though I was pretty certain I shouldn't be out running, walking felt like something I could probably handle. It was a cold morning but at least it was dry. I had planned to buy a cup of coffee and walk down by the beach to

242

watch the sun come up. Unfortunately, the sun wouldn't come up for about three hours, and it was nearly impossible to find coffee. World-class city that Vancouver claims to be, it is still nearly impossible to get a good cup of coffee at four in the morning. I had to settle for just walking and thinking about coffee.

I also thought about Carl and Tricia and my limited knowledge of Serbia and whether it seemed at all likely that the Serbian embassy would somehow be involved in the death of a teenaged niece of the consular general. It was certainly understandable that the ambassador would make every effort to cash in on his political connections to see a swift end to the case, but I couldn't accept it as coincidence that a black limousine was spotted by more than one person near the crime scene, at Mountain View cemetery where I was attacked and in the motor vehicle registry records of the Serbian consulate. By the time I had reached my apartment, I decided I needed to find out more about Tricia's family and their connections to Serbia.

Tricia's funeral was planned for one o'clock, and if nothing else, I planned to pay my respects. A memo had been distributed at school on Monday asking teachers of Grade Twelve students to be lenient with attendance and assignments on Wednesday, since a good number of kids would want to attend the memorial for their slain friend. As I approached St. Mary's funeral home on Joyce Street, it was clear the school's administration was correct: the parking lot was overflowing, and what looked like half the school's senior population was milling about outside. In fact, the proprietors of the funeral home had set up a large picnic tent in the rear of the building with two video monitors to handle the masses of people who had shown up to grieve and to show their support for the Bellamy family. The chapel itself was reserved for members of the family and closest friends.

I parked on a side street several blocks away and made my way back to the tent-covered rear parking lot of the chapel, where I was met with the surprised look of dozens upon dozens of J. Mac students. The low hum of conversation hanging over the assembled mourners dropped to hushed whispers as, once again, my presence drew unwanted attention. An uncomfortable quiet hung in the air for several moments, which I tried dutifully to ignore while I found a seat on a white plastic folding chair near the edge of the tent. The kids were mostly pretty good about not staring outright—and I smiled a pleasant acknowledgment at those who did—but I could feel the awkwardness. I had half thought about getting up and leaving when a familiar voice called out from immediately behind me.

"Hey, Mr. Patrick." Sarah Kolinsky was standing next to me, along with Jillian Ballantyne.

"Hi Sarah, Jill."

"Mind if we join you?" Sarah asked, pointing to the unoccupied seats next to me. In fact, most of the seats surrounding me had not been occupied, as though my battered and bruised body might somehow be contagious. Sarah and Jill were either really concerned about their academic standing in my class, or genuinely concerned about me. Feeling sorry for myself, I was kind of hoping it was the latter.

"By all means, if you can handle being ostracized." I realized I sounded like a whiner, but I rationalized that it might do them good to experience a little role reversal.

"Can I tell you something?" Sarah asked. I nodded my consent. "You look like shit." Sarah had long since demonstrated her ability to speak her mind. I had found her blunt opinions refreshing in class; at least she had opinions and was willing to share. Her current assessment was, like many of her in-class statements, entirely sound.

"Thank you," I laughed.

"We've been worried about you since Monday," Jillian assured me. "The class actually made a get-well card for you yesterday. If we'd known you were going to be here, I'd have brought it. We gave it to the principal to give to you."

"Thank you. I'm sure he's planning to bring it to me tonight or something," I lied. He was probably hoping I would just stay home for the rest of the year.

"He's here now," Sarah told me. "I saw him when we arrived."

I nodded my acknowledgment. I was less concerned about Don questioning my attendance at the funeral when I was absent from teaching and more wondering if my presence here would breed new hostility from my immediate supervisor. We made idle chit-chat, and for the first time in a long time I was feeling comfortable in my role as teacher. My two students sat with me and asked genuine questions about my health, and I took an interest in finding out a little about each of them while we waited for the service to start. Despite the circumstances, the need to be sitting under a tent awning and the cold November bite in the air, the few casual moments were a relief in the stressful week.

The service began a few moments later, and it was as horrible as I had expected it to be. There was much crying under the tent, and I suspected it was much worse inside the chapel proper. The microphones inside the chapel picked up and amplified the sounds of crying friends and family who had come to mourn collectively. I was holding it together pretty well—I would have described myself as stoic—until about halfway through the service, when a particularly loud moan followed by prolonged wailing was carried through the chapel's speaker system to the crowd outside. At the sound of what was likely the mother's lamentations, the few remaining dry eyes outside—mine included—gave in and joined the crowd of wailers.

As the service ended, I was glad I had made the decision to come. Many students, who had paid me little or no attention since I had joined J. Mac's teaching faculty, were suddenly seeking solace from a trusted adult, any trusted adult who was available. I certainly wasn't the only teacher from the school present, but there were many students in need of comforting, most of whom had likely never attended a funeral before, and certainly never the funeral of a friend. I used as many reassuring words as I could muster, attempting to think of individual words of encouragement for each of the students I spoke to. As one of my law students hugged me and told me through tears how much she could not believe someone her own age had been so tragically struck down, I spotted a familiar face over her shoulder at the far end of the outdoor tent, nearest to the chapel's rear doors.

Carl Turbot, dressed in funeral blacks, was standing leaning against one of the tent's support poles. I separated myself from my grieving students and made my way over to Carl. "What in the hell are you doing here?" I hissed at him under my breath.

He turned and faced me, recognition coming slowly to his face as though he momentarily did not know who I was. I realized he had been lost in his deep remorse. "Oh. Hi, Winston."

"Hi, Winston?" I was incredulous. "Jesus, Carl! You should not be here."

His spirits were sunken. "I had to come, Winston. I couldn't let her be buried and not at least pay my respects."

"Does Bonnie know you're here?"

"No," he admitted. "I told her I was going to help prepare some more lessons for my substitute."

"Nothing like working on rebuilding your relationship with a foundation of honesty." I sighed then continued. "Do you have any idea what your presence here looks like? Have you ever heard of the theory that the criminal always returns to the scene of the crime?"

"What?" Carl looked incredulous. "Don't tell me you've changed your mind."

"No, Carl," I harshly scolded. "I have not changed my mind. But I am working night and day around the clock to make sure you don't get put in jail for a crime you didn't commit. Your innocence by no means guarantees a good Crown prosecutor can't dump your ass into jail. The police will be watching this place, and your presence here will do nothing to help convince them that someone else is responsible for Tricia's death." I was fighting to keep my voice down, because I didn't want to draw any more attention to Carl's presence. Everyone seemed to be wrapped up in their own grief at that point, but with the police and media presence on the street, I knew it was just seconds before someone noticed him, especially with me standing next to him. We were, after all, celebrities.

Carl began to scan the crowd. "The police are here?"

I looked around too. "Of course they are," I assured him. Spotting both Furlo and Smythe on the sidewalk, I nodded subtly in their general direction. "There are the arresting officers right there." I wasn't sure they had seen us yet, but it was only a matter of time. Then something worse happened.

"You bastard!" a hysterical voice screamed from over Carl's right shoulder. Turning to face the chapel, I saw a heavyset woman with short, reddish-brown hair standing breathing fire at my client. "You would come here after what you've done!" She was surrounded by people in suits and dark dresses and the officiating priest.

"Mrs. Bellamy," Carl tried to begin.

"What kind of a monster are you?" she demanded further as heads around the building began to turn. Furlo and Smythe had heard Mrs. Bellamy's bellows, and I saw they were now heading our way.

"I wanted to tell you how sorry I am," Carl started to say.

"Carl," I gently admonished him, taking him by the elbow. "It's best if we just leave now." Mrs. Bellamy and her entourage were advancing towards us, and I feared for the second time that week for my physical safety. Working on Carl's defence had already trained my eyes for the inevitable scrutiny of the press, whose presence I had made note of when I had first arrived at the crowded funeral home. I'd managed to elude them on the way into the service (they had been keeping a respectful distance), but the sound of raised excited voices and the attention being drawn to us was beginning to draw the interest of reporters filing stories for their early afternoon news editions.

A middle-aged man, tall and with a thick head of handsome grey hair, stepped away from Mrs. Bellamy's elbow and now stood in front of us. He was expensively dressed, and I surmised that I was staring into the face of the Serbian consul general for Vancouver. "This?" he asked no one in particular. "This is him?"

"I don't believe we've met," Carl began sheepishly, confused but beginning to recognize the potential for danger that surrounded him. "I'm Carl Turbot." Carl was so stunned by the proceedings and I assume by his own grief, that he actually stuck out his hand to introduce himself to his slain girlfriend's angry relative. I tried more forcefully to pull Carl away from the growing fracas, but not before the man I assumed was the diplomat responded very undiplomatically to Carl's greeting. Before I could remove the offending hand, Tricia's uncle slapped it hard to the side.

"You piece of shit," he hissed Carl. "You do not belong here. How could you even think for a minute you would be welcome here? You killed my niece!" By the time he uttered the last sentence, he was shouting. At least he confirmed my assumptions about who he was.

"No," Carl protested. "No sir. I did not. I did not kill Tricia."

"Do not say another word. It's time to go," I ordered with as much force as I could muster above the growing din. But even as I was speaking, Tricia's mother had grabbed Carl by the arm and had begun to shake him violently.

"You took my baby away from us!" she hollered, hate burning in her eyes. "You deserve to be in that coffin, not her." I pulled at Carl, trying to shake him loose from Mrs. Bellamy's grip.

"Let go," I ordered firmly. I felt someone pull at my other arm and turned to see two young mourners who appeared associated with the family attempting to separate me from Carl. "You don't want to do that," I told them firmly. "Just let us go, and we'll leave." Mass amounts of shoving began to take place as more people struggled to join the jostling group around the front edge of the parking lot, some inevitably drawn to participate, others simply clamouring for a closer view of whatever was happening. From the corner of my eye, I saw Carl fall backwards, with Tricia's uncle falling on top of him, and I knew then that no one was likely to escape uninjured. Carl was shouting at his attacker to stop, all the while begging him to believe that he had no part in Tricia's death.

Before long I found myself on my hands and knees, pulling at Carl's upper body with one hand while simultaneously pushing at Mrs. Bellamy with the other. As I pulled, I let out a short yelp as another mourner, pushed by the growing throng of people, fell over on my back, causing great pain to my previously abused ribs. The yells and crying of people above my head grew louder as increased efforts were made to break up the beginning of a good old-fashioned parking lot brawl. Tricia's uncle had Carl in a kind of bear hug and was screaming angrily in his face. The cursing that had begun in English was now mixed with Serbian, but as with many angry people did when tempers flared, he resorted to his mother tongue. For Carl's part, his face was quickly turning red, and I realized he was literally being pinned down to the point of losing his breath. Letting go of Carl's arm, I began pounding furiously on the man's back and sides, trying to force him off my client.

The darkness that enshrouded us from above suddenly lifted, and I saw daylight again as the screaming uncle shot upward and away from us as though sucked up by a cosmic vacuum. No sooner was he yanked away from me than I felt Carl slip from my grasp, sliding upward and away from the protection I was attempting to offer. The shouting and shoving continued as four arms took hold of me, two on each arm, hauling me to my feet at the same time as they dragged me backwards, my feet not immediately finding purchase on the ground, causing me to slide in reverse like the new bride of a caveman. I looked over my shoulder and found Detective Jasmine Smythe pulling me away from the fracas. In front of me I saw her partner using his considerable bulk to thwart further advances by the angry mob of Tricia's relatives, yet at the same time showing remarkable restraint and even compassion— an attribute I wouldn't have readily attached to Michael Furlo. I snapped my head to the side to identify my other saviour and nearly laughed to see Andrea, her eyes scanning the crowd for further danger. In high school, some of my male classmates had accused me of needing a girl to defend me. Nearly twenty years later, it was still true.

The crowd was beginning to disperse as a couple of uniformed police officers entered the fray. There was still plenty of shouting, but Carl and I were being escorted away by Andrea, Smythe and Furlo. "Fucking brilliant," he was hissing, barely under his breath. "What the fuck are you two doing here?" Though I was adamant in my belief that Carl's presence was entirely inappropriate, it hadn't occurred to me that mine might be too. I was a teacher in the school. Didn't I have a right, if not a duty, to pay my respects to a fallen student? Of course, I also knew I had come with the intention of scoping out the family to see what kind of people they were, so my altruistic righteousness was ringing kind of hollow in my own head.

"Personally I was just hoping to run into you again. It's been so long since we've been able to chat." I didn't feel like arguing my right to attend a funeral, so I chose to pick a cat fight with Furlo instead.

"I'm more than willing to leave you to fend for yourself, String-bean," Furlo told me. "But I guess your little girly-friend here wouldn't like that." We had turned our backs on the crowd now and were trying to walk around the perimeter of the parking lot.

"String-bean? Girly-friend?" I asked mockingly. "My God, Furlo. How old are you?"

"You hang out with him voluntarily?" Detective Smythe asked Andrea.

"Ever since we were kids. It's some sort of residual Catholic guilt," Andrea replied wryly.

"You should think about converting to something else," Smythe smiled back at her. I thought that these two would make much better partners than Furlo and Smythe. I made a mental note to suggest it to Andrea, though I knew she wouldn't be interested. She was one of those cops who didn't work with a regular partner. She claimed to be a loner.

I could still hear the protests and complaints of Tricia's family and friends and over it all, the incessant wailing of her mother. A couple more police cars had arrived to assist in dispersing the grieving, angry crowd. People continued to shove and yell at police officers, obviously indignant that the law's representatives were harassing mourners who could not believe the victim's accused killer would show up at her funeral. I couldn't really blame them. I turned to have one last look at the crowd and stopped dead in my tracks.

"Andy!" I barked.

She stopped and turned around to follow my gaze. "What? What is it?" Furlo, Smythe and Carl all stopped and turned to see what had drawn me back towards the angry mob scene in the funeral home's parking lot.

"There!" I was pointing to the far side of the parking lot, not more than a dozen feet from where Carl and I had first been rescued by the trio of detectives. "That guy. The tall one in the black coat. With the blond hair. That's one of the guys who attacked me in the graveyard on Monday!"

"Are you sure?" Detective Smythe wanted to know.

"Absolutely. I recognize his face."

"From here?" Furlo sounded skeptical, but he was joining me as I began to walk in that direction. Being surrounded by three cops was making me feel bolder than I would have had I run into him again on my own.

"Yes. I'm sure. It doesn't happen to me all the time. It's sort of engraved in my memory." I was attempting to be snide, but my pulse rate had begun to quicken, and my speech wasn't sounding tough or cool. Andrea, Smythe and Furlo were springing into cop mode, and I realized they were barely listening to me.

Furlo turned and put both of his arms onto my body, stopping me like an unruly child. "Patrick. Go back to your car. Take your client and go home. Now."

"What?" I began to protest. I wasn't sure what I had been planning to do when I confronted the graveyard bully with my three tough friends, but I did know that I at least wanted to take part.

"Winston. For once, don't argue. Furlo's right. Please. Go to your car and let us do our jobs," Andrea told me. She had caught the eye of one of the uniformed officers in the crowd of mourners and signalled for him to come over. He recognized her immediately and trotted over. When he arrived, she gave him a succinct order that immediately negated any further efforts on my part to argue. "Escort Mr. Patrick and Mr. Turbot back to their cars. Please see they leave here safely." Carl, I noted, had said nothing during this whole exchange and seemed quite content to leave quietly. I was feeling less inclined now that I had a uniformed, armed guard.

"You bet," the young, burly police officer confirmed. He was dressed in Vancouver Police Department's new "blacks", having recently given up their decades-old blue uniforms, probably because the black uniforms made them look more "cop-like". The young patrolman's biceps and pectoral muscles appeared to stretch the uniform's fabric to its breaking point. Even without his gun, I would have liked to have confronted my attacker with this kid at my side. He turned and took me by the elbow in a manner he probably thought was gentle. "Mr. Patrick? Let's go, please."

Before I could say anything further, Andrea, Furlo and Smythe began walking quickly away, Andrea and Smythe heading around the perimeter of the crowd, Furlo heading through its middle towards my assailant. I knew the young cop was not going to permit me to

251

stay and watch. The tone in Andrea's voice had implied that Carl and I were in some sort of danger, and he was taking it as his personal mission in life not to let her down. She has that effect on people. I walked away with Carl and the cop and hoped that at least the assailant resisted arrest, and Andrea was forced to kick his ass. I knew Furlo could take him, but Andrea might let it get a little personal.

At my car, the officer stood watch as I fumbled for my keys and opened the driver's door. "Thank you, officer," I told him. "I'll be okay now. Perhaps you could escort my client to his car to make sure he's safe." The cop looked hesitant to leave me, since Andrea had not made it clear who he was mostly there to protect. But all cops read the newspapers, and he knew well enough that while I might have been the one who had gotten beat up—there was no hiding the fact given the lovely discolouration on my face—Carl was the one who would face the most danger at this gathering and would most likely need a cop by his side.

"Okay, sir," he told me politely. "Lock your door and head straight home."

"I will," I assured the young law enforcer. "Carl, I'll talk to you later. Go straight home and do not talk to anyone."

"Okay. Thanks, Winston," he replied, which seemed to be his constant refrain.

I settled down into the car and even started the engine for good measure, fastening the seat belt and watching Carl and the police officer in my rearview mirror. As soon as they were out of sight, I shut off the engine, hopped out and trotted briskly back the couple of blocks to the funeral home. I knew something had definitely happened, because the crowd was moving as one large throng in the direction of the parking lot where I had seen my attacker. Pushing and shoving through the sea of people, I couldn't help but feel just a little guilty at the commotion I knew I had partially caused. It wasn't exactly a dignified send off for Tricia, but I only felt a little guilty. After all, the guy who attacked me had started it. It was the same argument I had used to use when I fought with my sister as a kid.

When I reached the outer edge of the parking lot, neither my attacker, Andrea or Detective Smythe were in sight. But Furlo was. In fact, he was half lying, half leaning up against the door of a black limousine, struggling to get to his feet. A small crowd of mourners had worked their way over to him and were huddled around him, no one reaching forward to offer direct assistance, but no one making any moves away from the scene either. I pushed my way through the crowd and took hold of Furlo's arm. "What happened?"

"What the fuck are you doing here?" he demanded angrily. "I told you to go home." Such an ungrateful lout. He shook his arm violently, brushing off my assistance. He had pulled himself up, and already his eyes were scanning the parking lot in search of his partner. He tried to brush me aside as he moved away from the car. I trotted after him.

"Furlo, stop being a shit. What happened, and where the hell is Andrea?"

"Your buddy is with my partner. Your little Balkan friend cold-cocked me with a wrench or something when I tried to convince him to come in for questioning." Furlo was trying to act tough, but he was limping, with a bit of staggering thrown in.

"Which way did they go?" I asked, realizing I had inadvertently placed myself into an old Western movie. I followed Furlo as he staggered after his partner. "Furlo, for God's sake, you're not going to catch up with them. Sit down here and tell me where they went."

"And what the fuck are you going to do for them? Throw your body at him so he can beat the shit out of you again?" Two uniformed police officers had joined us and were looking with obvious concern at Furlo. The gash on his head from the blow had let out a lot of blood, which was just now starting to congeal. He was also getting progressively woozier—for lack of a better medical term—as he attempted to move forward.

I turned to one of the uniforms. "Call an ambulance," I said and kind of shoved Furlo into their waiting arms. His dizziness was obviously growing as he gave very little resistance and collapsed on the wet sidewalk. I broke into a light run for the first time since my attack and headed in the general direction Furlo had been attempting to go in before he realized he was in no position to go any further.

The endorphins began to pump as I felt my regular running rhythms kick in. It had only been a few nights, but my body was already going through some kind of running withdrawal. It was stupid to feel good, but momentarily I did. I ran easily the couple of blocks down Joyce Street away from the funeral parlor, looking in all directions for signs of Andrea and Smythe. I passed underneath the Skytrain station, briefly pausing to see if Balkan Man—the name I had just now developed for him—had attempted to make an escape using the city's rapid transit system. Passengers were going about the business of buying tickets and oblivious to any police action around them, so it was safe to assume nothing unusual was happening on the platform above. I was heading away from the station when something caught my eye to my left.

The John Labatt trail runs more or less beneath the Skytrain line, from New Westminster to downtown Vancouver. It is a haven for urban and suburban cyclists and rollerbladers, a paved destination trail for fitness buffs. At this time of year in this weather, it should have been deserted, but there was movement down the trail. I turned and headed down the paved path, in the direction of the bodies on the trail, kicking my running into higher gear, which was something I frequently did in Fartlek interval training but generally not in a double-breasted suit and dress shoes. Within a couple of minutes, I was able to clearly identify both Andrea and Smythe, still running at a good pace down the trail, and just ahead of them, a man in a long black coat attempting to get away. As the gap between the two cops and me closed, I could see the gap between the man in black and the two cops was closing as well. I still believed she was no match for me, but Andrea was a hell of a runner in her own right. I was almost right behind Smythe as Andrea, who had pulled ahead in the race between law and disorder, suddenly tackled her quarry onto the cracked pavement. I could hear the air rush out of him with a grunted expletive in a language I still couldn't identify.

Smythe was suddenly on top of Andrea and Balkan Man, attempting to push down their suspect to prevent him from doing to them what he had already done to Furlo. It didn't look to be too easy. He struggled, shouted, cursed, screamed and kicked. Andrea had rolled back onto her knees and was attempting to put Balkan Man into a chokehold. His neck was thick enough that even

Andrea's well-chiselled arms were struggling to complete the grip. Balkan Man got up onto his hands and knees and tried to shake Andrea off. Smythe drove her body, right elbow out, into Balkan Man's back. At the same time, Andrea had reached onto her belt beneath her suit jacket, now caked in mud and rainwater and pulled out a pair of police issue handcuffs, managing to slap the cuff on one of Balkan Man's wrists. The weight of Jasmine's body dropping onto his back had slowed his writhing down long enough for me to get up beside him. I swung my foot forward and upward, landing a solid kick to Balkan Man's midsection. He grunted again and seemed to weaken. I used the heel of my shoe to half kick and half push him over onto his side. From that position, Andrea and Smythe were able to finish cuffing his hands behind his back.

They both stood up and began to brush themselves off, though with the amount of water and mud now caked onto their funeral outfits, it wasn't really doing much good. "That's the kind of behaviour that gets cops cited for police brutality," Smythe said to me with just a hint of bemused scolding in her voice.

Andrea was not as genial. "I thought you were going to your car and going home." It wasn't a question, and because I am immature at the best of times, it got my back up.

"You thought wrong. What were you guys even doing at the funeral?"

"Protecting your ass, it turns out."

Smythe could feel the tension between two stubborn friends. "It's pretty standard procedure to attend the funeral of a victim. Apart from showing obvious respect and concern for the family, it isn't unheard of for killers to attend funerals of the victims. And look who we found: your client."

"You've already arrested my client. You were going to use a memorial service to try to bolster your case against him?"

"Save your moral indignation for the courtroom," Smythe replied, giving a wave to a number of uniformed police officers who were heading our way. "And don't try to tell me you weren't there having a look at the crowd for someone to provide 'reasonable doubt' on your client's defence." My God, I'm transparent.

Balkan Man groaned. "You also found someone else at the funeral, which could bring some credibility to your 'perp always returns to the scene' theory." I walked over to the man, whose pain appeared to be subsiding as his anger returned. "Hi there," I said in a friendly tone. "Remember me?" He didn't respond. "Yeah, that's right. I'm the guy you suckered out into the cemetery so you could repaint his skin tones." I pointed to my blackened eye to remind him of the damage he and his partner had inflicted.

"Fuck you," he blurted out.

"Wrong answer," I told him and gave him another half-hearted shove with my foot.

"Counsellor," Smythe barked. "If we attempted to interrogate your client this way, you would be all over us."

"That's different. I get overly dramatic when someone beats the shit out of me."

Andrea had spoken with the uniformed police officers who had joined us. The two men picked up Balkan Man off the ground with such force, his feet momentarily dangled in the air. I knew they weren't being so rough on him out of any particular love for me. He had assaulted one of their own. Cops get especially sensitive about things like that.

"Take him in, book him for assaulting an officer," Andrea told them.

"Add assaulting a lawyer to that charge too," I insisted.

"That's still under investigation," she informed me, "but we've got him dead to rights on this one."

As Balkan Man was led past, he looked carefully into my eyes. His were icy blue and they showed no fear. "You should watch your back."

I stepped in front of him with what little reserves of dignity I had managed to maintain over the past few days. "Even uttering the threat is breaking the law. Where you're going, you should watch your backside." I smiled. He began to writhe in protest at his captors.

We watched him get dragged away with the two officers, then began to follow at a discreet distance.

"It's amazing the way you connect with people," Smythe said.

Twenty-Four

I couldn't stand the thought of going back to work, but I knew it had to be done. After another sleepless night, I was back at it. My short return to physical activity during the post-funeral pursuit had at least inspired me to brave the elements and pound the pavement. The reception I received on my return was also, if not warmer, at least more courteous than the one I had received earlier in the week. Now I had pity on my side and a suspect in custody who would soon be charged for attacking both Furlo and me, though in the time he had been held, he had offered absolutely no indication of his specific motive for either attack or the identity of his partner in crime. It was easy to understand that if he was a close family member or friend, his emotions would be raw, but once it was established he was not immediate family, it just made Carl's case that much more puzzling.

Of course, it would be too easy to assume that having Balkan Man—whose name was established as Zoran Jonkovich—in custody would have gone far to convince Furlo and Smythe that Carl was less likely the prime suspect in Tricia's death. In fact, quite the opposite was true. Furlo and Smythe were working feverishly to gather evidence against him. I knew I would need to spend the weekend preparing Carl's defence and that we would probably push for a preliminary hearing to take place sooner rather than later. I was relying on Derek's expertise, since it was becoming increasingly obvious I was out of my league. We felt our case would be better served by trying to get a preliminary hearing under way as soon as possible, given that we considered the Crown to have a rather weak circumstantial case. The timing of a prelim was ultimately up to the Crown, but we would try to use what little influence we had to expedite the process.

By the time school let out on Thursday, most of the high school buzz around my presence had died down, and while students and even teachers in the hallways were still prone to casting awkward glances my way, most of my own students had grown accustomed to my gruesome visage within the first few minutes of class. True, our regular curriculum was interrupted because I could not very well pretend that nothing had happened and that they would just keep right on working. I had learned in my limited experience that any little event—even an upcoming school dance in the evening—could throw students for a loop. Something like their teacher being battered for defending another teacher on murder charges was a little more cataclysmic than a school dance.

Friday was much the same, but with less attention being paid to me. It was either a tribute to their resilience or a sad statement about their short attention spans. I managed to survive the day with little controversy, albeit with minimal contact with my teaching colleagues. The score was still running around 50/50: half of Sir John A. Macdonald's teachers were standing by Carl and kept popping by to offer words of support; the other half avoided me altogether. No matter how the trial, if there was one, turned out, teaching at J. Mac would continue to be uncomfortable for some time to come. Still, teaching was giving me a much-needed break from dealing with Carl's case. As much as I now believed he was being wronged, life was very complicated with his legal issues as my burden.

By the time the bell rang at the end of Friday afternoon, my mind was already on the minutiae of preparing a legal defense. This would involve a whole lot of time in front of law books, looking at theoretical means to defend a client. Given that I wasn't at all certain yet what the Crown's evidence would be, there was only so much concrete work I could do, but I did know Derek would suggest we tie up the first round of court preparations with pretrial motions such as the legality of gathering Carl's DNA sample from his classroom. I was right in telling Carl he could not be guaranteed any privacy in a public school room, but I might be able to make a good case about the admissibility of the evidence gathered in a public institution without first obtaining a warrant to search Carl's place of employ, even if that place of work was a public institution. There had to be some precedent out there somewhere.

In the meantime, I simply could not wrap my head around the direction the case had taken over the past week, particularly the vicious attack I had suffered. It wasn't uncommon for a grieving relative to take matters into their own hands—at least that's how it often plays out in the movies—but ever since I'd met Mr. Woo and heard about the black limo, then spotted my attackers getting into the same kind of car, I could not accept that large a coincidence. Vancouver may be a movie town, but there just aren't that many black limos floating around. And given that Balkan Man had shown up at Tricia's funeral, in my head I knew the answer to Balkan Man and Baseball Cap's involvement had to take me to one place.

Tricia Bellamy's family lived within walking distance of the school. I knew Sandi would tell me I was being irresponsible in regards to my own safety, and Andrea would tell me I was potentially interfering in a police investigation, but the police had thus far been unwilling to investigate in the direction I wanted. There was no way I was willing to risk walking and being attacked on the street, but as my last period class cleared out for the weekend, (one or two of them even admonished me to get some rest over the weekend because I looked like hell), I had already decided to drive to the Bellamy house and try to sit down and chat with her mother.

The house was bigger than I had expected, given the neighbourhood. A few years before it had become hip and trendy to start building new houses in pseudo-Victorian style, in an effort to reverse the style damage done by decades of cheap stucco that had come to dominate Vancouver's residential landscape. The Bellamy house had a decorative verandah running across the front, complete with squared pillars and two wooden steps leading to the front door. On the verandah itself, a wooden porch swing tried to give the impression of lazy evenings sipping lemonade and chatting with strolling neighbours. As I approached the front door, I almost changed my mind but knew that if I didn't get this interview over with now, I would blurt out my intentions to my best cop friend, and she would either talk me out of it or place a tail on me to prevent me from doing it. I took one final deep breath, as deep as my still-bruised ribs would permit, and rang the doorbell.

It had been two days since I had seen Mrs. Bellamy, and she didn't look any happier to see me than she had at her daughter's funeral. She was a woman whom one could generously describe as plump. Her eyebrows were locked in what I assumed was a permanent frown; she had the serious look of a woman who had seen much in her life and wasn't afraid to share her findings. It was unreasonable and callous to do so, but I took an immediate dislike to her.

"You," she accused me by way of greeting.

"Mrs. Bellamy. My name is Winston Patrick. I am legal counsel for Mr. Carl Turbot."

Her eyebrows furrowed into an even deeper scowl than I would have thought possible. "I know who you are."

I eyed her carefully for any indication she might attack me the way she had pounced on Carl two days earlier. When a moment passed during which my safety seemed assured for the time being, I pressed on. "May I come in? I really do need to talk to you."

An emotion somewhere between outrage and bemusement passed across her strong-featured face. I supposed she had a right to be indignant. Still, didn't good manners dictate she should at least respond? "Mrs. Bellamy, we will have to talk sooner or later. It might prove easier on both of us if we can clear up some issues now rather than later in court." She turned and walked away from me without another word. On the plus side, she did not close the door, which I took to be an invitation to follow her inside.

I closed the door behind me and followed her into the house. There was no carpeting on the floor, and Mrs. Bellamy's footsteps sounded loud and hollow as she clunked away from me. She walked heavily, and I figured if there was a basement suite in the house, the tenants would have to be hard of hearing, or they would never sleep as long as Mrs. Bellamy was up. Halfway down a wide entrance hallway, she turned to the right and entered a sitting room decorated in dark colours. The sofa-loveseat-chair ensemble was dark blue with hideously stencilled flowers on the fabric. They were the kind of furnishings you would find in a grandmother's house.

She finally turned to face me and uttered her first reasonably civil word to me. "Sit."

I did as I was told. The house was cold. There was no fire in the big brick-façade gas fireplace, and it felt like the furnace hadn't been on in some time. People deal with grief in a variety of ways, and warmth deprivation appeared to be part of the Bellamy ritual. I figured it would be pushing my luck to hope for tea or coffee to warm me up, so I opted instead to get right to business. "First," I began, "I know this will sound hollow to you, but I do want to express that I am truly sorry for your loss. I won't insult you by telling you I understand how you feel, but I know your pain must be unbearable, and I truly am sorry to have to come here today."

Mrs. Bellamy offered no response. She took a seat on the loveseat opposite the position I had acquired on the spongy sofa. Her eyes stared coldly across the room at me, and for a moment I wondered if perhaps she'd used up her repertoire of English in the brief conversation we'd had so far. Since she remained silent, I took the lead and plowed on.

"Mrs. Bellamy, I know my being here must seem inappropriate to you right now."

"You should burn in hell for coming here when you are defending that animal," she replied.

"I see." I had about ten flippant comments I could have made, but she was a grieving mother, after all. "I also know my beliefs are little comfort to you right now, but I'm going to share them with you anyhow." I paused to wait for some response but didn't receive one. The rest of the house was eerily quiet. If anyone else was home, there was no television, stereo or even footsteps to indicate it. "Mrs. Bellamy, I do not believe my client is responsible for your daughter's death," I continued.

"Then you are a fool as well as an animal."

"I understand why you want to be angry with me. I really do. The fact is I don't normally do cases like this. In fact, I don't take cases at all any more. But Mr. Turbot came to me as a friend and a colleague, and based on the evidence I've seen, it is clear to me he is not your daughter's killer." Her stare did not weaken in the slightest. It was starting to make me uncomfortable, and I could feel my body temperature rise slightly. "I am most interested in seeing her actual killer brought to justice."

"You knew Tricia?" she asked.

"Not personally, no," I admitted.

She leaned forward slightly in the seat. The edge of the loveseat creaked in protest as her considerable size caused the cushion to crush and the love seat's chassis to sink. "You mean 'personally' like your friend the science teacher knew her? I am glad at least to know that not all teachers find it acceptable to sleep with their students." That ruled out having to ask if she knew about Carl and Tricia's relationship.

"I did not come here to defend my client's actions in his relationship with your daughter. I am more concerned with Tricia and how she might have been acting just before her death."

"What do you mean 'acting?'" she wanted to know.

"Had she seemed upset? Did she talk to you about anyone who was upsetting her at school? Maybe someone new she had met who had bothered or threatened her?"

"The only thing that bothered her was that man. She sobbed in my arms, telling me how he had broken her heart. Stole the innocence from my baby, then threw her away when he was done with her. The heathen animal." Heathen? Interesting, I thought, but figured it was simply one of many invectives a grieving mother could use to describe my client. She spoke of Tricia in maternal terms, but she showed no emotion other than hostility at the memory of Tricia's confessions. I decided to change topics.

"Who is Zoran Jonkovich?" I asked.

She sat back on the couch but never once dropped her eyes from mine. "Why is Zoran of concern to you?"

"For starters, because he did this to me," I said, pointing to my purplish coloured eye. "He and his partner viciously assaulted me, Mrs. Bellamy, and he was at Tricia's funeral. What was his relationship to you and to Tricia?"

"Zoran is a family friend. That is all." She was emphatic.

"And no one ordered him to attempt to persuade me from defending Mr. Turbot?"

She suddenly stood up, rightfully indignant at my poorly veiled accusation. "Zoran cares deeply for us. Why would we send him to do such a terrible thing?"

I tried to make my voice sound calm and reassuring. "No one is suggesting you did, Mrs. Bellamy. But I'm wondering if there might be someone else who could have convinced him to take such a personal interest in the investigation."

Her breathing slowed down again. The sudden effort of hauling herself off of the couch had surely sent her heart into overdrive. "I would not know that."

"What does he do for a living?" I asked innocently.

"He is a chauffeur for my brother."

"The consul general for Serbia?" That touched a nerve for reasons I did not understand.

"You should go now. I do not want you in my house any longer."

I stood up to comply with her wishes. For all I knew, Baseball Cap could be sitting in the kitchen, waiting for a signal from her to forcibly eject me. "Okay. I am truly sorry to upset you." I reached into my pocket and pulled out one of my old business cards on which I had written my home telephone number. "If you think of anything else that might help us to determine who the real killer is, I do hope you will call me."

She took the card from my hand, looked at it only for an instant, then ripped in two and let it fall to the floor. "The police have their killer. I hope they kill him in prison."

I sighed. I've never been one to let go of an argument easily. "I know it is difficult for you to even conceive of this right now, but the evidence the police have against my client is limited. What's more, I have been gathering evidence that I assure you will prove my client could not have been responsible for Tricia's death." For just a brief moment, one of her eyebrows shot up onto her forehead, then returned to its scowling position. "I do hope you will keep that in mind and assist either me or the police in finding the person responsible."

"Get out," she told me and pointed to the door without bothering to show me the way. I was a quick study. I found it easily.

Closing the door behind me, I stood on the verandah for a moment and watched the endless November rain fall onto the streets. That had gone well. At least no one had beaten me up.

Twenty-Five

"Y\ou did what?" Andrea screamed when I talked to her on the phone later that night. I can't remember all of the expletives she used, but I do recall that a few of them were creative. My best friend could make a trucker blush with her vernacular when the mood struck. Fortunately, she was working through the night—lots of fun for a detective on a Friday night—so she was not able to come over and kick my ass in person. But she assured me if she found an off-duty officer with some time on his hands, I could expect a visit. At the very least, she warned me cryptically, our conversation was not over.

Having satisfied my need to turn the forces of law and order against me, I settled into what had become my comfortable Friday evening routine: walking back up to my favourite bistro, Chianti, for dinner and wine. Walking the three blocks to Fourth Avenue, I was greeted by the restaurant's usual line-up. I have found that walking with a great deal of purpose, as though I have every right to be cutting in, generally generated fewer hostile glares than trying to be polite. In truth, the restaurant would take reservations, but I have never been organized enough to plan that far in advance, and I knew Teri would find a place for me.

As though she sensed my pending presence, she was standing by the front counter as I entered the restaurant. "Oh my God," she declared, "will it be a table for one, or will the entire Vancouver press corps be dining with you?" There's really no point in going out for dinner alone if you're not prepared to suffer a little sarcasm at the hands of the serving staff.

"Top of the evening to you, Teri," I replied in my best impression of my father's Irish accent, still thick and growing after thirty-seven years in Canada.

"I was beginning to wonder if you were going to remember us little people, what with you being so famous and all."

"Will my newfound celebrity rank me a table in your busy establishment?"

"Always, Professor." She turned her back on me and proceeded to navigate the narrow passageways between tables. The nice thing was that even if you were dining alone, the tables were so close together you often felt you were part of someone else's party anyway. Towards the rear of the one room eatery, a lone table waited, and Teri led me to the chair facing the front, knowing me well enough by now to understand I could not possibly enjoy a meal while sitting with my back to the door. Too many viewings of *The Godfather* to tempt fate that way. As I sat down, she turned and walked away without a word. As part of our ritual server-patron dance, Teri always pretended I needed to carefully scrutinize the menu before ordering, though it was customary and expected that I would order whatever the combination special happened to be; tonight it was a half-order of curried chicken fettucine with a half order of ravioli Napoletana.

I knew this evening would be my only free time over the weekend. I had already planned to meet again with Carl and Bonnie Turbot in the morning to discuss the next stage of preparing for his defence. Derek had agreed to give up some of his Saturday morning casual work time to assist me. That was his way of being humble; in reality, we both knew Derek was going to be there so he could tell me what we should do next. But I also knew he would be gracious enough to make it look as though I was lead counsel.

Lost in thought, I barely noticed the carafe of wine that had appeared on the table next to the basket of warm buns the busboy had dropped off. I looked up at Teri, who stood waiting for me to sample her choice. "Do any of your customers get to choose what wine they're planning to drink?" I asked.

"You look like you've got enough decisions to make." Always the wise one. "This is new. It's a cabernet-merlot blend, and I knew you would get all snobby on me and wouldn't take my suggestion because you'd think that somehow because it's a blend it isn't worth your time. But you're just going to have to trust me on this one." She turned and left me pondering my wine at the table. Teri understood me, at least my wine snobbery, better than my ex-wife ever had. But damned it if she wasn't right. I wouldn't have ordered it. I took a small sip in order to escape my server's wrath, and damned it if she wasn't right again. It was very good. I should not have been surprised. Teri would not bring me bad wine.

Since my last visit to the restaurant, I was feeling much better about my client. My confidence not only in Carl's innocence, but in our ability to establish his alibi had grown considerably. If it came to a trial, we certainly appeared to have enough plausible evidence to raise reasonable doubt in a jury. I knew it wasn't my job to prove Jonkovich's complicity in Tricia's death; it was up to the Crown Counsel, but my subconscious was nagging me to figure out what his motive was. If his attack on me was to dissuade me from further investigating his involvement, I had to wonder why he would want to kill Tricia Bellamy, a family friend? Was it moral outrage that she was having an affair with Carl? If so, why not kill Carl? Was it jealousy? Was it possible he too had been romantically involved with Tricia, and that his was a crime of passion? Jonkovich was in his mid to late twenties as far as I could see, a little old for Tricia, but he was still younger than Carl. I really didn't want to expend a great deal of energy trying to build a case against Jonkovich, but his guilt might still prove to be Carl's best defence.

I gave up staring into space when Teri filled my field of view, plopping down into the chair across from me as she placed a plate of spinach salad in front of me. "If you keep looking so glum, you're going to be bad for business. I might have to ban you."

"Since when is the volume your primary concern?"

"No customers, no tips."

"Sitting around with customers means no tips from other customers. And now that I'm a teacher, you know I'm going to be a notoriously poor tipper. Especially in a contract negotiation year. There could be a strike."

"You might have to drink domestic wine."

"I'd sooner cross the picket line." That wasn't fair, of course. British Columbia had some fine vineyards producing some award-winning wine, but the wine snob that I was had a hard time buying anything local.

"So." She turned serious for maybe only the second time since I'd known her. "How is life in the F. Lee Bailey lane?"

I smiled at her. "I don't get paid as much."

She returned the smile. "I keep seeing you on the news. I heard about your attack. In fact, you look like hell, in a good way."

"Ahh, but you should see the other guy."

"Bruised knuckles?"

"And how. I'm really okay. I was even back running again."

"So not sleeping again." It was more of a statement than a question. I raised an eyebrow at her. We weren't that close. "Detective Pearson was in here for an early dinner before the evening shift started."

"You need to join a book club. Then the two of you could talk about something other than me."

"Don't get all shitty on me. She's just worried about you. You any closer to figuring out who really did this?"

I paused before answering, not because I needed to carefully consider my response but because I had filled my mouth with spinach salad. "Does this mean you believe me, the low-life defence counsel rather than the high powered crown counsel who seems to have the press on his side? I'm touched."

"Are you kidding me?" she asked rhetorically. "Would your heart be fully involved in anything less than a noble cause?"

"Ask my ex-wife."

"I wouldn't let you in here if it weren't so."

She stood up to return to her duties feeding the pasta-deprived people of Kitsilano. "Do what you have to do, Professor."

"If only I knew what that was. I sort of wish I had never gotten involved." I hadn't intended to sound self-pitying, but it came out that way.

Teri cocked her head at me with a sympathetic look. "You're

267

doing this because a friend was wrongfully accused. You also know that somewhere out there, the killer of a young girl wanders free. Neither of those things is acceptable to you, so you won't walk away and stay uninvolved. Rest not until your work is done, lest there be no real rest for ye."

Either the red wine was affecting me or her. "What the hell are you talking about?" I asked her.

She harrumphed and walked away, leaving me to my brooding, my salad, and most importantly, my wine. In short order, I suddenly felt very much alone. Though the food was probably excellent, I did little more than peck away at it. Teri brought me the bill and made one last valiant effort to lift my spirits, which were sinking rapidly towards downright morose.

"Hey," she announced, "this is not the smart-assed defender of wrongs and molder of our future generation I'm used to seeing in here."

"Nope," was all I managed to reply.

She actually reached forward and lightly placed her hand on my cheek. It was warm, and I found myself for a moment tilting my head so she was almost supporting it. "Don't let 'em get ya. You can't save the world if you don't look after yourself first." She brushed my cheek and lifted her hand away. She gave me one last wink and smile, then turned and walked away without saying goodbye.

Teri's compassion did not completely lift me from my funk, but when I got outside the skies had cleared and it was no longer raining. I suppose we all suffer from seasonal affective disorder to some degree, but I must have it worse than others. Just standing outside on Fourth Avenue, looking up and actually seeing a few stars, made me feel suddenly more alive. I took it as a sign that maybe all was okay in the universe. I made the trek back home to spend a couple of Friday night hours catching up on teaching duties.

I worked until around midnight, when two things happened: I completed all of the marking I had brought home with me, and I grew drowsy almost at precisely the same time. I crashed into bed where as usual, my mind would not cooperate. I dozed on and off throughout most of the next three hours. Around three thirty, I gave up and decided to treat myself to a good long run.

Of course, since I was now ready to run again, Vancouver was now ready to rain again, and rain it did. If the clouds parted for my walk home from the restaurant, it must only have been to catch their breath, because by the time I laced up, bundled up and made it down to the lobby of my building, the rain was coming down in ice-cold sheets. When you run as much as I do, you learn not to let a little thing like foul weather get in your way. As I took off heading west down Cornwall Avenue, I could feel the endorphin rush beginning much earlier than usual. A week of legal limbo, physical assault and spinning my wheels had left my body crying out for a good run, and I'd been able to give it barely a jog since my encounter with Balkan Man and Baseball Cap earlier in the week.

I made my way to Macdonald in what seemed like moments, following the usually busy arterial route up to Tenth Avenue before turning right and heading towards the university. The Saturday morning streets were all but devoid of life, save for the occasional taxi bringing the party-weary home. I shortened my steps without reducing my pace as I climbed the hill before hitting the university golf club, the dark forests lining the road along the endowment lands making me feel even more alone. The run was longer than I'd anticipated, but the more I ran, the more I could feel the cloud that had hung over me receding as the winter rains ran down into my face and washed away the sweat accumulating from beneath the band of my toque.

Entering the university proper, I still could not bring myself to turn back; my body was feeling the best it had in what seemed a long time. Turning left instead of right, I began the long journey down West Mall towards the student residences in which I had spent the first two years of my own undergraduate career, and where Andrea had first introduced me to late night/early morning runs to clear my head from the fog that often accumulated during exams. From the residences, I proceeded along the ring road, past the university's famed Wreck Beach, where it was unlikely I would find any nudists at this time of night or year. At thirty-five years old and a lifetime resident of Vancouver, I had still never found occasion or the balls—so to speak—to actually visit the city's only official nude beach.

I was pumping hard as I rounded the curve past the Museum of Anthropology, its shiny windows sparkling in the wet rain. It was almost a shame to feel so alive and full of vigour and have no one, not even strangers, to share it with. By the time I reached the turn-off leading through some of Vancouver's tonier homes down towards Spanish Banks and back home, I was beginning to tire and slowed my pace to a gentle jog. Downhill can be even more demanding on the body than up.

My body and mind were clear and wiped clean of the previous week's traumas as I increased back up to my solid running pace along the waterfront of Spanish Banks towards Jericho. On my right side, the forest sucked up what little light shone across the bay from the city, leaving me alone and feeling as I always did when I ran this part of the beachfront—just a little vulnerable. Picking up the pace, I saw a car approaching. With the events of the last week, I admit a sense of apprehension caused my chest to tighten. But I didn't want to let go of how good I was feeling on my early morning workout, so I refused to feel fear.

I actually averted my eyes from the car, looking instead out to sea and across to West Vancouver. Nothing to be afraid of, I told myself as I heard the car glide by on the rain-slicked streets. There was no mistaking the sound of the car slowing down, however, as it went by, or the sound of gravel crunching as it turned around. I willed myself to look over my shoulder as it slowly crept along behind me. The rain was pounding so hard, it was impossible to see the car's occupants or even its make. All that was visible was the two headlights piercing the dark along the ocean front road. I cursed myself for going on such a long run, realizing if I had run less, I would have had a lot more energy to make a break for it. On this stretch of the road, however, there was nowhere to go.

I picked up the pace anyway, increasing my speed and risking a quick glance over my shoulder to see if the car would drive by. It didn't. Instead the driver seemed intent on keeping pace with my movements on the road. The pounding in my chest increased, and I willed myself to stay calm, knowing that if panic set in, more energy would be expended and less would be available to help me lose whoever was viewing me as prey. About half a kilometre ahead was the beginning of a residential neighbourhood. If I could make it there, I might be able to lose the driver by hiding out in backyards or alleyways or even attract the attention of one of the residents for help.

The houses were just about in view, and I actually moved off the sidewalk onto the roadway, planning to dart across the street and into a front yard. The car had kept a short distance behind me but now sped up, as though reading my thoughts and sensing what I might do. I had almost darted out in front of it when it emitted a burst of red and white light, nearly blinding me as the massive wattage picked up the glare from the wet roads and the sheets of falling water. I almost stumbled into the car's path. My mind, still in panic mode, took several seconds to recognize that the flashing lights belonged to a police car.

I stopped running and doubled over, catching my breath as the car came to a stop alongside me. As my panic subsided, anger kicked in. What the hell did this cop think he was doing? Did he really think the average burglar was out jogging in the middle of the night in the pouring rain? Standing up, I walked towards the cruiser as the window lowered.

"Mr. Patrick?" a young cop I didn't recognize said to me through the wall of rain separating us.

"Yes?" I responded, shocked that this patrolman would know who I was on sight.

"Mr. Patrick. Would you come with me, sir?" he asked quite politely.

"Why?" I asked, suddenly a little suspicious even of this young police officer. His partner leaned over and looked out the window.

"Mr. Patrick," the partner said, "Detective Pearson called your house looking for you. When she couldn't reach you, she asked us to come along this way to look for you." He was a little older than me and didn't appear to be a bad guy in a stolen uniform and car. But then, that would be the point, wouldn't it?

"Is she okay? Is everything all right?" I asked.

"We really can't say," the first cop responded. "In fact, she didn't say why she wanted us to get you. She just told us to find you somewhere along this route and bring you to her. The back door's open."

I looked around and didn't see any witnesses to whom I could holler to get the licence plate number in case I turned up missing. Not seeing any other alternative, I agreed. I opened the back door and got in, feeling like a prisoner who'd just been picked up for exercising at an ungodly hour.

"You have no idea what this is about?" I asked again.

"No sir," the older partner responded. "We're sorry if we gave you a scare back there. We wanted to make sure it was you."

"That's okay," I told him, because I couldn't think of how else to complain. We rode the rest of the way in near silence. We drove further and further away from my Kitsilano neighbourhood, heading east towards my place of employ. It was hard to imagine why Andrea was having me picked up in the middle of the night, or where she might be having me taken until we began to approach a familiar neighbourhood.

My heart caught in my throat as we turned down a side street I had visited for the first time only a week ago, and I saw that the street was awash in flashing blue lights. Police cars, ambulances and even what I took to be a coroner's wagon filled the street in front of a recognizable residence.

Carl and Bonnie Turbot's house.

Twenty-Six

M y stomach sank as the police cruiser pulled up amidst the collection of official vehicles lining the street. Despite the driving rain and the early hour, neighbours stood huddled in doorways watching their continuing community drama unfold before them. From the corner of my eye, I could detect two news media vehicles, their telltale folded towers perched atop the vans.

The more senior officer opened the door for me—it was locked on the inside to prevent escape of those who normally rode in the back—and I stepped out into the mayhem. For a moment I stood to the side of the symphony of lights and sounds. My endorphin-heightened senses intensified my awareness of all of the elements going on around me. I made note of the ridiculous, shin-length rain slickers worn by the majority of police, most of whom seemed to have little to do except stand and watch. I also noted the sounds of police radio squabble, a sound I had always believed was heightened by Foley artists in the movies. Now I was aware of just how constant police band radio chatter really is. Having arrived on the scene from a different direction than when I had arrived on my own, the Turbot house appeared to me to be sitting at the wrong angle, as though their entire neighbourhood had been reversed by tonight's events. When I got my bearings, I began to move forward toward the house, drawn by the swarm of activity near the front door and an overwhelming sense of what I knew I would find inside. This amount of police interest wouldn't be generated by good news. The senior officer put his hand in front of me.

"Hold on a moment, Mr. Patrick," he told me. "I'm not sure you're cleared to go in there."

My indignation began to rise as I stood facing this burly cop in the pouring rain. "Why the hell did you kidnap me off the streets if I wasn't supposed to see what's going on here?" I demanded.

He looked at me sympathetically. Like most cops in Vancouver, he surely knew who I was and the major events of my life during the past week. "Just give me a minute, okay?" He stepped away from me and said something into the radio strapped to his shoulder. By now, my running jacket had long since given up any pretense of repelling the downpour. I could feel growing cold spots on my shoulders. Another minute went by, and I saw Andrea come out the front door, pushing through the throng of cops who seemed primarily to be seeking shelter under the overhang outside Carl's front door.

"Win," she called out to me. She waved me over. "Come over here." I smiled at the big, burly cop and pushed past him towards my friend. I felt like my association with her let me outrank a mere patrolman. Andrea stood in front of the house, seemingly oblivious to the rain running down her now flattened hair and forming rivers down her dainty nose. "They found you. Are you all right?"

"I was running."

"I figured." She stopped then to give me a physical once-over with her eyes.

"So?" I asked.

She shook her head slightly. "It's bad."

I looked past her towards the front door. "Is he dead?"

She nodded her head the other way. "Yes," she said simply. "I'm sorry, Win." I nodded my acknowledgment of her sympathy but couldn't think of anything to say. "Win?" she continued. I looked back at her. "Win. I'm sorry, but there's more," she told me. "They're dead. Both of them."

"Bonnie?" I asked, though I knew there was no one else she could be talking about.

"Yes. They're both in there."

I let out a long breath through my nose. I could feel my body's core temperature dropping, and I wasn't sure if it was just the rain or if I might be descending into shock.

Andrea stood with me quietly for nearly a full minute before she continued. "I wanted to tell you, once I saw that the media had shown up. They monitor our radios, and they're here like flies on shit. I didn't want you to see it on the morning news." She didn't need to explain why she had brought me there, but she did anyway.

I glanced over my shoulder at the two cameramen from two stations who stood recording the images around them. I knew they would wait the few hours in the rain until they could catch the always-important shot of the body bags being wheeled out. Let them wait, I thought. "Can I see?" I asked.

She continued to look at me closely, her eyes never wavering. "Are you sure?"

"Yep."

"Okay. You probably shouldn't stand out here being the centre of their shot anyway," she said with a slight nod towards the camera crews. She took me by the arm as though I was an old man, and we headed towards the front door.

Police officers and crime scene technicians parted for us, and I was aware of conversations stopping as we passed. By now, most of the assembled had grown accustomed to the spectacle of the crime scene; I was a new element to be examined. As we passed people, they respectfully lowered their heads. We entered the tiled foyer of Carl and Bonnie's shoebox house and paused for a moment before going up the stairs.

Andy gripped my arm tighter to signal me to stop. "Winston," she said solemnly. "It's pretty horrific up there. You don't really have to see this. You could just wait here, we'll ask you all the questions we need and then I'll have someone drive you home."

I thought about her offer. Did I need to examine Carl's body personally? I could take her word for it. They were dead. What was left to see? Though Carl and I could in no way be described as close, I still felt like I owed him something more. Or maybe it was a sick morbid curiosity that bid me press on, but having come this far I determined I was going to see it through. "No," I confirmed out loud. "I think I should see them."

Andy probably knew that would be my answer. "Okay," she

consented. "If at any time you need to leave the room, it's okay. Just watch where you step. The 'techs' are checking everything out right now."

I nodded my agreement, and we began to climb the stairs leading into the living room. The main sitting area was teeming with official personnel, some dusting for fingerprints around window ledges, others sorting through mail and paperwork, others simply standing in the background trying to look as though they had good reason to be there. It occurred to me that the homicide business might be overstaffed. As Carl's lawyer, I felt I ought to be supervising the process to ensure his rights weren't being trampled. Having never worked a death scene, I had no idea which things they were searching were appropriate under the circumstances and which might be an invasion of posthumous privacy. At this point, protecting his privacy seemed of little concern or value. Andy pulled slightly on my left arm, leading me down the narrow hallway whose distance now seemed longer than the first time I had walked it. We walked past the first door, the den where I had discovered confirmation of Carl's love letters to Tricia, and rounded the corner at the end of the hallway before Andrea stopped.

"You ready?" she asked. I nodded, and entered the doorway of the master bedroom.

Four technicians were in the room—three men and one woman, along with Carl and Bonnie Turbot. Both were dressed, thankfully, but little more could be said for any sense of normalcy. Bonnie lay face down, though her head was tilted to the side. The mattress was now a bright red colour; a bloodstain covered the entire top half. The pillow on which she lay had worked like a sponge, absorbing most of the blood and brain matter from the side of her head, where a sizable chunk of her skull was missing. She appeared to be staring, as though something had caught her attention at the last moment as she headed off to the next life.

Carl was what appeared to have attracted her gaze. He was sitting reasonably upright against the wall, just below the ledge of the window that faced the house next door. The wall, which had once been white, was unrecognizable given the amount of blood and brain matter that had exploded from Carl's skull, much of which was lying around him. Like his wife, Carl's eyes were open, not so much in stunned amazement but in almost resigned banality. If this was death, his eyes seemed to be saying, bring it on. I'm ready. His eyes looked back toward his wife, and the two corpses stared each other into eternity.

Andrea touched my arm again. "You okay?"

"Better than them." I stood transfixed, looking at husband and wife splattered in their bedroom. "Any guesses?"

She nodded, though the nod was more subtle, which told me she didn't really want to talk about it right there. She took my arm and was about to lead me over to a corner when two familiar faces appeared in the doorway.

"What the fuck is he doing here?"

I turned and responded. "Good morning, Detective Furlo. I was in the neighbourhood, and since my client had his head blown off, I thought I would drop by."

"Got yourself an alibi?" he sneered at me.

"Yeah, this would be a hell of a way to collect my legal fees."

"I'll bet."

"Not now, Furlo," Andy interjected, taking me by the arm and leading me out of the bedroom.

"How are you doing, Winston?" Detective Smythe asked me as we squeezed by. I shrugged in response and followed Andy into the kitchen. The two recent arrivals followed.

Andrea turned to face me, leaning up against the stove handle. "Winston, it looks right now like a murder-suicide," she stated bluntly, because she knew softening the blow can prohibit understanding.

"What?" I shouted. "You've got to be kidding me. Carl would not kill his wife."

"What about his students?" Furlo tossed out.

"Why are you even here?" I wanted to know. "I was under the impression this was Detective Pearson's case."

"It is," Jasmine Smythe said soothingly. "But clearly there is a relationship to our ongoing investigation, so we were called out."

"I don't think Carl even owned a gun," I protested. Carl Turbot had had some questionable practices and a less than honourable relationship with Tricia Bellamy, but in the short period we had grown closer, I had grown quite sure he had not been responsible for Tricia's death. And if he had been—I was suddenly second-guessing myself—it was a crime of passion. It had been nothing like the violence that had transpired a few feet away in the bedroom.

"Do you know that?" Andrea asked. She was all detective-like.

"Do I know that?" I asked, my head starting to swirl. "How would *I* know that?"

"You just said he didn't have a gun," Furlo chimed in. "Are you taking a guess, or did you have a conversation with your client about whether or not he owned a gun?"

It suddenly seemed obvious to me we had. Of course we had. Doesn't every good defence lawyer ask his client accused of homicide whether or not he owned a gun? Carl was a science teacher—and already I was recognizing him as being in the past tense—why in the hell would he own a gun? Everything I knew about Carl, or thought I knew about Carl, was coming undone as the image of his dead, exploded body kept flashing into my head.

"Winston?" Andy asked again, trying to break me out of my head-spinning stupor. "Did Carl ever talk to you about whether or not he owned a gun? Or are you making a supposition?" This felt like an inquisition. I was getting dizzy.

I opened my mouth to answer. "Conversations between Carl and his defence counsel are privileged," I heard a voice say, and I decided it was an articulate, intelligent and entirely appropriate response. It took me a full couple of seconds to realize I hadn't said it. We all turned collectively to find my co-counsel, Derek Cuffling, standing in the doorway to the kitchen. Even at this ungodly hour of the morning, Derek looked coiffed, calm and composed, dressed in pressed, pleated khakis, a sport jacket and London Fog raincoat.

"What kind of bullshit is that?" Furlo demanded.

"It's legal bullshit," I replied, figuring I ought to contribute something to the argument. "But he's right. Conversations between Carl and myself are protected by solicitor-client privilege."

"He's dead, you moron," Furlo grunted. "I don't think privilege is a big deal any more. He's probably not going to fire you."

"Doesn't matter," Derek responded. "Privilege extends past the time of death of a client." He walked closer to the group and placed a hand on my shoulder. "Are you all right, Winston?" It was starting to get annoying how many people were asking me that.

"I'm fine," I snapped. "What are you doing here?"

"I called him," Andy responded. "Thank you for coming, Derek."

"It's no problem. Good to see you again, Andrea. I wish it wasn't under these circumstances." The only times I had ever seen his composure crack slightly were when he was around Andy. He turned slightly to face the other detectives. "And this must be the infamous Detective Furlo."

"You look a little pricey to be playing second fiddle to teacher-boy here," Furlo responded in confirmation.

"You're right, Win," Derek said without taking his eyes off Furlo. "He is charming. Got any theories other than murder-suicide?"

"Not from me. Looks pretty obvious from my point of view," Furlo told him. Derek threw a question at me with his glance.

"I don't know," I answered. "It seems way out of character for him."

"I agree," Derek told the room. His voice had a way of filling the entire kitchen. It wasn't loud; it just had presence.

"What about Jonkovich?" I asked. "What's his status?"

Jasmine Smythe cocked her head. "He was released on bail."

"When?"

Furlo looked a little sheepish, turned and left the kitchen in the direction of the crime scene master bedroom. His partner continued. "This morning. He was bailed out this morning."

Andrea chimed in. "Wouldn't that be extremely ballsy coming here and whacking two people the day he gets out on bail? Why the hell would he do that? Why now?"

I began to think out loud. "Well, he's a family friend. Maybe when I talked to Tricia's mom today, he got really pissed."

"You did what?" Smythe and Derek blurted simultaneously.

"He was doing a little investigating," Andy tried to explain for me.

"It's my case," Smythe complained.

"But he's defending it."

"That's bullshit. He could be interfering with the investigation."

"Hey, don't give *me* shit!" Andy said. "He's the one who went over there. If I had known he was going to do that, I'd have cuffed him to his kitchen table."

Detective Smythe shook her head. "Christ, he could have gotten these two killed." She had finally spoken what had been nagging at the back of my subconscious since I had arrived. I could feel the colour draining from my face, and a wave of heat began to crawl up from my stomach, through my chest and into my head. I moved over past the counter to the obviously second-hand kitchen table on the other side, sitting down on a chair and resting my head on my hand.

"He's still in the room," I moaned. "You don't have to speak about him in the third person." The two detectives stopped bickering long enough to look over to me.

Derek intervened on my behalf. "Detective Pearson is right. Mr. Patrick is defence counsel in Carl Turbot's pending murder case. He had every right to question potential witnesses. Maybe this isn't the best time to have this conversation."

Andrea regarded me for a moment, then spoke a few soft words to Derek that I couldn't hear. Mostly I could hear the ocean in my ears. Finally, she came to me and said, "Derek's right, Win. There's nothing more you can do here. Why don't you let Derek drive you home? We can talk later."

When I felt like I could stand without falling or puking, I let Derek lead me past the throngs of cops, coroners and reporters, through the rain to his waiting car.

Twenty-Seven

Much of the remainder of the weekend passed without much registering in my head. Andrea tried to convince me I was in shock and that I should see a doctor. I tried to convince her I was way too cool for that. Neither one of us was very convincing. Neither was the evidence of Carl and Bonnie's killing pointing towards a murder-suicide.

By Andrea's own admission, the evidence was sketchy. The sheer force of firing a Glock 9mm semi-automatic pistol at close range would surely make it difficult for a suicide victim to hold on to his or her firearm. Still, the forensics people had found the gun very close to Carl, and it had his fingerprints all over it. Though there was no record of a firearm being registered to the Turbots, that didn't mean Carl didn't have a gun; it just meant that if he did, he had never bothered to register it with the police. Some estimates put Canada's gun collection at four times the number actually registered. The techies had also found residue from the gun's discharge on Carl's hands, more evidence he had been the one who had pulled the trigger. But without any eyewitnesses, much of what the police had to work with was conjecture. And without Carl being connected to anyone in high places, the autopsies on both him and his wife would be done when there was time to get them done. In the meantime, murder-suicide was the assumption being made by the investigative team.

Though the discovery of the bodies had come too late to make the Saturday papers, it had certainly made the Saturday morning news shows, and by evening, every newscast was leading with the sad story of the science teacher, distraught after murdering his student, killing his wife then himself. By Sunday morning, the *Province*, Vancouver's tabloid newspaper, was leading the charge of conjecture with page upon page of mostly "unnamed sources close to the investigation", describing in as much grisly detail as possible the horror that had unfolded in a "quiet East Vancouver neighbourhood." By pages three and four, the paper had rehashed the details of Carl's alleged involvement in Tricia Bellamy's death and, much to my chagrin, had found out the details of their romantic relationship. I didn't have to guess too hard the "unnamed police source" who had provided them with that tidbit of information.

I had a vague recollection of Sandi calling me on Saturday night. She expressed some concern for my general wellbeing once she had heard about Carl and Bonnie's death. I finally won an argument with her when I talked her out of coming over to comfort me. I was feeling sufficiently sorry for myself that not even Sandi could penetrate my gloom. The deaths of my client and his wife were affecting me much more than I thought they could. Carl and I had by no means grown close, but he was a friend. At thirty-five years old, I had not yet reached the point in life where one becomes accustomed to the death of friends, and even this one was more depressing than I would have thought possible. All day Sunday, I lamented his loss but did it entirely in private, battling my own need to grieve against a misplaced sense of guilt that I might be at least in part responsible for his death.

Suffice to say, the weekend was not productive. But by four thirty Monday morning, I was back up and running, determined I would hold my head up high and be at school as usual. The students of J. Mac had suffered enough loss over the past two weeks to last them a lifetime, and I felt a duty to at least be there to do my part to help them to understand it. Winston Patrick. Teacher. Lawyer. Grief Counsellor.

If the school had been uncomfortably tense with grief after the death of Tricia, it was magnified ten times Monday morning. As anticipated, the local media lined the sidewalks, talking to anyone who would venture an opinion, comment or tear up about their fallen science teacher and his now-public relationship with their classmate. Monday morning's papers had more than made up for their lack of a Sunday edition with even more information about both the homicides, publishing full biographies of all of the players, including myself. The way newspapers can dredge up old photos of me is a mystery that leaves me uncomfortable about the power of information storage systems. When I had returned from my early morning run, I had seen my law school graduation photo staring at me from the front of page one. Another paper, one of the national dailies, carried a photo scanned off the television news station it also owned. Convergence at its finest: the papers didn't compete with the TV news any more; they just bought it.

My first period class was quiet as they entered the classroom. I wasn't ready for the uncomfortable tension hanging in the air between me and my students. I guess I could not have expected them to be jumping up and down to see me—some of them had barely tolerated me long before this mess had begun. But I got the sense the students were almost afraid to be in the room with me, as though all of the horrible things that had been happening were a direct result of my presence, my bad karma infectious. It didn't do much to assuage the guilt already plaguing me. Intellectually, I knew the unfolding of Carl's fate had begun well prior to my involvement, but I couldn't shake the burden that if I had managed to convince the world of his innocence faster, he might still be here to bask in his acquittal. Now he never would be, and I was little closer to convincing anyone other than Derek and myself that Carl could not and would not have killed his teenaged lover and his wife.

When the first period ended, I found a familiar face standing in the doorway. Second period was my preparation period that day, so I had some time to chat.

"Good morning, Don."

"Good morning, Winston," the principal responded. It was only 9:45, and already his tie was loosened, his shirt crumpled. "How are you holding up this morning?"

"I'm all right," I told him. "You?"

He only nodded in response. He stuck his hands deep into his pockets, bringing his shoulders remarkably high up, until they nearly touched his ears. "Listen. I know this will sound kind of hollow, but I do want to tell you, I'm sorry. I know you and Carl had become, well, friends of sorts, and I am sorry for your loss."

"Thank you."

He nodded again, not quite sure how to begin the next chapter of his message to me. "It's been kind of crazy down in the office."

"I can imagine."

"I can't remember the last time I've had this many parents trying to talk to me on a single day. I finally had to take a break and get out of there for a while."

"Yeah." My attempts at empathy were weak, I admit. They did nothing to ease my boss's discomfort.

"I was kind of expecting you wouldn't be in today."

"You sound disappointed."

He sighed, and I could tell he was doing his best to avoid getting into an argument with me. "I just meant that with all that happened...it might be difficult for you to come in and face...well...see, everyone."

"Easier for me than Carl." No slack for you today, Don.

He walked towards me and sat down on the edge of the desk. "Winston. I think you probably need a couple of days off."

"I just had a couple. It's Monday."

"A couple more, is what we're suggesting."

"'We're' suggesting? There's a conspiracy of sick day advocates out there?" Don stood up and actually took a step or two back.

"No, Winston." He paused, choosing his next words carefully. People in positions of authority tend to do that when talking to lawyers. "I spoke with the director of personnel for the school board this morning. He agreed with me that it might be best for everyone, including you, if you took a few days away from the school, say for the rest of the week, until things quieted down a little."

I stood up suddenly, and Don actually stumbled backwards away from me. "Are you suspending me? Because you had better have a damn good reason."

He lifted his hands in defence. "No. No. Not at all." He turned around, pacing the short space in front of my desk with growing impatience. "For God's sake, Winston, this is hard on all of us, especially the kids. There's media vans everywhere, people calling for you, for me, demanding answers. I can hardly think you're in the best frame of mind for teaching, nor your students for learning. I'm just asking you to think about staying away for a few days until we can restore some sense of normalcy to the school."

I felt under attack and even implicated in the mayhem around the school, but a nagging voice at the back of my head was telling me the principal for once had a good point. People, students and teachers alike, were definitely uncomfortable around me. "I don't have any real sick time banked," I told him finally.

He looked at me with surprise. He even smiled slightly, just at one corner of his mouth. "You won't have to use sick time. Personnel is willing to figure out a way to just have you take a few days paid leave. The accountants will figure out which slush fund it's coming out of later."

"Okay," I told him. "When do I go?"

"I'll have a sub here for you this afternoon. If you want to get a few things ready for today, you can be on your way."

"I've been thrown out of better places."

Don considered me carefully. "Part of this is about you. We may have had our fights over the past week, but remember, I hired you. I wanted you here as a teacher, and I still do. We just need a little time, okay?" How often does a person get unexpected paid time off? I agreed it would be for the best. "And use the time to get some rest yourself," the principal told me as he headed for the door.

"I will," I assured him. Then I added. "And thanks, Don." Without turning back, he gave me a wave as he turned towards the main office.

By the time I had packed up everything I thought I would need to prepare for a week's worth of lessons, my preparation period was almost over, and lunch time was upon us. If the principal was right, my presence was making the day uncomfortable for just about everyone in the building. I decided it would be best to get out altogether before seeing anyone, which was unfortunate, because I knew there were at least one or two members of staff—Christine, for example—who would have offered me at least some kind of moral support. Right then I didn't feel like I had too many friends left in the world, but Don figured I needed rest, so rest it would be.

But by the time I was at my car, I had already placed a call to Derek.

I only had to drive a couple of miles from Sir John A. Macdonald Secondary before a noticeable change in the economic landscape was apparent. The Granville Corridor running south from Broadway towards the city of Richmond and the airport is where some of the Lower Mainland's best and oldest money resides. Though Granville itself is desirable only as a thoroughfare between the two urban centres, the streets perpendicular to it from Sixteenth Avenue south to around Thirtieth contain some of the most extravagant mansions and upper class real estate the city has to offer. It was where Sandi had grown up. The neighbourhood also was home to a number of consular residences, foreign governments having the only bank accounts sufficient to maintain such opulence. One wouldn't think Serbia's government would have the kind of cash available for its representatives to live lushly overseas, but there's no understanding how a government spends its money.

I pulled up outside a white, faux-colonial style mansion on 23rd Avenue. A black Jeep Cherokee sat idling by the curb. It was a standing joke between Derek and me that the road between Vancouver and Whistler was rarely in poor enough condition to warrant a four-wheel-drive vehicle and that he had become the quintessential yuppie. He refused to accept my socialist barbs and insisted the large vehicle came in handy for transporting young players from the soccer team he coached. I was still convinced he only coached the team to justify his pricey vehicle. I've always been skeptical of altruism. Derek stepped out of the truck as I rolled to a stop. My convertible Saab seemed downright proletarian next to his monster truck.

"Still thinking this is a good idea?" he offered as a greeting.

"Don't have any better ones."

"There's always sleep."

"I've heard of that. Of course, sleep always seemed so much

more important when I had a job to get up and go to." Derek threw me the type of glance a mental health professional would use when seeing scars on a patient's wrist. Even I had to admit I was sounding pitifully self-pitying. "Let's get this over with," I grumbled as I walked towards the Serbian consular residence.

"Andrea know we're doing this?" he added as he dropped into step beside me.

I smiled at him. "I'm sure I wouldn't be here if she did."

"She could stop you?"

"She has handcuffs."

"Ahh." He smiled with just a hint of self-indulgent pleasure.

"My God, Derek. Wipe the smile off your face. She's my friend, you know."

"Relax, boy scout. Just a quick mental holiday." Derek gave me an annoyingly friendly pat on the shoulder and pushed us towards the front door.

"What's the protocol at a consulate?" I asked. "Do we knock or just walk right in?"

Derek shrugged in response. "I don't do a whole lot of consular house calls. Knocking always seems like a pretty safe bet."

"Like a good Catholic upbringing would teach you."

"Or a Jewish one." Derek reached forward and rang the bell at the side of the oversized double doors. We waited silently for what seemed like a long time. Derek finally spoke as we waited. "Do you want me to do the talking?"

"Only if it looks like I'm running out of things to ask."

He chuckled. "How long do you think that will take?"

"A couple of minutes at most." We waited a minute longer. "Any chance there's no Serbians home?"

"It's a big house."

"Your neck of the woods."

"My place was much bigger." Even when I was trying to insult him, he always pre-empted me. The rain continued to pour down in its November way, and I was beginning to feel uncomfortably cold. I hoped they would offer us something warm to drink. Do they have hot chocolate in Serbia? Finally, the right hand door opened, and we were greeted by a young, dark haired man in a charcoal business suit. It seemed odd: I guess I was expecting combat fatigues.

"Yes?" he asked in a completely unaccented voice.

"We're here to see the consul," I began. "My name is..."

"I know who you are," he interrupted. "I'm wondering what it is that you want." Fame.

For the first time in a long time, I figured I would try to win him over with politeness. My snotty sarcasm had been winning me no friends of late. Derek stepped in. "Since you know who we are, the nature of our business should be readily apparent to you."

"As you can well imagine, this is a troubling time for the consul general. He has been most upset by the events of the past week. He is also very busy."

"He'll end up talking to us sooner or later," I threatened. I'd heard them say that many times on *Law and Order*, and it always seemed to work.

The executive doorman considered my threat for a moment, then decided he would let us in. It was more likely he didn't feel like standing and arguing with us any longer. Just the same, he left us standing in a white-tiled entryway at the foot of a spiral staircase leading away to mysterious second floor rooms. Since he had given no specific directions as to where we were to go until the consul general met with us, we decided to stand silently in the lobby, like kids outside the vice principal's office.

"Good morning." Derek and I both turned in the direction of the voice that had spoken behind us. The consul general was a man of about fifty years. He had amazingly thick white hair and he wore a charcoal-grey suit almost identical to the one the doorman had greeted us in. I wondered if it was a Serbian uniform. We exchanged pleasantries and introductions and Serbia's top man in Canada invited us to sit down.

"We're sorry to have to disturb you today," I began. "I understand you must be busy, and that this is certainly a time of grief for your family."

"Thank you," Bogdan Dantolovec replied. He sat on a single armchair across from Derek and me. "It has been a very difficult time." He studied us for a moment before continuing. "But I can understand why it is you would need to talk to me. I will be as helpful as I can."

"We appreciate that." I paused again before I continued. The room that I presumed was used for business was originally the living room in the house and was decorated to make visitors to this tiny piece of foreign territory feel the warmth of hearth and home. Above the fireplace, an old fashioned mantle clock ticked loudly and was one beat removed from the sound of the rain falling in the chimney. The mantle clock was many hours out of sync with my own watch, and it took me a moment to figure out that the clock was probably set to Serbian time. I realized the silence had drawn out when Derek gave me the gentlest of nudges with the toe of his expensive shoe, spurring me back into investigator mode. "I guess I have to start by asking you about your relationship with Tricia."

"What is that it you would like to know?" Mr. Dantolovec spoke as though I were asking a question about tourism in his homeland. If our visit was truly upsetting to him, he was doing a fine job of masking it.

I pressed on. "To begin with, were you close with Tricia?"

"I am close with all of my family. No parent or relative likes to say these kinds of things, but it is fair to suggest Tricia was one of my favourites, if one can have a favourite niece. I considered her one of my own."

"One of your own children?"

"Yes. I have none. My life has been in the service of my country. I have had little time for family, an issue I regret deeply, especially now that Tricia is gone."

"Sir, I know this is difficult, as it was for Tricia's mother when I spoke with her, but I have to ask you. Can you think of any reason why someone would want to kill Tricia?"

His right eyebrow danced quickly up onto his forehead, a trait that seemed to run in his family. "Do you mean other than your deceased client?" Score one for the consul general.

Derek intervened. "Of course, sir, it is natural you believe our client was responsible for Tricia's death. I also understand that our belief in Mr. Turbot's innocence is hardly sufficient to sway you, but if we could, for just a moment, work from the supposition that Carl Turbot was in no way involved in your niece's death, perhaps we might find some fresh perspective and information."

Mr. Dantolovec stared intently at us. "It seems redundant that you choose to pursue this matter even after the untimely death of your client."

"Mr. Dantolovec," I told him, "if we were not fervently convinced Mr. Turbot was innocent, you are quite correct that our continued involvement would appear frivolous. The fact we are continuing to seek answers even after we no longer have a duty to our client ought to at least demonstrate to you that we are truly determined to see Tricia's actual killer caught."

He nodded slightly in acknowledgment that our logic was in fact logical. "Okay. I will play along with your assumptions for the time being, though I believe the police already had their man. To answer your question, then, no. I cannot think of any reason why someone would want to harm my beautiful niece."

"Did you talk often?"

"It was a practice of my family life here in Canada that we attempted to sit down to Sunday dinner as many weekends as possible."

"That's nice," I threw in.

"Yes. It was. I have held this posting for many years, since Tricia was a young girl new to Canada. She grew up knowing this house as part of her own heritage."

"Did Tricia know Zoran Jonkovich?" I threw the question at him, figuring it was the hardball that would make him flinch. It didn't.

"Of course. Mr. Jonkovich has been in our employ since he came to this country three years ago. Tricia would have seen him here many times."

"Did they get along?"

"Why would they not?"

"You tell me." His tone had turned slightly adversarial, and mine instinctively did the same.

"If you are suggesting Zoran could have killed Tricia, you are completely mistaken."

I leaned my elbows on my knees. They were still damp from the quick jog from car to Serbian front door. "He beat the daylights out of me. Violence is not beyond the scope of his understanding."

"No one from my country is immune to violence. Mr. Jonkovich made an error in judgment when he came to meet with you in the cemetery. He was spoken to."

"That makes me feel much better."

"What my colleague here means," Derek interrupted, sensing that my emotions were, yet again, running out of check, "is that Mr. Jonkovich's assault against Mr. Patrick seems to indicate a very personal interest in Tricia. Sir, with all due respect, this question will sound in the poorest taste, but I have to ask. Is it possible Mr. Jonkovich and Tricia were romantically involved?"

"That is absurd!" our host practically bellowed. "You are so desperate to clear the name of the vermin that you represent that you would sully the reputation of my niece even further?" Neither of us could think of a good response to his rhetorical question, so we just let it hang there and waited for him to continue. "Is it not enough Carl Turbot has stolen the innocence of the poor child, now you believe her to be some kind of slut?" I was taken aback by his use of the word. It didn't seem the kind of language used in the diplomatic service.

Derek continued calmly, refusing to rise to Dantolovec's emotional level. "Again, sir, putting aside the idea that Mr. Turbot had anything to do with Tricia's death, is it possible Zoran Jonkovich and Tricia had ever been romantically involved? They were not that far apart in age, certainly less so than Tricia and Carl Turbot. Did they ever spend time together?"

Dantolovec's breathing quickened. He glared angrily across the coffee table at us. "Is it possible?" he finally replied. "Yes. They spent time together, and I believe you could characterize their relationship as friendly."

"Friendly enough that finding out about Tricia's relationship with our client could have spurred him to violence?" Derek continued.

"If Mr. Jonkovich were going to get violent with anyone, why would he not have attacked your client?"

"Maybe he did," I replied, since I was feeling left out of the conversation. "The evidence in our client's death is pretty inconclusive."

Dantolovec seemed to think about it. "No. I cannot accept that Zoran would attack and kill Tricia. If he were to take action, it would have been against the Croatian traitor."

"Excuse me?" I asked. "What Croatian traitor?"

"Your client."

This was news to me. "My client was Croatian? I didn't know that."

"Apparently there is much you did not know about your client."

"What does his Croatian heritage have to do with anything?"

Mr. Dantolovec looked at me as though I were a complete idiot. "The Croatians were traitors against our country. For years we worked hard to modernize and bring the Yugoslavian people into respectability as a nation. The Croatians in Bosnia and in Serbia violently betrayed their fellow countrymen."

There was fire in the eyes of the Serbian consul. "Forgive me, sir," I said, "but I was under the impression it was the Serbians who slaughtered hundreds of thousands of Croats, not the other way around." I tried to sound historically knowledgeable, but in reality I knew very little about the long-standing conflicts in the Balkans.

"Then you have been misled by your hopelessly anti-Serbian media. You could not possibly hope to understand the years of torment our people have suffered because of the Croatian independence movement."

"No sir, I could not." We stared back and forth at each other for a few seconds.

"How then do you think Mr. Jonkovich would feel, knowing that not only was Tricia in the bed of her teacher, but that her teacher descended from the families of people he had been fighting against?" Not so good, I supposed.

Derek spoke up again suddenly. "So you can see, sir, why we need to determine Mr. Jonkovich's whereabouts on the night of Tricia's death, as well as the night of our client's death?"

Dantolovec calmed down and seemed to accept again the logic

of Derek's argument. He nodded barely perceptibly. "Yes. While I do not believe that Zoran would do anything against Tricia, I do understand why you seek this information."

"May we talk with him?" I asked hopefully, though the thought of facing Jonkovich on what was technically not even Canadian soil did not thrill me.

"Certainly," was the response, "though I do not know where to find him."

"He's not here?"

"No. He is no longer in our employ."

"You fired him? Why?"

"We had our reasons. Suffice to say I was not impressed with the manner in which he conducted himself."

I took this as an opportunity to keep pressing forward. "Mr. Dantolovec, I have another question. Who was the other person that was with Zoran Jonkovich when he attacked me?"

His eyebrow shot up again onto his forehead before he replied. "I do not know. You will have to ask Zoran." He glanced at the Serbian timed clock on the mantelpiece. "Gentlemen, I have given you all of the time that I can. I am afraid that now I have other business to attend to. Good day." Without so much as a handshake, the Serbian consul general stood, turned on his heels and left us sitting on the sofa wondering what had suddenly happened.

"Well, that was weird," I said, rising from the sofa.

"He definitely didn't want to talk about Jonkovich's partner."

"Baseball Cap," I said as we headed out of the ornate living room towards the front door.

"What?"

"That's what I named him."

"Oh." We stepped out onto the front verandah of the diplomatic residence.

"Do you think we learned anything important?" I asked my wiser partner.

"I think we want to talk to Zoran Jonkovich. Soon." He headed towards his monstrous SUV and left me standing on Serbian soil watching the Vancouver rain.

Twenty-Eight

By the time I got home, I had decided the principal was right: I needed to rest. My head was swirling with the amount of information it contained and worse, the amount of information I didn't have. My plan was to simply get inside, get undressed and crash. It was only five thirty in the afternoon, but I felt like I deserved some pampering. A hot bath—no, I don't think that's too girly—maybe a little wine, then bed. I wondered if maybe there was too much wine in many of my plans, but I didn't care. I had earned it.

I turned the key in the lock and entered my darkened apartment. All I could see was the glow of the city lights coming through the blinds I had left open. The light cast was eerie, causing dancing shadows on the kitchen wall to the left of the entrance hallway. As my eyes adjusted from the dimly-lit corridor to the near complete darkness of my apartment, I noticed one shadow dancer was more three dimensional than the others. I was too late figuring out that the shadow had taken form before I felt it slam into me. I crashed into the double-mirrored door that hid my apartment sized washer and dryer. One side of the double door cracked in the centre, and I could feel the large shards of glass coming down. Seven years bad luck. How much worse could it get?

I slid to the floor along with the remnants of the mirror, landing on my ass and crunching glass beneath me. I rolled onto my side, conscious of the dark figure still standing over me. How come he hadn't fallen? He had still said nothing, and I slid my way along the hardwood floor in a feeble attempt to get away from him. I could feel more anger than fear rising like bile in my throat, and I was growing outraged that I was being attacked a second time, this time in my own house. My outrage didn't lend itself to getting the shit kicked out of me, so I still fancied flight as the best expression of my indignity. Sliding across the hallway floor into the living room, I did a mental inventory of my furniture and belongings in search of a weapon I could use to defend myself. On the coffee table ahead, all I could make out were file folders filled with my preparations for Carl's defence. Filing a brief right then didn't seem like much of a defence.

The darkened figure let out a grunt, and I turned just in time to see his right foot swing back in pre-kick mode. I rolled over onto my back to raise both my hands in protection. Inadvertently, I caught his foot in mid swing and while it did propel me backwards, it had the bonus effect of throwing the kicker off balance. With a crash that I prayed would be loud enough to cause my downstairs neighbours to come running, he slammed onto the floor, the top of his head making contact with the lower part of the wall separating kitchen from dining room. "Fuck!" he yelled as he hit the floor. The "k" in "fuck" was very pronounced, accented. By now I had learned to identify the Balkan accent. I'm nothing if not a quick study. Zoran Jonkovich was lying on my floor.

I quickly scrambled to my feet and backed my way towards the fireplace. In contemporary, modern condominiums, all fireplaces are powered by natural gas, so I couldn't even find anything useful like a fireplace poker to wield as a weapon. I tried an authoritative tone instead. "What the hell are you doing here?" I demanded. I thought I sounded convincing. Judging by the speed at which Jonkovich was getting to his feet to come after me again, I gathered he wasn't as impressed by how ferocious I was sounding. I tried to put the coffee table between us, and already my juvenile imagination was concocting cartoon like images of Jonkovich chasing me in endless circles around the glass structure until help arrived.

"You were told to stay out of this!" he hissed at me, his breathing only slightly elevated.

"Yeah, I recall. You know, you could have just left me a message."

"You are a fucker like your miserable client!" He made a half-hearted lunge in my direction, and I stepped quickly to the side to dodge him.

"How did you even get in here?" I demanded further.

He smiled again. "I learned many things when I fought under Karadzic."

"Who?"

"Karadzic. The man who led us in the fight against the Croatian pigs like your client." Great, I thought. A crazed murderer was going to kill me, but not before I got a fucking history lesson.

"Look, Jonkovich," I said soothingly, "you're already in a great deal of shit for your first assault on me, and on the police officer at Tricia's funeral. Don't make this any worse for yourself."

"Who will even know that I've been here?" That didn't sound promising.

"You're assuming I'm going to keep quiet."

"And you're assuming you'll be able to speak." Yeah. That was where I'd thought he was going.

"So you're going to kill me like you killed Carl? If I end up dead after you killed him and his wife, the police are definitely going to come looking for you."

He sounded genuinely surprised, if not amused. "Your friend killed himself and his wife, I heard."

"You heard wrong. You think I don't know that you killed him?" I was running out of conversational topics, and I was no closer to finding a weapon to use against the mammoth Serb limo driver.

"I wish I had killed him, what he did to Tricia. He is an animal."

"Hey, you know what? I'm getting a little tired of that angle. She was with him of her own free will. It may not have made him the teacher of the year or anything, but he didn't hold a gun to her head. Which is less than I can say about you, by the way."

"He stole her innocence!" he barked, raising his voice again. I kind of hoped that the angrier and louder he got, the more likely it was someone, somewhere, would think to check if I was okay. "What kind of man does not take responsibility for his actions?"

"What is it you wanted from him?"

"He took her childhood. She was a child! That pig Croatian defiled her then killed her, so she could not turn him in!" As he spoke, his fists were clenching, warming up for my face again. The bruise around my eye was just starting to fade. I didn't relish another one, though given the choice between another black eye and death, I would choose the former. I wanted to keep him talking, shouting.

"Tricia told you this?"

"I heard from the family. They were outraged that this could happen!"

"Tricia seduced him. She initiated the relationship, not the other way around!" It was strange defending Carl's honour like this, but I could not swallow my outrage.

"Liar!"

"She phoned him and harassed him, over and over again. He even bought a call screening box so he could get the police to go talk to her, make her stop with the phone calls. She was the crazy one, not Carl!" He shook his head, confusion and anger boiling up in him. From the look on his face, I could see he suspected what I was saying was true. "But you knew that, didn't you? You were the one who went into Carl's house and erased the phone numbers that showed Tricia was harassing him!"

"No!"

"And when you saw that Tricia was the aggressor, she was the one who had come on to him, you refused to accept it and you killed her. You killed her and you threatened me once the police conveniently pointed the finger at Carl. You wanted me to stop trying to defend Carl so you could get away with having killed her yourself! You're the animal, Jonkovich, not Carl!"

"No!" he screamed at me. "He ruined her! He is to blame, you fucking, pig-loving sleaze." He stepped up onto the coffee table and crashed down onto the other side, grabbing me by the collar of my jacket and slamming me backwards against the sliding glass patio doors. I struggled for all I was worth. It wasn't graceful or even very impressive, but I yelled, I kicked, I flailed until I spun sideways, falling over the arm of the sofa, Jonkovich thumping down on top of me.

In a second, I felt his hands around my throat, and I could feel searing pain in my Adam's apple. I reached up, pushing at his face with my waning strength. Jonkovich arched his neck back, nearly out of my reach. My head began to spin as the pain from his hands and the lack of oxygen began to rob me of consciousness. I was starting to fade away, one hand already dropping away from Jonkovich when I heard someone scream my name.

Almost immediately, the pressure lifted from around my throat as Jonkovich flung me aside onto the floor. I was able to lift my head and see Sandi standing in the doorway, her face stricken with terror. Summoning what little oxygen I could muster, I managed to open my mouth and hiss at her. "Run! Go!" For the first time in all the years I had known her, my ex-wife did exactly as I asked her, turning back towards the door she had found and left open. "Go! Run!" I told her before falling in a heap on the floor. The last I saw, Sandi turned right as she went out the door, heading towards the emergency exit at the end of the hall. Good for you, I thought, though I no longer had the voice to say it.

Jonkovich went down my entrance hallway after her, for the time being leaving me to my own devices. The only device I could think of was the phone, and I reached up and banged the cordless phone down in front of me. I managed to dial 911 but could manage no further communication as the air was just now slowly returning to my lungs, and I began to choke and cough. As Jonkovich entered the hallway, I heard a loud scuffle and then some shouting. I made a slow effort to stumble to my feet, and I had almost made it to the door when Barry, my downstairs neighbour, appeared in the doorway.

Grabbing me by the shoulders he demanded, "Are you okay?" I pointed towards the stairwell where I assumed everyone had gone. Barry just shook his head. "He's gone. He ran out onto the third floor, and we lost him."

"Sandi," I whispered, then slumped against the doorway with relief as she opened the stairway door with the assistance of Barry's roommate Dean, who led her shakily back down the hall. For the moment, at least, we were all okay.

*   *   *

It was like a reunion in my apartment: Furlo, Smythe, Sandi and, of course, Andrea. They had raced to my apartment after the first call went out on the air from the police dispatcher who took the 911 call. Within about a half hour, the uniformed cops had left. My neighbours—including Barry and Dean, who had attempted to apprehend Jonkovich—had decided that life in the Patrick pad was returning to normal, and they could return to their own corners of the building. I was having a hard time convincing Andy and Sandi that I was physically and emotionally okay after my run-in with my own personal attacker. Of course, I wasn't entirely convinced myself either, so small wonder they didn't believe me.

Furlo was squatting down, carefully examining the lock and deadbolt on my front door for about the hundredth time since he had arrived. "Man. He's good. There's not a scratch on this thing. Not a scratch." If it wasn't for the fact he was referring to a man who had tried to kill me—and had in my opinion most likely killed Tricia Bellamy, Carl and Bonnie Turbot—I'm sure the detective would have been downright amused.

"They teach them that in the Serbian army," I told him.

"The Serbian army had to pick locks? Why didn't they just shoot their way into houses? It was a war, after all."

"I don't know. I was just about to ask him when he put his hands around my throat. I was having a hard time with functioning speech."

"Would you forget about the door for a minute, Mike?" Andy asked with exasperation as she brought in a cup of tea from the kitchen. When she mothered me, I generally didn't mind, but I was feeling a bit sheepish about it in front of Furlo and Smythe. Intellectually, I knew they didn't view me as particularly macho, but I still felt a need to have some kind of virility. "How long would you say it took you to get from the Serbian consulate back to your place?"

I did the mental math. "No more than about ten or fifteen minutes, I'm sure. Even during rush hour, most of the traffic is heading the other way out towards Richmond, so it was pretty quick."

"So that essentially rules out the good ambassador siccing his driver on you after you left," Detective Jasmine Smythe opined.

"Ex-driver," I corrected. "He's been fired."

"Or so he says," Andy added. "Did he leave you alone in the house while the two of you were there?"

"We waited in the living room for a little bit. But that was before we met him."

"He hadn't had sufficient opportunity to dislike you," Furlo commented as he closed the door and tried the dead bolt. Again.

Even though I was tired, I tried to think of something clever in reply, but my thoughts were interrupted by the chirping of Smythe's cell phone. She stepped away to answer in the relative privacy afforded by the piece of floor directly in front of my refrigerator.

"So on the surface it seems likely Jonkovich was not acting on the instructions of Dantolovec," Andrea surmised.

"So it would seem," I agreed, though I could not shake the feeling the Serbian consular general was extremely agitated by our presence.

"Well, that's interesting," Smythe blurted, stepping back into the dining area while snapping her cell phone shut.

"They pick up Jonkovich?" Furlo wanted to know. I did too.

"Nope. No one's seen him yet. But he's a big, ugly fella. He'll show up. That was my contact in forensics. They've been going over the crime scene data, including other prints they found in the house. They've essentially ruled out a number—including yours." She pointed to me. "They also didn't find any prints from Jonkovich."

"Wait a minute," I protested. "Now you guys are leaning away from murder-suicide?"

"Too many other prints in the house for plain old homicide to be ruled out," Furlo confirmed. "But it looks like our boy Jonkovich wasn't there. He seems just to have a burr up his ass about you, Patrick."

"Or he was there, but didn't leave any prints," Andrea mused, since the deaths of Carl and Bonnie was, in fact, her case.

"Gloves?" I threw in.

"Ooh, you're good," Furlo replied. I had to give him that one; it was a pretty obvious observation.

"Fuck you," I replied. On the other hand, it was my apartment, and I was the victim of an attempted murder. If someone else wasn't going to start feeling sorry for me soon, I was going to have to do it all myself.

"Boys, boys," Smythe scolded. "We're not getting anywhere. Did he say anything else to you that points to him as Tricia's murderer? Or the Turbots, for that matter?"

"Just what I told you. He was irate and after me but..."

"But what?" Andrea wanted to know.

"You know, it's just weird. This is the second time Jonkovich has kicked the shit out of me, but I can't shake the sense he was somehow being genuine."

"In what way?"

"He was still pissed at me that I was defending Carl. Everything he said took him back to the fact that Carl killed Tricia. He really seemed to believe it."

Furlo spoke up again. "Maybe because he did. Your client is still the best bet we've got on Bellamy's death."

"Yeah. Yeah. I've heard that refrain, Furlo. We can agree to disagree on that for now. What's more important to me is that Jonkovich believed it too. If he killed Tricia and killed Carl, why the hell come after me too?"

"He's angry because he got fired?" I had almost forgotten Sandi was in the room.

"Yeah. But, killing me just points more suspicion at him. He was angry. In a rage. This was vengeful."

Andrea was nodding. "So he's got some hard-on for Tricia and is still enraged at Carl for her death and their relationship."

"Yeah," I agreed, "which tells me even more strongly that someone else killed Tricia. I just gotta figure out who."

Detective Smythe laid her hand on my arm. "No. No, you don't. That's our job." She was speaking firmly, telling me I should stay out of the way. But for the first time, it sounded like she was willing to acknowledge that my client hadn't been a killer. I smiled slightly. I had successfully defended him at last.

Twenty-Nine

I was a little surprised by the sound of a knock on the door. I don't get that many nocturnal visitors. I was still groggy as I approached the front door. The entrance hallway seemed longer than usual, as though challenging me to abandon my quest for the person on the other side of the door. I considered abandoning the trip altogether. I really just wanted to sleep.

Light seeped in from the hallway under the crack in the faux old-fashioned front door, leaving an eerie glow that only partially illuminated my bare feet. I noticed my feet in front of the doorway. As men's feet go, mine are actually pretty nice. It wasn't entirely surprising when I stole a glance through the peephole that I saw no one there. It was the hour that invites pranksters. I decided to open the door anyway, just to be sure I had not, in fact, imagined the knocking in the first place, though it had continued from the time I rolled over in bed until the moment I reached the front door.

She was there. It seemed unfathomable to me that one of my students could possibly know my home address. Surely the media wouldn't have released that information, though as I thought about it, I realized I had never bothered to get an unlisted address and phone number in the telephone directory. I tried to ask her what she was doing in my hallway, but before I could, she pushed gently past me and entered the apartment, causing me to step backward as she glided by.

I was mesmerized by her ease of movement, and her ability to seemingly float across the hallway floor. But her very presence in my apartment quickly enraged me. She had crossed a line. You don't show up at your teacher's house. Never. It isn't done, and her impertinence made me furious. Before she could travel much further into my apartment, I grabbed her by the arm, spinning her around to face me. Her eyes widened in surprise, even horror, at the rough way that I grabbed her. Inexplicably even to me, her sudden fear of me after her brazen gall at arriving at my home in the middle of the night only served to make me angrier. I wanted to demand an explanation, to order her to leave, but in the growing heat of the moment, I knew—I knew—she wouldn't listen to reason.

She opened her mouth to speak, but before she could even utter a syllable, two hands grasped her throat. To my utter dismay—and no doubt to hers—the hands were mine. Her eyes grew wider, part from fear, part loss of innocence that this teacher she had come to trust would take such violent action against her. Her naïveté inflamed my temper further, and I squeezed even tighter, watching in fascinated horror as my student grew weaker and weaker. Finally, after clutching desperately at my grip, her hands gave out, her eyeballs rolled backwards in her head and she dropped to the floor. For a moment, I looked down, cocking my head at the curious heap of student on my hallway floor. She looked humbled, as I thought she should after interrupting my rare sleep with her unexplained visit.

Gently, I lowered her into the trunk of the car, placing her carefully on top of the other students I had collected there. I stepped back from my car and smiled slightly, bemused at how many bodies the semi-compact trunk could hold. I wondered if the automaker would like to know how much cargo I was able to haul.

The park looked the same as I had seen it the first time. Quiet. Lonely. Surrounded by houses where nobody watched, and it seemed a fitting place to unload my car of its lifeless cargo. The bodies were light, much easier to move than I would have thought, given the term "dead weight", which suggested to me that carrying my dead students would have been difficult. But as easily as each had floated across the threshold into my apartment, they seemed to float in my arms as I carefully laid them to rest, one after the other, dead centre in the middle of the park. The night was still and quiet, and I reflected to myself how easy it had been. I felt little remorse. They had come to me willingly, after all.

Turning, I saw Don McFadden walking towards me from between the abandoned swings of the playground. He didn't look too angry. His face had that "I knew it" kind of smugness to it, and I knew he had decided he had been right about me all along: my connection to Carl had made me into some kind of monster myself. I shook my head at him, unable to think of a suitable explanation for the students lying at my feet. Don simply turned and walked away. As I looked down sadly at the victims at my feet, the telephone broke my seductive trance with its sharp shrill.

Rolling over in my bed, I picked up the telephone and mumbled "Hello?"

"You weren't sleeping?" came Andrea's voice.

I took a slow look around my empty room. "No," I told her. "When do I ever sleep?"

"That's what I figured. I also figured you'd go running. I'd rather you didn't go alone. I'll be there in half an hour."

"Fine," I told her and hung up without saying goodbye. Obviously, I needed to clear my head of some residual guilt.

Since Furlo and Smythe had acknowledged the possibility of another direction in Tricia's death, I was officially—especially as far as Furlo was concerned—"off the case." In one of those rare moments of camaraderie between Furlo and my best friend, Andy was also doing her level best to convince me my role here was complete. In other words: stay the hell out of their way.

On many levels, their advice made sense. My commitment to Carl was to give him the best legal defence for Tricia's homicide. Given that the lead detectives were now at least considering other possibilities, my job had effectively ended. If Carl were still alive, he would likely be released with charges against him being dropped. I needn't worry any further.

But I did. It wasn't helping that for the remainder of the week at least, I was not expected to go back to work. The media with their ever-growing abilities to monitor police information had made sure the attack on me had become public knowledge. The principal was near the point of suffering a heart attack at the thought of my returning and causing any more publicity for the school. The last thing I needed was someone else's death on my conscience.

Not being at work did afford me the luxury of time to reflect on how things had unfolded, and it had provided me with the rare evening of actually sleeping—at least until Andrea had phoned and interrupted my slumber, thank God. I had been scrupulously avoiding thinking about the possibility that I might have been wrong about Carl. Self-satisfaction is just not part of my makeup.

When Andrea arrived—it was still only seven in the morning— I threw caution to the wind and suggested we run over the Burrard Street Bridge into the West End, there to tackle the perils of the windswept English Bay and Stanley Park seawall. I could tell she was a reluctant participant, but if she was going to insist on babysitting me every time I left the house, I wasn't about to make it easy for her. While we ran, she attempted some light conversation, but my heart just wasn't in it. The more she tried, the harder I pushed us, figuring she couldn't talk if she couldn't breathe. By the time we reached the Third Beach concession stand, she was pretty insistent we turn around.

The whole time we ran, I couldn't get my mind off my most recent encounter with Zoran Jonkovich. I suppose that was natural: it isn't every day someone breaks into my house and tries to kill me. It's bound to stick with a person awhile. Still, his obsession with Tricia Bellamy bordered on the absurd. Even in her death, Jonkovich was determined to protect, what? Her honour? Her memory? As we neared the south end of the bridge, I ran a theory past my puffing protector self-designate. "I was thinking," I began.

"So I gathered since you've stopped harassing me about my stride."

"We have no physical evidence to tie Jonkovich to Tricia's death."

"Not specifically, though using gloves on a strangulation victim is not uncommon."

"But I just don't buy it. Other than his actions towards me, there is little to suggest he would have killed Tricia."

"Last night you told us Jonkovich appeared to be in love with Tricia. Don't you think this could be a crime of passion or jealousy?" We rounded the corner at the foot of the bridge onto Cornwall Avenue, past the White Spot restaurant that, in spite of my protests, had replaced the Baskin-Robbins ice cream shop.

"Then why not kill Carl rather than Tricia?" I asked rhetorically.

"We don't know he didn't. There were no prints at the Turbot residence that registered on our database o' bad guys. Someone planning to ensure his tracks are covered would surely use gloves during both crimes." Andrea always answers my rhetorical questions.

"But that's what's bugging me," I retorted. We slowed down at the corner of Yew Street, planning a leisurely cool-down jog for the last few blocks. "These murders were carefully planned. I'm no forensics expert, but it can't be a simple matter to make a double murder look like a murder-suicide."

"Which we still haven't ruled out," Andrea reminded me.

"Still," I said, slowing to a walk, "let's assume for a minute they're both homicides. The sequence doesn't make sense. If Jonkovich was in love with Tricia..."

"Was there anyone who wasn't?" she interrupted sardonically. "This girl cast one hell of a spell over the men in her life. I would like to have met her."

"I did," I replied glumly, recalling our one conversation together and illogically punishing myself for not resolving her dispute with Carl before so much harm befell them both. "She could certainly inspire passion. Which brings me back to my point: if Jonkovich was so in love with Tricia, why not kill Carl first, hoping to eliminate his romantic competition? A sense of betrayal is one motive, I admit, but these two crimes—killing Tricia and moving the body, the staged murder-suicide—were carefully planned. I'm not sure Jonkovich is up to that."

"He planned to be at your place when you arrived."

"Picking a couple of locks at best. And his attack on me *was* passionate. Not calculating. In fact, he might have been planning just to beat the hell out of me again. I probably goaded him into a rage. And he must have left his fingerprints all over me and my apartment."

We stopped on the sidewalk in front of my building. Andy's "bitchin'" Camaro, as she liked to call it, was parked out front. She acknowledged my skillful observation. "That's true. He could just be getting angrier, but you're right: the three crimes don't seem the same."

Maybe I had detecting abilities after all. Look out Spenser, here I come. "Which means we still need a suspect."

"No," she corrected me for only about the hundredth time, "*we*—not you—still need a suspect. Your job is done here."

"Yeah, yeah," I brushed off her admonition. "And I still say our best bet is Jonkovich's partner in my first attack—Baseball Cap."

"Your friend Mr. Wong..."

"Woo."

"...Woo," she repeated, "did mention two people in the limo that night."

"Which your friends Furlo and Smythe totally blew off in their quest to arrest Carl."

"Yes, but my point being, Jonkovich was the limo driver for the consul general. Assuming Baseball Cap did Tricia, who was with him in the car if not the man employed to drive it?"

She had me there. The head Serbian in Vancouver had denied even knowing, let alone employing anyone resembling Baseball Cap, and was now invoking diplomatic immunity to prevent close scrutiny of the embassy's personnel files. My thoughts were interrupted by a soft but familiar voice from behind me. "Mr. Patrick?" Turning, I saw Scott Harton from my senior law class walking towards us from under the front portico of my apartment building.

"What are you doing here?" I asked.

"I'm sorry. I needed to talk to you. I didn't know when or even if you were coming back." In the face of Scott's obvious discomfort, I told him it was okay and asked what he needed. He looked at me, then stole a glance at Andrea. She caught his none-too-subtle signal.

"I was just leaving," she told him with a look to me that asked if I wanted her to stay. Sensing that Scott had come reluctantly, I decided to talk to him privately. "I'll call you later," Andrea said as she turned and trotted to her car.

"Let's go inside," I told my student and pointed him towards the door.

*   *   *

Scott Harton looked nervously around my apartment as I directed him to a stool in front of my kitchen pass-through. Inviting him to sit on my overstuffed sofa seemed even less correct than having him here at all. Briefly, my mind flashed again to principal Don McFadden's face, as it would no doubt appear with the knowledge that a student had crossed this divide. Carl's relationship with his student had underscored the always-lurking danger of even perceived inappropriateness in teacher-student relationships. Scott's presence at my apartment would not be viewed as sound practice. He was male, true, but pedophiles do not necessarily discriminate between genders.

"I'm sorry to bother you at home," he began quietly. "I know I've crossed a line here." At least we were on the same wavelength.

"That's okay," I tried to reassure him. "I'm certain you would not have come if it wasn't important." He looked at me rather quizzically. I was dripping wet, dressed in Lycra running shorts—unflattering no matter what man you put them on—a sweatshirt, running jacket and a threadbare cotton toque. It no doubt clashed with Scott's image of me in shirt and tie. Most teachers at Sir John A. Macdonald don't dress that formally, but as a former lawyer, I had a closet full of dress shirts and inexpensive ties. I also believed it helped to separate me from the students; as youthful-looking as I narcissistically believed I was, I didn't want to be mistaken for a twelfth grader. I would sometimes "mix it up a little" by wearing jeans with my formal upper wear. Keep 'em guessing. "Pardon my appearance. Can I get you something to drink? I'm having orange juice."

"That would be fine, thank you." Teenager with manners. He gazed around the dining room—dining area really—and spotted a stack of papers on the table. "Those our constitution papers?"

"Yep. Having time off makes it much easier to catch up on marking."

"How'd I do?"

"Pretty well, if I recall. Your position on minority language rights was well defended, if a little anti-francophone."

"Thank you," he said again, then turned nervous as he realized where he was. A silence passed between us. I didn't want to push, but I didn't want to prolong his visit either.

"So. Did you come here to pick up your paper?"

"No," was his blurted answer followed by an uncomfortable laugh. "I came to talk to you about Tricia. And Mr. Turbot." Nodding, I waited for him to continue. He looked positively mortified. Clearly what he had to tell me made him very uncomfortable.

"How are you holding up?" I offered.

"Oh, I'm okay, I guess. I mean, Tricia was close with my girlfriend, and I liked her. I guess we were sort of friends. And I really liked Mr. Turbot. He was a great teacher." He looked past me out the living room window where, as usual, it was raining.

"What is it you wanted to tell me Scott? Whatever it is, it's okay."

He took a small sip of orange juice. "Jessica—you remember, my girlfriend—didn't think we should bring it up, especially now that they're both dead." He struggled to get out the last word, as though saying it would make their deaths still more irrevocable. "But now it sounds around school like the police are still investigating, and it doesn't sound like they have, you know, all the information."

He paused another moment until I gave him an encouraging nod. "What information are they missing?"

"God. Jessica doesn't even know I'm here. She's gonna be pissed, but I figured if I told you instead of the police, you could help me determine if the police need to know. I didn't know who else to talk to."

"That was solid, rational, legal reasoning. I'm still counsel for Mr. Turbot. Anything you can tell me may be helpful."

Studying me, he decided he could trust me. "Tricia. She got pregnant with Mr. Turbot."

I nearly choked on my orange juice. "Pregnant? Are you sure?"

"Yeah," he told me resignedly. "I am. Tricia had come crying to Jessica about it. Trish didn't know it, but Jess had told me. We tell each other almost everything." His last sentence appeared designed to show the depth of his and Jessica's relationship. Scott looked as though he had been caught kissing in the cloakroom. Of course, they don't really have cloakrooms any more. Where do elementary school kids steal kisses nowadays? It was one of those unusual moments when I was temporarily speechless. "Was it wrong of me to tell you that?" he continued. "I don't want Tricia's family to be hurt any more."

"No. No, Scott. You were absolutely right to come to me with this."

"How is it going to help?"

I thought about that for a moment. "I don't know, off the top of my head." I searched the recesses of my memory back to everything Carl and Tricia had told me. At no point did he refer to Tricia being pregnant. Of course, it was possible he didn't know, or that Tricia had come to him with the information, leading to his wanting to break it off with her. Which, of course, gave him another motive to kill her. Shit. Suddenly, a thought struck me. Jumping off my stool opposite Scott, I trotted across the living room to the legal file boxes beside the couch. I rapidly dug through one until I came across the file I sought. I riffled through a few pages, glancing at the information they contained.

"Mr. Patrick?" Scott asked. "Is everything okay?"

"Yeah, yeah," I told him absently. "Scott, are you sure Tricia was telling Jessica the truth?"

"Yeah. Tricia and Jessica are...were...best friends. What are you looking at?"

"This is a copy of the autopsy report on Tricia. It's preliminary, but it would have shown Tricia was pregnant."

"Oh, no, Mr. Patrick. She wasn't by the time she was killed."

"What do you mean?"

"Tricia had an abortion."

Thirty

The house looked the same, except for the dusting of snow that had fallen and was coating the trees in the front yard. Snow is a welcome reprieve from rain in Vancouver in the winter, but given that we rarely get anything resembling accumulations of the white stuff, it wreaks havoc on any and every roadway in the city and the surrounding suburbs. Sure, we have snowplows, but apparently not enough of them or enough employees to man them sufficiently to keep our roads moving. Thus, it had taken me considerably longer than normal to arrive at the Bellamy household.

I had been a bad boy, neglecting to inform Andrea, Smythe and Furlo of the substance of my conversation with Scott Harton the night before. If he was correct, and Tricia had been pregnant with Carl's child, it seemed at least a plausible motive for Carl wanting to kill his teenaged lover. I knew I would have to tell them eventually, but I needed a head start before I encouraged Furlo to push the investigation back in Carl's direction. Even given this possible new motive for my client, it still didn't account for who had killed Carl and his wife. I refused to believe in the murder-suicide scenario, but there was no way of being absolutely certain until the autopsy results were finalized. Despite the high-placed influence in hastening justice in the investigation of Tricia's death, there had been no such "rush" request from on high when it came to solving the double homicide of the Turbots. I crunched across the mushy snow that had not yet been cleared from the sidewalk leading to the Bellamy household. I had put on an old trial suit, hoping my businesslike appearance might grant me a warmer welcome than I had last received. My pant cuffs were already brown and damp, and the loafers would never be the same.

311

"What do you want?" Looking up from my gingerly placed footprints, Mrs. Bellamy already stood on the front porch beneath the snow-weighted overhang, a scowl across her face and wearing another bright, floral print pullover that would easily make her a target for pollination. Luckily for her, no self-respecting wasp would be out in that weather.

"Good morning." Always try the friendly approach first. "I was here before. I'm Winston Patrick."

"Go to hell!" she hissed. Though it was apparent Tricia's grieving mother was not about to throw open her arms for a welcome hug, neither did she turn away to leave me, proverbially and literally, out in the cold. I approached the three front porch steps tentatively.

"I am sorry to come here again. I know my presence can only cause you more pain."

"You know nothing of how I feel." Her eyeballs, like saucers, pierced daggers through me, and her nostrils flared as she spoke. In the winter air, steam chugged from her nose, like a bull about to charge. I would not have wanted to be on the receiving end of her attack, since she appeared to weigh about the same amount as the animal her breathing emulated. I saw a family resemblance, as though at one time Tricia's mother might well have worn the same beauty as her deceased daughter. But at that moment, it struck me that when Mrs. Bellamy passed on her looks to Tricia, they must have all drained to her daughter.

"No," I admitted, acutely aware of the growing cold spot on my right toe and hoping to at least talk my way inside. "I can claim no knowledge of your pain, but some information has come up about your daughter, and I want to discuss it with you."

"What kind of information?" She turned slightly, and I thought I saw her hoof, er foot, claw at the porch's baseboards.

"Mrs. Bellamy, please. You have no reason to care about my comfort, but I am wet and freezing, and I would really like to speak with you, preferably somewhere close to a fireplace." As she had on my first visit to the house, she turned her back on me and stalked into the house without closing the door. Experience had taught me this was as close to an invitation as I would get, so I followed her in, closing the door behind me and removing my surely ruined leather

312

loafers in the hallway as the grieving mother turned into the living room ahead of me. To my disappointment, the interior of the house was not a whole lot warmer than the exterior, and I wondered again if refusing to use the furnace was some kind of Balkan mourning ritual. Mrs. Bellamy sat down on the sofa next to the fireplace that, in keeping with the furnace, was not lit.

She said nothing but gave me a cold glare that, in mother mourning language, indicated she was ready for me to begin. I did. "I need to ask you a few more questions about Tricia."

"Why?" Fair question.

"I have received some new information which may help us determine who was responsible for Tricia's death." She stared at me with barely muted hostility, her eyes numbing me as much as the cold in the room was numbing my wet toes.

"Your friend killed my daughter." It didn't seem productive to go through this dance again, but I was on her turf so it didn't seem possible or polite to completely shut her down. She offered no further evidence in her argument, and after a moment of sustained silence between us, she seemed ready for me to continue.

"Ma'am, there is no delicate way for me to broach this subject, so I am just going to be blunt with you. It's obvious you are aware of the nature of Tricia's relationship with Carl Turbot."

"Last time you were here, you were not willing or able to confirm that."

"Last time I was here, my client was still the prime suspect in Tricia's death and was very much alive. Things have changed."

"I should say so." The slightest hint of a smirk broke at the edge of her mouth. I detected a note of smugness in her demeanour.

"I know I was not able to be completely frank with you before. Technically, Mr. Turbot is still my client, and as such, there are things I should not be discussing with you. However, some of what I have found out did not come from my client, and is therefore not protected under solicitor-client privilege." She chewed on this for a while.

"What is it you want to tell me?"

I took a breath before I let her have it. "You know Tricia had gotten pregnant." The slight smirk disappeared entirely from her face, and her stare turned colder still. I had deliberately phrased the information as a statement rather than a question. Mrs. Bellamy's expression confirmed the statement for me. "Had she told you about it?"

She continued to glare at me as she spoke, and I wondered for how long she could go without blinking before her eyes completely crusted over. "What do you know about anything?" she scoffed.

"I know your daughter was pregnant. I know she terminated that pregnancy. And I know Tricia claimed my client was the father of the baby."

"Claimed?" she nearly screamed. "Claimed he was the father? Your friend Mr. Turbot ruined my daughter's life. He stole her innocence and was nowhere to be found when she needed him." It was quietly puzzling that she still referred to Carl as "Mr." Turbot, despite her apparent belief that Carl had killed her daughter.

"Do you know that for a fact?"

"I am her mother! I know what my daughter was going through!" She stood with some significant effort and clomped her way over to the fireplace. Turning and glaring over her shoulder at me her hand brushed the fireplace tools suspended from a faux brass rack next to the chain mail grate that hung cold across the opening. A brief wisp of panic flooded through me as I pictured her picking up the poker and swinging it at my head. My head had been through enough lately. I arched my back deeper into the uncomfortable couch, mentally removing myself from potential blows.

"What I mean to say, Mrs. Bellamy, is did Tricia tell you directly that she was pregnant?" The overwrought woman paused before turning back towards the fireplace, staring into the long cold embers and dust that had settled into a pile beneath the grate.

"She didn't have to," she said finally. I let that sit for a moment before continuing.

"Why not?"

Slowly she turned to face me again, her eyes cold, spikes of ice. Any semblance of grief or remorse she might have been feeling at the start of the conversation had vanished, replaced by anger bordering on hatred. Her words came out with a palpable venomous drip. "Because the day she had the abortion, I got a call

314

asking how she was feeling since she was not in school."

"Is it unusual for the school to phone home about an absent student?" I honestly didn't know. I had never bothered to observe closely how the school secretaries dealt with absences.

"No," she said quietly, and her cold voice sent chills through the already frigid room. "But it was your Mr. Turbot who called. He asked me how Tricia's 'procedure' had gone, and if she was resting comfortably. I had no idea what he was talking about, and I told him so. Once he realized I didn't know what was happening, he told me he must have been thinking about the wrong student, and he hung up."

I thought about that for a moment. From my limited relationship with Carl, it sounded like the kind of sensitive and not-too-bright thing he would do. He knew she was having an abortion that day and called to make sure she was all right. "How did that lead you to think she was having an abortion?" I asked Tricia's trembling mother.

She walked slowly over to the couch again and collapsed into it. A small billow of dust exploded from the cushions. I had an urge to start cleaning. "I knew how she felt about that man. He was all she ever talked about. 'Mr. Turbot this' and 'Mr. Turbot that.' The man could do no wrong. It was as though he walked on water."

"And you knew they were having an affair?"

"A mother knows. I tried to talk to her about it, but of course she said it was not true. I even confronted him about it, and he just turned me away. He never even had the courage to admit it or deny it to my face. He just said he wasn't 'comfortable' talking to me about Tricia. Then when he phoned, I knew. I knew for certain what that Croatian animal had been doing to my little girl."

"Mrs. Bellamy," I tried to sound reassuring. "I can only begin to imagine how painful it must have been to learn your daughter was involved romantically with one of her teachers. But I have to ask: why does Carl's Croatian background—distant background from what I can gather—even enter into the picture? Would you have been any less angry if Tricia had been involved with a non-Croatian?"

"You don't understand."

"Try me."

"These people have been the cause of so much hatred against

315

and destruction of my people for hundreds of years. My Tricia knew that. She grew up knowing how the Croats sought only to steal from and kill the Serbs. How could she take up with one of them? Then to learn he had left his child in her. It was more than I could bear." Her last sentence had an ominous tone.

"What do you mean, 'more than you could bear?' What did you do?" She looked up at me again finally.

"I went to see my brother."

"Why?"

She looked me steadily in the eye. "Because he would know what to do."

* * *

The Serbian consul general's residence loomed as imposing as on my last visit, though this time it was more intimidating, given that I was approaching it alone, without my big old buddy Derek for moral support. Detective Andrea Pearson would be outright apoplectic at the thought of me visiting the top Serbian diplomat in the region unprotected. It was, after all, my previous visit to the official residence that had preceded Jonkovich's attack at my apartment. I was not convinced the two events were directly linked, but it did give me pause as I walked alone up the sidewalk to the imposing front portico of the opulent West Side residence. I didn't anticipate my visit would be unannounced after I left the Bellamy home, and the front door opened as I reached the front steps.

"Good day, Mr. Patrick," the deep voice of Bogdan Dantolovec greeted me.

"Good morning, sir. I'm sorry to bother you. I was hoping I could ask you a few more questions." It was strange to me that Dantolovec had met me personally at the door. Given his demeanour on our previous meeting, it seemed below him to answer his own door.

"I believe I made it clear to the investigating officers in both of these heinous cases that I have answered all of the questions that I intend to answer. I can not nor will I be compelled to be interviewed by your police or the Canadian government." His tone was considerably less friendly than it had been when Derek and I had first made his acquaintance.

"I represent neither," I tried to assure him. "Mr. Dantolovec, some information about your niece has been brought to my attention. If I know about it, it is only a matter of time before it becomes public information. Before any more harm or humiliation befalls your family, it might do you well to be prepared for what may come."

"Are you offering me legal advice?"

"I already represent a client."

"A dead one."

"Yes." He hesitated a moment, then turned and walked away from the door, leaving it ajar. It had to be a custom that ran in his family. I followed, closing the heavy oak door behind me. The latch made a disproportionately large click in the tiled hallway as it caught. I followed the sound of Dantolovec's expensive shoes as he departed the circular entranceway and headed towards an interior meeting room. We entered a different room from the one Derek and I had visited earlier in the week. The consul general turned his pinstriped grey suit towards me and pointed towards a distressed leather chair next to the fireplace. Unlike his sister's house, the fire in this room was lit, which pleased me no end. Looking at the damp cuffs of my suit, I was slightly embarrassed facing this career diplomat, whose impeccable attire probably cost as much as a month of my teaching salary. My ex-wife would have been humiliated by my slovenliness.

"My sister tells me you've been bothering her again, too," he began as he took the chair opposite me on the other side of the fireplace. We looked like two prime ministers posing for a photo op at a summit meeting. I figured I could destroy the image easily by simply kicking off my loafers and pointing my near frostbitten toes a little closer to the thawing power of the flame. It was even real wood, throwing off decent heat, unlike the decorative gas apparatus in my condominium.

"If bothering entails trying to solve her daughter's murder, I am a pest." I'm always ready to spar verbally when my feet are cold.

He studied me silently as if choosing his next words carefully. "Why is it that you believe a grieving mother would in any way be able to help you clear the name of your deceased client?" He sounded almost sad, as though my own stupidity caused him great consternation.

"I guess it's because ever since my client came to me with this problem he was having with your niece, new information just keeps popping up. And you know? The funny thing is, that just about every time there is some new little piece of information I gather, it seems that it was information Tricia's mother could easily have provided for me if she'd only bothered to take the time. I'm finding it difficult to understand why she has been so reluctant to be wholly truthful with someone whose purpose has been to solve her daughter's murder." I smiled innocently at the end of my speech.

"Your purpose," Dantolovec corrected, "has been to undermine serious police investigations in order to clear the name of a teacher who has sex with his students."

"Student," I corrected him. "I am not here to defend Carl Turbot's conduct with Tricia. In fact, quite frankly, I have found it very difficult to look past his obvious poor judgment and unacceptable conduct, except for one thing: he did not kill your niece. I think you know that." Now the Serbian ambassador to Canada looked slightly bemused.

"And why would you profess I know such an absurd fact?"

"Mr. Dantolovec, you have thwarted us at every turn. One of your confirmed employees attacked me not once, but twice. Another man, who joined Jonkovich in the original attack, spoke with a heavy Serbian accent. The Serbian population in Vancouver is simply not that large, and while you may find it a coincidence, the fact that you refuse the police access to the consular employee records simply leads me to the rather obvious conclusion that my other assailant was himself an employee of the embassy, or was at least working with the embassy's knowledge."

"As I've made clear to the police, I am under no obligation to answer any of their or your questions."

"At least not any legal or diplomatic obligation," I countered, my thrust and parry picking up steam. "Morally, there's a whole other argument to be made."

"A defence lawyer is going to give me an ethics lesson?" His voice was dripping with sarcasm.

"A diplomat withholding information about an investigation into the murder of his own niece is going to do lawyer jokes?"

Dantolovec leaned forward in his chair to continue our argument, then thought better of it. "I think it is time for you to leave, Mr. Patrick. You may find it hard to believe, but I do have more pressing matters than making small talk with you."

"Small talk?" I demanded, sensing my own voice rising with my ire. "I hardly think that seeking to solve Tricia's murder qualifies as small talk." Dantolovec rose from his chair, attempting to begin his exit sequence. "I simply cannot understand your reluctance to participate in bringing your niece's killer to justice." I was trying to keep him talking, so I wouldn't be thrown out.

"I would argue that her killer met justice!"

"Of biblical proportions? An eye for an eye? Is that your version of the way our legal system ought to work?" I demanded.

"That seems much more efficient than the way it works now." Dantolovec was standing now, towering over me with cold outrage in his eyes. I wanted to rise to meet him face to face but perversely figured that as long as I remained seated, it would be at least physically more difficult to eject me from this Serbian territory.

"And what about his wife?" I pushed further. "Does your version of justice require she be killed too?"

"That was a mistake!" he bellowed, then stopped himself and stepped back away from my chair. He stepped quietly across the fireplace from me and stood behind the leather chair identical to mine. Laying his forearms across the back of the chair, he lowered his head and sighed before lifting his eyes to meet mine.

When I could stand it no longer, I finally asked, "A mistake? Which part was a mistake, Mr. Dantolovec? The fact that Bonnie Turbot happened to be home when Carl was killed? Or the fact that the investigation into your niece's death did not go the way you wanted, so the second part of the operation became necessary?" Instead of answering, he raised himself from the leaning position he had been stooped in, came around to the front of the chair and lowered himself into it. He stared thoughtfully into the fireplace and seemed momentarily mesmerized by the sounds of the wood cracking and popping as the flames slowed, rested and waited for more fuel. The two of us sat trance-like in front of the ornate fireplace like a Rockwell painting. I had crossed a line. Our conversation had gone from one of gentle fishing for information to my outright accusation of criminal involvement. International incident, here we come. I wondered if the prime minister would call me. Following my host's lead, I too stared into the embers of the fire, doing my best to remain calm while anticipating anxiously where the conversation would lead us next. Clearly I had struck a nerve. Finally, Dantolovec spoke.

"You could not possibly understand," he sighed.

"You may be underestimating me," I countered.

His eyes left the fire, turning to face me, and the anger that had been in his face was gone. His face was awash only with sorrow, and he looked about two shades paler. "What they did was wrong. It was an abomination, and it was unforgivable." I didn't want to speak for fear of interrupting whatever train of thought he was riding, so I left a silent gap between his sentences. He was sounding a little bit lost, and I considered feeling sorry for him momentarily. "This has been so difficult for me. For us. For all of us."

"I mean you no disrespect, Mr. Dantolovec, but you are not the only one who suffered loss. My client and his wife had family who are grieving too. Carl's students have suffered the unspeakable loss of their friend and peer, followed by the brutal slaying of a teacher they trusted and respected." The Serbian official turned and stared glumly into the fire before speaking. The crackling and popping of the smouldering wood was dying, sounding less like fireworks and more like Rice Krispies, as I waited for further discussion. "Mr. Dantolovec," I prodded again, "you said what 'they' did was wrong. Who are you talking about?"

He turned to face me again as though I were once again the child asking why the sky was blue. "They? Your client and Tricia," he said with undisguised disgust.

I'm sure my face expressed some surprise at his inclusion of

Tricia in his sphere of blame. Heretofore I had assumed Carl was the singular target of the Bellamy family hatred. "You'll pardon my lack of understanding, sir, but it seems odd to me that you find Tricia's involvement with Carl Turbot as anything but a case of exploitation of a minor by her teacher."

"And you call yourself his lawyer? It's probably just as well he did not survive to face trial." He had a good point there. Dead or no, I was still supposed to be defending Carl. A slight smirk broke through the gloom on the consular general's face. "Tricia was not a child. She was sixteen years old when she began her disgusting affair with that man. She was practically a woman. She chose to defile herself as much as he chose to defile her." He looked me coldly in the eyes. I wondered if Tricia had inherited the cold stare gene that seemed to run in her family. I wondered if she had used it on Carl, and for the flash of a second I pictured it being the preceding moment to my client wrapping his hands around Tricia's throat and squeezing the very life from her glaring eyes, but just as quickly determined to push that thought out of my mind.

"As I said before, Mr. Patrick," he continued, "the biases perpetuated by your western media have caused you to see what's happened in my homeland from a singular perspective. What your client's people did to mine in pursuit of their independence was nothing short of wicked. That Tricia would have fallen in love with and carried the child of a despicable Croat was more than the family could bear."

"I mean you and your country's collective history no disrespect, and I'm certainly no expert on Balkan politics, sir, but I'm not even certain Carl Turbot ever visited the region, let alone was born there or had any particular political leanings towards the cause."

"It doesn't matter," he replied dejectedly.

"It should," I said, the heat rising in my bloodstream again like steam on cold morning pavement. The notion that several people may have been sacrificed not because of their relationship with one another, but because their togetherness somehow offended a centuries-old feud in another part of the world was causing my own sense of injustice to overflow. "She was a child, despite your assertion that she was completely responsible for her own actions; neither she nor my client deserved to be put down like stray dogs because of your beliefs that Serbs and Croats ought not to procreate with one another."

"Don't you dare to presume to lecture me on justice," he hissed, his own voice rising as he stood up from his expensive chair and took a few tentative steps towards me. For the first time I could remember in a long time, I did not retreat, another clear sign I was allowing exhaustion and emotion to drive my actions as much as he was. "How could you expect her mother—my sister—and my people to live with that kind of shame?"

"Because she had gotten involved with a man who somewhere down his genealogical tree had a few Croatian branches? No cause is worth the price she was made to pay."

"Tricia's own mother was the victim of violence from those so-called Croatian 'branches.' It is part of Tricia's heritage. She has herself been witness to unspeakable acts of Croatian violence." Oh, Christ, I thought. It just kept getting better. "Can't you see?" He was almost pleading now. "It was just more than any person, any family could take." The official I had viewed as so harsh, so commanding in presence looked utterly despairing. My experience as defence counsel had done little to prepare me for the moment in which I would attempt to wear down a witness into confessing their involvement in a crime. Generally, I was trying to keep them from doing so. I was temporarily flabbergasted.

At last I found my voice. "All right then. "So you killed Tricia and Carl."

He actually laughed at me. "What? That is absurd! Of course I did no such thing."

I chuckled back at him. "Well, of course not. A man of your position."

"You mock me now?"

"Seems as good a time as any."

He actually leaned over and poked me in the chest. It hurt. "I loved Tricia. I had nothing whatsoever to do with Tricia's death." I waited a moment for him to continue. He spoke only with his eyes, eyes that told me something surprising: he was surprised by my accusation. Truly surprised.

I was momentarily stunned. "Your sister told me she came to seek your assistance in 'dealing' with the Carl and Tricia problem."

He looked back at me intently. "She did."

I continued with disbelief. "And you're telling me you had nothing to do with Tricia's death?"

"Of course not!" he was practically shouting. I worried his outburst would bring reinforcements running. We both took a moment to breathe and stare at each other.

Finally, I could take it no longer. "You have yet to deny having anything to do with Carl and Bonnie's death." It was a statement, not a question, and Dantolovec treated it thus. He just looked at me sadly as though realizing for himself for the first time all that had transpired. Like Peter Parker, I suddenly felt my spider sense tingling. It seemed an opportune time to take my leave. Reluctantly rising from the comfort of the chair and the warmth of the fire, I faced my host one last time. "Well. It's been fun. Now that I know about your involvement, I feel pretty good about the job I've done for my client. When I get home, I'll call detectives Furlo, Smythe and Pearson and everyone will be happy."

"Your police have no jurisdiction over me. I think you know that." Damn it. He was right: I did know that. But in the smugness of the moment it had escaped my memory temporarily.

"Mr. Dantolovec, diplomatic immunity will only get you so far. Even if we cannot prosecute you here for your involvement, I am certain the Canadian government will find a way to have you sent packing back to Serbia, where they can try you under the Serbian justice system. Or am I to assume that 'Serbian justice' is an oxymoron?" In response, he shook his head from side to side in disbelief.

"You'll do no such thing," a voice said from the doorway to my right. Turning my head quickly towards the voice, a wave of panic descended like an Acme anvil onto my chest.

Baseball Cap.

Thirty-One

The first thing that popped into my head was that Andrea had been right: I kept overstepping my bounds and getting myself in over my head. I believe she had also mentioned something or other about putting myself into dangerous situations, but as usual, I had ignored her. I made a silent vow to apologize to her and assure her that from now on, I would listen to her advice. I hoped God was listening and would accept my plea bargain, despite his knowing that I rarely kept promises like that.

"Good to see you again," I opened. "Have you selected which part of my body you didn't do enough damage to that you'd like to pick up on?" Dantolovec seemed almost as surprised as I to see Baseball Cap at the door, but it was possible he was a consummate actor: despite its war torn history, surely Serbia had theatre.

"I believe Mr. Patrick was just leaving," the consul general told his underling. I could take a hint. I began to back towards the door on my only moderately shaking legs and prepared to exit post haste. Baseball Cap took a few steps towards me.

"Yes. I believe I will join him." The edge in his voice brought me quickly back to the day in the cemetery when he had tried to persuade me to abandon my defence of Carl. In retrospect, it looked like a good idea. Carl would be alive—albeit in prison—and I would likely be quietly teaching a communications or law class to a group of uninterested adolescents. We all make choices.

"Luka," Dantolovec spoke again, a warning tone in his voice. "I said Mr. Patrick is leaving. Please step aside." A power challenge was brewing between the men, and I was the unfortunate spark hovering dangerously near the fuse. Baseball Cap did nothing to follow the orders of the man I presumed to be his boss.

"No," he replied. "Mr. Patrick will be coming with me." Shit. No good could come of that.

"Listen, anything I know about you guys is likely pretty much covered by diplomatic immunity anyway. You really don't have anything to worry about." I heard a smidgen of pathetic desperation in my own voice, but it didn't really bother me right at that moment.

"Likely?" Dantolovec queried. He sounded like he might be the deciding vote on my living or perishing.

"I guess. Look, I slept through most of my course on international law. I don't travel much, so who figured I'd need it? But if diplomatic immunity and extra territoriality can't cover things like homicide, what the hell good are they?" Oh, oh. Rambling. Any second now, sweat beads would be visible on my brow.

"Not very convincing, I'm afraid," Dantolevec replied. "Besides, I don't relish the prospect of expulsion either." He paused to look at his hired muscle, reluctant, I suppose, to be even indirectly responsible for any further carnage. A conscience. Shaking his head disappointedly, he finally acquiesced. "Very well." He gestured his hand towards me, as though politely pointing out an overpriced, curious piece of artwork, and Baseball Cap took this as his cue to move towards me.

"Seriously," I tried one last time, "let's call it a day, boys. Can't we just agree to disagree? I could be on my way never to bother you again." The pleading in my voice was starting to get on my own nerves, but next to the hulking behemoth who had previously rendered me unconscious in a graveyard, I recognized that physical action on my part would be of limited value. Before I could decide if a bolt for the door was worth considering, Baseball Cap was beside me and had taken hold of my right arm with such force I thought it might come out of its socket. I may even have yelped aloud. Not surprisingly, my pain seemed of little concern to the man apparently named "Luka", who pulled me out of the ornately decorated living room and down the hallway from whence I had arrived. He pulled me roughly through a door in the hallway, and we found ourselves in a multi-car garage. Directly in front of us was the Serbian Consulate's vehicle of choice: the black limousine.

"Hey," I said. "That looks familiar." In response, Baseball Cap shoved me roughly through the back door he had opened with his free hand. I crumpled on the floor of the oversized car and turned around just in time to see the door slam shut. Like the police car I had so recently ridden in, this car appeared to have no door handles on the inside. I guess limo drivers in Serbia like to make sure that only they are able to open the door for their passengers. That ruled out escape, though I wasn't confident I could have brought myself to jump out of a moving vehicle, despite my predicament. I felt more than heard the engine come to life, and the semi-darkened garage got brighter as Baseball Cap opened the automatic door and headed out into the early afternoon fading light. Just to be on the safe side, I made sure that both doors had in fact been altered to keep me—or perhaps Tricia—inside. Finding they were, I settled onto the back seat for the ride. It wasn't often I got to ride in a limousine, and while I often thought it was a bit pretentious to be driven around in an oversized grandparent mobile, I had to admit the luxury of the ride did have some appeal.

Baseball Cap said nothing as he pulled out onto Granville Street and headed north in the opposite direction of rush hour traffic. Traffic was lighter than normal due to the snow, but it was just as slow moving. Along the sidewalks, several cars littered the sidewalks and driveways, where frustrated or out of control drivers had abandoned their vehicles and huddled in bus shelters, waiting for the public transit this crowd had likely never taken. While I had been inside the embassy, it had begun to snow again. There must have been two inches on the ground. The local economy would take a beating as nancy boy west coasters clung to their gas fireplaces and hot tubs and avoided unnecessary bouts of shopping.

"You taking me for dinner?" I asked, trying to strike up what was beginning to dawn on me would be my last conversation. "I know a great Vietnamese place. Or maybe Indian. You like tandoori?" Baseball Cap continued to ignore me like a student in a communications class. As the analogy crossed my mind, so did my students, and I felt at once sorry for them and saddened I wouldn't see them again. I had only known them a few months, but they had been through so much already with the death of Tricia and Carl. This would be an additional burden that was going to be extremely difficult for some of them to take. At the same time, I realized how much some of them had come to be important to me. I had been jaded, cynical and distant from the teenagers I worked with. Starting late in the profession, I figured I had years of catching up to do with some of my more bitter colleagues, but the reality was, quite a number of them had grown on me. Maybe it was because I was starting to feel old—and likely facing my imminent demise—that I enjoyed the thought of their youthful sense of life. Eighteen was a fun year. I envied them that, and I knew I would miss them.

I examined the floor for any telltale signs of violence that might have preceded my trip in the expensive car. Tricia had been strangled, but it was possible she had left some blood behind if she had been in the car. Of course, any really messy evidence would have long since been washed away; there was no way a man with fancy suits like the Serbian consul would ride around in a bloodstained limo. But I had read enough Patricia Cornwell to know blood could stick around where you least expected it. It was too bad they didn't have portable Luma Lights for traveling forensic investigators. I could have at least gone to my grave with irrefutable evidence that I had been right. It was important to me that I was able to declare "I knew it" when I reached the pearly gates.

"Do you have any particular destination in mind, or are we just cruising?" I tossed up to my driver. "Stanley Park is nice in the snow, if this thing has good traction." There was just no getting this guy to laugh. Baseball Cap turned left onto Broadway and headed in the general direction of home—my home. It was then I figured out what his intentions were. "You know," I told him, "you can only pull off that fake suicide thing so many times before people start to catch on."

We turned right on Burrard and headed down the hill towards Kitsilano. The Fifth Avenue Cinemas passed by my right, and the foreign films I would never get to see popped into my mind like a psychic vision. I was running out of witty comments to make as we got closer to my apartment, and my heart began to race for possibly the last time. My mind swirled with lame ideas of how I might bolt past Baseball Cap when he opened the door, and run into the night, screaming madly for help from the urban folk, who would ignore me. At best, I could count on my ability for distance running, despite the snow on the ground and my expensive shoes that were most definitely not made for mileage.

The limousine pulled slowly down the alley behind my building, parallel to the street out front. It had not yet been cleared of snow. Baseball Cap pulled in alongside the leaning cedar fence separating my condominium from the building next door. The car's engine shut off, barely noticeable it was in such fine tune, and Baseball Cap soon appeared at the door. As he opened it and reached in for me, I slid across to the opposite side of the seat. The last thing I planned was to make this easy for him. If he wanted me out there, he could damned well come and get me. He changed my mind when he pointed what seemed to be an inordinately large gun into the passenger space and grunted "get out." Whenever I see situations like this in movies or television, I always think the victim should simply refuse. You're going to get killed anyway, I always tell them. Why play along? But the reality is, when someone is pointing a gun in your face, I suspect most people become pretty pliable, if only in the interest of preserving their own lives just a few moments longer.

As I stepped out of the car, Baseball Cap slid the gun back into his deep jacket pocket but took me securely by the arm. I thought about yelling, but the strength with which he held my elbow focused all of my attention on that one spot of my body; I couldn't even think clearly enough to yell. Most of my neighbours weren't big enough to tackle Baseball Cap anyway, and none of them, I was sure, were armed. We approached the entranceway to the underground parking lot, and with a quick, deft movement, Baseball Cap reached inside my jacket pocket and removed my key ring, pointing it at the entrance panel and activating the automatic door. I stole one glance over my shoulder, vainly hoping someone would see us and suspect something was amiss, but all that remained in the nearly darkened alley was the limousine, calmly sitting with its hazard lights on as though the driver were making a casual stop to pick up his passenger. Baseball Cap knew exactly what he was doing. It came to me as we walked through the underground that he had been planning this for some time. My death was not an impulsive act.

We rode up the elevator in silence, and to my grave disappointment, no one got on at the main lobby floor. The pain in my arm where Baseball Cap continued to squeeze was causing my vision to blur. Unlocking my apartment door, he shoved me forcefully down the hallway, and I stumbled over my own awkward gait, momentarily falling to my knees and instantly grabbing my left arm that I sensed might be broken from the pressure he had applied. I turned around to see the door close behind me. Baseball Cap flicked on the kitchen light to the right of the front door, leaving the rest of the apartment in darkness. Homicidal mood lighting. He still said nothing but reached into his other pocket and began pulling on dark leather, form-fitting gloves, the kind worn by drivers who want to give the impression their car is more expensive than it is. I took the opportunity to clumsily pick up the cordless telephone from my coffee table. Baseball Cap was entirely disinterested in my efforts, and it only took a second to realize why: as I pressed the "Talk" button, I received no dial tone. My telephone had already been disabled. I looked back at Baseball Cap, who was calmly using a handkerchief he had produced from somewhere to wipe down his gun, I assumed to remove any fingerprints he had left prior to donning gloves. The confirmation of my original assumption about his plans to rid himself of me blazed into the front of my consciousness.

"There will come a point when you will kill one too many people. Sooner or later, they will trace this back to you. It always happens." Keep him talking, thought I. As long as I was talking, I was still alive. Small victories, but I had little else to hope for.

"Not always," he replied serenely, and the look on his face showed he might actually be enjoying this. It struck me that Baseball Cap had probably killed far more people than just Tricia, Carl, Bonnie and me. He had a practiced fluidity in his preparations, walking towards me, gun at side, with a gracefulness that belied the gravity of my situation.

"Maybe not where you're from, but here in North America, we sort of pride ourselves on catching killers. Moralistic perhaps, but we just can't let go of the notion that 'Thou shalt not kill' is absolute."

"I believe you have another expression that the only absolutes are death and taxes." He smiled at his own dark humour.

"A scholar," I commented, half under my breath. "I wish you'd read some philosophy instead of serial killer manuals." He chuckled at my gall. "Not to change topics," I ventured further, "but how in hell did you get Zoran Jonkovich to help you dispose of Tricia? He was completely in love with her. He was convinced Carl had killed her."

"Who do you think convinced him? He knew your friend was fucking the young girl. It was killing him. When she became pregnant, I thought he might kill your friend himself. It was all I could do to restrain him."

"But Carl didn't kill Tricia. You did. How did you explain having her body in the stretch limo when he helped you place her in the park?"

He smiled again at me. "Love is blind. All he knew was Carl had killed Tricia upon learning of her abortion. We did not want the family to be shamed by having her found at his house."

"And he was content to let Carl go to prison rather than exact his own revenge?"

"At least until you and your co-counsel began to make it look like prison might not happen. Then we had to take drastic measures." He examined the room slowly, planning the best angle at which to stage my suicide.

"Killing an innocent, beautiful girl didn't bother you at all?" My own questions were beginning to sound like desperate pleas, anything to prolong my execution.

Baseball Cap laughed again. "Innocent?" He sounded incredulous. "You people have portrayed the little slut like she was some kind of angel. A victim."

"Are you saying she deserved to die?"

"She would have anyway. She slept around."

"She had an affair with one teacher."

He laughed again. "You are so hopelessly naïve the way you portray your young. You think your friend was the only one who took an interest in Tricia? You are dead wrong. Your friend did her. Fellow students did her. I did her. Even her beloved uncle did her. I never once heard her complain."

"Jesus Christ," I muttered, and realized Tricia's life had been much worse than I had originally believed. "And you all knew about this? Her family was aware of all of this?"

"Of course not. But I have been around the family a long time. I find how much they don't know about each other amusing." He smiled at his own clever secret. "And Zoran. He naïvely believed that once Carl Turbot was out of the way, true love with Tricia would flourish. What a fool." He stood with his back to the living room's picture window and suddenly pushed me forcefully to the couch. His movements were mechanical, methodical. He was able to toss me around effortlessly like a rag doll. Both Andrea and Sandi had been right after all. I was too skinny.

"For God's sake," I pleaded, stuttering, "If Tricia wasn't the sweet innocent girl we assumed she was, what the hell did she do that was so bad you finally had to kill her?"

"Your friend. Carl. The Croat."

"She's dead because she slept with someone from the wrong side of the Balkans? That's fucking insane."

"You are not the one who would have to live with the shame, knowing about it for the rest of your life."

"Why the hell would you be shamed?"

He shook his head regretfully, disappointed he could not make me understand. "Not me, Mr. Patrick." He looked past me at the wall behind, squatting slightly to peer past my shoulder as though planning the trajectory.

"You people are crazy." I was almost crying now. "You don't have to do this."

"Hey," he said wistfully, "we all must make a living somehow." Along with my life flashing before my eyes, understanding went bolting by also.

I wanted to ask more, but he had decided we had talked long

enough. He suddenly dropped one knee onto the couch and pushed his huge left hand across my chest, pressing me heavily into the sofa cushions. I struggled gamely, but his bulk was overbearing, rendering me unable even to lift my arms.

"As I told your friend, you will feel only the shortest pain. It will be over before you know it. I won't make you suffer." At that, he smiled, showing that despite his killing profession, he did, in fact, have a heart. With the gun still in his right hand, he pressed harder against me and pried open my jaw, jamming the pistol into my mouth. I could taste the steel of the barrel, cold and smooth, as what I assumed was the gun sights pressed up against the top of my mouth. "Shhh," he whispered to me softly. "It's all right." My eyes were wide, and I could hear muffled grunts emanate from within me as I tried vainly to scream. I tried snapping my head back and forth, but that only jammed the gun further back, and I could taste my own blood as the gun cut into the walls of my throat. "It's almost over now," he continued, cooing as if to a child about to receive his first vaccination. Tears streamed down my face, and I looked into his eyes one last time, silently pleading for a last second reprieve. He pushed the gun hard, jolting me backwards as he released the pressure from my chest and leaned slightly back himself, probably to minimize the splatter that would damage his expensive suit. I couldn't bring myself to close my eyes. My last act of defiance was to stare my death in the face. Baseball Cap looked over his shoulder.

I heard all four shots, followed by the sound of breaking glass and immediately felt relief that the pain was, as promised, very limited. My throat continued to burn, and my spinning mind fought to grasp all that was happening in these final seconds of its usefulness. As my mind started to focus, it asked me the question: why four shots, and as the seconds ticked by I found my eyes continuing to focus around my apartment until they settled on the gaping, man sized hole in my living room window. Dazed and lost, I turned to face the direction I had last seen Baseball Cap look and instead of my killer saw Zoran Jonkovich, standing, gun in hand, looking past me out the hole which my mind was starting to tell me had been made by Baseball Cap.

I was too tired, still too terrified to speak, able only to stare up at him in wide eyed terror. "The bastard!" he proclaimed, talking not necessarily to me. "He killed her. It was him, and I let him play me for the fool I was. Fucking idiot!" I continued to stare at my unlikely saviour, wondering if he had indeed rescued me, or if he wanted to kill me himself. Questions formed in my mind, but they could not travel down to my mouth to be asked. "I cannot believe I trusted him. Them. They treated me like family when I had none. And for what? They are animals!" He was talking to me now, though he seemed as dazed and unfocused as I was. Seconds that seemed like hours ticked by, and I sat stupidly on the couch staring at the gun in Jonkovich's hand. He seemed to see me finally and broke into a strange smile. "How ya doing?" he asked.

I was still unable to find my voice but was recovering enough to glance down to ensure I hadn't, in my perceived last few seconds, pissed in my pants. To my utmost surprise, I had not. I was beginning to rise from the couch when the front door to my apartment crashed open and Detectives Furlo and Smythe rushed through, guns drawn. "Drop it," I heard Furlo yell fiercely, and in my confused state, I could not figure out why they would be angry at Jonkovich until I remembered he was still holding the gun he had used to kill Baseball Cap. As the door blasted open, Jonkovich had turned, levelling his gun at the two approaching police officers, and a standoff had begun. "Put the gun down," Furlo commanded further, taking up position in the hallway just feet away from Jonkovich, who had backed away towards the window.

Jonkovich looked to me then back at the two police officers. "Put the gun down," Smythe said soothingly, falling into the good cop routine to counter her partner's aggression. "It's over. It's time to talk. No one wants to get hurt." Jonkovich did not waver from his pseudo-military stance, the gun pointed squarely at Furlo's chest.

"You can't get us both," Furlo warned. "Don't make this any worse than it is."

Jonkovich turned his head slightly to catch my eye, and he smiled slightly in my direction. I found my voice for the first time since the gun had violently flown out of my mouth. "Jonkovich, don't," I said quietly.

Glancing back at the officers, he slowly began to lower his gun, then suddenly and quickly turned the gun and pointed it instead at me, pulling back the hammer and preparing to shoot. Before he had the chance—which I knew he would not take—shots sounded from both Furlo and Smythe's guns, and Jonkovich was pounded backwards by bullets, crashing into the remnants of my living room window that, unlike his partner, held him. His body slumped downward from the window, leaving a blood-red stain smearing down the remaining glass.

"Shit," Furlo said quietly, holstering his gun then turning to me. "You all right?"

I honestly didn't know. I stole one morbid glance at Jonkovich's face staring up at us with no surprise, no fear in his wide-open eyes. He was smiling.

Thirty-Two

I made some half-hearted protests that I did not need to go to the hospital, but the truth was, I was glad to get out of my apartment, at least until they removed Jonkovich's body. Several hours passed before doctors and nurses decided I was sufficiently out of shock to leave Vancouver General, and the crime scene technicians had gathered enough evidence that I was permitted back home. It probably wasn't a good idea. Just being in the room, staring at the assassin-sized hole in my window and the blood-stained hardwood floor was depressing. Does blood stain wood? At least the technicians had had the generosity to wipe the blood smears from the windowpane. God bless Windex.

The living room and kitchen area were abuzz with people, notably Furlo and Smythe—without their weapons, apparently standard procedure after a shooting— and Andrea. Sandi and Derek had been summoned to the hospital to make sure I was okay and to provide transportation home. A couple of uniformed officers huddled around in the hallway, lest there be anyone else left alive who might still want me gone.

All present heads turned as Sandi, Derek and I entered. Andy deemed it her duty to be the first one to come forward and hug me. "How you doing?" she asked. "You didn't need to come back here tonight. You probably won't be able to get anyone to fix the window before morning."

I shrugged nonchalantly. "Oh, well, I've always wanted air conditioning." Below the window, an area of yellow police tape had been cordoned off, restricting access to the indentation in the grass where Baseball Cap had plunged three stories. Most estimates figured him to be dead from the four shots likely before he left the window and most certainly before he hit the ground. It was almost too bad. Despite the passage of time since the incident, I was having a hard time feeling charitable towards him. I glanced at Furlo and Smythe. "How did you guys get here so fast?"

Jasmine Smythe looked sheepish. "We were out front."

"Why?" I wanted to know.

"We were watching the building," she replied, avoiding my gaze with obvious discomfort. My confusion must have been obvious. "In case Jonkovich came back."

I looked at them quizzically. "Jonkovich was in my apartment when I was dragged in here by Baseball Cap."

"Who?" Sandi suddenly was interested in the conversation.

Smythe filled her in. "Luka Gersen. He worked for the Serbian embassy, at least unofficially."

"How is it that you didn't see Jonkovich coming in?"

It was Furlo's turn to look contrite, perhaps for the first time in his life. "He must have come through the back door. Like you did. We weren't aware of any activity until Gersen did his reverse swan dive out the window."

I felt myself suddenly indignant. "Oh, he used that sophisticated method of deception known informally as 'the back door'? Yeah, I can see how that might have gotten by you."

"Believe me, we don't feel good about it either," Smythe responded lamely.

Andy interjected on her colleagues' behalf. "They were here on their own time, Win. The department wouldn't authorize surveillance for you. Otherwise we would have had people all around the place."

I digested that for a moment. "I'm not important enough for the VPD to keep around, I guess." The late hour and my fatigue were causing me to descend into self-pity mode. I slumped down onto a stool in front of the kitchen pass-through. Sandi sat down next to me and draped her arm over my shoulder. My ex-wife bordered on radiant, despite the late hour and the gruesome crime scene. It gave me weird comfort to have her sitting next to me and fawning over my beaten state.

"Looks like giving up your practice didn't give you the happier life you were looking for," she said. She always had a way of killing a good moment.

"We've had BOLO's out for Jonkovich since he hit your place last time. We figured we would be able to pick him up before he did anything stupid. Looks like he was planning on finishing the original job he started a few days ago." A hint of anger seethed through Andrea as she gave me this information.

I shook my head slowly in disbelief. "He stopped Baseball Cap from killing me." I still couldn't bring myself to use his name. He would forever be Baseball Cap to me.

"Only after he realized he'd been screwed over." Derek had waded into the conversation with that high-priced legal analysis. "So there's no doubt in your mind that Gersen was paid for his, umm, work?"

I nodded slowly. "That's what he said. Someone trying to pick up the consul general?" I asked Andrea.

She looked back at me with disappointment. "Not going to happen. While you were at the hospital, the inspector himself went down to the consulate. He was refused admittance. No one answered the door, although it was clear people were inside. We've posted people outside to watch what happens."

"But you can't go after the consul general himself, even though he was the cash man?"

"That's right," she confirmed. "We can't even confirm he is the cash man. Department brass are speculating that he's preparing to head home. If not, a request will likely be made by the feds to have him removed. But we can't prosecute."

"International diplomacy at its finest," Furlo scoffed. "We could build a rock solid case against Dantolovec, and his immunity status lets him walk."

I wanted to make a snide comment about their previous rock solid case against Carl Turbot but thought better of it. I didn't have the energy for verbal sparring with a man whose opinion I had no respect for anyway. Instead I turned to the best legal mind that I knew. "There's no way around this?"

Derek shook his head. "Not by us. Conceivably, the Minister of Foreign Affairs could make a request that we get to keep him here for trial, but there's nothing that would require the Serbian government to comply. Then, Andrea's right: Canada will ask him to leave. Whether or not he's prosecuted back home is up to the Serbs. There's been a huge improvement in law and order in that country, but Dantolovec is a well-connected, high-placed government official. I wouldn't bet the farm on him doing any time."

"Not to mention," Smythe added, "the only witness to the fact he was paid by the consul general isn't going to be talking. I suspect Gersen won't have left a standard financial paper trail we could use to even build a case against him."

"So that's it, then?" Sandi asked. It was an appropriate question. It was hard to believe that after five violent deaths, no one would face justice. A quiet moment hung over the group assembled in my living room. The hole in the window was allowing cold air to blow through my structurally and emotionally damaged living room. There was nothing more we could do, certainly not that night. I felt a need for some kind of closure, but looking around the room and feeling the cold air blowing over me, I knew I wouldn't get it tonight. I should probably just leave and go stay at a hotel.

Within a few minutes, Furlo and Smythe left, and just friends—if you can call Sandi that—remained in my death-stained apartment. It was quiet, and I wanted red wine, but the hospital had given me some kind of sedative to quell the shock. According to all present, that ruled out alcohol. I remained sitting on a stool by the kitchen, not able to bring myself to head back into the living room, let alone to sit on the couch. I knew I would have to get rid of it. The bloodstains could probably be cleaned, but I would always know exactly where they had been. It wouldn't be a pleasant dinner conversation with prospective female friends either. Left alone save for the two police officers stationed outside my door, we could find nothing to talk about besides the events of the past couple of weeks.

"You know," Derek finally said from the armrest of one of my living room chairs where he had been sitting contemplating. "I still don't quite get why Dantolovec would want Tricia killed. If everything we believe is true, he had a 'relationship' with her too."

Andrea looked over at him. "That might just give him more motive to get rid of her. Maybe she was going to expose him. If the truth about her relationship with Carl was coming out, maybe Tricia thought this was the time to tell Mom or someone about what good old uncle had been doing all those times she stayed over with relatives."

"It's positively sick," Sandi added. "I know it sounds completely naïve, but I just can't believe someone could do that to his own niece. I don't care how beautiful she was, the man is a perv. Someone should take him out back and shoot him."

"Please," I groaned melodramatically, "don't give anyone any ideas." The tension in the room actually dissipated a little, and a couple of us chuckled.

"Seriously though," Sandi went on, "I can think of few things worse than what she went through."

"No one should ever have to experience that," Andrea confirmed, "especially as a kid."

"And her mother," Sandi added, and she paused and rubbed her non-existent tummy, where someday she would begin to show her own child. "Women who go through this kind of trauma feel shame their entire life. I know if my daughter went through all Tricia did, I couldn't bear the thought of her suffering the psychological scars all her life." Another cold gust of wind blew into the room, bringing with it that unique Vancouver mixture of rain and snow. I looked past Sandi out the missing window towards English Bay, just a few blocks away at the ships moored out in the cold harbour. I must have gone away for a good few seconds, because when I tuned back in to the people around me, they were looking at me with some concern.

"Win?" Sandi said. "You all right?"

I shook my head. "Shit," was all I could muster.

* * *

I am stubborn, but I am no fool. When I could stand my apartment no longer, I finally acquiesced, rejecting all offers of shelter except Andrea's. By the time we had reached her place, morning was upon us, but the effects of the hospital's sedative were still with me. I crashed in Andrea's spare bedroom, but within an hour, my racing mind had wakened me. Andrea, I was glad to see, had not gone off to work. She wasn't happy when I woke her up, but when I told her what I wanted to do she was up, showered and dressed within minutes, a skill Sandi had never come close to mastering.

We pulled up to the same East Vancouver house I had visited twice before, and I didn't even try to persuade Andy to wait in the car. After the attempts already made on my life, I knew she wouldn't, and I didn't really want her to. I'm no tough guy, and this morning I didn't even feel like pretending. As we walked up the path in front of the house, the front door opened. "I guess I have been expecting you," said the woman at the door, turning again on her heels and walking back into the house without closing the door in what had become her pattern of invitation into her home. I glanced at Andrea, who nodded her assent, and we both followed Mrs. Bellamy into the house. We wandered down the same hallway into the same cold living room where I had last been yelled at by the grieving mother. Andrea walked one small step ahead of me, and her eyes scanned across the room. Her hand was inside her purse, where I knew she would be carrying her weapon—although she was officially off duty. As if sensing her apprehension, Mrs. Bellamy nodded towards Andy's purse. "You can relax, officer. You will not be needing that. I have no means nor any intention of harming you." Looking at her, she did not appear to be much of a threat, and Andy relaxed. A little.

"You know who I am?" Andrea asked.

"I saw you at the funeral." Mrs. Bellamy turned her attention back to me. "You have been busy."

"I guess I could say the same of you." An hour's sleep and some of my surly sarcastic self was returning. "Your brother was protecting you quite well."

She tossed her hand in the air, dismissing the very thought of her high-powered sibling. "My brother could do no good. He knew what was happening with Tricia. He could have, should have taken care of her. But he viewed things differently. He viewed Tricia differently."

"So you knew?" Andrea asked her. I threw a cautious look at Andrea. If she was going to ask questions, she should be reading Mrs. Bellamy her rights. She shouldn't even be in the room hearing whatever this conversation was going to be. But I didn't want to be defence counsel at that moment. Not for her.

"I knew," Mrs. Bellamy confirmed, unconcerned about Andy's questioning.

"How?"

She looked back at Andrea. "She told me. A daughter talks to her mother." Mrs. Bellamy's voice was laden with ice, and I could not imagine a vulnerable young girl wanting her as a confidante. She did not ooze motherly concern or comfort. Tricia's life must have really been going badly for her to turn to this hard, cold woman. I could see too why she would have been attracted to the gentle warmth of Carl's personality, and I felt a renewed twinge of grief for both of them. Reluctantly, she gestured towards the same chair I had occupied during our last meeting. I complied as she sat down again on the couch opposite. Andrea remained standing.

"When last we spoke, I was led to believe you were shamed because of who Carl was, not because of Tricia."

She looked at me, and I felt her hostility and hatred rising to the surface and floating across the freezing room to me. "It was not easy to decide who was shamed worse, her or me."

"Because she had been abused?" I demanded.

"Because she turned to that animal teacher friend of yours for comfort. For love."

"And she was probably getting so much of it from you."

"You know nothing!" she hissed at me.

"I know that because your daughter was abused by her uncle, you felt she would not be able to handle the shame. When she turned to a Croatian man, you decided you could not handle the shame. You had your own daughter killed because she sought love and support from a man whose crime in your eyes was not that he had an illicit affair with your daughter, but that he was Croatian."

"My whole life growing up, I was tortured by those people." Andrea's eyes were darting quickly between Mrs. Bellamy and myself, no doubt continuing to determine whether either of us was at risk.

"And you're here now. You came here for something better. But you could not let go. For God's sake, you killed your daughter, not because she was in love with a teacher, but because she was in love with the wrong teacher. And you claimed the Croatians were barbaric." She stared coldly at me, and I recognized that no matter how I put this, in her eyes she had committed a righteous act. "So you had your brother send out Gersen after her."

"No," she said quietly. "My brother is a coward. He could not involve himself in something that might sully his precious position and risk his high-flying lifestyle. My brother wanted to deal with your client only. He would not have had the stomach to put Tricia out of her misery. Luka worked for me."

"You paid him?" Andrea asked.

She did not answer but continued to stare at me. I leaned forward in the chair next to the still non-functioning fireplace.

"Here's what I don't understand. If Carl's family history made him so bad, why not just kill him? Why kill Tricia?"

She almost smiled. I sensed those were rare occurrences. "You call yourself his friend, and you would have me kill him?"

"Spare me the self-righteousness. You killed him anyway. Or at least your little friend did."

Her slight smiled broadened at her own private joke. "He would not have, were it not for you."

"Don't kid yourself. Gersen wasn't that clever, and I'm not that good a lawyer. Any defence counsel Carl would have ended up with would have found the same weak case I did. Eventually the outcome would have been the same."

"Or at least you tell yourself that to ease your conscience."

"And you've avoided my question. How does a mother—even a bitter, hostile one like yourself—arrange the death of her own daughter? How could you?" My own tone had taken on the same self-righteousness I had accused her of, but mine felt justified. At least to me.

342

It was her turn to lean forward, placing both her flabby arms on her knees as she stared across the small space between us. "She felt shame for what had happened to her. That she had been abused, time and again. But she felt no shame for what she did, what she made with Carl Turbot." She paused, and I felt her next words more than heard them. "Instead she shamed me."

I stood up abruptly. "I'm gonna go now." I looked at Andrea and shrugged my shoulders as a question mark.

"You go on ahead. The uniforms are outside. Furlo and Smythe should be there too."

"You called for backup?" I asked, teasing.

"Told them to give us five minutes or so, then be here."

"You're not so tough after all."

"Nope. Just smart. You could learn from me."

"No, thanks," I replied and left her in the room with Mrs. Bellamy sitting staring after me in the cold living room. I left the door open as Mrs. Bellamy had and smiled at the two police officers on the front porch.

Walking down the front path, I could just make out the beginning of Andrea's speech informing Tricia's mother of her rights: "Dobrila Bellamy, you have the right to remain silent..." As I sat down in the front seat and started the car—cranking the heat way up—I gave a wave to Furlo and Smythe, who were just then stepping out of their unmarked but obvious police cruiser.

Thirty-Three

There was only one day remaining in the week, but I had stayed away long enough. Fridays are paradoxically never the best days at school. The kids can see the three o'clock light at the end of the tunnel and are even less focused than Monday through Thursday. My presence in the building only added to the unusual sense of unrest that had befallen the school in the past few weeks. Principal Don McFadden was the first to show up at my classroom door. With my return, he was no longer the first vehicle in the staff parking lot.

"Welcome back," he told me as he popped his head into the room.

"Thank you."

"I didn't expect to see you so soon."

"You sound disappointed."

"No, it's just that..." He stopped himself. "We're not about to get into an argument already, are we?" I gave him my most gracious smile.

"I hope not."

"Listen," he continued, "I know this must have been a difficult time for you."

"Yep," I confirmed then decided to acknowledge, "you too."

"Yeah," he said, shifting his brief case to his other hand. "Anyway. I'm glad that you're okay." That was about as emotional as he was likely to get.

"Thanks, Don." He walked off in the general direction of the office as Christine Wilson from the English department stepped in.

"He's right. We didn't expect you back so soon."

"I hope everyone's not disappointed."

She gave me the first smile I had seen in the building in a long time. "Nope. Some of us might even be glad to see you."

"I'm not sure my students will feel the same way."

"Are you kidding me? After all the press you've gotten? You're going to be some kind of hero around here for a while. Enjoy it while you can. They'll turn on you again eventually."

"No doubt." We paused.

She leaned on the doorjamb before continuing. "Do you like hockey?"

"Yeah."

"The Leafs are in town tomorrow night."

"You have tickets?" I asked her.

"No, but I have a big TV. I thought you might want something home cooked for a change." She smiled with what might have been a hint of coquettishness.

"You cook?"

"Literary queen. Culinary genius. I got it all."

"How could I resist?"

"I can't imagine. I'll talk to you later." She left the room, and I looked sadly over the stack of assignments that would require my attention throughout the weekend. Clearly my students had managed to progress along just fine without me. I gave myself thirty seconds of self-pity then tried to figure out what I would do with the rest of the day. It didn't really matter. Most of my students were only interested in hearing me recount as much as I possibly could of my brush with death, and I tried to oblige them without adding anything too graphic they ought not to hear. I was willing to let them focus their attention on my doings, if only to distract them for a while from the deaths of Tricia and Carl.

By the end of the day, I was fully ready for the weekend. I opened the door to my apartment and immediately turned on the light, looking slowly around the large, airy space. My apartment window had been fully replaced, and professional cleaners had made sure that not even a trace of blood remained on the hardwood floors in the living room. Only the pictures in my mind would be evidence two people had died in that room.

Kicking off my shoes, I opted not to check messages on my voice mail. I knew who would have called without having to check: my mother, Andrea, Sandi, my mother, Derek, Andrea and my mother—in that order. I needed to be alone to get used to my own space again. Logically, I knew I should put my place up for sale and find somewhere without the ghostly baggage hanging over it, but I've never been all that logical in my life decisions. It was already dark and I knew that tomorrow I should be shopping for Christmas, at least until I went to Christine's for dinner and hockey. I unpacked a small stack of papers to read and, avoiding the couch, went straight into the bedroom and flopped down on the bed. Flipping on the TV for some background company, I was only halfway through the first paper when I did something I had not done properly or for long enough in what felt like a very long time.

I slept.

David Russell is a long-time member of the arts community in Vancouver, British Columbia. He has worked in stage and television, including performing as a company member with the world champion improvisation company the Vancouver Theatre Sports League for over fifteen years, where he continues to perform today. He hosted a youth television program on the Global Television network and was host for six years of a Vancouver-based talk show.

Russell has written freelance for a number of publications, including *Maclean's, The Vancouver Sun, The Province* and the award-winning online news site *The Tyee*, and others.

In addition to writing and performing, Russell teaches high school law and history. He lives with his wife and daughter in Coquitlam, British Columbia.